M000049822

BEST OF THE EROTIC READER
VOL. II

BEST OF THE
EROTIC READER

VOL. II

ANONYMOUS

BLUE MOON BOOKS
NEW YORK

Published by
Blue Moon Books
841 Broadway, Fourth Floor
New York, NY 10003

ISBN 1-56201-216-9

Manufactured in the United States of America

CONTENTS

BEST OF THE EROTIC READER
VOL. II

The Lascivious Monk

Slowly we walked, not in the tree-lined paths but among the open garden beds where the rays of the sun were the hottest. The only protection Madame Dinville had was a little fan. I had nothing, but I suffered my tortures stoically. The Abbot was laughing at our foolishness, but he soon became discouraged after we went around several times. I still could not guess what Madame Dinville had in mind. Also, I could not understand how she was able to stand the burning heat which I was beginning to find unbearable. Little did I realize that rich reward I was to get for my faithful service.

Our stubbornness in continuing the walk soon bored the scoffing Abbot and he retired. When we were at the end of one of the paths, Madame Dinville led me into a pleasantly cool little arbor.

'Aren't we going to go on with our stroll?' I innocently asked.

'No, I think I've had enough sun,' she replied.

She regarded me searchingly to learn if I guessed the reason for the promenade, and she perceived that I had no idea of the blessing she was intending for me. She took my arms which she squeezed affectionately. Then, as if she were extremely tired, she rested her head on my shoulder and put her face so close to mine that I would have been a fool not to kiss. She made no objection.

'Oh, oh,' I thought to myself. 'So that's her game. Well, nobody will disturb us here.'

In truth, we were in a sort of labyrinth whose obscurity and turnings and windings would conceal us from the sharpest eyes.

Now she sat down under a bower on the grass. It was the ideal setting for the purpose I was sure she had in mind. Following her example, I seated myself at her side. She gave me a soulful look, squeezed my hand, and reclined on her back. Believing that the moment had come, I started to ready my weapon when all of a sudden she fell sound asleep. At first, I thought it was only drowsiness caused by the heat and that I could easily rouse her. But when she refused to wake up after repeated shakings, I was simple enough to believe in the genuineness of a slumber that I should have suspected because of its promptness and profundity.

'My usual luck,' I swore to myself. 'If she fell asleep after I had quenched my desires, I wouldn't mind, but to be so cruel at the moment when she had raised my hopes so high is unpardonable.'

I was inconsolable. There was sadness in my heart as I regarded her. She was dressed like the previous day, that is to say, with the diaphanous blouse which revealed her unbelievable breasts, that were so near and yet so far. As the strawberry-tipped orbs rose and fell, I longingly admired their whiteness and symmetry.

My desires were almost at the breaking point, and I felt the urge to wake her up, but I dismissed the desire for fear that she would get angry. She would have to awaken eventually, I reflected, but I could not resist the urge to put my hand on that seductive bosom.

'She is sleeping too soundly for her to awaken at

my touch,' I said to myself, 'but if she does, the worst that she can do is scold me for my boldness.'

Extending a quivering hand to one of the inviting mounds, I kept an anxious eye on her face, ready to retreat at the first sign of life. But she slumbered peacefully on as I lifted her blouse up to her neck and let my fingers graze the satin-smooth contours. My hand was like a swallow skimming over the water, now and then dipping its wings in the waves.

Now I was emboldened to plant a tender kiss on one rose-bud. She still did not stir. Then the other was given the same treatment. Changing my position, I became even naughtier. I put my head under her skirt in order to penetrate into the obscure landscape of love, but I could not make out anything for her legs were crossed. If I could not see it, at least I was going to touch it. My hand slowly crept up the thigh until it reached the foot of the Venusberg. The tip of my finger was already at the entrance to the grotto. I had gone too far, I decided, but having reached this point, I was more miserable and frustrated than ever. I was so anxious to see what I was touching. Withdrawing the intruding hand, I sat up again and regarded the visage of my sleeping beauty. There was no change in her placid expression. It seemed that Morpheus had cast his most soporific poppies on her.

Did my eyes deceive me? Did one of her eyelids twitch? I felt a sense of near panic. I looked again, this time more closely. No, the eye I thought had momentarily opened was still tightly shut.

Reassured, I took new courage and began to gently lift up her skirt. She gave a slight start, and I was positive that I had awakened her. Quickly, I pulled the skirt back down. My heart was pounding as if I had narrowly escaped a disaster. I was terror-stricken as I sat again at her side and feasted my eyes on her admirable bosom. With relief, I saw that there was not a sign of returning life. She had just changed position, and what a delightful new position it was.

Her thighs were now uncrossed. When she raised one knee, the skirt fell on her stomach, revealing her hirsute mound and cunt. The dazzling sight almost intoxicated me. Picture to yourself a rounded leg encased in a frivolous stocking held up by a dainty garter, a tiny foot in a saucy shoe, and thighs of alabaster. The carmine red cunt was surrounded by a ring of ebony black hair and it exuded a scent more heady than the rarest incense. Inserting my finger in the aperture, I tickled it a little. At this, she opened her legs still wider. Then I put my mouth to it, trying to sink my tongue to the very bottom. Words cannot describe the straining erection I had.

Nothing could stop me now. Fear, respect and caution were thrown to the winds. My passion was like a torrent, seeping away everything in its path. If she had been the Sultan's favourite, I would have fucked her in the presence of a hundred eunuchs armed with sharp scimitars. Stretching my body over her and supporting myself with my hands and knees so that my weight would not arouse her, my member gradually disappeared into the hole. The only part of me touching her was my prick which I gently pushed in and pulled out. The slow but regular cadence enhanced and prolonged my ineffable bliss.

Still carefully watching her face, I gently kissed her full lips from time to time.

But the raptures I was experiencing were so great

that I forgot my caution and fell heavily on the lady, furiously hugging and embracing her.

The climax of my pleasure opened my eyes which had been shut since I had entered her, and I saw the transports of Madame Dinville, joys which I was no longer able to share. My somnolent friend had just clutched my buttocks with her hands, and raising hers which she convulsively wiggled, she dragged me down hard on her quivering body. I kissed her with the last of the passion I had left.

'My dear friend,' she moaned in a failing voice, 'push a little more. Don't leave me half way to my goal.'

I felt renewed vigour at her touching appeal and resumed my enjoyable task. After barely five or six strokes more, she really lost consciousness. For some unknown reason, that excited me and I quickened my tempo. In a matter of seconds, I reached the peak again and fell into a state like that of my partner. When we revived, we showed our appreciation of each other with warm kisses and tight embraces.

With the fading of passion, I felt I had to withdraw, but I was embarrassed for I was unwilling for her to see the sorry condition my prick was in. I tried to hide it, but her eyes were fixed on me. When it was out, she grabbed it, took it into her mouth, and began to suck it.

'What were you trying to do, you silly boy?' she murmured. 'Were you ashamed to show me an instrument you know how to use so well? Did I conceal anything from you? Look! Here are my breasts. Look at them and fondle them as much as you want. Take those rosy tips in your mouth and put your hand on

16

my cunt. Oh, that's wonderful! You have no idea of the pleasure you're giving me, you little rascal.'

Animated by the vivacity of her caresses, I responded with equal ardour. She marvelled at the dexterity of my finger as she rolled her eyes and breathed her sighs into my mouth.

My prick, having regained its pristine rigidity from her lips on it, wanted her more than ever. Before putting it in her again, I spread open her thighs to feast my eyes on that seat of delight. Often these preliminaries to pleasure are more piquant than pleasure itself. Is there anything more exquisite than to have a woman willing to assume any position your lascivious imagination can conjure? I experienced an ecstatic vertigo as I put my nose to that adorable cunt. I wished that all of me were a prick so that I could be completely engulfed in it. Desire begat even more violent desires.

Reveal a portion of your bosom to your lover, and he insists on seeing it all. Show him a little firm white breast, and he clamours to touch it. He is a dipsomaniac whose thirst increases as he drinks. Let him touch, and he demands to kiss it. Permit him to wander farther down, he commands that you let him put his prick there. His ingenious mind comes up with the most capricious fantasies, and he is not satisfied until he can carry them out on you.

The reader can imagine how long I was content nuzzling that appetizing aperture. It was a matter of seconds until I was again vigorously fucking her. She eagerly responded with upward thrusts to match my powerful lunges. In order to get farther in, I had my hands on the cheeks of her derriere while she had her legs wrapped around my back. Our mouths, glued to

17

each other, were two cunts being mutually fucked by two tongues. Finally came the ecstasy that lifted us to the heights and then annihilated us.

It has been said that potency is a gift of the gods, and although they had been more than generous with me, I was squandering my divine patrimony, and I had need of every drop of the heavenly largesse to emerge from the present engagement with honour.

It seemed that her desires were increasing in proportion to the loss of my powers. Only with the most libertine caresses was she able to turn my imminent retreat into still another victory. This she accomplished by getting on top of me, letting her full breasts dangle above my face and rubbing my failing virility with her cunt which seemed possessed of a life of its own.

'Now, I'm fucking you!' she joyously cried as she bounced up and down on me. Motionless, I let her do what she wanted with me. It was a delightful sensation, the first one I had ever enjoyed in that way. Now and then, she paused in her exertions to rain kisses on my face. Those lovely orbs swayed rhythmically above me in time with her repeated impaling of herself. When they came close to my mouth, I eagerly kissed or sucked the rose nipple. A streak of voluptuousness shuddering through my body announced the imminence of the supreme moment. Joining my transports to hers, I gushed just at the moment she did, and our juices mingled with the perspiration on our bellies.

Exhausted and shattered by the assaults I had launched and withstood for more than two hours, I felt an overwhelming desire for sleep and I yielded to it. Madame Dinville herself rested my head on her

18

abundant bosom, wanting also to enjoy some rest, but with me in her arms.

'Sleep, my love,' she murmured as she wiped the perspiration from my forehead. 'Have a good sleep, for I know how much you need it.'

I dozed off immediately, only to awaken when the sun was sinking on the horizon. The first thing I saw when I opened my eyes was Madame Dinville. She looked at me cheerfully, interrupting the knitting she had occupied herself with during my slumber to dart her tongue in my mouth.

She made no attempt to conceal her desire for a resumption of the sport, but I had little interest. My indifference irritated her. It was not that I was disinclined, but if it had been left up to me, I would have preferred repose to action. But Madame was not going to have it that way. Holding me in her arms, she overwhelmed me with proofs of her passion, but they did not arouse me, even though I tried my best to stroke the dead fires within me.

Disappointed at her lack of success, she employed another ruse to relight my extinguished flames. Lying on her back, she raised her skirt to her navel, revealing the object of the desires of most men. She well knew the effect such an exposure would produce. When she suggestively jiggled her buttocks, I felt something stirring in me and I placed my hand on the gift she was offering me. But it was only a token gesture of passion. As I was negligently titillating her clitoris, she was feverishly massaging my prick in a hysterical cadence dictated by her feverish eagerness. When my prick finally stood up, I saw her eyes sparkle in triumph at her success in reviving my ardour. Now aroused by her caresses, I promptly bestowed on her the tokens of my gratitude which she zealously accepted. Grasping me around the waist, she bumped up and down under me so violently that I ejaculated almost automatically, but with such raptures that I was angry with myself for having ended the joy so promptly.

Now it was time to leave the arbor which had been the scene of such transports. But before returning to the chateau, we took several turns in the labyrinth to allow the traces of our exertions to disappear. As we were strolling, we naturally chatted:

'How happy I am with you, dear Saturnin,' she remarked. 'Did I live up to your expectations?'

'I am still relishing the delights you were good enough to grant me,' I gallantly replied.

'Thank you,' she said. 'But it was not very wise of me to have surrendered to you the way I did. You will be discreet, won't you, Saturnin?'

I retorted that if she thought I was capable of betraying to others what joys we had, she must not have a very high opinion of me. She was so pleased with my astute response that she rewarded me with a long, lingering kiss. I am sure that I would have been rewarded much more richly had we not been in a spot where we could be seen. As an additional gratitude, she pressed my hand on her left breast with a meaningful expression.

Now we quickened our pace as the conversation languished. I noticed that Madame Dinville was anxiously looking from side to side and wondered why.

But who would have thought that after such an exhausting afternoon, she still wanted more? She wanted to crown the day with one last engagement, and she was on the lookout for some stray servant.

The reader will probably think that she had the devil in the flesh, and he would not be far off the mark.

She tried to revive me with her tongue and mouth, but the poor thing was lifeless. Sad but true. To attain her goal, what did she do? That is what we are going to find out.

As a youngster just getting to know the ways of the world, I flattered myself that I had made an auspicious debut and that I would be lacking in respect if I did not see her to her rooms. That done, I felt I could take my leave by giving her a final kiss for the day.

'What's that?' she demanded in a surprised tone. 'You're not leaving, are you? It's only eight o'clock. You stay here. I'll arrange things with your Cure.'

The thought of avoiding Mass appealed to me and I was agreeable to her interceding for me. Making me sit on the bed, she went to lock the door and returned to take her place at my side. She looked at me intently without uttering a word. Her silence disconcerted me.

'Don't you want to any more?' she finally said.

Because I knew I was finished, I was so embarrassed that I could not force out a word. To admit my impotence was unthinkable. I lowered my eyes to conceal my shame.

'We're all alone, dear Saturnin,' she said in a coaxing voice, bathing my face with hot kisses which just left me cold.

'Not a soul in the world can spy on us,' she continued. 'Let's take off our clothes and get into my bed. Come, my friend, down to the buff. I'll soon make the stubborn little prick stand up.'

Taking me in her arms, she actually carried me and deposited me on the couch where she disrobed me in a feverish impatience. She soon got me in the desired condition, that is to say, naked as the day I was born. More out of politeness than pleasure, I let her have her way with me.

Turning me on my back, she started sucking my poor prick. She had it in her mouth up to my testicles. I could see that she was in ecstasies as she covered the member with a saliva that resembled froth. She did restore some life to it, but so little that she could make no use of it. Recognizing that that treatment was of no avail, she went to her dressing-table and got a little flask containing a whitish fluid. This she poured on her palm and vigorously rubbed it on my balls and prick.

'There,' she said with satisfaction when she finished. 'You aren't through yet by any means.'

Impatiently I waited for the fulfilment of her prediction. Little tingles in my testicles raised my hopes for success. While waiting for the treatment to take effect, she undressed in turn. By the time she was naked, I felt as if my blood was boiling. My penis shot up as if released by a powerful spring. Like a maniac, I grabbed her and forced her on the bed with me. I devoured her, scarcely permitting her to breathe. I was blind and deaf. Sounds like those of an enraged beast came out of my mouth. There was only one thought in my mind, and that was her cunt.

'Stop, my love!' she cried, tearing herself from me. 'Not in such a hurry. Let's prolong our pleasures and elaborate on them. Put your head at my feet, and I'll do the same. Now your tongue in my cunt. That's it. Oh, I'm in heaven.'

My body, stretched out on her, was swimming in a sea of delight, I darted my tongue as deep as I could into the moist grotto. If possible, I would have sunk my entire head into it. Furious sucking on her taut clitoris produced a flow of nectar a thousand times more delectable than that served by Hebe to the gods on Mount Olympus. Some readers may ask what the goddesses drank. They drank from Ganymede's prick, of course.

Madame Dinville was clutching my backside with both her arms while I squeezed her pneumatic buttocks. Her tongue and lips wandered feverishly over my prick while mine did the same to her nether parts. She announced to me the increasing intensity of the raptures I was causing her by convulsive spasms and erratically spreading and closing her thighs. Moderating and augmenting our efforts, we gradually progressed to the peak. We stiffened as if collecting all our faculties to savour the coming bliss to the full.

We discharged simultaneously. From her cunt gushed a torrent of hot delicious fluid which I greedily gulped down. Her mouth was so filled with mine that it took several swallows to get it all down, and she did not release my prick until she was sure that there was not a drop left. The ecstasy vanished, leaving me in despair at the thought it could not be recaptured. But such is carnal pleasure.

Back in the pitiable state from which Madame Dinville's potion had rescued me, I beseeched her to restore me again.

'No, my dear Saturnin,' she replied. 'I love you too much to want to kill you. Be content with the joy we just had.'

Not overly eager to meet my Maker at the expense of another round of pleasure, I followed her example and put on my clothes.

Feeling that Madame Dinville was not displeased with the way I had comported myself, I asked her if I would be permitted to play our games again with her.

'When do you want to come back?' she answered, kissing me on the cheek.

'As soon as I can and that won't be soon enough,' I declared spiritedly. 'How about tomorrow?'

'No,' she smilingly refused me. 'I have to let you get some rest. Come and see me in three days' time.' (She handed me some pastilles that she said would produce the same effect on me as the balm.) 'Be careful how you take them. Also, I don't have to tell you that you are not to say a word about what we did.'

I swore eternal secrecy, and we embraced one last time. So I departed, leaving her under the impression that I had presented her with my virginity.

Fanny Hill's Daughter

Dear Madame:

As you would doubtlessly be the first to inform me, drawing on your own rich experience, there is no certainty in our profession from one hour to the next, let alone for any longer time.

'Twas on the sunniest of afternoons that the dread blow fell. Miss Kitty and I returned from visiting the stores, with our arms full of bundles and anticipating a most lively and pleasant evening, to find my gallant protector's orderly awaiting my arrival in the little room downstairs off the front door. His name was Hogg, and he was sufficient gross to rate it e'en had his parents not wished it on him at birth.

Usually a merry enough dog and inordinately devoted to my master, on this occasion his expression was melancholy enough to wring tears from a statue and aroused in my breast the most exquisite alarm, a sensation soon fully justified by the missive he solemnly handed me.

It was sealed and addressed in my protector's hand, and I feared to open it lest it contain I knew what not awful tidings. Yet mustering my courage under the regard of the devoted Hogg and Miss Kitty, I ripped loose the seal and read—

Most honourable mistress,

It is with the most galling sensations of remorse and regret that I take pen in hand. For ye have brought me nought but pleasure and have merited

26

far more from me than the troubles, self-inflicted by mine own outrageous weaknesse, in which I must now ask you to share . . .

I shall spare you the rest of that awful missive, Madam. Suffice it to say that, in part-payment of a gambling debt contracted at Whyte's my protector had sold me to a Mr Ian MacTavish of Edinburgh.

Nor was I to see my beloved young protector again, for, unable either to face the tragic scenes of parting with my person which must have ensued had he returned to the lodgings we so happily shared till that unhappy day, and being likewise unable to face the thought of forfeiting his honour by refusing to make good the wager he had so rashly entered into and so unhappily lost, he stayed away from my presence, remaining in barracks until I was safely (from his point of vantage) ensconced on the Edinburgh stage two mornings later.

In truth, had it not been for the kind consolations of Miss Kitty, well laced with the sound sensibility that is so much a part of her, I might well have destroyed myself in my grief and terror. For to be thus disposed of, via the turn of a card or the cast of a dye, like a dog or a Blackamoor slave, by a young man to whom I had cheerfully granted my greatest treasures without thought of return . . .

Chere Madame, words fail me!

As it was, had not Miss Kitty reminded me of the cruelty and unfathomable mystery of Man, I must indeed have succumbed. Nor did she content herself with mere verbal solace, but saw to it that my trunks were well filled with furs and furbelows, and that I was further equipped to meet Fortune's whims with two hundred golden guineas and a hamper well stocked with flesh, fowl, chocolate, two bottles of tawny port and other provenances against the rigours of travel—albeit so deep was my distress at the sudden downturn in my fortunes that I was scarce aware of the extent of her assistance.

To Miss Kitty's great kindness, for which I fear I was then insufficiently grateful in my wretched bewilderment, I must, in all good faith and gratitude, add your own sage instruction, Madam, on the frailty of Man and on the readiness of women to expect the worst from these most fickle of all created creatures.

E'en now, I must confess I find it hard to accept the fact that a protector as openly loving and affectionate as Lieutenant the Honourable Roderick Weymiss of His Majesty's Coldstream Guards should venture my person on a play at Whyte's. Is it for such fecklessness and ingratitude that we conceive the creatures in our bellies and give them birth and tender rearing . . .?

But enough of such disgressives, and on with the account of my fortunes.

Of the Honourable Ian MacTavish, my purchaser, I had but little time to record my impressions, for my life with him was of the briefest and least consequential—albeit fraught with the most veritable perils and excitements whilst it endured.

He picked me up in a rented hack two mornings following my receipt of the fateful message from Mr Weymiss, delivered by the porcine Hogg, to convey me to the Edinburgh stage, on which we were to ride in company to the land of Scotland, a land I had never before laid eyes on, and of which I had heard a great many things to make me distrustful, nay even afeard.

28

The Honourable Mr MacTavish was as tall as a flagpole and as lean as an Irish peasant in a famine year—yet withal not of unprepossessing appearance, save for a great red beak that thrust through and above his muffler like the prow of a Bristol merchantman.

His pale blue eyes looked rheumily down on me, as I stood in Miss Kitty's doorway, surrounded by my trunks, and said to her as she stood beside me, 'Is this the baggage I have engaged?'

In my confusion, I believed he spake not of mine own self but of the trunks, cases and hamper with which mine hostess had so generously provided me. Thus we were off on the wrong foot right away, as I had hardly been accustomed to being thus referred to in front of my face.

But the Honourable Mr MacTavish was no man to stand on argument, and I was whisked away in his rented hack before we had time to exchange so much as a single pleasantry.

All he told me during our half-hour journey to the Royal Scotsman, the tavern whence the Edinburgh stage departed, was, 'If ye'r as plump in bed as Weymiss claims, ye'll hae na troubles with me.'

Which, I must say in all humility, hardly constitutes a wooing, even for a gentleman of Scotland dealing with a young lady of pleasure like myself. Pray tell me if you find it otherwise, Madam, and I shall be more than ever in your debt.

However, if remiss in the courtesies of courtship, my purchaser soon proved himself more than eager in the performance of the role himself, and lived up fully to the reputation of his compatriots from north

29

of the Tyne for ensuring the receipt of that which he had purchased to the final farthing.

For the departure of the coach being delayed due to the tardiness of a passenger of importance, the Honourable Mr MacTavish wasted no time in hustling me into a small room off the ordinary where, by tipping a potboy tuppence, he thought to have privacy in order to, as he bluntly put it, 'try the worth of the goods.'

He made me lie down on a narrow, horsehair couch insufficiently cleansed of the vomit of one or more of the previous eve's revellers, as the noxious fumes that assailed my nostrils made unpleasantly clear, pulled up my petticoats and made ready to enter me without so much as a by-your-leave, unbuttoning his breeches to display a virile member that resembled more the central trunk of a stout bramble bush, so greatly was it knobbed and gnarled, than any organ of Man.

Nor was my already distraught spirit put further at ease when, grasping this ugly but all-too-practical tool in the very nick of time and squeezing its lumpy surface tightly in my fist, it gave evidence of a yellowish discharge that told me all too clearly its owner was suffering from the lesser of those two plagues of Venus that so sorely beleaguer both sexes in the exercise of their natural pleasures, and that in its most active and virulent form.

Having small wish to visit upon mine own self such an unpleasant ailment, I pleaded with him to leave me alone, at least until his trouble had abated, but his blood was up and he was in no mood to brook any delay in seeking immediate satisfaction of his most manly appetite.

Only at the last instant did I recollect the trick of

which you must be well aware, and in which Madame Berkeley schooled me, the trick of knocking the large vein in the side of the prick with a fingernail, thus causing the sturdiest of male emblems to resume its sorriest condition (not that the condition of my new protector's was not sorry enough to begin with).

In any event, he subsided, albeit with wrath, and made for to strike me with his stick, uttering great outcries about insubordination and ingratitude to which I paid small heed. I stood up to him, however, and informed him in no uncertain terms that I would announce to the world his condition and what he intended doing to me whilst in it—at which he resigned himself to muttering fury and, at last, rebuttoned his breeches to my great relief.

Had I but a moment further in which to ponder my plight, I doubt not that I should have left him then and there, and let my recent protector get out of his debt of honour to the MacTavish as best he could.

But all my possessions, save the golden sovereigns in my purse (which was concealed in my muff) and the clothes I wore on my back, were already aboard the Edinburgh stage, and I had small desire to render myself once more destitute in so short an interval of time. On top of this, the Eminent Gentleman for whom the stage was held arrived, and demanded we be off at once, as he was in a great hurry to tend to his affairs in the north. So I was bundled aboard with little chance to speak, or even determine, mine own mind.

Ne'er in all my born days did ever I see a gentleman of such surpassing ugliness as this Eminent Gentleman, who took a seat directly opposite me, resting his chin on his elegant knuckles and his elegant

31

knuckles on the carved ivory top of his elegant ebony cane, splaying wide his knees with utter disregard of the comfort of those passengers who sat on either side of him.

Save for the ruffles at his wrists and throat, he was attired wholly in black broadcloth, his gentility attested to by his total lack of jewelled adornment (for certes none but a very great gentleman has courage thus to appear in public without evidence of his property in jewellery or insignia of some sort). Only his buckles were of fine, polished silver that winked reflection of each passing sunbeam that entered the stage-coach windows as we jogged along, drearily enough, over the rough surface of the St. Alban's road.

His face, beneath his great black cocked hat, which filled with gloom that entire portion of the stage in which he sat, like some gigantic bird of melancholy prey, was lined and seemed, as if carved in putty by some overzealous Canova, and his deep-sunk eyes remained fixed on my face and person as if held there by a lodestone. So ugly, in truth, was this august personage, that my new protector, the Honourable Mr MacTavish, appeared actually young and handsome in comparison.

Mr MacTavish was all too evidently impressed by the honour of riding with so obvious a Personage of Importance. Albeit I was considerably taken up by the evident interest which the eminent stranger took in my person (which he made no effort at all to hide), I could not but be aware of the starts and fidgets of my new protector as that worthy conjured up conversational opening gambits, only to decide that each in turn was not a proper ploy and remain silent, his mouth opening and closing like that of a goldfish swimming idly in its bowl.

Not until we were more than an hour beyond Charing Cross did Mr MacTavish find his gambit and seize upon it. Our coach had just travelled over a pot-hole which caused it to tip so severely that we were all but hurled into one another's laps, all save the elegant stranger, whose cane, firmly planted on the floor of the stage, held him firm as Gibraltar itself against the human tide that assailed his flanks.

In overt admiration, my protector then addressed himself directly to *l'eminence noir*, remarking, 'I'll wager ye'r no descendant of King Canute, sirrah, for, mighty monarch that he was, with all his powers he was unable to halt th'advance of the waters.'

Save for a single eyebrow, which rose mayhap a half-finger, the elegant stranger in black gave no response—at which, believing him deaf, my protector repeated his words, shouting at the top of his lungs.

The stranger flinched ever so slightly. He removed one smoothly gloved hand to the ear nearest the MacTavish and patted it lightly, as if to be certain the appendage remained yet in place and attached to his head.

Then, employing an utterly world-weary drawl and pronouncing his syllables as if he were addressing a child, the eminent one spake to me and remarked, 'If ye'r companion is addressing himself to me, I'll thank ye to translate his words—for surely, with all those rolls of his rrr's, he employs some barbarous *patois* which I, alas, find myself utterly unable to comprehend.'

I had noted my new protector's heavy Scottish burr, but had lacked either the wit or courage to call him

33

on it as this stranger did. At which The MacTavish grew so incensed that he roared it a third time, in the voice of a Caledonian lion, if indeed such a creature exists.

The elegant eyebrow went up again, the wearied lips pursed slightly, and the gentleman in black uttered a single syllable directed at me . . . '*Please!*'

So I repeated it more gently for him, at which he afforded me a tiny smile of such confidential import (as if, indeed, we shared a secret from which the rest of the world was locked out) that his ugliness quite vanished beneath the assurance and glow of his personality.

Then at last he replied, in the most exquisitely insolent drawl imaginable, ' 'Tis well for you that no wager exists, for ye'd have lost, my dear fellow. I'm a descendant of the late King Canute on the side of my great-great grandmother, thirty-three times removed, and have in my house a small bucket of that very sand which was wet by the tide that refused to obey his royal command. Should ye care to call and view it, ye'll find it still damp.'

'Had I wagered, I'd hae won, sirrah,' cried my protector, now beside himself with fury. 'Damp or not, ye'll have difficulty proving the sand was not culled from the sands of the Thames only last week.'

'If ye please, my dear, will you again translate?' the gentleman in black inquired of me, and of course I complied, enjoying my rude protector's exposure for the man of ill parts he most assuredly was (may his soul rest in Presbyterian peace, where'er it lies!).

When I had finished, he smiled at me again in confidence, and replied, 'Tell the good fellow then, sweet lady, that he'll have just as de'il a time proving th'opposite. *Hah*!'

With this, the elegant gentleman in black, disregarding the MacTavish's apoplectic sounds of stuttering fury no more than t'were the lullaby of a nursing mother, composed his chin upon his knuckles once again and, after one slow wink at me, closed both his eyes and, to all appearances, fell fast asleep, in which condition he remained despite the rude jolting of the stage until our halt for dinner at St. Alban's, whereat he disappeared into a private room, while my discomfited protector could not bring himself to spend more upon our fare than was afforded by the ordinary.

At this, once again, I was reminded of the parsimony for which the Scottish folk are all too well renowned, and began to fret myself anew about th'uncertainties of my present estate. Furthermore, I wondered how a man to whom even a farthing appeared so dear had discovered the courage necessary to play for high stakes at Whyte's.

As yet, the problem appeared unanswerable, and I could but lament inwardly over the cruel twist of fortune that had served to place me, helpless, in his niggardly claws!

My hopes that he might prove a protector of weak or lagging appetite vanished as I watched him dismember the joint placed before us, and gobble it so rudely that I was forced to feed upon scraps left swimming in the grease and gravy.

Nor did he forego the pleasures of the bottle (since all drink, like all food consumed along the way was included in our passage). Yet this latter proved, in truth a blessing, for so deeply did he indulge that he soon fell asleep and snored loudly upon my shoulder virtually all the way to Luton, at which town, bone-weary, we alighted for supper and to pass the night.

It was here that a most curious happening occurred, one which has since proved all-important in its influence upon my present fortunes and estate.

My protector and I retired to a private room (it appeared that, for once, the greater parsimony of displaying me, his most expensive purchase, in the ordinary after dark or sleeping with other passengers and paying guests in one of the common bedrooms, overcame the lesser parsimony of paying extra for more secluded lodgings), where I steeled myself to endure the inevitable and, again in accord with my wise training for a young woman like myself to put the best face possible upon it.

Yet my apprehensions were to prove groundless, for even while we dozed and jolted in the stage en route to my northern exile, a kindly Providence, assisted by a more earthly agency, was moving in my behalf. At first alighting and retiring to our chamber, we were both so boneweary and travel-fatigued that our only thoughts were of easing our aching flesh and bones and of removing the dust and stains of our journey (at least myself, for the MacTavish shewed neither desire nor inclination toward cleanliness).

A scullery girl fetched me two pails of steaming hot water (for which my protector, grumbling at such extravagance, forced me to pay myself out of mine own small store of silver), in which, with the aid of a cloth and soap, I was able to wash after a fashion. Ye may be sure I took care not to remove any essential articles of clothing lest, despite his groans of aching weariness, I should arouse his lust prematurely.

The tavern food proving unsuited to his palate

(and, it must be confessed, to mine own as well), the MacTavish fell to demolishing the contents of the hamper with which Miss Kitty had provided me to such hearty avail that soon all that remained were a few oddments of bone and gristle, and mayhap, a few fingers in one of the two bottles of tawny port.

At this point, my protector felt quite well disposed toward me (and why not?), offering me praises for having come so well provided with sustenance, and belching his appreciation. He laid hands upon me as if to buss me in fatherly fashion (yet the manner in which his hands strayed to the roundness of my breasts and buttocks and lingered there gave me cause to doubt that his affections were wholly paternal in aim or origin), vowing that ne'er had mortal man been blessed with such a bonny mistress.

At this point, there came a knocking at the door of the room, and with a curse at such untimeliness, my protector reluctantly moved to answer it.

A manservant stood there, bearing a tray on which stood a cobwebbed bottle of fine old scotch whiskey, and a note. The manservant stood there, awaiting an answer, while The MacTavish scanned it and remarked, ' 'Tis indeed an unco display of courtesy on the part of your master. Pray gie him my thanks and appreciation.'

Impassively, the manservant replied, 'Mr Selwyn requested me to inform you, sir, that upon my return to his quarters, he will toast your health from the contents of a like bottle and wishes you to do the same for him.'

'Tell him his wish is fulfilled,' said my protector. 'You might add that I feel in no way discountenanced, upon learning his identity, at having been bested in verbal intercourse today by a gentleman of such renowned wit.'

When the manservant had gone, The MacTavish, all aglow at having received such a tribute (to say nothing of free whiskey), pulled out the cork and poured a stout measure into one of the wineglasses, lifted it to its donor and downed it straightaway.

'*Wurragh!* 'Tis powerful stuff!' he gasped, shuddering throughout his entire great frame as it went down. His eyes turned on me, bright red from the effusion of blood brought on by the force of his reaction, and he opened his ugly mouth to speak whereat to me.

Yet, once again, he was speechless, as on the coach that morning. For his face went slack, his eyes rolled upward, and he fell prone upon the carpet with a horrid sound and a shaking of the building itself.

I was hard-put to it to know what to do, but before I could cry out for help, the manservant had reopened the door and, putting a finger to his lips, enjoined me to silence. Nodding in satisfaction at sight of my unconscious protector, he removed the bottle of whiskey and the glass from which the MacTavish had drank and, placing them under one arm, offered me the other.

'My master awaits ye, ma'am,' he said with great courtesy. 'Permit me to shew ye to him.'

I hesitated, fearing dire consequences from the unexpected action I had so recently witnessed, and said, 'What have ye done to him?' Is he dead?'

'Only till morning, ma'am,' replied the manservant. 'And when he awakens, I'll warrant his head and stomach contain far too many woes for him to think of anything else for another twenty-four hours.'

Still I hesitated, but not for long. After all, my present situation was hardly one to my liking, and almost any change in protectors was bound to be for the better. So I said, 'My things! I cannot leave them behind. Nor can I well hope to return to my gentleman after this. He'd think me guilty of complicity and have my hide.'

'Ye'r things I'll see to myself at once,' he promised. Then, eyeing me, 'As to ye'r beautiful hide, I'm certain my master will treat it with proper affection and tenderness.'

'You are insolent,' I told him, smiling, for his good humour was infectious.

'Ain't it in truth a terrible thing?' he countered with feigned remorse. Nor was I surprised to learn that his name was Patrick.

The chamber to which Patrick took me was—need I say it?—far more roomy and sumptuously furnished than that which the penny-pinching MacTavish had hired for the night. It was well carpeted and held a large four-poster bed and a number of tables and chairs, as well as an elegant commode disguised as a low-boy. In the most comfortable of the armchairs sat my *vis-a-vis* of the stage still fully attired in his elegant black travelling clothes, at his elbow on a large tray the remains of a comfortable repast.

Eyeing me with the closest attention, he smiled and said, 'I trust a change of companions does not meet with ye'r disapproval, my dear. I must say that ye'r a most uncommon fine young woman, mightily ill-matched indeed with that barbarous Scotsman ye wore on ye'r elbow.'

Albeit I am well and dutifully aware of the fact that girlish ways sit ill with the deportment of a mature young lady, as I by now bethought myself, there was that in my new friend's manner and delivery that forbade me aught but to giggle most unbecomingly. The mere thought that I had been wearing The MacTavish on my elbow proved beyond resisting.

Mercifully, Mr Selwyn, for such was his name, did not appear displeased by my reaction, albeit he failed to respond in kind. A sparkle in his eye informed me that he enjoyed my pleasure.

When I could speak, I said most demurely, 'Milord, it would ill become me to show disrespect for the gentleman who gained my person fair and square.'

'My I inquire just how this ill-favoured son of Caledonia won ye?' He inquired. 'And do not call me milord, for I am not of the peerage.'

'Pray then, how shall I address you?' I inquired.

The faint smile reappeared. 'Ye may call me Mr Selwyn,' he replied most graciously. 'And may I reiterate my question?'

'I was informed by messenger, but two days ago, that my master lost me to The MacTavish at picquet—at Whyte's.'

He studied me in silence before remarking, 'By Gad, ye must be Roddy Weymiss' woman! He spake mightily well of ye before he pressed his luck too far.'

I lowered mine eyes with what I hoped was becoming modesty, and Mr Selwyn paused to inhale a pinch of snuff, which he withdrew from a most elegant chased-silver box adorned with rubies and sapphires. He uttered a snorting sound, which I at first mistook to be a sneeze, but which I realized later was his manner of laughter—for Mr Selwyn *never* sneezes whilst taking snuff, a reaction he holds to be most vulgar.

40

In kindly tone, he said, 'The young idiot! Risking such a prize on the turn of a card!' Then, after a pause, 'Well Weymiss' loss, Selwyn's gain.' And, in a most considerate manner, 'My dear, please tell me frankly and with the utmost candour—has any warm sentiment developed between the man MacTavish and ye'rself in the course of ye'r brief acquaintanceship?'

I replied. ''Tis most thoughtful of you to ask, Mr Selwyn, for indeed such a sentiment has indeed developed, at least as regards my feelings for Mr MacTavish.'

'*Amazing*!' An expression of regret flickered over his impassive features, to be followed by one of incredulity. 'I find it hard to believe, my dear—nor do I mean to cast any doubt upon ye'r truthfulness. But with such a man in so short a time. . . .'

'None the less, 'tis true,' I replied. 'I developed the warmest hatred for Mr MacTavish that I have ever conceived for any human being.'

'That, my dear,' he said, permitting himself a smile of pure relief, 'deserves a toast. Will ye join me?'

'I'd like nothing better,' I replied, and at Mr Selwyn's bidding, Patrick fetched glasses and poured us both full measures of whiskey from a bottle that looked suspiciously similar to that which the MacTavish had drunk the gift-draught that laid him low.

'Fear not,' said Mr Selwyn, reading my mind all too accurately. 'Better yet, let Patrick drink from ye'r glass, since he is playing a part in our little comedy.'

'Indeed he has—a part for which I am most grateful,' I told them.

'Ah, Patrick's important scene is yet to be

41

performed,' said Mr Selwyn. We looked on while the burly manservant drained my tumbler and received its contents with no visible ill-effect—after which, Mr. Selwyn and I drank a toast proposed by Mr Selwyn, to a hope that the MacTavish slumber long and soundly through the remainder of the night.

We drank another toast to my comeliness soon after, in which I was happy to join, then a toast to the recent good fortune of Mr Selwyn (by which, I took it to mean his good fortune was the acquisition of mine own poor self), the while Patrick was absent from the chamber upon some business his master proposed.

Upon his return, my new protector, (for such I rightly took him to be) said to his man, 'Patrick, are ye ready to play the game?'

' 'Twill be a pleasure sir,' replied Patrick, his dark eyes devouring me with what I felt to be unseemly lust in the presence of his master.

Then, turning to me, Mr Selwyn said, 'I trust ye'll not be offended, but I have found it to my advantage to adopt a most wise and intelligent policy of the Empress Catherine of Russia.'

'Indeed, Mr Selwyn . . . ?' I spake warily, for I could feel it in the atmosphere of the room that some most unusual request was about to be made of me.

'She maintains at her court in St. Petersburg a most accomplished young Scottish peeress who bears the nickname of *l'epreuveuse*—the tester. Whenever the Empress desires a member of her bodyguard or of a visiting embassy, she first sends this woman to his bed to discover if he has the qualities requisite to the Empress' own pleasure. 'Tis said both women are of

42

a remarkable similarity in this regard, just as Patrick and I are as like as peas in a pod.'

'You wish me to bed with Patrick before bedding me yourself?' I asked.

'If ye do not wish to be returned to the tender mercies of Mr MacTavish,' Mr Selwyn replied, most gently withal, yet with unmistakable intent. 'In any event, I'd see you naked before going on with the game, my dear, if only to ensure the genuineness of ye'r indubitable charms.'

In truth, I was in no way displeased at the prospect of displaying my charms and accomplishments for the edification of so amiable and elegant a gentleman as Mr Selwyn, but I could not resist casting a sidelong glance at the manservant who was to put me to the test and said, 'If Patrick is willing. . . .'

My new protector, Mr Selwyn, is not a man who gives way to laughter upon slight pretext. He has since told me on many an occasion that it well behooves a gentleman who would be considered so by his peers to display any emotion at all, either in public or private. Yet, at my poor foolish remark, he put back his well-powdered hair, opened his mouth and gave vent to a series of bellows and roars that momentarily alarmed me lest he had suffered some sort of fit, until I saw the tears streaming down his cheeks.

Nor, *chère madame*, could I perceive why my innocent jest should have given rise to such an extreme reaction, albeit within minutes I got the full point in more senses than one. For, having removed my clothes and posed prettily before Mr Selwyn, who ogled my dugs, my belly and my cunny as if he had ne'er before viewed their like (which, indeed, he has since claimed he never did), I turned toward Patrick, who came up beside me and discovered that the Hibernian was not only willing but ready.

Madam, ne'er in all my born days did I see such a tool. Where Lieutenant the Honourable Roderick Weymiss' shaft was long and rifle-thin, and that of his boon companion, Lord Peter Ronsabell's was short and thick as a Coehorn, Patrick's was their combined match in both dimensions. One glance at its immensity, and I shuddered at the thought of so massive an instrument probing my delicate inner parts, and would have protested its entry vigorously had opportunity but offered.

For the rest, Patrick was stoutly made, and his bones well coated with smooth flesh bearing but little hair—all told a most attractive couch companion albeit I found it difficult to contemplate any portion of him at that moment save the alarming codpiece I was destined to contain. I felt the great strength of him as he plucked me from the carpet like a piece of cloth and laid me on my backside on the unopened bed—whose tufted spread did threaten under the pressure of our combined weights to dot my tender flesh with more dimples than nature e'er intended.

Patrick toyed with my tits and cunny skilfully enough to prepare us both for combat, and I encircled his mighty lance with a timorous fist, nor were my fears in any way allayed by the fact that palm and fingers could scarce encompass its girth. Albeit I did my best to guide the purple crocus blossom of his stout maypole within the portals of my cunny, terror forbade mine own juices greasing the mouth of the tunnel, and his best efforts availed him nothing.

Undeterred, he laughed and kissed and cozened me as I were a doll, so helpless did he hold me in the strength of his embrace, ultimately upending me and rolling beneath till I full straddled him with his mighty blossom still prodding amain at my un-oiled gates. Whereat he unleashed his hold of my waist with one hand and put it to his mouth and spat upon it gently. He then slid it beneath my centre-piece and annointed his great mace, then held me as in a gentle vice and lowered me slowly upon it . . . and, lo! almost ere I knew what was happening, his crocus was well within my tunnel and forcing its way slowly upward into the very heart of me.

I cried out as its great girth bid fair to stretch my poor passageway past the bursting point, and looked at Mr Selwyn for aid, but that gentleman's eyes were glued upon the *pièce de resistance* of our performance, and he neither saw nor heard my plea for mercy. His eyes were fixed on our fused centre parts as if they were about to pop like great ripe currents from their caverns in his skull.

So great, indeed, was my discomfort, that I wriggled with all my might to escape the agony of my impalement upon Patrick's giant codpiece, and thereby was either done or undone depending upon the eye of the beholder—for the motion involved caused my juices to start flowing in a great suffusion, and what had been a mortal agony was transformed quicker than words can say it into a delight beyond any I had known before and scarce to be endured.

I cried out again, but not for succour this time as nature and Sir Isaac Newton's Law of Gravity caused Patrick's penetration of my poor small body to become deeper still, and our most private hairs met and mingled in the broth and froth of our passion. I soon felt his rigidity increase, and his machine grow turgid until it bucked within me, and his love-juice spurted to rebound from the very top of my womb, whereat he, too, cried out and fell limp, and what had so short a time before filled me with discomfort beyond endurance soon dwindled till it threatened to leave behind an empty, gaping void no more to be borne than its impalement.

With gentle moans, I settled myself more closely still upon his waning member, rubbing and rotating mine own private parts around it until, as if by magic, its retreat was stemmed, and soon a rally got under way again filling me to a bursting point I no longer feared or wished to avoid—quite the opposite, I confess it.

Resting a moment after the rebirth was complete, I looked again at Mr Selwyn and laughed and thrust out my tongue at him, a gesture my elegant new protector, with the most seemly gravity, returned in kind, thereby causing me to love him the more dearly. But at this point, Patrick returned to life with a great upward movement in a circular motion that sent reason, in truth all other sense and sensibility, dancing merrily away, and we clouted and clipped and clasped and clambered upon one another like mad moujhicks from Tartary's plain indulging in some heathen ritual wherein cunny and codpiece replace the altar of our Lord.

Since Patrick had already discharged his cannon once full within me, his powder took far longer to ignite on the second round of pleasure, and we worked one another over vigorously with the utmost delight until it seemed we would fair be drowned in our own sweat and other effusions, and sheer mutual exhaustion bid fair to put an end to our pleasure without its appointed conclusion, at least as far as stout Patrick was concerned, for I must confess, *chère madame*, that I attained paradise so many times I felt myself threatened with becoming a permanent resident of that celestial sphere.

Then, with a mighty heaving and thrusting and groaning, my tester achieved that which he so vigorously sought, and this time I was far too spent to seek to retain his spear at rigid attention within me, nor could I have done so e'en had I possessed the strength.

When we had rested for a while, drained of all desire, and naked on the spread that now resembled an ocean in mighty turmoil, so great was its confusion, rather than the calm sea it had been at the outset of our great trial, Mr Selwyn most considerately asked Patrick if he felt me qualified to service the master as well as the man. To which, Patrick could reply but with a heart-felt groan, at which Mr Selwyn professed himself entirely satisfied, as he was with what he had witnessed of our protracted bout.

He then had me bathe and e'en towelled me off afterward himself, paying especial attention to those parts of my poor body that had been most actively engaged, and pronouncing them charming. Whereat he told me I must dress, for that we had a hard journey still ahead of us that night.

'I am not afeard of your MacTavish,' he assured me solemnly. ' 'Tis just that I have long since learned to deem discretion in these matters by far the better part of valour.'

'As ye wish,' I replied, not even wondering what new turn my fortune was to take, so spent, was I from my two turns with Patrick, and, rendered so languid

47

by the warm water of the bath Mr Selwyn had had the tavern scullery maid heat and pour.

Had he suggested we take off for Timbucktoo itself, I doubt not that I should have assented without question. So I dressed with such care as conditions permitted and accompanied him downstairs in the inn.

Patrick awaited us, on the box of a three-quarter-front carriage, and I must confess myself both relieved and mightily impressed to discover my dunnage securely strapped, along with Mr Selwyn's, on the rack at the rear. My heart went out both to my new protector and to his man for affording me a symptom of their care and comfort in regard to myself, as well as for the pleasures the man had afforded me in the inn. Forsooth, any fretting that might have troubled me at forming an alliance with a man as obviously mature as Mr Selwyn was allayed by recollection of how inexhaustibly his servant could minister to my needs and foibles, so much so that any lingering sorrow at loss of Lieutenant the Honourable Roderick Weymiss and his charming companions was quite allayed.

Maudie

After dinner that night Charlie begged to be excused. Sitting alone in the little smoking-room, he began to think out his plans.

At that moment one of the pretty maids came in without knocking.

'Oh, mistress's compliments, sir, and she'd forgotten to give you the key of the wine and spirit cupboards; there they are. I'll open them.'

She brought out the necessaries, also a pile of books.

'Mistress says you might like these, too,' she giggled. 'Let me show you the best,' and she flicked over the pages of an obviously very erotic book, full of coloured plates of lust in every form. 'Saucy, aren't they? Look at this.'

It portrayed three couples, hopelessly mixed up, tongues, lips, cocks and cunts in helpless and joyful confusion.

She put her hand on Charlie's shoulder, playfully flicking his ear, and bending over kissed his forehead, pressing her breasts against the back of his head.

'I'm glad you've come,' she cooed; 'so are all the girls. We like you. I'm going to bring your hot water up to-night; mind you're awake.'

Charlie couldn't help it. He pulled her round on to his knee. She put his hand under her clothes herself, and wriggled.

'It's all right,' she said; 'no one will come in. This is what I'm best at,' and she slipped between his legs and undid the fly buttons with her teeth.

50

'You little devil!' was all Charlie could say.

A confused, gurgling noise was the only answer—his prick seemed to be half way down her throat.

He nervously fingered her head—she had deliciously soft hair—and gave himself to an abandon of lust.

She gently tickled his balls till his cock seemed to throb like a motor bicycle engine, and, well, it couldn't last for ever; he spent like Niagara.

The pretty girl threw back her head and gulped it down.

'I say, old chap,' came Tubby's voice from behind, 'you're beginning soon, y'know, and you've got the nicest, by God, y'have, and, I say, your aunt's looking for you, and she's going to stay the night, and what the devil are we going to do, what, what!'

The pretty maid stood up, blushing, and hung her head.

'You'd better be off, my dear,' said Tubby; 'and, for heavens sake, be careful what you do or say when that old lady's in the house.'

When they were alone, Charlie apologised.

'Oh, don't worry about *that*, old chap. You can do what you like to the girls, but it's your aunt—quick, for God's sake put those books away: I hear a rustle.'

Charlie was just in time. Lady Lavinia was in the room just as the cupboard door slammed.

She sniffed at the collection of liquors.

'As I thought, drinking, and *solitary* drinking. Why couldn't you be like your friend and come in the drawing-room for a little music?

'And what's this?' She picked up a maid's cap from

the floor. 'One of the *servant's* caps! What's it doing here?'

'Oh, I suppose she must have dropped it,' answered Charlie, pettishly. 'I'll come down to the drawing-room now. It'll be bed-time in a few minutes.'

In the servants' quarters of the house, discussion as to the identity and *raison d'être* of the new guests ran rife.

Young men of the world like Charlie were no new thing, but Aunt Lavinia—in such a house—well!

'Such particular instructions I've had to clear her room of anything saucy,' said the old housekeeper, gossiping in her room with the butler and the chauffeur; 'and I'm to take 'er tea myself: let none of them 'ussies go near.

'It makes me fair nervous, it do. Not that I altogether 'old with these games 'ere, but we're all in it, with our eyes open—oh, dear, *if* she should see some of them pictures.'

''Twould be a to-do, and no error,' said the butler.

'And the good lady she tink Mr Bertie so good young man vos—ha! ha!' and the chauffeur laughed viciously. 'She into what you call a 'ornet's nest got, is it not?'

In the greater servants' hall speculation was also rife: guests seldom arrived at that house except in very large parties, in motor loads at a time, as a rule. And as for mistress bringing home a single young man, she hadn't done such a thing for years.

No one had seen his condition when he arrived except the chauffeur, who had maintained a dogged silence. He had been told to do so, and his job was too good to lose.

52

They were a free and easy lot in the upper servants' hall at Maudie's, with a very large preponderance of women, mere girls, many of them, and all pretty. In fact, the house was ridiculously over-stocked with females. There was nothing for them to do save when the very big parties were on, and then they were more required for the photography than anything else.

There were only two men, both deft-handed servants, and both French, and a French-American cook, who was rather a wet blanket on the general irresponsibility of the girls. There remained the page-boy, and several other young boys and girls who helped in the scullery.

The girls did not care much for the two Frenchmen, and the cook thought of nothing at all but inventing new dishes; hence the joy with which Charlie was received.

It was an appetising scene. Everything in the house was done, and the girls sprawled in varied alluring *déshabillés*—it was a hot night, and drawers and chemise, or chemise only, or drawers and vest, and one or two, vest only. Two were quite naked. The room was very comfortable to lounge in, and Maudie didn't care what happened so long as she was waited on quickly. Two girls remained dressed, ready to see their mistress and Lady Lavinia to bed when rung for.

The page-boy was in general request, fetching coffee and cigarettes, and came in for a good deal more petting than was good for him. In fact, he was quite *blasé*. The warm caress of a semi-naked divinity had *no* effect on him.

They disappeared to bed by degrees, till only Elsie and May were left.

'Are you going to take the new gentleman any hot water?' queried May.

'Yes,' answered Elsie.

It was she who had come into the smoking-room.

'May I follow you?'

'A good half-hour after me. I tell you, dear, I need something badly; I haven't had my legs opened for a week, and it's just about time. You come in later, and we'll see what the two of us can't make him do: he's got a rare big 'un.'

'Right'—and they sealed the compact with a kiss.

There are few things prettier than the sight of two pretty women who are both lustful, and who really care for each other, kissing as if they meant it.

Tubby rolled over in bed, and grunted, then he kissed his bedfellow, and was immediately asleep. Maudie sighed. She had had a great deal too much of this of late. She thought over the events of the day, and longed for Charlie. For one wild moment she recollected how firmly Tubby slept, and contemplated making a dash for Charlie's room—but prudence prevailed. She mustn't jeopardize the future. She took up a book, *Nadia*, a lustful romance, and tried to read herself to sleep, but in vain. Her blood boiled, and at last she woke up Tubby roughly.

'Tubby, dear, I *must* and *will* be fucked,' she said. 'You hardly ever touch me, and yet you expect me to be true to you. Come on.'

Tubby acquiesced sadly. His extreme stoutness made it quite impossible for him to attack in the old Adam and Eve fashion. He had to do it as the beast of the field. He got out of bed and turned Maudie over its edge. Then, without seeming in the slightest enraptured by the sight of her snowy white buttocks, he deliberately plunged his sausage-like machine into that gap which should only have been reserved for connoisseurs.

Of course he liked it: he was very healthy, and full of good food and wine, and his penis swelled enormously as his strokes increased in vigour. Maudie lay on her stomach, her pretty little face buried in the lace-edged pillow, and her brain, behind her closed eyes, just a blissful vision of Charlie.

Oh! if it had only been Charlie!

The fact is known that sometimes women who, when madly lustful for particular men, are forced to be carnal elsewhere, derive really more pleasure from the beautific dream of their fancied darling, who in a vision is responsible for the flesh spasms which the unseen operator manipulates, than they do when the real darling is in the saddle, so to speak.

Maudie certainly loved it, and she was only just conscious enough of what had happened to bite her tongue to stop crying 'Charlie' as the last violent stroke from her fat lover sent a hard-shot torrent right up to the doors of her womb.

'My God,' she thought, 'I really believe Tubby has copped me this time.'

She hastened to syringe, a precaution she seldom took with her fat lover.

Tubby, on his part, sank exhausted into an armchair.

'You've fair whacked me this time, petlet,' he gasped. 'I've never had a fuck like this with you before. What's come over you?'

The dream was still in Maudie's brain as she answered vaguely, 'How—how can you help it, when you love so much?'

When Tubby did turn off to sleep he dreamed rapturously. Maudie, too, slept well: she was thoroughly tired at last. These physical and mental fucks combined are pretty fairly damaging to the vitality.

Lady Lavinia, when the pretty maid had helped her out of her clothes and given her a nightdress, the decorations of which ill coincided with the elderly widow, removed her wig, put her teeth in a glass, and sniffed round the room.

She could not but approve of the comfort. No detail necessary to coax comfort to the weary or lazy bedgoer was missing.

Maudie had put it to her very delicately that if she had neuralgia—or anything—there was 'something' in the cupboard.

She had a look, and found, in addition to the 'something', a pile of books, one of which she picked out at random.

It was prettily bound, and called *Nemesis Hunt*. She took it back to bed with her, had a very hearty drop of the 'something', and opened it.

A good many readers of this book may have read *Nemesis Hunt*. They will remember that that charming and loquacious lady somewhat lets the tail go with the hide in her confessions. A fuck is called a fuck, and there is *more* than fucking in the naïve three volumes.

Lady Lavinia's eyes dilated as she read. Once before, in the very early days of her married life, she had been shown a book like this by her husband, and she remembered now, with a sigh, *what* a night they had subsequently had.

Her first impulse was to throw down the book in anger, the consciousness of her position, her reputation, flashed through her brain, but—curiosity prevailed, and Lady Lavinia, firmly adjusting her glasses, took another strong sip of the 'something', and started seriously in to read the first volume of *The Confessions of Nemesis Hunt*.

When young, she had been very pretty, and had been much courted. She had loved admiration, and had flirted above a bit.

Her short married life with the late earl had been a long round of love and lust, and frank sexual enjoyment, but his sudden death had brought about an equally sudden revulsion of feeling.

Lady Lavinia had turned suddenly very good, mid-Victorian good. She had mourned her husband, and put a great deal of mournfulness into other people's lives by doing so—as have other illustrious widows.

Now there came back a rush of something—it must have been Georgian—and she let down the drawbridge.

At the end of the fifteenth page of Nemesis Hunt's pleasant confessions, she decided to leave on the morrow, *but* return.

Nemesis was put under the pillow, and in that very ultra-modern house there slept what may be described as a memory of Cremorne.

Charlie Osmond went to bed with mixed feelings. He had had a very good time: he had a prospect of future life in view, which he rather welcomed—*but*, he wanted to be with Maudie—not to be immoral, but to talk. It flatly bored him to go to bed.

Outside, the Thames valley looked very peaceful. The dogs, the chickens, everything slept, except Charlie, *and* Elsie and May, who, after seeing to the little wants of Lady Lavinia and Maudie, bided their time for an invasion into Charlie's room.

That worthy had his suspicions of impending events. He did not lock the door, but sat by the window in his pyjamas, and gazed peacefully out over the moonlit garden and river.

It was altogether rather too nice, too idyllic, and—well—the door opened, and Elsie came in without knocking.

She was fully dressed, and carried a tray with hot water and glasses.

Charlie laughed.

'I somehow expected you,' he said; 'but do you know it's very wrong. You don't know what I am, whether I'm married or not, or *what* trouble this might get me into.'

Elsie laughed.

'Well, I've done it,' she said. 'I meant to from the first moment I saw you. Give me a cigarette and a drink, and let me come and sit in the window, and you won't be bored for the next half hour, I can promise you.'

Elsie curled up on the corner of the window-seat, the moon full on her delicate little features, lit the proffered Albany cigarette, sipped a little of the whisky and Rosbach, and grinned, frankly grinned.

'I suppose you think it frightful cheek,' she suggested.

'Well, I can't say I don't like your cheek,' and he kissed it.

Elsie kissed him back on the lips, and took off her bodice. She had very pretty arms, and a gold bangle with a purple enamel medallion, worn just above the left elbow, did not make them less attractive.

She had a little more of the Three Star Bushmills, stood up and slid her skirt off: then her chemise—she wore no petticoats—and to cut a long story short, her next sitting-place was on Charlie's knee, and the next kiss had nothing to do with cheeks.

Charlie lifted her on to the bed. Even then, though she was exasperatingly pretty, he could not help thinking of Maudie.

She curled over him, slowly, deliberately and maliciously taking both his hands in hers, and rubbing her soft cheeks against his.

There must be something in telepathy, for at the moment, the precise moment that Charlie reconciled himself to a connection which he *knew* would be nice, but which he really did not want, save for the exquisite pleasure in thinking that Elsie's arms were Maudie's, that latter lady saw in a blue mist of ecstacy the image of a very loving Charlie—poor Tubby being merely the engine-driver who drove the imagination of her recklessly lustful brain.

Charlie let himself frankly go. There was no light in the room at all bar the shafts of the moon, filtering through the swaying trees. The silhouetted skyline and the delightfully placid atmosphere made Charlie lazy.

He had some recollection of little tickling fingers swiftly undoing the strings of his pyjamas, little tickling fingers also playing with an already erect member, naked arms twisted round his neck, firm, plump legs twisted round his thighs, and—well—he was in—well in—and those soft cheeks were most lustfully pressed to his.

Maudie had been very loving, *but*—all said and done—as he felt all his love juice being sucked out of him, *this*, Charlie couldn't help admitting, was better still.

He came in a long rhapsody: the girl jerked the eiderdown over them, and snuggled up. He didn't know whether she meant to stay the night, or not, or what the morals of this peculiar house permitted, but it was *very* comfortable.

He was just going to sleep when the door opened very quietly, and *another* girl came into the moonlight.

Charlie gave up. He remembered where he was, and determined to die game. The 'other girl' apologised laughingly, and the original giggled in the sheets.

'You don't mind May, do you?' she said.

'No,' was Charlie's answer; 'but it's got to stop at May, you and May. If I've got to go through the whole *personnel* of the establishment, I give up.'

May did not answer—but just, just seemed to *slide* just as Elsie had done—out of her clothes, and into bed.

Poor, but happy Charlie—he realized quite what a squeezed lemon must feel like—but he valiantly did his duty.

May was more placid than Elsie, more tender, more caressing, perhaps, but Charlie's cock was just as stiff as he felt his balls right against the soft buttocks of his new love.

It was a long fuck and a delightful one. Elsie, wicked little devil, gave every help in her power.

She flung back the clothes, and there they lay, three naked bodies in the moonlight. There was no artificial light save the glow of Elsie's cigarette end.

Elsie slipped the pillow down so that her little friend's bottom was just correctly raised, and, as Charlie knelt between May's legs, guided his penis dexterously in.

May, of course, was shaved, in the fashion of everyone in Maudie's mansion, and Charlie began more and more to appreciate the added charm of the hairless cunt, as he thrust his fingers between their bodies and felt the soft, warm, smooth flesh.

Elsie crept right on top of them, her head between Charlie's legs, so that her tongue swept over and over his swelling balls. As his cock slipped in and out of May, her fingers played with it. May had a large cunt, and Elsie's little finger could slip in beside Charlie's cock.

Her cunt was on his backbone, and on that she frigged herself—he felt the warm love moisture much about the same time as he spent himself in May.

He didn't recollect the actual end, didn't recollect anything till a stream of daylight dazzled him into being, and he found himself alone—with a little note pinned on each side of his broad pillow.

Each read the same: 'Thanks *so* much.'

Only the handwriting and the signature were different. One 'Elsie'—the other 'May'.

Pauline the Prima Donna

Among the persons attending the rehearsal I noticed a stranger who immediately made a strong impression on me: a very handsome man, well dressed, with an intelligent face. When the tenor sang a false note, he leaped to the stage, took the score, and sang the passage with such passion and so much expression and taste that the whole cast was enraptured. I have never heard a voice his equal; it sent shivers of delight the length of my spine. Everyone applauded wildly and the tenor cried, 'After you, sir, it would be a profanation for me to continue!' And with that he ripped up the rest of his score.

I asked Monsieur de R. who he was and if he was Hungarian.

'You are asking me more than I can tell you,' he replied. 'His card carries the name Ferry. He could be Hungarian, English, Italian or Spanish, as well as French, German or Russian. He seems to speak all languages. I have not yet seen his papers, and the only thing I know is that he has just arrived from Vienna, that he is received at court there, that the English ambassador has recommended him to his *chargé d'affaires* for something or other, that he has dined with the manager of the royal theatre, and that everyone is happy to have him at dinner. I think that he is on some sort of diplomatic mission, and I know that he is living at the *Hotel de la Reine d'Angleterre*.'

Ferry remained to the end of the rehearsal and we were introduced. He was a perfect and gallant gentleman, and I had to watch myself closely when speaking with him.

I was always free in the evening when I had a long rehearsal in the afternoon or morning, and someone had recommended that I go often to the theatre in order to hear good Hungarian spoken. So that night I attended a performance accompanied by Madame de F. At the first intermission I had the pleasure of an unexpected visit from Ferry. He excused himself for coming to see me so quickly, but I begged him to stay. He paid me several compliments, saying he liked my voice very much, that I had good stage presence, that my costumes and makeup were excellent, etc., but he never spoke a word of love. He was simple and polite, never common and never importunate, and I resolved then and there to make a conquest of this man before the women of Budapest society got to him. I immediately brought all of my charm and coquetry into play, thinking to win him rapidly and, as he asked permission to pay me a visit soon, I thought that I had already won. I was soon to discover my error.

We finally did speak of love, but in a very general way. However much his eyes were eloquent, his tongue remained mute, and if his words left me in no doubt of how much I pleased him, he never so much as hinted at asking the slightest favour. When he pressed my hands upon arriving or leaving, he did it almost nonchalantly, without attaching the least bit of significance to it.

Finally, even so, I managed to steer the conversation to his past loves, and I asked him if he had made many conquests and if he had ever been seriously in love.

'I take the beautiful where I find it,' he replied. 'I believe that it would be an injustice to bind myself to a single individual and I think, in theory, that marriage is the most tyrannical institution in society. How can a man of honour dare to offer that which does not depend solely on his good will? Generally speaking, I believe that one should never promise anything to anyone, and you will never find a soul that can say to you truthfully that I have once promised him something. I do not even promise to come to a dinner when I have been invited; I content myself simply with acknowledging the invitation. I never gamble; chance is too great a power for me to give it the opportunity to defeat me. And that is why I never promise a woman to remain faithful to her. She must take me as I am if she takes me at all. If she is willing to share my heart with others, she will find plenty of room. That is the reason that I have never yet made a declaration of love to a woman; I always wait until she tells me simply and frankly that I please her enough so that she can no longer refuse me anything.'

'I imagine that you have already come across many such persons,' I said to him, 'but I cannot understand how you have been able to love them. It seems to me that a woman must be extremely imprudent to dare take the first steps in an affair, without waiting for the man to assume the initiative and make the overtures.'

'And why, may I ask?' he replied. 'Does not a man prefer a woman that loves him enough to dare to break all the laws of conventionality to one that simply plays a role? Women who demand the man's initiative are only going to give in at last in any case. A man infinitely prefers a woman who knows how to sacrifice her vanity to a woman who only knows how to be a coquette. Bitterness often pushes a man to revenge himself on a woman who has made him languish a long time, and when she finally cedes to him what he wishes, he will be unfaithful to her and leave her.'

'And those unfortunate young women that cede to the first attack of the man, do they also merit his vengeance?'

'I have never revenged myself but on coquettes, and I would certainly not like to seduce a young, innocent girl. I have never done it either, although God knows I've had the opportunities. Each woman that I have had has offered herself to me without my asking anyone to sacrifice her virginity. Each of them was free to choose, and they said to themselves, 'Should I prefer him who pursues me and who does not please me, or him who pleases me and says nothing?' And each of their choices fell upon me. They managed to free themselves from the foolish scruples that their mothers, aunts and other frustrated spinsters had taught them from childhood, and they played their game in the open. None of them ever regretted it, for each knew the risks she was running; I explained to each one that, though she could possibly become a mother, even so I would never marry her, that I loved other women as well as her, and that she might never see me again. Tell me, was I honest or not?'

I could not deny it, but I also told him I would never dare to make a declaration of love to a man.

'Then,' he said, 'you will never love a man. For love in a woman entails sacrifice, and I will never show the slightest favour to a woman that will not give me the proof of such a love.'

He had answered everything I had asked; I knew now that he would never make a declaration of love to me. However, it was evident that I pleased him. Why else did he visit me so often? He preferred to be in my company rather than go out for the evening. Nevertheless, I hesitated. I wanted to make the declaration he wished, but I wanted to do it in such a manner as to save myself as many blushes as possible, and I hoped to find a means during the carnival. I didn't know if he thought me experienced or not but, in any case, virginity obviously had no particular charm for him. What he would have liked would have been a virgin as corrupt as a Mesalina. Unfortunately, there are no such virgins.

I did not know if I ought to confide in someone and have them act as an intermediary. I finally talked to Anna. She told me that although Ferry had already succumbed to another woman, she would do everything possible to win him for me. Above all, however, she wanted to know if he were going to participate in the orgy which was to take place in the brothel.

Several days later she brought me the news that Ferry's mistress was the Countess O. Her chambermaid had overheard the initial conversation between the two. He had proposed exactly the same conditions to the countess, adding to the two that he had mentioned to me as being necessary—that the woman must make the overtures and that she must not count on his fidelity—a third: that each woman who gave herself to him must be completely nude. When a woman accorded everything to a man, he asserted, there was no reason for her not to reveal herself completely. The countess had accepted.

I do not know if I could abandon myself in that

fashion, even if I were to be in love. I am very liberal on that point; however, I cannot free myself from a certain prudishness which, innate or acquired, still dominates me. I have not yet learned whether this facet of my character is common to all women.

In the meantime, Anna told me that, though Ferry would undoubtedly participate in the orgy, as he had been invited by three women, he had not promised definitely, for it was against his principles.

The evening of the orgy approached rapidly. Anna, Rose and Nina helped me to finish my costume and try it on. It was made of a sky-blue silk, very heavy, with insertions of white gauze and brocaded gold flowers. My buttocks and, in front, my breasts and my belly, from the navel to three inches below my grotto of delight, were uncovered. On my feet I was wearing a pair of crimson velvet-tipped sandals. My collar was the ruffled lace one sees in portraits of Mary Stuart. The sleeves of my dress were elbow length and embroidered in gold. An Indian shawl, also in gold, was fastened about my waist and my hair was adorned with multicoloured marabou feathers.

I did not want to wear my own jewels, as they would have given away my identity, so I left them with a Jewess, who lent me some others. Besides this, I carried a staff with a gilded penis in erection on its tip, and wore a mask that covered my whole face except for the mouth and eyes. The colour of my hair was not unusual enough to betray me, although there were very few women who could claim locks as rich as mine. In all, my costume was in very good taste and quite original.

The 23rd of January, Anna and I went to the house on the Goldstickergasse, I wearing a heavy cloak over my attire. When we arrived, Anna left me in the vestibule and I was received by Resi Luft. Although the hall was already well filled and the orchestra playing, the first men I saw upon entering were Monsieur de F. and the baron. They were almost entirely nude, wearing only a sort of skimpy bathing suit in clinging silk, and they wore no masks. My entry, meanwhile, had created a sensation. I heard the women murmuring, 'There is the one that is going to beat us tonight! . . . My, she is pretty! . . . That one is made of sugar, and how I would love to eat some of it! . . .' And the men were even more excited. The most beautiful parts of my body—my breasts, my arms, my calves, my buttocks, and my sex—were all bare or scarcely veiled. I waited not a second, taking the opportunity to seek out Ferry immediately. I finally found him dancing with a woman dressed in white tulle scattered over with roses and lilies, for she was supposed to be a nymph. Her body was fairly well proportioned, but not as beautiful as mine. Another woman had her arm around Ferry's hips. She represented Venus, and the only articles she wore were a belt of gold, a few diamonds and a crown in her raven black hair. She held the great, erect sceptre of her partner in her hand, and I must admit that I have never seen as large nor as handsome a lance as his. It was of an extraordinary size, as red as the sandals that were the only clothing of its master, and it shone as if it had been dipped in oil. The rest of Ferry's body was a gleaming white, tinted here and there with pinks and roses. Not even an Apollo, a Belvedere or an Antinous could have been as handsome or as well proportioned as he, and I trembled at the sight of him. My eyes were so busy devouring him that I stopped involuntarily before the tableau of which he was the centre. His Venus had a very pretty body, very white, but her breasts were slightly pendulous, and her violet-lipped grotto was too open, too ravaged by love.

Suddenly Ferry's eyes found and rested on mine. He smiled very slightly and said, 'Very good. That is much the best method by which to take the initiative.' He then broke away from his women and came towards me, bent his head down to mine, and whispered my name in my ear. I blushed scarlet beneath my mask.

The orchestra, separated by a great screen from the revellers, broke into a waltz, Ferry took me by the waist, and we whirled into the maelstrom of couples. The contact of all those bodies, burning and brilliant, male and female, infatuated me. All the members of the men were fully erect and, during the dance, turning towards a common goal. Kisses bubbled everywhere, and an exquisite perfume began to float upwards from the closely clasped bodies. I was dizzy with joy. I felt Ferry's dagger touch me suddenly, butting its head like a maddened bull against my sex. I pressed myself against him, spreading my legs so that he could enter lower down, but he did not attempt it, asking me instead, 'Are you ever jealous?'

'No!' I responded quickly. 'I want to see you like Mars and Venus.'

He left me quickly and took Venus, who was dancing with another man. Meanwhile two of the girls of the house, Vladislava and Leonie, brought out a stool covered with red velvet and placed it in the middle of the room. Venus bent over it, leaning on it with her hands, and Ferry attacked her from the rear.

71

Vladislava and Leonie then knelt at the feet of the combatants, the first spreading Venus' lips, the other tickling Ferry's testicles. Ferry gave Venus such a riding that she was soon groaning in ecstasy; I was now feverishly stripping myself. I now stood entirely nude before him and asked, 'The mask too?'

'Keep it,' he said and, withdrawing his rod from the goddess, shooed her off with a smack on the behind so that I could take her place. My knees turned to rubber. Ferry then kneeled before me, tonguing me so masterfully that I thought I would surely discharge; finally he attacked me from the rear as he had my predecessor. I noticed then that his rod was the splendid rose colour of the symbol on the staff I had carried to the ball.

It was too much! Venus and another woman were sucking my breasts, a third was kissing me and thrusting her tongue between my lips to suck and bite, while Leonie was kneeling between my legs and tickling the base of my font with her tongue. My senses whirled, my breath rasped in my throat, and my whole body trembled; everywhere hips, thighs, arms and buttocks burned me, and from my font flowed a whirling stream like whipped cream, jetting into the mouth of Ferry, who drank it to the last drop. Then he leaped to his feet once more with a bound and drove his great sceptre into me to the root. All my nerves, which before had been distended, now knotted with desire; my temple of pleasure was on fire; the shaft of stone ravaged me like a knife. How that man could ride in the joust of love! Sometimes he completely withdrew his weapon, rubbed the head against my lips, then thrust it in again suddenly and violently. I could feel the tiny opening of my hymen attempting to absorb the enormous head of his mace; it held it tightly, as if in a vice, until he completely tore it violently open. He repeated this game several times, his movements accelerating and becoming more abandoned, while his rod expanded even more. He was no longer master of his desires, and he leaned heavily upon me. His fingers bruised my thighs, his mouth sank into my shoulder, and his tongue sucked the blood. Suddenly I felt his jet inundate me and overflow my sex.

I thought that I had lost the game, that all was over, but at once he began afresh, his weapon a prisoner in my cavern of joy, regaining its vigour little by little. He kept up the assault and I responded with ardour. The duel continued, but more carefully, more slowly, to the applause of the spectators, who had now formed a circle around us. Thrust followed thrust at regular intervals; I suddenly felt an electric shock that nearly paralyzed me—a great jet even more scalding than the first ripped through my body.

Once more he was to prove his strength to me, his love and his virility. The spectators became delirious when they saw him withdraw his sword from the scabbard for the third time and for the third time thrust it back in to renew the combat of love. They began to cry, 'All good things come in threes!' This time the game lasted a good quarter of an hour and they watched it to the end. Ferry was indefatigable, but the crisis had to arrive sooner or later and our joy was infinite. He inundated me with his sperm, carrying our passion to undreamed of heights. I was no longer standing on my own feet. Several of the girls of the house were supporting me, while from all sides, I felt nothing but nude flesh. Women were covering me with kisses and biting my nipples, while Ferry, still standing behind me, clasped me in his arms.

Finally they left us alone. Ferry clasped me once more and then offered me his arm to take me to another room. 'On the throne! On the throne!' cried several voices, for there had been erected at one end of the hall a sort of throne made of an ottoman covered with red velvet and surmounted with a canopy of purple. It was there that they wished to carry us in triumph, to indicate that we had won first place among all the combats of love. Ferry declined in my name, thanked them for the honour, and said that if it were permitted he would prefer to take a short rest. Thereupon the woman who was dressed as Venus took us into the banquet hall, but the table was not yet prepared.

'Isn't there a private room somewhere where my Titania (he called me thus, for he said that I was most beautiful of the beautiful) can rest quietly for a minute?'

'Resi Luft ought to have several,' replied Venus. 'I will tell her to ready one for you.' She disappeared and soon returned with our hostess. At sight of her, we burst into gales of laughter, for she had followed our example and was completely nude. She was old, enormously fat, and incredibly greasy, a perfect twin of that famous queen of the South Sea Islands, Nomahanna. Oh, those great reddish rolls of flesh and that timber forest beneath her belly! But somehow she proved appetizing yet, for I understand that she found several men to taste her charms and to let themselves be swallowed up in that sea of flesh.

She let us into a small room near the dance hall,

from where we could watch the progress of the bacchanal. There were several couples still dancing, but most of them preferred a more serious occupation. We could hear the murmur of voices, the sound of kisses, the panting of men, and the sighs of women. I was sitting on the knees of my lover, and becoming more and more excited by what I could see, when something hard and hot rose against my buttocks. I did not need to guess what it was.

'You are not ready to start again?' I asked him, covering his mouth with kisses.

'And why not, may I ask?' he said, laughing. 'But would you refuse if I shut the door and asked you to remove your mask? I want to be able to see the sensuality and the pleasure in your face.'

He was not the tyrant that I had thought. This despot of mine was as mild and caressing as a shepherd. I went to the door and shut it. Then I turned, took off my mask, and threw myself on the bed. I spread my thighs, pushed myself up on my elbows, and awaited my cavalier. He didn't hesitate a second before ramming home his lance, and this time there was no one to disturb us. I saw only him and he saw only me.

Can I possibly tell you what I felt? No, I think not. It will have to suffice to say that we drank three consecutive libations to the gods of love, and I simply cannot tell you the joy I felt at having these all by myself and in privacy. When the crisis approached, his eyes fixed themselves on mine and took on a savage expression of desire. We rolled breast to breast, stomach to stomach, arms and legs entwined like serpents. At the end, we lay side by side, his sceptre still inside my case, our eyes closed, resting and finally falling asleep. We lay in this ecstasy a good half-hour until the sound of the revels reaching their peak awakened us. I dressed hurriedly, forgetting my mask, which Ferry took and put on my face, and we reentered the hall.

The orgy had indeed reached its height. You could see nothing but groups of bodies, in every imaginable pose, made up of two, three, four and five persons.

There were two groups that were particularly complicated. One was composed of a man and six women. He was lying on his back on a plank across two chairs. He was running one girl through with his lance; another was sitting on his chest while he licked her grotto; his hands were tickling the fonts of two other girls; the remaining two were being invaded in their sensitive spots by his big toes. These last two were actually playing less; they were there only to complete the group and had to pretend to be satisfying themselves.

The other group was composed of Venus, who was stretched across one man who invaded her from the front, while another attacked her rear, an opening much smaller than the first. In her two hands she manipulated the organs of two other men. The fifth man, a giant from Rhodes, knelt on two chairs above the head of the first, who sucked his shaft of love. The climax was achieved at the same time among all six of them. It was undoubtedly the best group.

A third group was made up of two women and one man. One of the women was lying on her back, the other on the stomach of the first with her legs tightly wrapped around the hips of her partner. They were both spread voluptuously, biting and licking each other. The man dressed like Hercules, forced his lance

76

first into one and then into the other, and I was curious to see how they would share his vital fluid when the time came. As it turned out, it was a reasonable and just division; neither received more than the other. When the crisis struck he did not lose his head, but doled the nectar out equally. The one on the bottom received the first.

Every man and woman at this ball took part in the activities. No one remained a wallflower. Everyone was a combatant at least twice, and Ferry among the men and I among the women were in the best form.

Venus, the Countess Bella, and I were the only women who had so far remained masked. Later on I learned that Venus was a woman famous for her affairs and I discovered her identity. She never, however, removed her mask. The Countess Bella was a veritable fury, a female demon. She cried in a loud voice, 'Look! Look! Don't you know that I am a whore, a real whore!' She then made a tour of all the ladies of the house, giving them candy, fruit or champagne. At the table, she drank a full tumbler of brandy that a man had poured for her and rolled dead-drunk onto the floor. Resi Luft dragged her into a room and locked the door, while Bella tried to break it down. Finally she went fast asleep. Later, two of the whores went to see if she were still sleeping and found her flowing from every opening like a leaky barrel. They put her on a bed and she slept until four the next afternoon.

The supper was in every way worthy of the orgy. Several persons slept on the table, and there were not more than two men besides Ferry who were capable of comporting themselves decently. The others were left standing by, hanging their heads sadly. Finally the prizes were distributed. Ferry was proclaimed the king, followed by one who had played the harmonica very well, and a third who had given out a lot of candy. My chief rival, the Princess O, whom I had found in Ferry's company, had finished him off very well. I tried to get him to drink until he was drunk, thinking that it was a chance of reviving him, but he refused. However, he did down one more glass of brandy before the orgy terminated at four o'clock in the morning.

Ferry and I, Venus and several other women went home. The rest were drunk and passed the remainder of the night at Resi Luft's.

On the whole, I noticed that the girls of our hostess conducted themselves better than the other women. They had been asked to take part in the ball by the men beforehand and all continued into the bacchanal that followed except Leonie. However, it was said that she was actually a member of the nobility, and that she had left her parents, members of an old Viennese family, to come directly to Resi Luft and practise her adopted *métier*.

Ferry accompanied me to my apartment, where Rose was still up awaiting me. She did not go to bed until I finally asked her to, and need I tell you that for Ferry, who was himself again, and I, the war of love was not yet over for that night?

I was splitting my pleasure, during those days in Budapest, with two persons, Ferry and Rose. The former was my declared lover while the latter served to vary my excitements.

One day Ferry surprised me by saying that until he had met me he had never known real love, that his long-held principles were no longer as solid as they once had been, and that he could now admit his fidelity. If I wished, he added, he would now consent to marry me. Despite the allure of such a proposition, I refused and was forced to refuse many times again when he continued to put the proposition before me. I was too afraid of killing our love by attaching other bonds to it, for I firmly believe that both the church and the state have made marriage a tomb for love. The memory of the happy life of my parents did not serve to reassure me, for I felt that that had been pure chance. Very simply, I loved and the secret of our pleasures only served to augment my love. Ferry appreciated and finally adopted my views.

I abandoned myself completely to love. I loved no one but Ferry and, thanks to his prudence, no one suspected our relations and my reputation did not suffer in the slightest.

Rose, however, had much more to complain of. Ferry took no notice of her to speak of, and I rarely had a night free to spend with her. Realizing this, and since I was not a victim of any kind of jealousy, I asked myself if it would not be wise to push her into the arms of Ferry also. The taking of her virginity with the aid of my rubber instrument that night had not been completely successful, for the membrane had resumed its former position and she was once more as good as new. You are probably going to say this is impossible, but I assure you that several months after the episode with Anna and Nina I attempted to insert my finger into her cavern and found my way blocked. I made her lie down on the couch and examined her grotto very carefully under a lamp. She spread her legs and I saw an entry that was completely round, with a little partition that was quite hard and completely inelastic. It reminded me of the presentation of a virgin at the panopticum on St. Joseph's Square near the fair of Budapest . . . I am not religious and I am only telling you what I saw.

I asked Rose if she would like to have a lover like Ferry, and she replied that when she had me she did not want any man. She said that if she had to sacrifice her virginity to a man she would be doing it only for my pleasure. Ferry did not seem to her any more desirable than any other man she had known.

Very few women know the pleasure of watching the combats of another couple and very few men feel anything but scorn for a woman who gives herself to another man before their eyes. Ferry and I were exceptions.

Ferry had often asked me to give myself up to another man before his eyes, but I had always refused, thinking that he wanted to quit me and that he was only looking for an excuse. I had not yet begun to believe that it was only pleasure he was after. However, he told me of many examples of the same thing, citing in history the cases of Gatta and Melatta, the Venetian heroes who never made love to their wives until they had abandoned themselves to another man. Finally I was convinced, and we decided that Ferry should teach the art of love to Rose and that afterwards I would do the same with a young man.

I had a great deal of difficulty in convincing Rose that she should take part. She threw herself into my arms, crying and saying that I no longer loved her, and I had to try to prove the opposite. I kissed and sucked her front, I bit the nipples on her breasts, I excited her so that she panted with desire. Then Ferry helped me to strip her and soon she was nude before us. Ferry kissed her tenderly and passionately, stroking her foaming grotto with his shaft of love until finally the moment arrived. He picked her up and carried her to the bed where he placed several pillows beneath her behind. She spread her legs involuntarily and he kneeled between them. The little fake was trembling in all her limbs, but she had her eyes closed so that we should not see how much she really wanted the pleasure that was about to come. I kneeled on another pillow so that her head was underneath my stomach. She immediately pressed me with her left hand while her right held tightly to Ferry, to whom I had turned my stern. When Ferry finally broke through Rose's membrane she bit me violently. Even this pain was wonderful. Neither Rose nor I could prevent from crying out in ecstasy; Ferry alone was silent.

Rose was so violent in her pleasure that Ferry could hardly stay aboard her. She bucked, groaned, then cried out passionately or cooed like a dove. We lay there, one on top of the other, one within the other, and our burning bodies smoked in the bed. I forced my nose deep into Rose's armpit and lay there, drunker than if I had been drinking all evening. Our ecstasy was infinite.

Little by little we recovered and left the soaked bed. Ferry advised us to take a bath at once, which we did. In Budapest, I had made a hot bath a daily luxury, for I found that it always revived me immediately, no matter how fatigued I was by either love or work, and it did no less for us this time.

Ferry was a master of love. He knew every means for increasing and renewing pleasure. And this time he was no less imaginative. When Rose and I got out of the tub and began to dry ourselves, he stopped us and told us instead to rub soap and oil over our bodies. This we did, and our bodies became as slippery as those of two eels. Then he had me lean over the bathtub while he hoisted Rose to his shoulders. In this position, with her facing him, he attacked me from the rear, not through the ordinary tunnel, but through a neighbouring one that up until then had been virgin to me. He had smeared it well with oil, making his entry much easier. However, it did hurt a little.

While he was thus occupied, he put his arms around me and forced his fingers in through my cavern and I could feel his hands inside me almost reaching his shaft. Only a thin layer of skin seemed to separate them. Sensuality was, at that point, much stronger than pain and I was completely ravished by desire. In the meantime, Rose slipped onto my shoulders so that her temple of love was now before my mouth. The game was exquisite and we all came at the same time. However, Ferry would have finished his play much sooner than either Rose or I if he had not kept his head. For he was forced to stop and remove his arrow from my quiver several times in order to remain master of himself. Each time that he returned to the assault a sharp pain which quickly turned to a quenching sensuality filled me. It was thus that he attacked five or six times before we were all reduced to intoxication. Rose's fountain overflowed its banks. In the meantime the flow from Ferry's weapon inundated my interior and my own source sprang forth.

I can never remember having had an experience like that again. It was undoubtedly the height of my sensuality and I will never be able to forget that game in my life. We finally parted and went to Rose's bed to sleep, for mine was still afloat. We lay down, Ferry in the middle and the two of us pressing on him from both sides.

Ever since that night I have never been able to understand jealousy in women. It no longer seems to me reasonable and natural that these things do not happen more frequently in our civilized countries, for I am convinced that copulation and desire have for their object, not the perpetuation of the species, but simply the experiences of sensuality.

The very next day Ferry reminded me of my promise and assured me that if I carried it out no one should ever know. He told me to accompany him on a short trip.

It was spring and the weather was magnificent. Ferry told me we would leave Budapest on the day after the next, and he spent the intervening twenty-four hours entirely with me.

We left the city on a Sunday at two o'clock in the morning. Taking Ferry's private carriage instead of a train or boat, we travelled the rest of the night until we reached Nessmely around eight in the morning. There we left the main highway, crossed Igmand, and arrived at around noon in the famous forest of Bakony. At an inn in the middle of the forest we found a table already prepared for us. There were several rather sinister and evil looking men about, and I thought that they were perhaps robbers. Ferry talked with them a few moments in Hungarian and I asked him worriedly what they were up to. He told me that they were just some poor devils that lived in the wood, and that I had nothing to fear. In the afternoon, after we had eaten, we climbed back into our coach, this time preceded by five horsemen.

We no longer went as fast as we had, for the road was very bad and narrow. Finally we arrived at the densest part of the forest and once more alit from our carriage. We walked the rest of the way and the coach was driven to a building which I could barely see through the trees and which looked like an inn. The horsemen preceded us, parting the branches for our passage, and we finally reached a beautiful glade with a large and deep stream. We rested there and ate, and an hour later, two men appeared. One was about thirty-four or thirty-five and was built like a Hercules. His face was savage but very regular, almost handsome. The other, scarcely twenty, was as beautiful as Adonis. Ferry presented the two men and told me I would now taste the thrills of love with them, that I had nothing to fear, and that neither knew who I was nor had the slightest relation with the outside world.

The Hercules immediately stripped, but the young man blushed and hesitated. Ferry gave him a sharp command and he followed suit. I undressed slowly and Ferry told me that I should abandon myself completely, because the more passionate I was the more pleasure he would take in the sight. However, knowing his thoughts, I resolved to be as dissolute as possible. I called the two men and took them by their lances. The little mushroom of the young man immediately became a branch of oak that reached all the way up to his navel. The giant's sword had unsheathed itself as soon as I had undressed. I took the young man's weapon and started to tickle the end of it but as soon as I touched it I received the full flow of his burning discharge. In the meantime, the giant lifted me by my buttocks until my behind was touching his stomach and, without my guiding him, thrust his lance straight into my shell. I thought he would penetrate right up to my throat, his weapon was so long. His blows fell slowly, measuredly and powerfully, and I thought at each shock that I would swoon. However, I never loosened my grasp on the young man's shaft and it soon grew hard and strong once more.

'Is it good?' Ferry asked me. He was not yet undressed himself.

I could only reply to his answer with my eyes. I almost fainted with delight and my lock gates began to open wide until they finally released my precious nectar, flooding the giant's great shaft. However, he continued without tiring, and worked a good half hour before he began to feel his crisis approach.

'Don't give her any children!' cried Ferry, laughing.

'Don't worry! Where I'm going to end up you'll never find a baby growing!'

And with that, he removed his redoubtable staff from my shell and I thought I would die from pain when he forced it into the neighbouring hole. He gave only two thrusts when the juice from his loins flowed in a jet that lasted at least a full minute. It repaid him well for his long labour and finally he withdrew his dart. He had so skinned me that I could not at all sit down and scarcely walk. He carried me to the stream and washed my wound with his fingers, thereby soothing my pain, but I still could not walk a step. I was very sorry not to have accorded the young man more pleasure, but I had solaced him twice.

I remained about an hour in the water, then the

giant took me in his arms and three men helped him dress me. They finally took me into the house where Ferry put me to bed.

Can I describe to you vividly enough the three days that I passed in that forest? I changed lovers every day and even more often than that, for there were nine brigands. And the third day we celebrated with a great orgy with the peasants from nearby. Agrippina would have envied our saturnalias. These peasants were as skilful and adroit as the aristocrats of Budapest.

I had plenty of time to rest up during the rest of my vacation and Rose alone accompanied me. I left Ferry after many tender farewells, but it was necessary, for many more debauches would have surely killed me.

A Man with a Maid

'I was very angry with my maid this morning and it would have delighted me to have spanked her severely. Now, would such delight arise from satisfied revenge or from being cruel?'

'Undoubtedly from being cruel,' I replied, 'the infliction of the punishment is what would have given you the pleasure, and behind it would come the feeling that you were revenging yourself. Here's another instance—you women delight in saying nasty cutting things to each other in the politest of ways; why? Not from revenge, but from the satisfaction afforded by the shot going home. If you had given your maid this morning a box on the ears you would have satisfied your revenge without any pleasure whatever; but if I had been there and held your maid down while you spanked her bottom, your pleasure would have arisen from the infliction of the punishment. Do you follow me, dear?'

'Yes, I see it now,' Alice replied, then added archly: 'I wish you had been there, Jack! it would have done her a lot of good!'

'I sometimes wonder why you keep her on,' I said musingly. 'She's a pert minx and at times must be very aggravating. Let me see—what's her name?'

'Fanny.'

'Yes, of course—a case of 'pretty Fanny's way,' for she certainly is a pretty girl and a well-made one. My dear, if you want to do bottom slapping, you won't easily find a better subject, only I think she will be more than you can manage single-handed, and it may come to her slapping your bottom, my love!'

Alice laughed. 'Fanny is a most perfect maid, a real treasure, or I would not keep her on—for as you say, she is too much for me. She's very strong and very high-spirited, but wants taming badly.'

'Bring her some afternoon, and we'll tame her between us!' I suggested seemingly carelessly.

Alice started, raised herself on her elbows and regarded me questioningly. I noticed a hard glitter in her eyes, then she caught her breath, coloured, then exclaimed softly: 'Oh, Jack, how lovely it would be!'

I had succeeded! Alice had succumbed to the sudden temptation! For the second time her strain of lascivious sexuality had conquered.

'Shall we try?' I asked with a smile, secretly delighted at her unconcealed eagerness and noting how her eyes now were brimming over with lust and how her lovely breasts were heaving with her excitement.

'Yes! Yes! Jack!' she exclaimed feverishly, 'but how can it be managed?'

'There shouldn't be much trouble,' I replied. 'Take her out with you shopping some afternoon close by here, then say you want just to pop in to see me about something. En route tell her about this room, how it's sound-proof, it will interest her and she will at the same time learn information that will come in useful later on. Once in here follow my lead. I suppose you would like to have a go at her?'

'Oh! Jack!' exclaimed Alice, her eyes sparkling with eagerness, 'will you fasten her down as you did me?'

I nodded.

'Yes! Yes! let me have a turn at her!' she replied

vivaciously. Then after a pause she looked queerly at me and added, 'and will you . . . ? at the same moment significantly squeezing my prick.

'I think so—unless of course you would rather I didn't, dear,' I replied with a laugh; 'I suppose you have no idea whether she is a virgin or not?'

'I can't say!' Alice replied, blushing a little. 'I've always fancied she was and have treated her as such.'

'And what sort of treatment is that?' I queried mischievously, and was proceeding to cross-question Alice when she stopped me by putting her hand over my mouth.

'Well, we'll soon find out when we get her here,' I remarked philosophically, much to her amusement.

Next afternoon, after seeing that everything was in working order in the Snuggery, I threw open both doors as if carelessly, and taking off my coat as if not expecting any visitors, I proceeded to potter about the room, keep a vigilant eye on the stairs. Before long I heard footsteps on the landing, but pretended not to know that any one was there till Alice tapped merrily on the door saying: 'May we come in, Jack?'

'Good Heavens, Alice?' I exclaimed in pretended surprise as I struggled hurriedly to get into my coat—'come in! how do you do? where have you dropped from?'

'We've been shopping—this is my maid, Jack'—I bowed and smiled, receiving in return from Fanny a distinctly pert and not too respectful nod—'and as we were close by, I thought I would take the chance of finding you in and take away that enlargement if it is ready.'

By this time I had struggled into my coat: 'It's

quite ready,' I replied. 'I'll go and get it, and I don't know why those doors should stand so unblushingly open,' I added with a laugh.

Having closed them, noiselessly locking them, I disappeared into the alcove I used for myself, and pretended to search for the enlargement—my real object being to give Alice a chance of letting Fanny know the nature of the room. Instinctively she divined my idea, and I heard her say: 'This is the room I was telling you about. Fanny—look at the double doors, the padded walls, the rings, the pillars, the hanging pulley straps! Isn't it queer?'

Fanny looked about her with evident interest: 'It *is* a funny room, Miss! And what are those little places for?' pointing to the two alcoves.

'We do not know, Fanny,' Alice replied, 'Mr Jack uses them for his photographic work now.'

As she spoke, I emerged with a large print which was to represent the supposed enlargement, and gave it to Alice who at once proceeded to closely examine it.

I saw that Fanny's eyes were wandering all over the room, and I moved over to her: 'A strange room Fanny eh?' I remarked. 'Is it not still; no sound from outside can get in, and no noise from inside can get out! That's a fact, we've tested it thoroughly!'

'Lor', Mr Jack!' she replied in her forward familiar way, turning her eyes on me in a most audacious and bold way, then resuming her survey of the room.

While she was doing so, I hastily inspected her. She was a distinctly pretty girl tall, slenderly but strongly built, with an exquisitely well-developed figure. A slightly turned-up nose and dark flashing eyes gave her face a saucy look which her free style

91

of moving accentuated, while her dark hair and rich colouring indicated a warm-blooded and passionate temperament. I easily could understand that Alice with her gentle ways was no match for Fanny; and I fancied that I should have my work cut out for me before I got her arms fastened to the pulley ropes.

Alice now moved towards us, print in hand: 'Thanks awfully, Jack, it's lovely!' and she began to roll it up. 'Now, Fanny, we must be off!'

'Don't bother about the print, I'll send it after you,' I said. 'And where are you off to now?'

'Nowhere in particular,' she replied, 'we'll look at the shops and the people. Good-bye, Jack!'

'One moment,' I interposed. 'You were talking the other day about some perfection of a lady's maid that you didn't want to lose—' (Fanny smiled complacently)'—but whose tantrums and ill tempers were getting more than you could stand.' (Fanny here began to look angry.) 'Somebody suggested that you should give her a good spanking—' (Fanny assumed a contemptuous air)'—or if you couldn't manage it yourself you should get someone to do it for you!' (Fanny here glared at me.) 'Is this the young lady?'

Alice nodded, with a curious glance at Fanny, who was now evidently getting into one of her passions.

'Well, as you've nothing to do this afternoon, and she happens to be here, and this room is so eminently suitable for the purpose, shall I take the young woman in hand for you and teach her a lesson?'

Before Alice could reply, Fanny with a startled exclamation darted to the door, evidently bent on escape, but in spite of her vigorous twists of the handle and shakings, the door refused to open, for the simple reason that unnoticed by her I had locked it! Instantly divining that she was a prisoner, she turned hurriedly round to watch our movements, but she was too late! With a quickness learnt on the football field, I was onto her and pinned her arms to her sides in a grip that she could not break out of despite her frantic struggles: 'Let me go! ... let me go, Mr Jack!' she screamed; I simply chuckled as I knew I had her safe now! I had to exert all my strength and skill for she was extraordinarily strong and her furious rage added to her power; but in spite of her desperate resistance, I forced her to the hanging pulleys where Alice was eagerly waiting for us. With astonishing quickness she made fast the ropes to Fanny's wrists and set the machinery going—and in a few seconds the surprised girl found herself standing erect with her arms dragged up taut over her head!

'Well done, Jack!' exclaimed Alice, as she delightedly surveyed the still struggling Fanny! The latter was indeed a lovely subject of contemplation, as with heaving bosom, flushed cheeks, and eyes that sparkled with rage, she stood panting, endeavouring to get back her breath, while her agitated fingers vainly strove to get her wrists free from the pulley ropes. We watched her in victorious silence, waiting for the outbursts of wrathful fury which we felt would come as soon as she was able to speak!

It soon came! 'How dare you, Mr Jack!' Fanny burst out as she flashed her great piercing eyes at us, her whole body trembling with anger; 'How dare you treat me like this! Let me loose at once, or as sure as I am alive, I'll have the law on you and also on that mealy-mouthed smooth-faced demure hypocrite that calls herself my mistress indeed!—who looks on while a poor girl is vilely treated and won't raise a finger to help her! Let me go at once, Mr Jack! and I'll promise to say and do nothing; but my God!—' (here her voice became shrill with overpowering rage)—my God! if you don't, I'll make it hot for the pair of you when I get out!' And she glared at us in her impotent fury.

'Your Mistress has asked me to give you a lesson, Fanny,' I replied calmly, 'and I'm going to do so! The sooner you recognize how helpless you really are, and will submit yourself to us, the sooner it will be over; but if you are foolish enough to resist, you'll have a long doing and a bad time! Now, if I let you loose, will you take your clothes off quietly?'

'My God! no!' she cried indignantly, but in spite of herself she blushed vividly!

'Then we'll take them off for you!' was my cool reply. 'Come along, Alice, you understand girl's clothes, you undo them and I'll get them off somehow!'

Quickly Alice sprang up, trembling with excitement, and together we approached Fanny, who shrieked defiance and threats at us in her impotent fury as she struggled desperately to get free. But as soon as she felt Alice's fingers unfastening her garments, her rage changed to horrible apprehension: and as one by one they slipped off her, she began to realize how helpless she was! 'Don't, Miss!' she ejaculated pitifully. 'My God! Stop her, Sir!' she pleaded, the use of these more respectful terms of address sufficiently proclaiming her changed attitude. But we were obdurate, and soon Fanny stood with only her chemise and undervest left on her, her shoes and stockings having been dragged off her at the special request of Alice, whose uncontrolled enjoyment of the work of stripping her maid was delicious to witness.

She now took command of operations. Pointing to a chair just in front of Fanny she exclaimed: 'Sit there, Jack, and watch Fanny as I take off her last garments.'

'For God's sake, Miss, don't strip me naked!' shrieked Fanny, who seemed to expect that she would be left in her chemise and to whom the sudden intimation that she was to be exposed naked came with an appalling shock! 'Oh, Sir! For God's sake, stop her!' she cried, appealing to me as she saw me take my seat right in front of her and felt Alice's fingers begin to undo the shoulder-strap fastenings which alone kept her scanty garments on her. 'Miss Alice! ... Miss Alice! don't! ... for God's sake, don't,' she screamed, in a fresh access of dismay as she felt her vest slip down her body to her feet and knew now her only covering was about to follow. In despair she tugged frantically at the ropes which made her arms so absolutely helpless, her agitated quivering fingers betraying her mental agony!

'Steady, Fanny, steady!' exclaimed Alice to her struggling maid as she proceeded to unfasten the chemise, her eyes gleaming with lustful cruelty: 'Now, Jack!' she said warningly, then let go, stepping back a pace herself the better to observe the effect! Down swept the chemise, and Fanny stood stark naked!!

'Oh! oh!' she wailed, crimson with shame, her face hidden on her bosom which now was wildly heaving in agitation. It was a wonderful spectacle!—in the foreground Fanny, naked, helpless, in an agony of shame—in the background but close to her was Alice exquisitely costumed and hatted, gloating over the sight of her maid's absolute nudity, her eyes intently fixed on the gloriously luscious curves of Fanny's hips, haunches, and bottom!

I managed to catch her eye and motioned to her to come and sit on my knee that we might in each other's close company study her maid's naked charms so reluctantly being exhibited to us. With one long last look she obeyed my summons. As she seated herself on my knees she threw her arms around my neck and kissed me rapturously whispering: 'Jack! Isn't she delicious!!' I nodded smilingly, then in turn muttered in her ear: 'And how do you like the game, dear?'

Alice blushed divinely: a strange languishing voluptuous half-wanton half-cruel look came into her eyes. Placing her lips carefully on mine she gave me three long-drawn kisses, the significance of which I could not possibly misunderstand, then whispered almost hoarsely: 'Jack, let me do all the . . . torturing and be content this time, with . . . fucking Fanny . . . and me too, darling!'

'She's your maid, and so-to-speak your property, dear,' I replied softly, 'so arrange matters just as you like: I'll leave it all to you and won't interfere unless you want me to do anything.'

She kissed me gratefully, then turned her eyes on Fanny, who during this whispered colloquy had been standing trembling her face still hidden from us, her legs pressed closely against each other as if to shield as much as possible her cunt from our sight.

I saw Alice's eyes wander over Fanny's naked body with evident pleasure, dwelling first on her magnificent lines and curves, then on her lovely breasts, and finally on the mass of dark curling moss-like hair that covered her cunt. She was a most deliciously voluptuous girl, one calculated to excite Alice to the utmost pitch of lust of which she was capable, and while secretly regretting that my share in the process of taming Fanny was to be somewhat restricted, I felt that I would enjoy the rare opportunity of seeing how a girl, hitherto chaste and well-regulated, would yield to her sexual instincts and passions when she had placed at her absolute disposal one of her own sex in a state of absolute nakedness!

Presently Alice whispered to me: 'Jack, I'm going to feel her!' I smiled and nodded. Fanny must have heard her, for as Alice rose, she for the first time raised her head and cried affrightedly: 'No, Miss, please, Miss, don't touch me!' and again she vainly strained at her fastenings, her face quivering and flushed with shame. But disregarding her maid's piteous entreaties, Alice passed behind her, then kneeling down began to stroke Fanny's bottom, a hand to each cheek!

'Don't, Miss!' yelled Fanny, arching herself outwards and away from Alice, and thereby unconsciously throwing the region of her cunt into greater prominence! But with a smile of cruel gratification, Alice continued her sweet occupation, sometimes squeezing, sometimes pinching Fanny's glorious half-moons, now and then extending her excursions over Fanny's round plump thighs, once indeed letting her hands creep up them till I really thought (and so did Fanny from the way she screamed and wriggled) that she was about to feel Fanny's cunt!

Suddenly Alice rose, rushed to me, and kissing me ardently whispered excitedly: 'Oh, Jack! she's just lovely! such flesh, such a skin! I've never felt a girl before, I've never touched any girl's breasts or . . . cunt . . . except of course my own,' she added archly, 'and I'm wild at the idea of handling Fanny. Watch me carefully, darling, and if I don't do it properly, tell me!' And back to Fanny she rushed, evidently in a state of intense eroticism!

This time Alice didn't kneel, but placed herself close behind Fanny (her dress in fact touching her) then suddenly she threw her arms around Fanny's body and seized her breasts: 'Miss Alice! . . . don't!' shrieked Fanny, struggling desperately, her flushed face betraying her agitation. 'Oh! how lovely! . . . how delicious! . . . how sweet! . . .' cried Alice, wild with delight and sexual excitement as she squeezed and played with Fanny's voluptuous breasts! Her head with its exquisite hat was just visible over Fanny's right shoulder, while her dainty dress showed on each side of the struggling agitated girl, throwing into bold relief her glorious shape and accentuating in the most piquant way Fanny's stark nakedness! Entranced, I gazed at the voluptuous spectacle, my prick struggling to break through the fly of my trousers! Fanny had now ceased her cries and was enduring in silence, broken only by her involuntary 'Oh's,' the violation of her breasts by Alice, whose little hands could scarcely grasp the luscious morsels of Fanny's flesh that they were so subtly torturing, but which nevertheless succeeded in squeezing and compressing them and generally in playing with them till the poor girl gasped in her shame and agony: 'Oh! Miss Alice! . . . Miss Alice! . . . stop! . . . stop!' her head falling forward in her extreme agitation.

With a smile of intense satisfaction, Alice suspended her torturing operations and gently stroked and soothed Fanny's breasts till the more regular breathing of the latter indicated that she had in a great degree regained her self-control. Then her expression changed. A cruel hungry light came into her eyes as she smiled wickedly and meaningly at me, then I saw her hands quit Fanny's breasts and glide over Fanny's stomach till they arrived at Fanny's cunt!

Fanny shrieked as if she had been stung: 'Miss Alice! . . . Miss Alice! . . . don't! don't touch me there! . . . oh! . . . oh! my God, Miss Alice! . . . oh! Miss Alice! take your hands away! . . .' at the same time twisting and writhing in a perfectly wonderful way in her frantic endeavours to escape from her mistress's hands, the fingers of which were now hidden in her cunt's mossy covering as they inquisitively travelled all over her Mont Venus and along the lips of the orifice itself. For some little time they contented themselves with feeling and pressing and toying caressingly with Fanny's cunt, then I saw one hand pause while the first finger of the other gently began to work its way between the pink lips I could just distinguish and disappear into the sweet cleft. 'Don't, Miss!' yelled Fanny, her agonized face now scarlet! While in her distress she desperately endeavoured to defend her cunt by throwing her legs in turn across her groin, to Alice's delight—her tell-tale face proclaiming the intense pleasure she was tasting in thus making her maid undergo such horrible torture!

Presently I noted an unmistakeable look of surprise in her eyes; her lips parted as if in astonishment, while her hand seemed to redouble its attack on Fanny's cunt, then she exclaimed: 'Why Fanny? What's this?

'Oh! Don't tell Mr Jack, Miss!' shrieked Fanny, letting her legs drop as she could no longer endure the whole weight of her struggling body on her slender wrists, 'don't let him know!'

My curiosity was naturally aroused and intently I watched the movements of Alice's hand which the fall of Fanny's legs brought again into full view. Her forefinger was buried up to the knuckle in her maid's cunt! The mystery was explained, Fanny was not a virgin!

Alice seemed staggered by her discovery. Abruptly she quitted Fanny, rushed to me, threw herself on my knees, then flinging her arms round my neck she whispered excitedly in my ear: 'Jack! she's been . . . had by someone . . . my finger went right in!'

'So I noticed, darling!' I replied quietly as I kissed her flushed cheek. 'I think you'd better let her rest a bit now, her arms will be getting numb from being kept over her head; let's fasten her to that pillar by passing her arms round it and shackling her wrists together. She can then rest a bit; and while she is recovering from her struggles hadn't you better . . . slip your clothes off also—for your eyes hint that you will want . . . something before long!'

Alice blushed prettily, then whispered as she kissed me ardently. 'I'd like . . . something now, darling!' Then she ran away to her dressing room.

Left alone with Fanny, I proceeded to transfer her from the pulley to the pillar; it was not a difficult task, as her arms were too numb (as I expected) to be of much use to her and she seemed stupified at our discovery that her maidenhead no longer existed. Soon I had her firmly fastened with her back pressing against the pillar. This new position had two great advantages: she could no longer hide her face from us and the backwards pull of her arms threw her breasts out. She glanced timidly at me as I stood admiring her luscious nakedness, and waiting for Alice's return.

100

After a short pause she whispered: 'Oh! Mr Jack! let me go! . . . I'll come to you whenever you wish . . . and let you do what you like . . . but . . . I'm afraid of Miss Alice today . . . she seems so strange! . . . oh! my God! she's naked!' she screamed as genuine alarm as Alice came out of her toilet room with only her shoes and stockings on, and her large matinee hat, a most coquettishly piquantly indecent object! Poor Fanny went red at the sight of her mistress and didn't know where to look as Alice came dancing along, her eyes noting with evident approval the position into which I had placed her maid.

'Mes compliments, mademoiselle!' I said with a low bow as she came up.

She smiled and blushed, but was too intent on Fanny to joke with me. 'That's lovely, Jack!' she exclaimed after a careful inspection of her now trembling maid. 'I like that much better, Jack.' Then catching me by the elbow, she pushed me towards my alcove saying: 'We both will want you presently, Jack!' Looking roguishly at me: 'So get ready! But tell me first, where are the feathers?

'Oh, that's your game!' I replied with a laugh. She nodded, colouring slightly, and I told her where she would find them.

I had a peep-hole in my alcove through which I could see all that passed in the room, and being curious to watch the two girls, I placed myself by it as I slowly undressed myself.

Having found the feathers, Alice placed the box near her, then, going right up to Fanny, she took hold of her own breasts with her hands, raised them till they were level with Fanny's, then leaning on Fanny so that their stomachs were in close contact, she

101

directed her breasts against Fanny's, gently rubbing her nipples against Fanny's while she looked intently into Fanny's eyes! It was a most curious sight! The girl's naked bodies were touching from their ankles to their breasts their cunts were so close to each other that their hairs formed one mass, while their faces were so near to each other that the brim of Alice's matinee hat projected over Fanny's forehead!

Not a word was said! For about half a minute Alice continued to rub her breasts gently against Fanny's with her eyes fixed on Fanny's downcast face, then suddenly I saw both naked bodies quiver, and then Fanny raised her head and for the first time responded to Alice's glance, her colour coming and going! At the same moment, a languorous voluptuous smile swept over Alice's face, and gently she kissed Fanny, who flushed rosy red but as far as I could see did not respond.

'Won't you . . . love me, Fanny?' I heard Alice say softly but with a curious strained voice! Immediately I understood the position. Alice was lusting after Fanny! I was delighted! It was clear that Fanny had not yet reciprocated Alice's passion, and I determined that Alice should have every opportunity of satisfying her lust on Fanny's naked helpless body, till the latter was converted to Tribadism with Alice as the object.

'Won't you . . . love me, Fanny?' again asked Alice softly, now supplementing the play of her breasts against Fanny's by insinuating and significant pressings of her stomach against Fanny's, again kissing the latter sweetly. But Fanny made no response, and Alice's eyes grew hard with a steely cruel glitter which boded badly for Fanny!

Quitting Fanny, Alice went straight to the box of

feathers, picked out one, and returned to Fanny, feather in hand. The sight of her moving about thus, her breasts dancing, her hips swaying, her cunt and bottom in full view, her nakedness intensified by her piquant costume of hat, shoes and stockings, was enough to galvanize a corpse: it set my blood boiling with lust and I could hardly refrain from rushing out and compelling her to let me quench my fires in her! I, however, did resist the temptation, and rapidly undressed to my shoes and socks so as to be ready to take advantage of any chance that either of the girls might offer; but I remained in my alcove with my eye to the peep-hole as I was curious to witness the denouement of this strangely voluptuous scene, which Alice evidently wished to play single-handed.

No sooner did Fanny catch sight of the feather than she screamed: 'No! . . . no! Miss Alice! . . . don't tickle me!' at the same time striving frantically to break the straps that linked together her wrists and her ankles. But my tackle was too strong! Alice meanwhile had caught up a cushion which she placed at Fanny's feet and right in front of her, she knelt on it, rested her luscious bottom on her heels, and having settled herself down comfortably she, with a smile in which cruelty and malice were strangely blended, gloatingly contemplated for a moment her maid's naked and agitated body, then slowly and deliberately applied the tip of the feather to Fanny's cunt!

'Oh, my God! Miss Alice, don't!' yelled Fanny, writhing in delicious contortions in her desperate endeavours to dodge the feather. 'Don't, Miss!' she shrieked, as Alice, keenly enjoying her maid's distress and her vain efforts to avoid the torture, proceeded delightedly to pass the feather lightly along the sensitive lips of Fanny's cunt and finally set to work to tickle Fanny's clitoris, thereby sending her so nearly into hysterical convulsions that I felt it time I interposed.

As I emerged from my alcove Alice caught sight of me and dropped her hand as she turned towards me, her eyes sparkling with lascivious delight! 'Oh, Jack! did you see her?' she cried excitedly.

'I heard her, dear!' I replied ambiguously, 'and began to wonder whether you were killing her, so came out to see.'

'Not a bit of it!'· she cried, hugely pleased, 'I'm going to give her another turn!' a declaration that produced from Fanny the most pitiful pleadings which however seemed only to increase Alice's cruel satisfaction, and she was proceeding to be as good as her word when I stopped her.

'You'd better let me first soothe her irritated senses, dear,' I said, and with one hand, I caressed and played with Fanny's full and voluptuous breasts which I found tense and firm under her sexual excitement, while with the other, I stroked and felt her cunt, a procedure that evidently afforded her considerable relief although, at another time, it doubtless would have provoked shrieks and cries! She had not spent, though she must have been very close to doing it; and I saw that I must watch Alice very closely indeed during the 'turn' she was going to give Fanny for my special delectation, lest the catastrophe I was so desirous of avoiding should occur, for in my mind, I had decided that when Alice had finished tickling Fanny, she should have an opportunity of satisfying her lustful cravings on her, when it would be most desirable that Fanny should be in a condition to show the effect on her of Alice's lascivious exertions.

While feeling Fanny's cunt, I naturally took the opportunity to see if Alice's penetrating finger had met with any difficulty entering and had thus caused Fanny the pain that her shrieks and wriggles had indicated. I found the way in intensely tight, a confirmation of her story and statement that nothing had gone in since the rape was committed on her. Although therefore I could not have the gratification of taking her virginity, I felt positive that I should have a delicious time and that practically, I should be violating her, and I wondered into which of the two delicious cunts now present I would shoot my surging and boiling discharge as it dissolved in Love's sweetest ecstasies!

'Now, Alice, I think she is ready for you!' I said when I had stroked and felt Fanny to my complete satisfaction.

'No, no, Miss Alice!' shrieked Fanny in frantic terror, 'for God's sake, don't tickle me again!'

Disregarding her cries, Alice, who had with difficulty restrained her impatience, quickly again applied the feather to Fanny's cunt, and a wonderful spectacle followed; Fanny's shrieks, cries, entreaties, filled the room while she wiggled and squirmed and twisted herself about in the most bewitchingly provocative manner, while Alice, with parted lips and eyes that simply glistened with lust, remorselessly tickled her maid's cunt with every refinement of cruelty, every fresh shriek and convulsion bringing a delightful look on her tell-tale face. Motionless, I watched the pair, till I noticed Fanny's breasts stiffen and become tense. Immediately I covered her cunt with my hand, saying to Alice: 'Stop, dear, she's had as much as she can stand!' Then reluctantly she desisted from her absorbing occupation and rose, her naked body quivering with aroused but unsatisfied lust.

Now was the time for me to try and effect what I had in mind, viz, the introduction of both girls to Tribadism! 'Let us move Fanny to the large couch and fasten her down before she recovers herself,' I hastily whispered to Alice. Quickly we set her loose, between us we carried her, half-fainting, to the large settee couch where we lay her on her back and made fast her wrists to the two top corners and her ankles to the two lower ones. We now had only to set the machinery going and she would lie in the position I desired, namely spread-eagled!

Alice, now clutched me excitedly and whispered hurriedly: 'Jack, do me before she comes to herself and before she can see us! I'm just mad for it!' And indeed with her flushed cheeks, humid eyes, and heaving breasts this was very evident!

But although I also was bursting with lust and eager to fuck either Alice or her maid, it would not have suited my programme to do so! I wanted Alice to fuck Fanny! I wanted the first spending of both girls to be mutually provoked by the friction of their excited cunts one against the other! This was why I stopped Alice from tickling her maid into spending, and it was for this reason that I had extended Fanny on her back in such a position that her cunt should be at Alice's disposal!

'Hold on, darling, for a bit!' I whispered back, 'you'll soon see why! I want it as badly as you do, my sweet, but am fighting against it till the proper time comes! Run away now, and take off your hat, for it will now be only in the way,' and I smiled significantly as I kissed her.

Alice promptly obeyed. I then seated myself on the couch by the side of Fanny, who was still lying with eyes closed, but breathing almost normally, and bending over her, I closely inspected her cunt to ascertain whether she had or had not spent under the terrific tickling it had just received! I could find no traces whatever, but to make sure I gently drew the lips apart and peered into the sweet coral cleft, but again saw no traces. The touch of my fingers on her cunt however had roused Fanny from her semi-stupor and she dreamily opened her eyes, murmuring: 'Oh, Sir, don't!' as she recognized that I was her assailant, then she looked hurriedly round as in search of Alice.

'Your mistress will be here immediately,' I said with a smile, 'she has only gone away to take off her hat!' The look of terror returned to her eyes, and she exclaimed: 'Oh, Mr Jack, do let me go, she'll kill me!'

'Oh, no!' I replied as I laughed at her agitation, 'oh, no, Fanny, on the contrary she's now going to do to you the sweetest, nicest and kindest thing one girl can do to another! Here she comes!'

I rose as Alice came up full of pleasurable excitement as to what was now going to happen, and slipped my arm lovingly round her waist. She looked eagerly at her now trembling maid, then whispered: 'Is she ready for us again. Jack?'

'Yes, dear!' I answered softly. 'While you were away taking off your hat, I thought it as well to see in what condition her cunt was after its tickling! I find it very much irritated and badly in want of Nature's soothing essence! You, darling, are also much in the same state, your cunt also wants soothing! So I want you girls to soothe each other! Get onto Fanny, dear, take her in your arms; arrange yourself on her so that your cunt lies on hers! and then gently rub yours against hers! and soon both of you will be tasting the sweetest ecstasy!! In other words, fuck Fanny, dear.'

Alice looked at me in wonderous admiration! As she began to comprehend my suggestion, her face broke into delightful smiles; and when I stooped to kiss her she exclaimed rapturously: 'Oh, Jack! how sweet! . . . how delicious!' as she gazed eagerly at Fanny. But the latter seemed horrified at the idea of being submitted thus to her mistress's lustful passion and embraces, and attempted to escape, crying in her dismay: 'No, no, Sir!—oh, no, Miss!—I don't want it, please!. . .'

'But I do, Fanny,' cried Alice with sparkling eyes as she gently but firmly pushed her struggling maid onto her back and held her down forcibly, till I had pulled all four straps tight, so that Fanny lay flat with her arms and legs wide apart in Maltese-Cross fashion, a simply entrancing spectacle! Then slipping my hands under her buttocks, I raised her middle till Alice was able to push a hard cushion under her bottom, the effect of which was to make her cunt stand out prominently; then turning to Alice, who had assisted in these preparations with the keenest interest but evident impatience, I said: 'Now dear, there she is! Set to work and violate your maid!'

In a flash Alice was on the couch and on her knees between Fanny's widely parted legs—excitedly she threw herself on her maid, passed her arms round her and hugged her closely, as she showered kisses on Fanny's still protesting mouth till the girl had to stop for breath. With a few rapid movements she arranged herself on her maid so that the two luscious pairs of breasts were pressing against each other, their stomachs in close contact, and their cunts touching!

'One moment, Alice!' I exclaimed, just as she was beginning to agitate herself on Fanny, 'Let me see that you are properly placed before you start!'

Leaning over her bottom, I gently parted her thighs, till between them I saw the cunts of the mistress and the maid resting on each other, slit to slit, clitoris to clitoris, half hidden by the mass of their closely interwoven hairs, the sweetest of sights! Then, after restoring her thighs to their original position closely pressed against each other, I gently thrust my right hand between the girl's navels, and worked it along amidst their bellies till it lay between their cunts! 'Press down a bit, Alice!' I said, patting her bottom with my disengaged hand; promptly she complied with two or three vigorous down-thrusts which forced my palm hard against Fanny's cunt while her own pressed deliciously against the back of my hand. The sensation of thus feeling at the same time these two full fat fleshy warm and throbbing cunts between which my hand lay in sandwich fashion was something exquisite; and it was with the greatest reluctance that I removed it from the sweetest position it is ever likely to be in, but Alice's restless and involuntary movements proclaimed that she was fast yielding to her feverish impatience to fuck Fanny and to taste the rapture of spending on the cunt of her maid the emission provoked by its sweet contact and friction against her own excited organ!

She still held Fanny closely clapsed against her and with head slightly thrown back, she kept her eyes fixed on her maid's terrified averted face with a gloating hungry look, murmuring softly: 'Fanny, you shall now . . . love me!' Both the girls were quivering, Alice from overwhelming and unsatisfied lust, Fanny from shame and horrible apprehension!

Caressing Alice's bottom encouragingly, I whispered: 'Go ahead, dear!' In a trice her lips were pressed to Fanny's flushed cheeks on which she rained hot kisses as she slowly began to agitate her cunt against her maid's with voluptuous movements of her beautiful bottom. 'Oh! Miss . . .' gasped Fanny her eyes betraying the sexual emotion that she felt beginning to overpower her, her colour coming and going! Quicker and more agitated became Alice's movements; soon she was furiously rubbing her cunt against Fanny's with strenuous down-thrusting strokes of her bottom, continuing her fierce kisses on her maid's cheeks as the latter lay helpless with half-closed eyes, tightly clasped in her mistress's arms! Then a hurricane of sexual rage seemed to seize Alice! Her bottom wildly oscillated and gyrated with confused jerks, thrusts, and shoves as she frenziedly pressed her cunt against Fanny's with a rapid jogging motion: suddenly Alice seemed to stiffen and become almost rigid, her arms gripped Fanny more tightly than ever; then her head fell forward on Fanny's shoulder as an indescribable spasm thrilled through her, followed by convulsive vibrations and tremors! Almost simultaneously Fanny's half-closed eyes turned upwards till the whites were showing, her lips parted, she gasped brokenly: 'Oh! . . . Miss . . . Alice! . . . Ah . . . h!' then thrilled convulsively while quiver after quiver shot through her! The blissful crisis had arrived! Mistress and maid were deliriously spending

110

cunt against cunt, Alice in rapturous ecstasy at having so deliciously satisfied her sexual desires by means of her maid's cunt, while forcing the latter to spend in spite of herself, while Fanny was quivering ecstatically under heavenly sensations hitherto unknown to her and now communicated to her wondering senses by her mistress whom she still felt lying on her and in whose arms she was still clasped!

My Conversion

Back in the Babylon which has the most corruption of any city in the world simply because it has the most people, I wore myself out paying calls on every coquette and scoundrel in Paris. For more than two weeks nothing eventful happened. I was bored to tears. I gambled and lost. I saw that my sustenance would be gone if I continued, and so I considered flight to avoid the temptation of the tables. It was a momentous decision which I carefully weighed.

Already the sun was gilding the crops and the Graces were retreating to the copses. And all the women were flying to the countryside. Their example decided me and I followed them. You can be sure that like a busy bee I sucked only the juiciest blossoms. Nevertheless, it was tedious.

You know as well as I those enchanted palaces that line the shores of the peaceful Seine. I went there and found nothing.

Finally, I went to the Marne where rise walls built by our forefathers. Their imposing aspect seems to proclaim that kings reside there. But no. It is merely the abode of the brides of Our Saviour, the convent of ***, whose abbess is the aunt of one of my acquaintances. She has been told that I am likeable and I am welcomed with open arms. You have no idea of the excitement I cause when I arrive. The pretty little nun coquettishly adjusts her wimple when she sees me. All rush to the visiting room.

When Madame Abbess appears, all vanish out of

respect. What a voluptuous figure she has. I could almost eat her.

She has just reached her fifth lustrum. To the flower of youthfulness is joined the blossom of perfect health. A glittering face with eyes blacker than jet, a rose-bordered mouth, and teeth of ivory that she permits me to admire. There is something of the flirt about her which her garb cannot conceal.

When she notes the lust in my eyes, she says to me teasingly: 'Are you another Abelard?'

I don't know what to say. But I know that I am going to fuck my Abbess or know the reason why. The compliments we exchange are prettily turned on her part and gallant on mine. Soon we are chatting as if we had known each other for years. My God! Now I have an erection that is killing me. It is the result of gazing too intently at those seductive breasts.

I shall not speak of the parties that were given in my honour or the recitals. There could be heard my sonorous male voice blending with the titters of the timid novices. A satyr is loose among captive nymphs, in effect. In vain do they try to flee, but there is something about me that stops their steps. As they totter, the squeals they emit are not those of fear.

What a wonderful thing to find yourself in a seraglio of twenty little nuns who vie with one another in loveliness. Their eyes reveal a tender languor. Several of the innocents have twitches they have never before experienced. How sweet they look. Let's fuck. Let's fuck. Oh, my prick, show what you are capable of. Hail Venus! Hail Priapus!

Contemplating such matters, I toss about in my bed. I am unable to sleep because of my excitement.

The next day, Madame the Abbess is slightly indisposed and keeps to her bed. I receive permission to pay my respects in her apartment.

What has come over me? She is as lovely as an angel. I forget why I have come. She extends her hand to me as she asks about my health. With passion I kiss that hand. She gives a sigh. Another sigh is my response. We are alone. Her half-closed eyes, her fluttering eyelashes, the distension of her stomach, and the palpitation of an alabaster bosom still covered by an inopportune veil embolden me. 'Julia! Julia!' Such are the first sparks of our fires. I kneel at the side of the bed with my burning lips on the hand that I did not relinquish. She makes no attempt to snatch it away. Heavens! She has fainted. She is dying. I summon her servants with screams of terror. Salts, waters, scents!

'That's one of Madame's dizzy spells,' cries one of the maids.

But it is not her final attack. After a quarter of an hour, she returns to her senses, pale as a sheet. Her pallor, however, is that of a woman in love. Several tears have dampened her beseeching eyes. Finally, we are by ourselves again.

'I apologize for these attacks which nearly kill me. The doctors cannot seem to diagnose them.'

I note the colour returning to her cheeks. Her pulse becomes normal. My heart is pounding as I approach her. Several disarranged pillows offer me a pretext. As I advance my hand to straighten them and hold her up—oh wonder of wonders!—her opulent bosom is offered to my view. The sight intoxicates me. I press my amorous mouth against her amorous mouth. My tongue gives her quivers of voluptuousness. Gradually, I make my way to the sanctuary. A finger penetrates it. It gives a twitch, one which excites her still more. What ineffable bliss!

'Sweet Jesus!' she moans. 'I can't stand this wonderful feeling. I think I am expiring.'

The sensations are too much, too new. Unable to withstand the shock, I sink back in a faint. She is worried to such an extent that she rings for her maid. When I come to, I find myself in their arms. Their efforts to revive me are so successful that the petite maid, on seeing the condition I am in, deems it wise to retire. The Abbess and I reiterate a thousand times our vows to love each other eternally, and after each oath, we seal it with the appropriate ceremony.

I am nourished with the strongest broths and foods. I spend the day as I did the morning, and the night is just as joyful. The following days, diversions without number are prepared for me—hunting, fishing and games. Such thoughtfulness strengthens my ties to the Abbess even more firmly. She is lascivious without being coarse. She takes my advice and my lessons inflame her. Her lovely svelte and flexible body and her shapely legs enlace me, melt into my body. Only in my arms does she enjoy repose.

I would have been true to her, but the flesh is weak. Young hearts are pining for me, and should I let them wither and fade away? No, I am too compassionate.

I establish a schedule—my nights are with the Abbess and my days are occupied otherwise. The dormitories and cells are all open to me, and I take advantage of it. The first one I fuck is discreet.

Discreet? You must be joking.

I am not. It is with the maid who restored me. And that's the truth. She was in charge of my meals. One day, I was so excited by the chase that I return late.

She is not expecting me. I enter her cell. Guess what meets my eyes.

She is sprawled out in a big armchair with her robe lifted up to her navel and her legs spread wide apart. With a great deal of enthusiasm she is manipulating—a dildo!

I shut the door quickly. Precipitately, she drops her petticoat and leaves the spear in the wound. With a deep blush, she stands up and starts to walk away with her thighs squeezed closely together. The devil inspires me. Taking her under the arms, I free Priapus who soon finds refuge deep in the centre of the comfortable chamber. She makes a feeble protest.

'My dear, I caught you in the act. And I am going to finish what you started. Don't worry. I won't betray you.'

I lay her on the couch, where I perform the sweet task twice.

'God bless you,' she sighs when it is over.

One day, the Abbess beckoned me and led me to a cell. Putting her finger to her lips, she pointed to a peephole and motioned me to have a look through it. I did as I was bid and saw Sister Stephanie in the adjoining cubicle.

Dear Sister Stephanie—such a romantic name. Young, rosy cheeked and ash blonde, she reminded me of a bouquet of flowers with her gentle charming voice and her veiled look which seemed to conceal so many tender secrets.

And the cell. It was a weird world, a bizarre enclosure whose walls were not limed with white but with blue, a sky blue that was almost ethereal. The ceiling, too, was painted with the same azure while the floor was of carefully waxed white planks. The bed looked comfortable.

What was out of place in the nun's cell was a Christ nailed to an oversized cross bracketed to the wall, but the figure was not that of the emaciated Saviour that is so familiar. He was a robust male with powerful pectoral muscles. Moreover, the body was made of a material with an astonishing resemblance to human flesh. I saw Stephanie touch it and her finger sank in.

As for the face of the Christ, the expression was one of ecstasy, a profane rapture that had absolutely nothing to do with religious exaltation. It was a handsome face, masculine and virile. The nostrils and lips were sensual, and there was a glitter in the eyes.

The door opened and in stepped Angela, one of the more delicious of the novices, who was warmly welcomed with a kiss.

'What lovely hair you have,' Stephanie remarked.

'And how about yours, Sister Stephanie?'

'I am rather vain about it.'

'But I thought when you took your vows, you had to have your head shaved.'

'Yes, you do. But if you get on the good side of the Mother Superior, she gives you permission to let it grow and fix it any way you like. It goes without saying that you can't let it show. Certain nuns would understand these special marks of favour.'

'Show me your hair,' Angela demanded.

Without any hesitation, the woman removed her wimple, and a cascade of tresses tumbled down over her shoulders. Silky curls, elegant waves fell on the white starched collar that formed a part of her costume.

After a gasp of unfeigned admiration, Angela asked permission to brush it.

The girl sat down facing the sister and began to brush the hair with measured strokes. Suddenly, Stephanie kissed Angela's lips with her moist mouth. At first, the girl shrank back but then surrendered her lips and tongue. In a trice her body was embraced. I could see that her sex was being ignited. The sensation must have become even more unbearable when Stephanie caressed the yearning breasts through the blouse. Then, baring them, she took the nipples in her mouth and sucked them slowly and avidly.

'I think I have wet myself,' Angela murmured.

Finally, Sister Stephanie disrobed, exhibiting her nude body with arrogance and hauteur. She possessed opulent round breasts, a thick fleece, smooth thighs, and delicious buttocks.

With deft nimble hands, she quickly divested the girl of her clothing, pushed her back on the bed and began to fondle her ardently.

I could see that Angela had lost touch with reality and I surmised that this was the first time she was experiencing true voluptuousness. Her twitches soon became violent convulsions.

She sank back in a faint from the force of the sensations. But she recovered under the tingling caresses that the sister was bestowing between her open thighs with her agile darting tongue. Then I heard the enamoured sighs, the squeals of joy, and the prolonged moans of pleasure which announced the arrival of the supreme sensation.

They fell back in exhaustion, but I kept my eye glued to the aperture. After a few moments, Stephanie rose and left the bed. I followed her with my eyes as she went to the Christ, pressed herself to it, embraced his muscular thighs, and licked his face. Now she stepped back and began undoing the loin cloth. When it dropped down to the floor, I observed to my astonishment that crucifixion did not necessarily cause loss of virility. And what virility! It was a long member which swayed and vibrated, a foully atrractive object the like of which I had never seen. Although it was monstrous, I found it strangely attractive, and I could recognize that this organ nestled between hairy bloated sacks could promise a woman certain raptures.

Stunned with amazement, I watched Sister Stephanie slowly impale herself on the colossus. As she let herself slowly down it, she shuddered and gave little groans. Now she slowly jabbed herself with it in a regular cadence. The cheeks of her buttocks were tightly closed to augment the sensation.

Now the nun began an almost motionless dance which ended with a loud shout followed by a long obscene rattle.

Let's pass over in silence several rather ordinary incidents. I fucked Sister Lapine, Sister Magdelon, Mother Bonaventure, etc. The dormitory, the garden, the dispensary and the chapel are all the theatres of my exploits. But let's discuss the novices.

They are five, and among them, Sisters Agatha, Rose and Agnes stand out. They are the most adorable creatures imaginable. The first two are inseparable and play with each other for lack of anything better to do. Agnes is in love with me, but she hides her feelings and weeps to herself. One day, I find the means to share her room with her.

'What's wrong with you, Agnes?' I demand of her.

'I really don't know.'

'For the last week, something has come over you. You are completely different. You used to laugh and be so much fun, but now you just look out into space and sigh. Tell me what's wrong. Or don't you trust me, who loves you so much?'

She flushes. 'You do love me? If only that were so.'

'Have I offended you?' I ask, taking her hand.

'Please leave me. I don't feel well.'

She rises.

'I see that you are afraid of me. Perhaps I am hateful to you. I think it is about time for me to leave.'

'You're not going?' she cries.

Poor child. She's mine. No further effort is needed. I shall soon have her.

The head of the novices provides me with a good opportunity a few days later. You will recall that she is a good friend. The choir is supposed to sing a motet, but the music-master does not come, and so she confides Agnes to me for the rehearsal.

As soon as the good sister closes the door on us, I resume my attack: 'Lovely Agnes, are you always so cruel?'

She lowers her eyes.

'How unhappy I am. Only God knows how much.'

She raises her hands to heaven.

'Agnes, you have made tears come to my eyes.'

'What do you think about me. I have been crying my heart out.'

Her tears fall fast and heavy.

'Let us console each other. If we don't, I shall die.'

'No,' she sobs. 'You cannot die. It is I who shall have to.'

I take her and put her on my knee with her head against my face.

'Agnes, it is only you whom I love. Tell me that you love me, too.'

'You wicked man, how can you have any doubt about that?'

Her mouth grazes my lips. The child does not recognize the significance of the outbursts of her heart. Her hour is come. I cover her with kisses. I transfer into her heart the fire that is devouring me. I make her drunk with caresses and kisses. When I remove the last of the veils, I am stunned by the treasures that are revealed. Modesty no longer holds me back. She no longer knows what she is doing. Like a flash of lightning, I strip her bare. The scream that Agnes lets escape is the signal of my victory.

You are probably thinking, fool that you are, that she makes a painful face and puts on airs and that she is despising me as her rapist. On the contrary, she thanks me from the bottom of her heart, the poor child. It is true that I merit the praise, for the fortress is damnably difficult to take.

Afterwards we begin work on her part in the motet. When the Mother Superior returns, Agnes is singing with the voice of an angel. As for myself, I am scorched and scalded. But twelve hours of repose heal my scars.

What a way to spend your time.

What do you mean, you fault-finder?

I'm scolding you because you are wasting your time without getting any money.

Oh, I forgot to tell you that the Abbess was the soul of generosity. No woman has ever been so bountiful. Now that your fears are calmed, let me continue with the account of my exploits.

Sisters Agatha and Rose are deserving of my homage. The elder cannot be more than eighteen. The former, possessed of an irrepressible spirit, has the devil in her flesh. Rose is more thoughtful but gay at the same time. These two children are united by a mutual understanding. The Abbess, whose jewels they are, told me in confidence that more than once she allowed them in her bed to appease their desires. The excesses they gave themselves up to! When I give them dancing instruction, we do all sorts of silly things.

'Sisters,' I say one day, 'would you be good enough to show me the games you play with each other.'

'What games?' demands Agatha as Rose blushes.

'If I knew, I wouldn't be asking you.'

'Well, Rose, I think he means hide-and-seek.' She begins to giggle.

'There's nothing hidden,' I tell them sternly. 'I saw everything.'

'What?' asks Rose in consternation. 'You saw? Agatha, we are lost.'

Both begin to weep.

'Dry your tears,' I order them. 'I promise I won't say a word.'

That reassures them somewhat. Besides, what they have done is considered in a convent only a little sin.

'But how were you able to spy on us?' Agatha timidly asks me.

'I really didn't see you. A little genie told me what you were doing.'

'A genie?' she exclaims.

'A genie? echoes Rose.

'Yes, a genie who comes to me every day. (I can barely stifle my roars of laughter.) I'll introduce you to him on the condition that you teach me your game and that you listen to what he has to say.'

'What? Does he speak, and how?'

'We talk to each other in sign language. I'll explain later.'

'Let's see.'

'Yes, let's see,' chimes in Rose.

'Easy,' I warn them. 'Wait until I summon him. In the meantime, perhaps you would like to show me your game. . . .'

(I had my reasons, but never has my jinni been so recalcitrant. I did my best to spur him to action, but nothing occurred. Finally, the imp arrived. Here is what happened. I produce the Monsignor, which makes Agatha's eye pop. She springs towards it.)

'Oh, Rose, I have it in my hand. Look at how beautifully it is fashioned. But it doesn't have any nose!'

'Help me to hold it lest it fly away.'

Rose clutches it.

'How quickly it came.' She tries to unhinge it.

'Young ladies, just a moment. Don't you see that it is just a little snail. It's in its shell.'

'That's so,' Rose says. 'Look at it in its cushion.'

'I've never seen a snail like this one,' Agatha comments.

'It's probably from China.'

'Where are its feelers?'

I am dying of fear lest I should be emancipated in their tender hands.

'I think he wishes to speak,' I tell them.

125

'We would like to hear him,' they reply.

'I have to warn you that if you get him angry, he will go away and never return. Now, mum's the word.'

I grasp Agatha and throw her on the bed. She is a brave little thing, not uttering a word. In a moment, I have her skirt up to her waist. Wild with curiosity, Rose flutters around.

'Agatha, is he speaking?'

'Oh, yes. I have never heard such eloquence. I don't think I can stand it any more.'

'What is he saying?'

It goes without saying that she has other things to do than reply. The little she-devil wiggles so divinely that I am about to begin all over again, when Rose, unable to contain herself any longer, grabs me. The overheated perspiring genie emerges from the carnage and begins to work on Agatha's companion. Although she is not as vivacious, she is almost mad with voluptuousness. But she has that rare quality I have always appreciated in a woman—the door of the sanctuary closes after the sacrifice without leaving me time to go limp. By now, neither of them is plying me with questions. They are in a state of utter ecstasy. As for myself, I take keen enjoyment in their confusion. We no longer speak of the game. They realize that they have been fooled, but they hold me no grudge.

I am at the peak of bliss, although somewhat fatigued. Every time I consider giving up the game, the devil comes out of his hiding-place and spurs me to new efforts.

Life becomes heaven and hell. You remember that three goddesses fought for one apple. Well, imagine what it is like when twenty little eager nuns compete for one man.

My friend, you have no idea of a female republic whose doge is the Abbess. The majority of the girls have been enrolled in the celestial militia against their wills. Although they are the wives of an ethereal being, they still have corporeal desires. The result is a charnel revolt, a conflict between the senses and reason, between the Creator and the creature. All that stimulates the passions, irritates desires and inflames imagination. That is why the girls get spasms and nervous attacks. They can't be praying all the time.

The normal object of their adoration is the confessor. If there are two, they share the fold, each hating the other cordially. If there is only one, the lambs fight among themselves for his favours.

'What! Over an old monk?'

'Yes. Over an old monk. They would do anything for him, for at least he is of flesh rather than wood or metal.'

Consequently, in these abodes of peace and innocence, one enjoys all the comforts of hell.

If only you knew the ruses the girls employ to sneak their lovers over the walls. I could tell you of the horrors of the despotism the vicious old women wield over their charges. There take place orgies worthy of being described by Aretino. When they are married, they have been initiated into every vice imaginable.

The murmurs of discontent are becoming louder. The governing body holds a session. Fault is found with the Abbess who demands that her tastes and pleasures be respected. The reverend mothers are all ears as they eavesdrop. The little innocents are trembling with fear. The way they all look at me leads me to believe that I'll be the scapegoat. For fear of losing me, the Abbess stoutly defends me. The complaints

127

are brought to the attention of the Bishop and thick-witted priest, who announces that he is coming in person to restore order in a house into which Belial has insinuated himself. I am ready to face him, but my dear Abbess persuades me that if I stay, she will be ruined. Loaded with sugar and gold, I make my departure. There is scarcely a dry eye when I leave.

The House of Borgia

Cesare stretched himself at ease on the red plush couch which had been put at his disposal. Around him, his principal officers shared with their leader the privilege of being the guest of the Chief Councillor of the city. Outside, the cannon was quiet, the citadel comfortably besieged. Full-scale assault operations could wait until tomorrow. The army needed rest and a little entertainment.

Throughout the city the brothels were doing fine, wine-flushed business. And any woman who showed herself willing was feeling the full pent-up strength following days of abstinence on the part of the visitors between her thighs. But, as usual, Cesare had forbidden violence. Any man reported stealing a citizen's unwilling wife or raping a reluctant maiden would be made an example of for all the town to see.

Within the mansion of the Chief Councillor, gypsy music was playing. A band of well-dressed nomads were strumming their guitars and tambourines. There was controlled passion in the music and in the dark, gypsy faces. There was ill-controlled passion, too, in the loins of Cesare's officers. This man, their host, had promised them, later, the full benefits of the high-class brothel which was virtually his harem. They were anxious to relieve this ache of longing in their lower regions.

Cesare toyed with his glass, sipping the rich, sweet wine with which his host had bolstered a magnificent meal. He was thinking of Lucrezia, wishing she were here, now, so that they could retire to a quiet nook and enjoy each other with the furious abandon of the days before he had left for the French Court.

'How do you like my gypsy orchestra?' his host asked, leaning across from his neighbouring couch.

'Excellent, excellent, but they look a little domesticated.'

'You mean they are well dressed, well fed? But of course. They have become quite famous these last few months. Everybody is paying big prices to have them play and dance. Their days of dirt and rags are over.'

He swallowed a glass of wine in one long draught.

'But if you talk of domestication, wait until you see Maria. Domestication! I'd like to see the man who could domesticate her. Violence, passion, sensuality! They ripple in her limbs when she dances, they reach to you from her breasts, they writhe in her buttocks. And yet she's not for sale. Oh, they've tried to rape her—many a man in torment. But she carries a stiletto and knows how to use it, they say. She's a proud one. I have to rush to my mistress in excitement after she's danced, and then I try to imagine she's the divine Maria who won't be bought.'

Cesare listened, idly swishing the wine in his refilled glass and letting the music flow in him. The old dotard, he was thinking; the thought that he couldn't have her would make him pay grovelling homage to the ugliest old whore.

'Well, when does this proud creature deign to appear?' he asked.

'Immediately if you so wish it.'

The host clapped his hands and gave orders to a servant, who disappeared, gliding over the rich carpets which covered the tiled floor, into the other

131

rooms which led off from a portico at the far end of the main dining hall.

After a few minutes, he reappeared, gave a few whispered instructions to the leader of the gypsy ochestra and withdrew.

The music changed suddenly to a wild, passionate flamenco in true Spanish style, the notes hurtling and gyrating one after the other in a loud, fiery torrent. There was a sudden strumming of chords and then a lowering of tempo and pitch. The guest officers glanced up from their conversation and wine. There was a foreboding in the music which immediately attracted all attention. While they stared, not knowing quite what to expect, but certain that something was going to happen, a figure danced slowly in from the shadows of the portico, a shadowy movement at first, growing into a flame of red and black, becoming a beautiful girl who swayed sensually in before the gypsy band which accompanied her.

There was an instant tension in the assembly. Men who had been engaged in, at least, the semblance of war for more than a week or two, flushed over with the tightening of desire. Cesare put down the glass with which he had been describing circles in the air.

'You hardly exaggerated,' he said quietly and in some surprise.

'Almost worth a stiletto in the ribs if one could be certain of achieving one's fill before the death blow, eh?' chuckled his host.

Cesare Borgia didn't reply. His thoughts were away on the hips that revolved gently, the breasts that were taut from her upstretched, slender brown arms. Her face seemed to spark and blaze with pride and a controlled sensuality; her dark hair swept back, dropping, long onto her shoulders; broad brow over dark, almond eyes, a straight nose which flared lightly at the nostrils, long, full lips which opened often in intense concentration as she danced, a good, clear chin which was round and smooth under her mouth; and then the neck, long and unexpectedly well-developed as she came forward into the light, full and with the slight ridge of a vein; below the black lace frill of the tight-bodiced red dress she wore, the breasts which forced out the yielding stuff in strong, taut lines, the slim waist which moved and writhed inside the dress, the skirt tight over her hips, enclosing her buttocks in a tight embrace and then flaring out loosely around her thighs to permit her freedom of movement.

'Superb, superb,' Cesare murmured aloud and his host smiled with a pleasure that conflicted with his mask of almost miserable longing.

The music gathered in crescendo and the girl made a full, twirling tour of the room, skimming the tables of the spectators with her flying skirt. She seemed to see nobody. At times her face was serene and ethereal, at others working with passion as if she were in the throes of sexual intercourse. The men seemed to come to life, out of the still, electric petrification her arrival had induced. They slithered forward on their couches the better to see. There were odd comments of coarse appreciation uttered without a withdrawal of the eyes watching her every movement, every crease and tension of every part of her body under the flaming silk dress.

The Duke of Valentinois watched with the others. He felt his heart pounding and that empty sucking in his stomach. She was as beautiful as Lucrezia, this

133

Maria, the gypsy; as beautiful at the other end of the scale, each of them perfection of their own kind.

His eyes ran over her avidly. As she swayed toward his end of the room, slim arms flowering in the light of the candles around the walls, he watched her breasts, full and alive under the slender covering. They bulged and moved in unison with her movement. The points of her nipples jutted, large and voluptuous from the summits of the warm mounds of flesh behind them. He let his glance fall, taking in the slim waist, so slim that it moved all by itself inside the dress as if it wanted no part of these protecting clothes. And then the tight containment of those hips, the rounded belly, which could be cupped with a hand, the protrusion of hipbones, well-fleshed and bulging against the silk, the lines of the strong, sexual thighs and then the slim, lightly-muscled calves that twirled below the whirl of the skirts.

'Beautiful, beautiful,' Cesare whispered.

His host leaned toward him, hotly.

'You must forgive me,' he muttered. 'I can't bear to stay. It is a mistake for me to be here at all and I must take my leave in a few moments. If there is anything you or your officers require of me, you have only to ask my servants. They will show you to your quarters and to the source of your future enjoyment.'

His breath had come with difficulty and when Cesare looked at him he saw that his face was almost crimson and his eyes drawn in anguish.

'My poor Chief Councillor,' he whispered sympathetically, 'I understand your predicament. To have such a delight within your house and be unable to sip of the ecstasy she promises is hard indeed. But I crave

134

one boon before you leave—that I may be permitted to try my gallantry with the lady.'

There was a note of envy in the Chief Councillor's tone as he gazed into Cesare's handsome, commanding face.

'By all means,' he said, 'and I wish you success. Perhaps a conquest would soften her heart toward others who would give their souls to share her bed. I will see that she joins you alone after the entertainment and that you are not disturbed.'

With that the Chief Councillor rose, not waiting even to hear his guest's thanks, and slipped from the banquet hall as if he were afraid he would in some way disgrace himself if he delayed his exit a single second.

Grinning to himself, Cesare turned back to the spectacle. The music was throbbing, drugging the room with its heavy insistence. The girl had her back to him, arms high above her head, hips swaying, heels tapping on the marble floor. The outlines of her buttocks pressed and relaxed in firm ovals against the seat of the dress. Each seemed to move of its own accord, rounded and naked, inviting lustful attack. She whirled and flitted forward with flying, little steps, toward Cesare's table. Her eyes seemed to catch his for an instant. He held them and they bored back at him until slowly he dropped his gaze and stared meaningfully at the triangular crease of her dress between her thighs. When he glanced up again, her eyes were still on him, but flicked away immediately, her head bowing to the ground in concentration.

A hot glow consumed Cesare, slowly, from his genitals. He had no thought of failure. The meeting of their eyes had established the beginning. He would, as always, win.

For a moment, he took his eyes from the scene to witness its effect. His officers were hypnotized. Some faces were scarlet, others white with desire: a band of civilized men, suddenly naked and primitive in the face of elemental sexual passion. The difference between most of them and himself, Cesare knew, was the difference between himself and the Chief Councillor: that he would not give his soul to possess this woman. It was, also, this very aloof quality which communicated itself even in moments of intimacy, which gave him his extraordinary power of attracting and, if desired, maintaining the interest of the most difficult and independent of women. Cesare had learned from his sister, Lucrezia, the intricacies of intrigue and attitude that women were capable of; he had, perhaps, been fortunate in learning from her the necessity of keeping himself beyond the snares which they set, of keeping himself whole in mind and emotions, of being always the master.

Now, catching again the eyes of the beautiful gypsy girl as she danced toward him, letting his eyes rove insolently over her breasts as if he were stroking them with his eyelashes, he felt certain that she was his. He could hardly wait to hold those buttocks naked in his hands and drive his strength and mastery between her naked thighs into the conquered lips that waited softly to receive him.

It was very warm in the banquet hall—as if all those who had left had jettisoned their heat before departure. Not all the candles still glowed smoothly into the gloom, only a few at odd points around the walls

136

cast deep and slightly moving shadows. There were two red candles flickering on the table and they threw a warm, flattering light on the faces of Cesare and the gypsy girl.

'A little wine,' Cesare was saying, as he filled her glass again.

She took her long-stemmed glass and sipped, looking at him over its rim. Her eyes were warm, and so friendly that they would have turned over the Chief Councillor's heart had he been there.

'They say that you will soon be lord of all Romagna—perhaps of all Italy,' she said softly.

'Gossip,' Cesare said. 'But it may be true.' He smiled. 'My chances would be greater had I your power of reducing men to willing slavery.'

'Gossip,' she retorted, 'if we speak of men. I can think of many I would not put in that category.'

'Our poor Chief Councillor is slowly dying of suffocation—suffocation of his desires.'

'He is like a cow,' she said. 'He chews his food and watches me with great, gawking eyes. When he desired me he had to send a servant to try to procure me so afraid was he that I might spit in his face.'

Cesare took a long gulp of wine.

'Are all as unlucky as he?'

'Did he not tell you I'm not to be bought?'

'I'm not talking of buying.'

She raised an eyebrow at him over her glass and smiled. She gave no answer and Cesare put his hand on hers on the table, gently but firmly.

'You remind me of my sister Lucrezia,' he said.

'But isn't she blonde?'

'I mean that you are perfect in your particular beauty as she is in hers. I am told, too, that she is perfect in bed. As for that, I would never be able to compare you.'

He watched her closely. But she didn't take his words amiss. Clearly he was not in the same class as the Chief Councillor, nor had she removed her hand from his.

'What happens when you want to give—and not be bought?' he asked.

'These are very personal questions—I had heard you were very direct,' she said, still smiling.

'It's the only way to know people,' he replied. 'Hedging and social protocol are all very well in their place.'

'Yes,' she said and she turned her hand in his and entwined their fingers gently. 'I have given very rarely,' she went on. 'I only give when I'm moved, otherwise it's not worth the pestering which would follow from all those who assume that because a woman gives she is free to all.'

She had leaned forward slightly and Cesare could see deep down between the swellings of her breasts. The skin was a tawny flame-colour and as smooth looking as parchment. He let his eyes run from her breasts up over her shoulders and that strong, voluptuous neck. When his eyes reached hers she was looking at him without the smile. It had been replaced by a look he recognized—Lucrezia's look of desire. In those few seconds he thought with amazement that she must always have looked like this. That even in rags, running the streets of the slum quarters in her youth before she joined the gypsy band, she looked this same lovely, haughty, sensual woman who might, at that time, have given herself to anyone who was prepared to make her rich, to give her the life of a lady. He wondered that no rich merchant, straying on his horse through the poor quarter, had caught a glimpse of her—probably with half a breast naked through her rags and tatters, or a side view of a straining buttock. She could, by now, have been at the court of kings.

'What are you thinking?' she asked softly, the desire still heavy in her eyes. 'Why do you look at me like that?' He looked at the dark shadows below her high, smooth cheekbones, his glance lingered on those full lips which had hardly moved as she spoke.

'I was thinking that you are, perhaps, more beautiful even than Lucrezia,' he said quietly.

'She would not be flattered to hear you say that.'

'She would probably retort by claiming that she was far superior in the boudoir.'

'But even after tonight you would have no way of comparing us—you would never have slept with her.'

Cesare stood up, slowly, not taking his eyes off the girl. Mingled with his unexpectedly easy triumph was a sly amusement at her peasant assumption. He was tempted to tell her, but the moment was not to be spoiled and, in any case, her tongue might wag.

He walked around the table toward her and she stood up with her lips parted, waiting. When he reached her and caught her face in both his hands, her body swept in and wriggled against him. Sparks seemed to fly in his body. God, he thought, it's almost as if she divined and were determined to prove herself the better. The flesh, smoothly, glossily almost, covering the fine bones of her face was hot under his fingers. There was a delicate perfume of roses about her hair. Her lips were moist and gave like a sponge, opening under his. They seemed to swallow his

139

mouth—and then her tongue, smooth as milk was panting into his mouth, exploring it, brushing against his own. Along his whole length he felt the warm slender solidity of her body pressing and moving slightly—the weight of her breasts protruding, the smooth roundness of her thighs brushing and clinging to his, her hips and that excruciating abdominal area which pressed against his confined genitals and slithered against them hotly. He pulled his mouth from hers and she let it go reluctantly. Audible little pantings breathed through her lips, now released, as he moved down her neck, sucking it, biting it, drawing a pattern of little red marks on the velvety skin. He reached her shoulders, the top halves, naked halves, of her breasts, which bulged and wanted to escape and soar forth for him in their entirety. As he bit her breasts gently, her abdomen, that triangular section between her strong thighs, squirmed furiously against the mound of his genitals which she could feel in an erect hump beneath his clothes.

'Let's go through to the private chambers,' he whispered.

'No, now—here!' she said passionately.

He pushed her gently back toward the divan from which he'd watched her dancing earlier in the evening. The Chief Councillor had promised they would be alone—and what did it matter if a servant did tumble onto them? Guilt and fear were for the weak and subordinate.

She fell back onto the couch and he lowered himself down with her. She put her hand on the covered heat of his penis and he felt its trembling, demanding pressure with a wild surge of immediate desire. He began, quickly, to slip off her clothes and she helped

140

him, breathing heavily, looking at him with deep, fire-filled eyes, concentrating on ridding herself of the garments that hid her body from him.

In a matter of seconds she was stretched out on the couch, more naked than in the days of flimsy rags and Cesare's mouth was avidly sucking her large, erect nipples, as his hands flared over her body, exploring its firm, beautiful contours while his penis seemed to throb and hum like a hive of bees.

Her breasts were taut and high in spite of their size. The nipples that he sucked crowned them in a dark, hard summit which seemed to epitomize her desire; the hard bosses yielded and flipped back in rubbering resilience and seemed to reach out to him in pleading desire for assuagement. Below her breasts her hard, narrow waist was the pivot for her writhing hips. No bones showed in her hips, the flesh was full and rounded, the little bulge of her abdomen heaving in and out with its crest of fine, dark hair. Her sensual, well-holding thighs pressed and slithered against each other, opening wide from time to time as Cesare's hands moved over her flesh. Between them, dark rose lips, moist and ready, were crushed with her movement.

Cesare's penis felt wet inside his clothes and the throbbing was unbearable. When, without opening her eyes or stopping the convulsions of her lost body, the girl put her hand again on his penis and began to squeeze and caress it, he stood up quickly and began to tear off his clothes.

She lay there, her breath exploding from between her parted lips, her thighs tight together as if to keep the sensation locked tightly in. She opened her eyes after a few seconds and watched Cesare baring his body. Her eyes were in anguish and her hands, which had moved up to the breasts on which the heat and fury of his lips remained, twitched gently.

Feeling the warm air strike his suddenly naked flesh with a cooling draught, Cesare looked back at the girl's body as he stripped. She was beautiful as a Greek statue and burning with sexual life. He could worship a body like that—except that he didn't worship bodies. He had a sudden irreverent thought of the envy the Chief Councillor would feel when he knew. What that man would give to be here now in his shoes—or rather in his skin.

Nude at last, with his penis soaring ruggedly out and up at an acute angle with his belly, Cesare moved toward the couch. She watched him come, her eyes flowing over his face and from it down over his lightly haired and muscular chest to the slim hips dominated by that great boom of penis with its narrowing, fiery tip. As he reached the divan she reached up and grasped it and icy darts shot through his belly and clashed in his genitals.

He lay down beside her and she stroked and caressed his prick and smothered his lips with hers, flicking her tongue in what seemed an almost involuntary spasm of sensuality.

Cesare pressed her dark head back onto the couch. The rose perfume was all around like an ethereal cushion and her dark hair brushed softly against his face as he sank into her lips and sucked them and her tongue into his mouth. Her flesh was hot and receptive, trembling against his as he slid his hand down over those firm, reaching breasts and the belly with its little indentation and then over the fine hair which was warm and soothing to his fingers, and so between

142

those hot and slightly sweating thighs, right at their topmost point where they merged into the hot arch containing the point of desire.

She gasped as his hand reached the lips of her cunt, gasped into his mouth and was unable to keep her lips against his with the sudden sensation. She dragged her head away and turned it so that her cheek lay along the divan, pressing into it as if she were resisting some torture.

Through the loose, wet flesh, his fingers wandered and into the suddenly tight and opening hole which he found.

'Oh, oh!' she gasped and bit her lips under his passionate, watching eyes as he lay with his cheek against hers. Her hand on his prick redoubled its activity and she began to stroke him gently, moving her fingers lightly on the hot, stiff flesh.

He felt her thighs moving and then opening widely and her crotch rose up slightly toward him, facilitating and demanding the entry of his searching fingers into the moist channel at whose entrance they dawdled. He pressed in, wiping a finger around the elastic rim and plunging on into the depths of the cavern beyond.

'Oh, oh, oh, oh!' Her face on the couch swung back at his and she released his prick and held him tightly with both arms as she kissed him wildly and rubbed her face all over and around his.

Cesare could feel his prick, hot and waiting, pressing up against her hip, the cool, yielding flesh of her hip. He moved in against her, crushing it against that flesh, rubbing his loins against her, moving one of his thighs half over hers.

His finger, now, had penetrated all the way and he could feel the smooth, viscid roof of the cavern. Her thighs alternately clamped his hand in the pressure of a vice and released it, sweeping apart in a wild, passionate gesture. She was panting continuously and punctuating the panting with little moans as he moved his fingertip gently against the roof of the cavern.

Her lovely lips were trembling and her nostrils were slightly flared the way he'd noticed them as she concentrated on her dancing. She had closed her eyes and the long lashes made tremulous shadows on her cheeks. Her long, slim hands ran convulsively over his body, not seeming to be controlled by her at all.

Cesare moved another finger into her vagina and she cringed away and then pushed back on the double prong which filled her. He allowed his fingers to roam all over and through the moist channel of her sex and then slowly withdrew them and searched for the tiny stub of her passion. He found it, hard and erect. It evaded him from time to time as he caressed it, slipping away into the fleshy folds of her lips.

The touch of his fingers on her clitoris had sparked even greater depths of passion reaction from her. She had caught his penis again and squeezed it hard. She ran her fingertips over his balls as far down as she could reach. She brought up her head and bit his neck and lips. She was like a tigress.

Caressing her, tantalizing her, bringing her to a pitch of excitement, with his own thunderous, growing passion as a controlled background, Cesare felt her thigh slipping and digging under his trying to get him to mount her. Her arms pulled his face onto her chest over against her breasts which strained up, digging him with erect, large nipples.

'Now, now,' she murmured. 'Do it now.'

Overcome with a nervous excitement, now that the

moment had come, as if afraid of the power of his own passion, Cesare hesitated, drawing his fingertips up her hard, little clitoris for a few seconds longer until she was groaning with ecstasy.

'Please, please, now, now, now,' she begged, hardly able to utter the words, squeezing blindly on his rod of flesh.

Cesare slithered over onto her. She made a superb, warm cushion for his body. Her thighs swung wide apart as she felt the knob of his penis tickling against the lips of her vagina. She gripped both his shoulders very tightly with her hands which quivered with emotion.

Cesare wriggled on her, longing to plunge in but enjoying the sight and sound of her passion and desire.

He felt her release a shoulder and then her hand came down under her thigh and felt for and found his penis. She held it gently, seeming to hold her breath, too, at the same time, and guided it at her wide-open cunt.

Right, now, at last, Cesare thought in a sudden, fierce, violent joy. He thrust in with a long, excruciating grind, all the way in one long, agonizing movement. She drew up her thighs with his penetration and her hands bit into his shoulders.

'Aaaaaah!' The ecstatic groan dragged out from between their lips at the same moment. With her it continued on a slightly lower key, a continuous, gentle, lost groaning. With Cesare it broke down into a shunting accompaniment of groans and pantings for breath as he drove in and in, crashing and plundering, right to the soft, giving wall of the cavern's roof.

Her thighs which had opened, giving him wider access, and moved back toward her shoulders giving him depth, came down and clasped his hips, moving and slithering against them as he pistoned in and out. Her breasts flattened and rounded under his varying pressure and her eyes opened to look with abandon into his as her groaning lips sought to touch, to bite, to kiss his face, any part of his face.

His loins aflame, consumed in the ecstatic relief of her moist, claiming containment, Cesare felt her passage plucking sensation from his prick along its whole length. Her channel fitted him like a glove, smooth and with a gentle pressure which became stronger as the tip of his organ coursed right through to its end.

Already he could feel pressure building up in his pulsating staff. All that preliminary titivating had prepared his prick for a quick release.

Under him, squirming and mouthing noises, the gypsy girl, too, was building up to the intense final pressure. Her arms moved around him, over his shoulder, down his back, to his buttocks which she could just reach. She pressed on them exhorting him into her and her legs swung up suddenly and entwined his thighs and then up further and gripped his waist.

Cesare slipped his hand under her full, soft buttocks which strained down firmly in his hands and then relaxed, soft again. He reached underneath, feeling her thighs from behind and she gasped anew as his fingers entered the long slit of her vagina, pulling the lips gently apart, brushing in with his hard length of penis.

Her head began to move from side to side on the divan. Her legs released his waist and swung down, flattening into the couch and then gripped him again before falling away, almost at right angles to her body.

Her crotch was running with moisture. Cesare's fingers slipped from it and ran up the crease between her buttocks. He pulled the buttocks apart and she gave a start of passion through her moaning. He plunged a finger against the tight, warm, puckering of her anus and felt it give and his fingertip break through to soft, tender flesh.

'Oh, oh, oh!' she gasped again and again.

She began to writhe as if in a paroxysm. It must be now, Cesare was able to think as he drummed into her, pulling back and then thrusting in his whole length in a slow, grinding crush.

She opened her eyes and looked at him desperately. Her eyes seemed to be speaking to him, loving him, wanting him, abandoning herself to him. Her mouth opened and her tongue came out—a long, point-tipped, moist and perfectly smooth tongue. Cesare lowered his lips to hers and bit the tongue gently. He ground in with slow, strong strokes. He could feel his penis swelling in a hot tingling expansion. He couldn't keep his mouth on hers and drew up, his hands under her buttocks, pulling them up off the divan, against his loins.

She wriggled furiously, her shoulders quivered, and her breasts under his eyes. She groaned and looked at his eyes in a last gleam of passion and then her mouth opened in a great circle, her head dropped back, her thighs clasped him and she emitted a loud, aching gasp and another and another, dwindling away into body-racking sighs.

Still holding her buttocks in his hands, fired by the sight of her fulfilment. Cesare, himself, trembled on the brink of release. His penis was chafing against the flesh of her passage and his loins were screwed up in a

147

turmoil of pre-explosion. Her beautiful body, heaving with passionate sighs, was in his hands. He looked down and saw her thighs hanging over his hands as he held her bottom, and saw his prick, inflamed and wet, disappearing into her red, loose lips. Her breasts swayed and heaved below him and that narrow waist was heaving too, above the hips that he held up slightly off the bed.

He thrust savagely in and felt his knob growing and growing as if it would burst into a thousand pieces. He ground slowly, slowly, extracting every iota of sensation from the long, slow stroke. His breath was rising up from his chest, rising up through his throat at the same time that his knob was expanding in unbearable torture. He felt the quick fire dart in his loins and come racing through. His mouth opened wide as the breath finally, suddenly, reached it. He shattered his sperm up, up into her belly as the breath broke from his throat, twisting his mouth out into an agonized explosion. He felt the pressure of her thighs renewed, fleetingly, heard a faint gasp echoing a recognition of his orgasm.

For several seconds he pumped into her, seeming to loose all the juices of his pent up body into that lovely, waiting receptacle. Then, slowly he collapsed on her warm, cushioning flesh and felt her arms encircle him gently and her lips, light and tender on his cheek.

Later, nude still, she preceded him as they walked to the private chamber Cesare had been allotted off the banquet hall. Watching her buttocks swaying and rounding under the slim, taut waist, Cesare wondered if the Chief Councillor meant it when he said it would be worth getting a stiletto in one's ribs if one could be sure of fulfilment first. Looking at her thighs, slenderly moving under the rounded voluptuousness of the buttocks, he felt pretty sure he meant it.

The Joys of Lolotte

The evening, though seeming like eternity, passed pleasantly enough. At supper, which was served in our rooms, I ate with gusto. My mother said she had to write a good many letters that evening. I was terrified lest she stayed up part of the night, which sometimes happened, but Félicité, with no less foresight, had seen to that. She found a way of telling me about it and laying at rest a worry that she evidently shared with me.

'Don't worry,' she said. 'I have added a reasonable dose of Madame's sleeping draught to her wine. I assure you she will quickly drop off over her writing paper and feel the need to go to bed.'

Her stratagem worked as it was meant to. My mother had been at work for scarcely half an hour when, yawning, abstracted and overcome with sleep, she rang for Félicité to help her undress.

'Really,' she said to her lady's maid. 'I feel quite tipsy. It can't be what I drank at supper. It must be an excess of happiness—a sentiment that my heart has become unaccustomed to lately.'

'Happiness no doubt has something to do with it,' the cunning Félicité replied. 'But, without noticing, Madam also drank rather more than usual tonight.'

'I don't believe so.'

'I was surprised myself but Madam lightly drank off a second carafe of wine.' (This was quite untrue.)

'Is that really so?'

'I assure you, madam. Anyway, have a good rest.'

152

'I am so sleepy I can hardly keep my eyes open; good night, Félicité.'

'Good night, Madam.' She drew the curtains. 'I wish you happy dreams. We, too—believe me—are going to have a good night after the happy events of the day.'

'I hope so, my children.'

'Good night, Mother.'

'Good night, Madam.'

We still had an hour to ourselves. Lord, how slowly the time passed. I was terribly impatient. Leaping from my seat to the window every few moments like a squirrel, I got even more tired and restless; by turns, I questioned Félicité, called her names and even hit her because she said, though with a laugh, that perhaps instead of expecting a man, we should prepare ourselves to discover that the idea of an assignation was the treacherous trick of some wicked hussy trying to compromise us with my mother and the Mother Superior.

At heart, however, Félicité, who was able to control herself better than I, was no less hopeful; what she said was merely to rein in my petulance a little and to give herself the mischievous pleasure of contradicting me.

But, in the end, when I went to the window for perhaps the hundredth time, what joy! I caught a glimpse of something moving in the garden . . . the object came closer; I called Félicité over. . . . First we saw a figure, then a ladder approaching our window. . . . How my heart was beating!

The ladder was put in position; the figure moved away and then returned. Good grief! It was . . . it was . . . only a nun! All at once my blood ran cold and fury replaced hope and desire. It would not have needed much for me to push over the ladder and hurl it, together with the figure on it, into the garden.

How unjust a person can be and how blameworthy if he acts rashly. How dreadful it would have been if I had been the cause of the charming creature that was coming to call on us breaking its neck.

The habit was straightaway cast off by our gentleman visitor (for it turned out that he really was male): ardent caresses were at once bestowed impartially on the mistress and servant.

'You understand, of course, my darlings, that midnight rendez-vous in a nunnery are not made for sentimental romances. More than once I have over-heard your intimate conversations and listened to your discussions. I know full well what you think and what you desire and I shall supply what you need.'

We had already had our bodices and skirts removed, because his hands had not lagged behind his speech in carrying negotiations forward. What an expert undresser of girls he was, to be sure!

'Let's get to work quickly and jointly. Let's shut the windows, draw the curtains and shade the lights. Let's not stand on ceremony and let us drop all inhibitions.'

At this point my shift was removed; I was immediately seized below my buttocks and lifted up so that my downed *honey-pot* could be freely kissed. I was released; now it was Félicité's turn and her magnificent breasts were gratified by the most ardent caresses. My own, alas, had not been treated like that—there was still too little of them. Now he returned to me. I was carried to the bed. At the same moment, Félicité's shift dropped to her feet. The hussy knew full well to what extent the advantageous display of her many charms would redound to her credit. The young man's reaction was striking—like that of Pygmalion prostrating himself at the feet of his Galatea taking her first breath. Félicité was hugged, covered with kisses all over—literally all over—and laid on the bed beside me. At almost the same moment, the young man was as stark naked as we were ourselves. But for the absence of wings, he was an angel or rather as one would imagine Apollo or Belvedere but with a *prick*! Heavens, what a *prick*! It was the first I had ever seen in the flesh and, alas, I have never had the good fortune to see another like it.

Imagine the embarrassment of a young worshipper, burning with desire, about to offer up his sacrifice, who has at his mercy on the altar two victims, one of whom is only a servant but mature, ravishing and perfectly made for enjoyment, whereas the other is her mistress but a mere sketch of a future masterpiece, having little to set against the charms of her attractive rival apart from the fantastic advantage of her virginity. While it is known that the latter is a powerful bait for many gallants, there are a great many others whom it does not interest in the slightest: the true man of pleasure attaches little value to the specious pleasures of self-esteem. So I had no reason to think that if the choice between us had been perfectly free the scales would have come down in my favour.

Félicité, it must be said, did nothing to persuade him that she should be awarded the apple, because I seemed to desire it so much, too much perhaps. The role of my inferior, my domestic servant, was to

155

discourage both the young man and myself from follies which—while we were together—she could tolerate but which could still be avoided as long as a shred of principle could still set limits to my fiery desires. The role of the Adonis was to avoid humiliating either of us; mine ought to have been not to demand so transparently, by my looks and attitude, that the flame that was progressively consuming me should at last be extinguished.

I wanted it so much; yet, I did not. I wanted to brave whatever might be coming to me; yet, I was afraid. The brat who had set her mind on being penetrated and had imagined that in her furious desire she would be capable of seizing the first hobbledehoy who came her way by the trousers—this foolish creature, I say, became increasingly reluctant as luck appeared to favour her more and more.

Let us cut a long story short. Félicité, lightly passed over, was neglected in my favour. The angel of pleasure, covering me with his heavenly body, said to me,

'Us two first, my little darling. For the first time, I can't promise you much joy. But I hope soon and often to reward you for the pleasure you will give me. Kiss me.'

What transports and what fire I put into that kiss, which was my only response!

'All the same, ask yourself,' he said after touching my little crack, 'will your miniature charms be able to sustain the rough assault of this, which is out of all proportion to them?'

I had seized it and my hand was scarcely able to encompass it: it was long in proportion, hard and hot.

'Shall we put it in?'

'Oh yes, please do,' I replied, throwing all caution to the winds. 'Do your best, sir, come what may.'

'She wants it,' he said smiling at Félicité.

'You're going to kill her,' she replied. 'Hold on a minute; I'll preside over this dangerous operation; let me do it, I'll direct it myself. Good heavens, what an enormous thing! No, Mademoiselle, with your sixteen years and your eye of a needle you'll never accommodate this enormous fellow.'

'Just go on, my dear, do your best.'

After that, the happy young man gave her free rein to do what she wanted. He was preoccupied with my kisses which stoked his fires and submitted to the attentions of the maid who, after applying the whole of a pot of cold cream to our playthings, finally placed the enormous button against the narrow button-hole. But in vain did she hold it open, in vain did she strangle the glans of the enormous *prick* in its hood to make it more pointed; she could not make it penetrate even a fraction of an inch.

He pushed; I lunged against him—but it was all to no avail. Our conjunction proved impossible.

But still, you cannot with impunity for long have your lips glued to those of a charming girl, with your *prick* in the hands of another beauty and rubbing against a maidenhead. As a result of these delicious experiences, the electric current of pleasure could not fail to affect the young man and a torrent of hot *spunk* gushed forth. Félicité believed that a joint effort, aided by the life-giving fluid, would at last break down the barrier.

'Push, my children. It must go in—now or never.'

We pushed hard enough to do ourselves a grievous

injury. All in vain. The precious ejaculation occurred entirely outside me and I was not even broached.

'Fate is cruel,' my young man said calmly as he changed position, 'but just regard it as a postponed fixture. I know precisely, my little darling, what you need; tomorrow—without fail—there are going to be two of us and you shall have what you need. And that contumacious maidenhead will give way, I promise.'

He was still speaking to me when he was already mounted on Félicité and attacking her most sensitive spot. She was surprised—or pretending to be—at this abrupt transition and wanted a little more ceremony—but he would have none of it.

'What, in front of Mademoiselle?', the hypocritical hussy said when it was almost too late, 'at least wait till I snuff out the candles; she must not watch this infamy.'

'God damme, if this were a public square, at noon, in front of the queen, I wouldn't let go of any part of you.'

'Quite right,' I interrupted, putting on a brave face in spite of my misfortune, though I was still a little out of countenance on account of the game with me having been abandoned so quickly.

To console myself a little at least. I feasted my eyes on the majestic entry of this beautiful *prick* into the maid's receptive and docile sheath. How could I possibly have borne anything of such dimensions! Even she made a bit of a face but every heave of her hips and haunches made another good inch of the formidable cylinder disappear and before long I saw both brave champions engaged, so to speak, skin to skin.

Tell me frankly what you think, true lovers and knowledgeable connoisseurs of all things voluptuous.

Is there anything on earth so fine, so admirable and so exciting as the sight of two perfect bodies being united by the introduction of a *prick*, bursting with health, into a *cunt* palpitating with lust? This ivory, this lily, these roses, this ebony, or this gold, all moving, colliding, struggling ... what a spectacle for the gods! They have made the eyes of the vulgar multitude chary of looking on while such things go on in order that they might enjoy them in privacy. But the elite of us mortals is made to share the sublime pleasure of those directly taking part. Everyone who *fucks* is a base ingrate if he does not in his heart have the ardent desire to let others watch what he himself does with such delight.

What you have missed, gentle reader, is not seeing, like me, the superb Félicité moaning with pleasure and rocking with her gentle movements the demi-god tumbling about on top of her! Oh, how inadequate this description is compared with the most beautiful scene of *fucking* that the human mind can conceive!

Not only did I not want to miss the most insignificant detail that my avid eyes could see; I also had to grope above and below—in all directions. I admired the almost chilly spheres in the element of fire surrounding them, contained in their elastic, wrinkled bag, which at one moment rubbed against the lower corner of the *cunt* and the next, separated from it by the entire length of the *prick*, the ridge of which almost appeared outside, as if to impress me with the adroitness with which it immediately re-sheathed itself up to the very *balls*. What grace, what harmony there was in the vigorous work of these two expert creatures!

By accident, I created for myself a small part in this voluptuous scene and my success in it made me quite proud. My fingers, lightly walking over the buttocks, thighs and genitalia of this Adonis appeared to give him great pleasure; nor was I niggardly in my stimulating attentions when I realized how much he enjoyed them.

'Oh, yes! Like that,' he said. 'Go on tickling, my little darling; tickle them well; one day they will amply repay you for what you are doing now.'

By degrees, Félicité warmed to her task. 'I am going to come but if you come at the same time, I'll be lost: we are more likely to make two babies than one. Can you slow down a bit?'

'I'll see to everything, don't worry.'

'Your word of honour?'

'You have it.'

'All right, then.'

At this point her movements became awesomely agitated and now she did everything herself.

'Give me your lips, my lover. Kiss me, my angel! Oh, my God! What a glorious *fuck*!'

This sacred word was followed by silence, enforced by the fury of the kiss by which she held her lover's entire mouth engulfed in hers. She gathered him to herself by the arms and legs and held him close, trembling. This ecstatic state lasted a good two minutes; it continued even when all her limbs weakened and the prisoner at last regained his freedom. He used it at once to accomplish his own task. A moment of the same ardour that had been displayed by Félicité now brought him to his crisis. She, immobile, her arms spread out, her head turned on one shoulder and as if in a faint, took no notice of anything. All the same, true to his word, the happy young man did not fail to withdraw at the decisive

160

moment. The thick fleece of the maid was liberally sprinkled but I observed that the unction, now more limpid, flowed less freely than earlier on with me. The beautiful young man's kept promise was rewarded with the tenderest of caresses. Now we washed; all three of us needed to badly. Félicité tidied up the bed a little and we warmed ourselves up in it, putting the dear creature who had just worked so well for our happiness in the middle.

Who was he? We were dying to know. But our curiosity was not to be satisfied yet.

Don't worry, my children.' he told us. 'One day I shall be able to tell you by what chance I became the spoilt child of this nunnery, in which—to be sure—I have many clients beside yourselves.'

'Would you believe it?'

'I cannot tell you more at the moment; but you should know that here, my dear children, you are more or less . . . in a brothel and that at this very moment there are six or seven males scattered about the sleeping quarters of this nunnery. There is apparently a god for fornicators and this god gives his special protection to a community so fervent in its worship of him; all the same, so much blatant scandal goes on here that one day—possibly quite soon—all this *fucking* may blow up in our faces.'

I suddenly had an idea. If, as he said, there really were six or seven males scattered about the sleeping quarters at that moment, would it not be possible to look for one more suitably built for my requirements, who could deputize for our visitor . . . I wanted to convey this thought to Félicité at once, so I asked our lover to raise himself slightly to enable me to whisper this lubricious thought in her ear.

161

'What a randy devil you are,' the malicious maid cried out aloud. 'Do you think the nuns have less of an appetite than you and are going to take the titbit out of their own mouths to feed you? And do you expect Monsieur to go out pimping for you? That, assuredly, is too much to expect of our gallant.'

'How delicious she is,' he said, hugging me. 'I don't think it's too much to ask at all. I'd be honoured to take the job on. Oh, my little darling, what a great name you'll soon be making for yourself in the world of *fucking*. I already regard you as one destined to take the blue riband of fornication and I already adore you on that account. What a pity, though' he added, 'that it won't be me . . .' (at this point he passed his hand over my little *cunt*) 'no, it's impossible.'

'Alas, what a dreadful shame!' I replied and sought out his monstrous engine. I surprised it at rest and in the shape of a swan's neck. But like a sleeping snake inadvertently touched by the heel of a huntsman, it no sooner felt the touch of my curious hand than it proudly raised its head and immediately recovered its old majesty. This made me sigh even more sadly, 'Oh, what a great shame.'

'Well, as for me,' Félicité, who was now caressing it as well, butted in gaily, 'I found it so good that if it had been any less long, or stiff or hot, I would have said even more fervently than you two: "Oh, what a shame!" '

'I've got something quite amusing to suggest,' our charming friend, whom our conversation had made randy again, said, 'which would occupy the two of you very pleasurably for a quarter of an hour.'

'Both of us?' I exclaimed with pleasure. 'Ah, my love, do tell us how.'

'I'll stay where I am' (he was on his back) 'and the charming maid will kindly sit astride me facing the foot of the bed . . . Yes, that's it' (Félicité was already mounting him) ' . . . she will be so good as to put it up her. Ah, lovely! At the same time, the little one will also bestride me facing in the same direction . . . yes, that's it and yield her pretty bottom to my observation and her little *cunt* to my kisses . . . marvellous!'

His suggestions were carried out as he made them. How readily a man is obeyed when it is pleasure he orders!

Félicité already had him up her, up to his *balls*; my *quim*, made more sensitive by our fruitless attempt earlier, was lightly moving round the loving tongue of the Adonis . . . Oh, ye gods! What charm the magnet of sex added to gamahouching, with which, of course, I was already familiar from my sessions with Félicité. What a surfeit of joy I felt when I allowed my hands to wander round the perfect hips and *arse* of the lucky maid, seeing her rise and subside rhythmically the better to be rammed by the full length of that magnificent engine. What a moment it was when he and the two of us, electrified to the very marrow of our bones, commingled the sounds of our luxurious agony!

But, above all, what a piquant variation was introduced by Félicité's whim when, finishing first, she did not think only of her own happiness and for a moment liberated this great *prick* which she had inundated with her own *cunt-juice* and at once enslaved it again more narrowly two inches away. From the very first stroke, it felt at home in the new scabbard and was able to run its course there.

'Come, my master, 'Félicité said passionately. '*Fuck*

your Félicité in the *arse* like this, *bugger* her for all you're worth. Give her all you have. In this hole there's nothing to fear. It can safely lap up all your heavenly *spunk*.

I saw her make an effort to get penetrated deeper still and her attempt was happily crowned with success.

Our jolly friend evidently had nothing against this form of pleasure because he intensified his action with his mistress and, as for me, I felt myself being *sucked off* with greater vigour. After some time, we both swooned. Félicité, duly charged and discharged, drooped forwards, her face against the feet of her lover, whose syringe was still active and spreading its drug.

But already this once so proud *prick* was losing its noble countenance. I touched it and separated it from the impure orifice in which it was lodged. It now resembled a flower which a fresh breeze had made sway in the air, its head now this way, now that; all the same it still fascinated me. Had it not just emerged from so questionable a place, how much I should have liked to kiss it.

The self-esteem of a gentleman of quality will not allow him to prolong a scene which is beginning to drag. So, our hero (no longer as heroic as before) got up almost immediately and donned his nun's habit again. Then, having promised without fail to come back next day *accompanied by a friend of the appropriate size for me*, he returned to his ladder and withdrew as happy as a sand-boy. We congratulated ourselves on having enjoyed so much pleasure with so little trouble. But our senses were sated, our eyelids drooping and we soon fell into the most profound sleep.

The Memoirs of
Madame
Madelaine

New York! Mecca toward which every country girl in America turns her face or her heart! City of fabulous wealth and untold poverty. City of exquisite refinements and gross depravities, of churches and bawdyhouses, of wide streets and narrow souls. In brief, a city of contrasts and contradictions. Anyway, this was the year 1907—a long time ago. Perhaps things have changed since then.

New Year's Eve Charley and a number of the boys were going on what they designated a 'slumming cruise' and I was invited to come along. As the party contemplated touching on some rather rough places, and the company of a woman might cause embarrassment, it was devised that I should masquerade as a man. Each had some bit of masculine haberdashery to contribute.

All in all, I made up rather successfully as an attractive, though slightly hothouse-grown young man. The greatest problem was the disposal of my long, thick hair, which I thought I could conceal but temporarily beneath a soft checkered cap. I was assured, however, that at the places we were going to visit, gentlemen did not remove their hats—or rather, there would be no gentlemen.

I even spent some time practising to speak in a lower register. My voice being naturally somewhat strong, this was not difficult. Yet at times I struck tones that were much too musical to pass for other than those of a Priscilla or a 'pansy'.

That evening was a haze of tobacco smoke and alcoholic fumes, a succession of fancy and cheap cabarets, with their corresponding demi-mondaine habitués, a medley of shouts, songs and tooting horns, with sex stories presenting a continual obligato.

At about 1 a.m. we were encamped in a somewhat quieter type of rendezvous, where the great number of unescorted ladies—and more particularly their boudoir costumes—made it obvious that drinks and music were not the only commodities for sale here.

No sooner were we all seated at a large corner table than a number of these ladies gathered about us. I was surprised to note that many of them were astonishingly good-looking and all had some considerable fund of bodily charm. The slight contempt that I had had for men who patronized prostitutes vanished immediately. Somehow I had always felt that only those women who were insufficiently attractive to ensnare permanent mates ever resorted to this profession. But now, with this proof positive before me, it seemed more likely that only those whose charms were too slight to insure numerous successive admirers would steer for the safe harbour of marriage with its stagnant waters. True, some of them seemed rather hard, vulgar specimens. But marriage is more likely to contain great numbers of viragos than this profession whose purpose is to please—and I was beginning to learn that there are degrees of refinement even among the votaries of Venus Pandemos.

One of their number, the youngest by appearance, singled me out for · her especial attention. My embarrassment could be better imagined than described—particularly, when my companions, realizing the humour of the situation, urged her on to overcome my 'bashfulness'.

The lady in question was a delightful young thing of about my age and size, with titian-red hair and eyes of a strange dark blue that bordered on green. Beneath the diaphanous black silk combination, that was all that she wore, could be discerned the pink-white prominences of her pretty form, the firm tract of her belly and a pair of pert, luscious breasts that seemed so deliciously edible that even I, who should have felt a minimum of response to such charms, experienced a deep impulse to bite into them—just to feel those tiny cherry nipples upon the back of my tongue with the surrounding ivory flesh caressing my lips. Her thighs and legs, though they demanded less attention by very reason of the fact that they were entirely bare except for the uppermost segments, were as shapely as any I had seen. A string of jade beads and a pair of tiny scarlet slippers completed her clothed protection—and little enough it was.

Sitting beside me on the wall-seat, she made herself agreeable to me in what I supposed was the conventional manner.

'You are a very handsome boy,' she said, with a slight accent that I immediately surmised as French, running her fingertips in a peculiarly subtle manner up my thighs. 'You would make a very pretty girl,' I winced, but smiled at her in lieu of the words I dared not speak.

'But I like you,' she went on. 'Do you wish to kiss me?' I shook my head. 'No? You're afraid of me? Come now, I won't bite you. Give me your arm. Now—put it around my waist, so. And your hand—here. Like that? Nice, isn't it? Make you feel

168

like doing anything? No? Then your other hand.' She pursed her pretty red lips patiently. 'Put it here on my thigh, so. You like that? Nice and warm, isn't it? Well, *do* something!' This time with a tiny trace of exasperation. 'I'm not your maiden aunt. You can move your hands a little bit. I won't slap you.'

Complying, I closed one hand over the firm little hillock of one of her bosoms, while with the fingers of the other hand that lay in her lap, I felt timidly about, sensing, through the silk of her combination, the crisp tiny clump of pubic hairs that rustled at my touch. Simultaneously, her deft, naughty little hand crept up my trousered thigh again to my corresponding part, feeling about for the expected result in vain. Of necessity, the phenomenon she desired was impossible; but little did she suspect that the strangeness of the situation was arousing me more than her caresses alone could affect any mere man. And if a penis had been the indicator of my suppressed excitement, I am certain it would have burst every last button on those borrowed trousers I wore.

But finding no index to my state, and therefore, reasonably deeming it a mark of her insufficiency, Nanette (for that was her name) pushed my hands from her, much to my regret, and spoke petulantly.

'You don't like me! I am too ugly for you perhaps. You want me to leave you and send one of the other girls?'

'No, no! I like you,' I ventured to say in low tones that were fortunately made hoarse by my sensual commotion. Whether the assumption of male clothes had worked a sexual transformation within me and my feelings were those of a man for a woman, or whether I had brought to light a heretofore concealed homosexual tendency or not, I cannot say. A simpler explanation would be that the presence of anything associated with sexual pleasure—and lord knows this creature's every curve and fold spoke only of the extremest sensual ecstasies—would stimulate male or female alike, by being interpreted associatively either actively or passively, as the case might be. 'I would like to fuck her' or 'I would like to be her when she gets fucked' is the idea.

Whatsoever the reason though—and too much reasoning is inimical to joy, I must remind myself again and again—I was anxious lest I lose the company of this luscious girlie, and forgetting myself completely, threw my arms about her neck and placed on her mouth a fierce, salacious kiss. I was pleased to find that her ripe moist lips were fresh and sweet, with that vague ambrosial perfume that women can give but cannot receive in kissing a man—and I was not averse when she prolonged the delicious contact by introducing the scarlet tip of her tiny tongue into my mouth. I am not idly employing metaphors when I write that during those few fervid moments my very heart sprang to my lips.

It was only after this compromising admission that I became aware that my companions, though they had been occupying only the periphery of my consciousness, had focused on me at least half their entire attention. They were nudging each other and laughing delightedly at my performance, not for a moment dreaming that it had not been entirely unwilling.

'Would you like to come upstairs with me, dearie?' Nanette whispered when she noted how discomfited I was by the onlookers. I shook my head negatively.

'Would you like to take me home with you then?' I shook my head again.

'Then we can spend the night together at a hotel. I will be so very nice to you. Everything. Yes?'

Again I shook my head. By this time, the boys gathered from my repeated 'no's the way the land lay, and considering it a rare joke, boisterously gave aid to her cause, urging me to go upstairs with her.

'Go ahead, Lou. She'll make a man of you!' Such were the jibes cast at me. At last, to put a stop to this roistering, which already was attracting the attention of all present, and to spare the little lady the public insult that my continued refusal would now be, I nodded my head in assent. She took my hand happily and led me away; but not without my turning back to give my blackest look to my companions for subjecting me to this unspeakable embarrassment.

At a sort of office in the rear, Nanette was thrown a towel and a key—much like the procedure of renting a bathouse at our beaches—and I was handed, imagine, a rubber sheath. Instantly falling out of role, I threw the condom back and continued on. My petulance drew only a polite smile from the madam and an 'As you will, sir.'

On the stairs, I decided it was time to disclose my real sex and bring to a close this comedy of errors. I tapped Nanette on the shoulder and stopped halfway up; but somehow, the words I would have spoken did not come. Perhaps the strange excitement, or fear of an emotional outbreak on her part, or perhaps curiosity as to the outcome, inhibited me. She merely took me by the hand once more and dragged me on, saying. 'Don't be afraid, child. It'll do you a lot of good. And you'll be glad you came. I like it too. For my sake you will do it; because you are a very nice boy and already I love you.'

We entered a brightly lit but plainly furnished room and the key was turned in the lock. Against the wall was a large heavy bed with fresh white linens. Over the lowermost part of the sheets, however, was spread a strip of dark blanketing—probably as a footrest for those who didn't stay long enough to remove their shoes.

'Now we are alone, honey,' Nanette addressed me as I continued to stand near the door. She approached, embraced me tightly, and rolling her waist and hips against my middle with a tense, slow movement that once more made me regret that I possessed no more projectible antenna with which to savour this contact, she placed a long hot kiss upon my mouth. I returned it with sudden, abandoned fervour.

She stepped away from me. A slight shake of her body, and the flimsy black silk under-garment that had been her sole costume slipped down from off her shoulders till only the upstanding heights of her breasts sustained it; another motion, and it slipped down to the station of her full wide hips; another, and the cloud of silk glided shyly down her thighs and settled slowly about her tiny slippered feet.

There she stood before me, nude—an apparition of beauty that not even Chrysis of old could have surpassed when she disrobed for some burning, hand-some lover in the moonlit groves behind the temple of Aphrodite.

What divine flesh! How lovely a form! I would have envied her inconsolably, had not the thought flashed upon me that I could not have loved that gorgeous body one half so passionately, so desirously, if it had been my own. From her gracious neck to her swelling, rounded young breasts my gaze went to the snowy valley between that widened downward to the broad delicious plain of her belly; the dimpled navel; the well-shaded triangular patch, overspread with curling silken hair of the richest, sable—beneath which began a scarcely discernible rift that shaded modestly down and inward to seek shelter between two plump fleshy thighs of just that proportion which is not too much for grace and yet enough for love's luscious demands.

A moment she stood for my admiration, then turning away, presented to my intoxicated view less consciously, another side that put me in deep quandary as to which, front or back, was the more beautiful. The rear of her thighs, more curved, more fleshy, more lascivious than the front, where, in close conjunction they plumped out in a pair of the most delicious white buttocks conceivable, would have stricken dead with desire any sodomist worshipper of Venus Callipyge.

Briskly, and to reassure the fearful young man that I still was to her, she bent over a sort of *bidet pour abolutions intimes*, and with an apologetic smile to me, proceeded to quickly soap and wash her private parts. Grotesque as this action may have been in reality, yet it in no way interrupted or dispelled the tense atmosphere of desire that enwrapped me. On the contrary, if I had been a man with all that belongs to a man, so inflamed by her suggestive squatting position would I have been, that I would have rushed upon her and impaled her soap and all, then and there!

Humming a little tune and watching me intently,

she gently dried herself with the towel, leaving her pubic hairs more silky, more curly and delightfully tousled than ever. Then, throwing herself on her back across the bed, she drew up her legs, spread wide her thighs and awaited me.

Irresistibly I was drawn near. The fascination of the vista spread before me held me breathless with a strange wild pleasure. Through the dark silky curls of her mount of Venus could be seen, like the setting sun through foliage, the merest suggestion of vermilion. And beneath that, the veritable red-centred velvety cleft of flesh itself, with its soft lovely little lips, shading gradually inward from palest pink through intermediate delicate tones of red to deepest carmine—expressing a harmony of line and colour, of softness and vividness, that Renoir at his best has never attained.

But alas! I could do not more than gaze upon it. Nature had sadly failed to bless me with the wherewithal to give that darling cunny that which it pouted for.

For a while the adorable creature continued in her expectant attitude. At last, seeing that not only had I not made proper application of the essential specific, but had not yet even disclosed it, she sat up on the edge of the bed and sighed patiently.

'Still bashful, eh? Well, come sit beside me. Either you've had too much of women or none at all. Which is it? Are you a virgin?'

I nodded affirmatively. All too truly.

'Well, well. I should feel honoured. You are my first beginner. But I thought nature would take care of herself and tell you what to do. Come closer. Put your arms around me. Now play with me while I get you ready.'

She bit her lower lip, and with a pretty little frown of earnestness, began studiously to attack the front buttons of my trousers. I was mortified beyond words. What could I say, after leading her on so far? I could only await the inevitable.

The last button was opened. Her pretty little hand insinuated itself into the gap with becoming awkwardness, felt about with increasing anxiety for the stiff bar of flesh, the male *ne plus ultra*, that should have sprung to her grasp, but was not there.

Instead she encountered only the soft silk of the feminine underthings I had retained despite my disguise. Grope as she might, there was not even the meagerest suspicion of the affirmative intrument she was no doubt sufficiently acquainted with to certify the absence of.

'Mother of God!' she exclaimed in horror, rapidly making the sign of the cross over her nude bosom. 'What kind of man are you? Have you been castrated? Were you born this way? And those silk underclothes—Ugh!'

I could only hang my head in shame.

'Why don't you answer me?' she went on. 'Are you deaf and dumb too? Why do you come here to waste a poor girl's time, you—you dirty catamite!' And she slapped me sharply across the cheek.

Still I could not articulate a sound. Bursting into tears of discomfiture and shame, my head still hung low, I pulled off the cap that till now I had kept jealously on my head. The loosely piled up tresses of my hair tumbled about my face and bosom like a shower of autumn leaves.

175

'Good Jesus, help me!' exclaimed the pious Nanette in amazement at this denouement. 'A woman! Or can it be a further deception of the devil?'

'No—a woman.' I spoke for the first time. Still sceptical, the good Nanette, with native directness, whipped down my already fully opened trousers, and searched through the tangle of my silk chemise till she found the conclusive proof of my statement.

Laughing delightfully now, with relief and appreciation for the jest, she placed a kiss on the bare smooth skin of my thigh, a quick little kiss that set us both blushing furiously.

'And a very pretty woman, too. My faith—but you surely fooled me.' She was looking me up and down, her eyes ever glistening and dancing with interest. 'But I don't care. I'd rather you were a woman anyway. I don't like men. They're just my business. But you—there was something about you that I liked from the beginning.'

Her bright smile was irresistible. 'You too, Nanette; there was something about you that made me really almost fall in love with you. Even now I wish I were a man.'

For the first time in that whole hectic evening I felt happy and released from the strain of carrying on my pretence. Kicking the trousers off from my ankles, I lay back upon the soft bed.

'Why don't you take those stiff ugly clothes off, dearie?' Nanette suggested. 'You've only been up here a few minutes. Your friends are probably busy with the other women and have forgotten all about you.'

I complied, while she considerately helped me off with the now hateful coat, vest, shirt and heavy shoes.

176

In a moment I was lying comfortably on the bed with nothing on but a pale green silk chemise.

'You are built beautifully,' Nanette said in low, admiring tones. I returned a similar compliment, but she ignored it, engrossed only in me.

'Your breasts are so full and rounded,' she went on. 'How did you ever keep them out of sight without a corset? They must be much softer and more compressible than mine. Mine are hard and firm. Feel.' And she led my hand to one of her globes of ivory, which may have been firm, but hard, never.

'Do you care if I touch yours?' she asked now, rather anxiously. I assented.

To complete her comparison, she gently slipped my chemise down off my bosom to my very hips—and then, suddenly abandoning the pretext of polite conversation, she threw herself upon me, fondling, kissing and biting my breasts with the fierce ardour of a lover and murmuring, 'I love you! I love you!'

The strange, perhaps abnormal, emotion, the merest suggestions of which I had felt before, now flamed forth in an overwhelming fever that must have out-temperatured Nanette's hot lips at every point where they met my flesh. My will melted away. I lay, grateful and passive to her caresses. Vaguely, I wondered at the forceful affirmativeness of her passion; as for myself, I still felt only deliciously feminine—although in my consciousness a gathering undertone insisted on mad, wild pleasures, the more forbidden, the more perverted, the more blasphemous to codes of man or God, the better!

My Nanette was leaning over my outstretched form at right angles to it, thus giving herself access to every part of me. Using her hands no more than if she had

177

had none, she continued covering me with hot kisses. Now she leaves off sucking my nipples to tongue the tiny ticklish depression of my navel, leaving a path of deliciously wet kisses in her wake.

On every exposed part of my body her lips worship. Now she is venturing lower to my hips. At this extra-sensitive zone her kisses cause my abdomen to contract sharply, spasmodically, again and again.

All over my belly again and down toward my thighs her kisses trail delightfully, setting off little titillating explosions of sensation through my whole body. As she goes lower, and lower still, she pushes before her with her head the loose silk chemise that lies lightly in her path—still not deigning to use her hands. I aid her by slightly raising my hips and buttocks from the bed, and thus she drives this last flimsy garment down before her with her kisses, down every fought-for inch to my thighs, and to my very knees.

Now up my thighs, and as deeply between them as she can reach, her lips and tongue run their delicious way. Gradually, I allow her to force my legs apart. Unceasingly she kisses and bites the inviting soft white flesh of my between-thighs, closer, closer to my awakening centre.

Panting with passion, she arrives at the edge of the very spot; then, exhausted by her continual kissing, she rests, burying her face deep in that strategic area where thighs at their most luscious meet belly and mossy mound and velvety cunt.

Full upon the sensitive seat of all my sensations her hot breath comes, in panting blasts like the scalding draft of a blacksmith's bellows. Up from my vulva to my very womb the heat spreads, firing further my already burning senses to a white unendurable heat, bringing down generous vaginal secretions and lubricants that are but oil to the flames. Uncontrollable as a nervous tic, my cunny is shaken by little spasms, and my hips begin writhing about in upward spirals. I cannot long endure her inaction. I am a soul in torment.

At last my exquisite female lover resumes. Boldly her mouth seizes upon the lips of my tender cunny and places full upon it a long luscious kiss. My clitty is galvanized into quivering erectness, and I almost scream with delight. Now I know my torment is past, that this way lies ecstasy and relief—that Nanette is not simply engaging in fruitless caresses and abortive titillations.

But no. Her dear mouth abandons the vital spot that so deeply craves her attention, and goes awandering again. Heavens! Why does she torture me so? Has she found that part distasteful? Or is she merely teasing my senses with prolonged suspense?

Happily it is the latter—else surely I would have died from that excessive, stinging desire.

Her pretty ruby lips once more make the circuit of my body, everywhere stirring up nervous reactions and reflexes that I had never before so much as dreamt of.

I open my eyes, which till now have been closed, to more fully concentrate upon the universe of sensual delights within and upon the surface of my body. Nanette too, it appears, is sustaining the full lash of desire. Her whole form, though flushed with internal heat, is shivering and vibrating with a strange nervousness.

Up till now her attention is all to me. But now, as her lips once more steal downward to the home base, she brings her whole perfect nude body around and upon me, in a reverse position, not for one moment abandoning the stimulating, titllating aggravation of her mouth.

The wondrous treasure of her glowing form is now suspended over me as she supports herself, her hands on each side of my thighs, her knees bestraddling my head. For a moment I glimpse down the vista made by the quickly narrowing space between our parallel naked forms—above my quivering abdomen. And overhead, her plump white thighs, crowned at their juncture with her now widespread pouting cunny, ripe, luscious and scarlet as a freshly severed pomegranate, and padded for protection of its delicate membranes with soft, curly hairs.

Our bodies at last in contact, flesh to flesh, our breathing now becomes synchronized with the rise and fall of breasts against diaphragm and diaphragm against breasts. Nor do her lips relinquish their activity for one moment during this transaction.

Her arms now slip under and embrace my thighs to bring my middle the closer to her. A moment she reaches down to whisk my chemise from off its last post on my lower legs, and now I am free to throw my limbs wide apart. Awhile longer she circles my anxious centre with a barrage of kisses. Now her face burrows deep between my fleshy thighs, and then—good God, what ecstatic relief—her mouth seeks and finds unerringly my palpitating cunny!

A sucking kiss upon the very clitty itself makes me nearly swoon with joy. Now her tongue softly but firmly ploughs down through the whole groove of my cunt, gently parting the adhering lips and laying open new sensitive zones, new nerve cells, for her ineffably wonderful lingual caresses. What an exquisite feeling pervades all my senses! Oh, gods and men, how I pity you for not having such a deep membranous organ as a cunt with which to experience this superheavenly exquisite delight. For no prick, be it ever so large and sensitive, can have that quantity of mucous nerve-netted surface that a woman's cunt is blessed with and that makes possible such subtle sensations as the sacred ritual of the cunnilingus alone can give! Oh gods and men, I exclaim again, I would not have accepted all the wealth of ancient Carthage in exch-ange for that one first lapping stroke of joy-giving tongue in my cunt!

Up to this moment, though Nanette's exquisite little quim was directly overhead, the inertia of modesty had restrained me from making any overtures comparable to hers, and I had kept my head slightly averted. But now, as more rapidly her agile tongue stirs up my boiling passions below, I, in gratefulness and in plain unadulterated lasciviousness, reach up with my arms, encircle her buttocks so conveniently near, and draw her quivering coral cunt down, down toward my face, to my panting mouth, to my waiting, lolling tongue. Her soft velvety thighs settle close about my cheeks. Immediately before my eyes are the lovely swelling prominences of her buttocks, the skin, even at this close range, whiter and more flawless than I had deemed possible. Between them, her pretty little bum, puckered delightfully, of a sepia tinge that faded to pink, to white, as its harmonious ridges melted into the gracious snowdrifts of her bottom. Below, separated from it only by a narrow little partition of pink flesh, the mystic grotto of love itself, leading in, inward, to woman's most vital organs and the wondrous womb of life; but more immediately showing a perfect ellipse of the most luscious vermilion that gaped invitingly at its widest, and melted together, just the other side of a small but inescapable projection, the clitty, in a little rift that lost itself in the abundant silky shrubbery of the Hill of Venus.

I raised my mouth to this delightful valley of love. If ever I had imagined qualms or compunctions about what I was on the verge of doing, they vanished instantly. Was it Juvenal, that old smart-acre, who insinuated, 'The breath of pederasts is foul; but what of those who lick the vulva?' If so, it is because his country was bathless and his women unwashed. No doubt his own mouth, unacquainted with the tooth-brush, was nothing to write odes about. But in this modern day, a woman's personal hygiene is an accepted fact, and the vaginal cavity may be as clean or cleaner than the oral.

Nanette's delicious quim possessed only the faint wholesome, personal odour of a young and healthy woman. This was subtly blended with the artificial perfume of her adjoining parts, and the whole gave a delicate local aroma that was stimulating and inde-scribably pleasing to my senses. Avidly I breathed it in, as I plunged my tongue into the exquisite crimson cavern. The warm, moist membranes, ineffably smooth and soft, gave as much caress to my lips and mouth as I in turn gave them.

In the meantime, my beloved Nanette is by no means idle. Now deftly and rhythmically, now with the uncontrolled fury of passion, her tongue weaves in and out among the folds of my inner cunt, now straight up and down through the full length of the tender cleft, now across, now in zigzags that run from end to end, now in little circles that concentrate on my clitty and put me wholly out of my mind with unendurable pleasure, now in sweeping ovals that stir up wide rippling waves of divine ecstasy, waves that somehow spread, not in circles, but in ever-widening ellipses that take in more of my entire being.

Unconsciously, at the other end, I adopt the rhythm and actions that she employs—and all that I describe as one doing was done and felt by each and both of us. In tense pleasure, she tightens her thighs against my cheeks. Instinctively I draw up my knees from the supine position and wrap my thighs tightly about her head, thus enabling me to bring her whole beloved face in closer to my tender parts.

Now dear Nanette is moving her whole body to the rhythm of lapping tongue, rising and falling to meet every caressing stroke. Soon I am adopting the same tempo, my hips and ass writhing madly up and down to follow the fullest presence and pressure of her tongue.

Demonically inspired by passion, my teeth seize fiercely, though restrainedly, the erect palpitating little bulb of her clitoris and press firmly into it. Nanette gasps with the extremity of her pleasure; as I gently nibble the sensitive projection, I can hear her murmur in a muffled manner:

'Ah! Mon Dieu! Que je t'aime!' In her excitement she lapses into her native language. The sound waves, spoken directly into my cunny, send peculiar vibrations through all my bone structure.

Recovering, Nanette reciprocates in even finer measure. Opening wide her hungry mouth to encompass the whole, she sucks in with her lips and breath all the succulent folds of my cunt. Already blood-gorged and sensitive to the utmost, this action overcharges the blood vessels and nerve cells almost to the bursting point. At the same time, the vacuum made by her delicious sucking suddenly causes my whole vagina and womb to contract with a strange tingling that wrenches and cramps my entire being in an agony of delight and brings down an inundation of the sweet secretions of love as if this were already my climax. I would have screamed if I could, but Nanette's dear part hushes me with its luscious caress.

For long, deliciously agonizing moments she holds that strange mouth-suction, during which I am in no less than a state of suspended animation. Then, having wrought in that part the maximum of hyper-sensitivity possible, she suddenly releases her magic oral grip and proceeds as if to devour me with mouth, lips, tongue and teeth. A series of deep tremors shake me, so surcharged is my whole nervous system with all these kissings and teasings and bitings and suckings.

But relief is at hand: dear, desirable, delicious relief from those tortures of love, which are no sooner ended when we wish only to renew them again and again. She now ceases her hungry random attack, and with scarcely an interval, takes up with her tongue a hand to hand duel with my bounding clitoris. And with what magnificent swordmanship! Back and forth with light but firm and ever-quickening little strokes, the sensitive tip of her tongue does battle with the even more sensitive little sentinel of my Palace of Pleasure. Not the fraction of a moment's respite does she give him. Scarcely has he rebounded, much less recovered, from one stroke than another and another and another falls to his share.

Doughty little clitty, who often enough in more common battles can vanquish and outstand in fight many a strong penis five hundred times his size—we cannot hold you to blame for your quick surrender! For what prick or clitoris, be it ever so stubborn, could long withstand that steady rain of caresses given by the moist tip of Nanette's deft, subtle tongue?

More and more rapidly the little strokes come, till the electrifying sensations that follow each come so close together as to blend into one continuous, ever-increasing, candescent ecstasy that wafts me softly skyward, as if on the magic rug of an Arabian Night's tale.

Try as I will, my own unpractised tongue cannot meet the pace she sets. And now, as the dear climax heralds its approach in my deep, violent gasps, my tongue strikes blindly, jerkily, missing strokes with every panting exhalation that is torn in sharp blasts from my writhing body. Only dear Nanette continues steadily and unflinchingly, though she too proclaims by the desperately irregular wrigglings of her buttocks that her dissolution is near.

Together now! Oh, to come together! To weld our ecstasies into one! My tongue and lips and teeth lap and kiss and bite wildly with every current of delicious pleasure that shoots through me! With difficulty I hold her madly writhing cunt to my mouth. All our universe becomes a tangle of dripping tongues and soft, warm cunt-flesh, of legs and thighs and buttocks—the whole mad scene illuminated by more and more frequent flashes of red-glowing sensation.

Suddenly, in this welter of pleasure, already superlative beyond conception, comes that infinitely superior, super-superlative of the climax!

Oh! What mortal pen can describe those divine orgasmic transports for which kingdom, life and honour are well lost? Only from the violent external manifestations can the inner turmoil be surmised. My whole body twitches in the supreme agonizing pleasure—and as the apex is reached, my thighs close so stiffly and tensely about my dear Nanette's head that I would have hurt her sadly, had not her face been cushioned by my own well-padded cunt and soft parts. As is, I crush her mouth inward to me and hold her as in a vice to put a stop to those unendurable titillations—for already my orgasm has sufficient momentum to finish of itself. But she manages to continue the fierce motion of her tongue. I am completely out of my mind! My alarmed senses scream out and struggle to retain consciousness in this turmoil of stimulations and new sensations; but despite all this, there is one obsession—to continue my own active part and to drag my companion down after me into this maelstrom of intense pleasure, to drown with me in all these swirling joys.

Madly my tongue continues lashing away, while I grip her form to me in every part. As one being now, we writhe in our embrace. Another moment, and I can tell from the sudden stiffening of her body and the sharp contraction of her cunt that she is with me! Then, and not till then, do I feel that the real apex of my own crisis is at hand.

Two long low moans go up from our tensely tangled form. First blinded, then entirely overcome, by the tremendous conflagration of sensations, I faint dead away—for long sublime moments of which, alas, I can give no report.

My joy-clouded brain begins to clear. We lie quivering and twitching in each other's arms like persons mortally stricken; but in truth we are still swimming in head-over seas of bliss. We have survived the delicious danger, and the delirium and tumult of our senses subside.

For a time we lie thus, breathless and happy, more languorously savouring the delightful afterpleasures of love. Our bodies relax, my thighs fall away from her head; Nanette's white naked form now rests upon me softly, her belly upon my breasts, a welcome blanket of gently palpitating flesh. Her cunt still lies upon my lips, but my tongue is withdrawn. As I open my eyes, till now closed in ecstasy, I can see that its folds are glowing with a more flaming vermilion than ever; but its so recently irritated membranes are now bathed and soothed by a generous flood of fine mucous. Through the vista of her still-widespread thighs and buttocks, I see the gas chandelier on the ceiling burning with what seems a dimmer flame. It is not my passion that is dimmer, however, for my mind is yet full of memories and desires for what is so recent; it is only that my eyes, their pupils contracting with languour, present the outer world thus dully in contrast to the brightness of sensation within. Oh, to lie with her forever! To sleep perhaps awhile, and then to awake to renewals of this subtle ecstasy!

Nanette is the first to stir. Much to my regret she removes her beloved body from over me and automatically resumes her dress of shoes and black silk chemise. I proceed to follow suit, but she halts my progress, covering my breasts with a round of tender kisses.

Then, full upon my mouth, still full of the dear moisture of her cunny, she places a luscious kiss.

187

Alternately we suck each other's lips and tongues, exchanging the sweet secretions of our mouths. As for myself, I find a deliciously wicked erotic stimulant in the thought that I am thus drinking from her lips the joint lubrications of our secret parts.

Reluctantly she begins to help me on with my clothes. Then suddenly, in a little flurry of passion, she falls to her knees as I sit on the edge of the bed and parting my thighs, she places upon the lips of my cunny what is meant as a grateful farewell kiss. Then, noting that it is still very wet, she compresses the lips together with her fingers, and leaning over it again, sucks away the moisture that she thus squeezes from it. Next, regretting the early completion of this pleasing task, she impulsively undoes her work by inserting her tongue and kissing it more moistly than ever.

Still unable to tear herself away from this most delicious part of me, she lingers on, saying good-bye again and again, fondling, kissing, admiring it, on her knees before me.

'A pure sweet virgin cunt! How long it is since I've seen one of those! To think—it has never been touched by man. That dear velvety maiden membrane—let me run my tongue once more across its delicious smooth surface—while it's still there! And those unfledged, unstretched lips, how nicely they kiss me back! And your lovely little joy-button, so small and sensitive and undeveloped. Oh, I must nibble it off!'

She suits the action to the word. It does not take a great deal of such delightful toying to reawaken my desires. My clitty stands up when spoken of with so much flattery. Nor does the gentle nibbling of her small regular teeth tend to lessen its self-consciousness. Little ripples of pleasure begin spreading from my cunny to my spine—But why worry the patient reader with a new recounting of what has just gone before? Only the delicious act itself bears repetition, and not with my inadequate words of attempted description. Suffice it to say that whether she had originally so intended or not, she accepts my gentle invitation to continue when I place my hands about the back of her pretty head and hold her more snugly to my reawakened cunt.

Scarcely a minute after she has begun, I come deliciously. But this climax I recognize as being just a part of my first thrill—a sort of warm wringing out of the remains of the earlier bacchanalia of pleasure—and so with continued importunities of my writhing hips, I wrap my thighs about her neck and shoulders and imprison her to a continuation of this delightful stimulation. Not at all unwilling, darling Nanette goes on, centering her dear labours of love exclusively upon my spongy little clitty for efficiency. I lie back on the bed and experience again her divine gamahuching. This time it takes a longer time for me to come—perhaps all of ten minutes—but, oh, dear reader, so delightful is the process of going to that 'come' that I am almost sorry when I arrive and it is all over. No—I lie. That third thrilling orgasm, though thinner, as it were, and less pervading (perhaps because of the familiarity with the paths over which the sensation has so recently blazed its way) was even sharper and more violently enjoyable than both those that went before. It left me sobbing and moaning in an overwhelming agony of bliss that—well, I am glad that I promised not to describe it, so completely would it defy my pen.

As I dressed, we exchanged our full names and became better acquainted in the more usual sense of the words. Also, we agreed to meet again in the early future.

Downstairs, I found that my marvellous adventure had occupied scarcely half-an-hour by the clock. Charley was sitting about disconsolately, consuming scores of cigarettes, alone except for a woman of the house who was wooing him in vain. All the other boys had retired with their respective choices and had not yet come down.

His eyes brightened when he spied me; but he was gloomy and sullen again when I sat down beside him.

'What kept you up there so long? A joke's a joke; but not when it's carried too far. One would think you were really up to something. What were you doing?'

'Oh—just chatting, to waste time. I didn't want to be the killjoy of the party and keep you from getting yourself a woman.'

'But don't you see, Louise?' he said earnestly, covering my hand with his and looking at me intensely with his handsome, pleading eyes, now seemingly shadowed by deep anguish, 'don't you see that I want no woman but you? I'm waiting for you. And damn it, I've been faithful to you for more than this half-hour that you've been gone.'

I blushed violently. My conscience was not clear.

'Charley,' I said, 'I'm afraid I'm scarcely worthy of this, your deep affection and unshaken faithfulness.'

He must have thought that he detected a note of sarcasm in my words, for he said roughly:

'Never mind, baby. I'm waiting.'

Randiana

I found at the age of thirty that I was only on the threshold of mysteries far more entrancing. I had up to that time been a mere man of pleasure, whose ample fortune (for my father, who had grown rich, did not disinherit me when he died) sufficed to procure any of those amorous delights without which the world would be a blank to me.

But further than the ordinary pleasures of the bed I had not penetrated.

'The moment was, however, approaching when all these would sink into significance before those greater sensual joys which wholesome and well applied flagellation will always confer upon its devotees.'

I quote the last sentence from a well-known author, but I'm far from agreeing with it in theory or principle.

I was emerging one summer's evening from the Café Royal, in Regent Street, with De Vaux, a friend of long standing, when he nodded to a gentleman passing in a 'hansom' who at once stopped the cab and got out.

'Who is it?' I said, for I felt a sudden and inexplicable interest in his large lustrous eyes, eyes such as I have never before seen in any human being.

'That is Father Peter, of St Martha of the Angels. He is a bircher, my boy, and one of the best in London.'

At this moment we were joined by the Father and a formal introduction took place.

I had frequently seen admirable *cartes* of Father Peter, or rather, as he preferred to be called, Monsignor Peter, in the shop windows of the leading photographers, and at once accused myself of being a doll not to have recognized him at first sight.

Descriptions are wearisome at the best, yet were I a clever novelist given to the art, I think I might even interest those of the sterner sex in Monsignor Peter, but although in the following paragraph I faithfully delineate him, I humbly ask his pardon if he should perchance in the years to come glance over these pages and think I have not painted his portrait in colours sufficiently glowing, for I must assure my readers that Father Peter is no imaginary Apollo, but one who in the present year of grace, 1883, lives, moves, eats, drinks, fucks, and flagellates with all the *verve* and dash he possessed at the date I met him first, now twenty-five years ago.

Slightly above the middle height and about my own age, or possibly a year my senior, with finely chiselled features and exquisite profile, Father Peter was what the world would term an exceedingly handsome man. It is true that perfectionists have pronounced the mouth a trifle too sensual and the cheeks a thought too plump for a standard of perfection, but the women would have deemed otherwise for the grand dreamy Oriental eyes, which would have outrivalled those of Byron's Gazelle, made up for any shortcoming.

The tonsure had been sparing in its dealings with his hair, which hung in thick but well-trimmed masses round a classic head, and as the slight summer breeze blew aside one lap of his long clerical coat, I noticed the elegant shape of his cods which, in spite of the tailor's art, would display their proportions to the evident admiration of one or two ladies who, pretending to look in at the windows of a draper near which we were standing seemed riveted to the spot, as the zephyrs revealed the tantalizing picture.

'I am pleased to make your acquaintance, Mr Clinton,' said Father Peter, shaking me cordially by the hand. 'Any friend of Mr De Vaux is a friend of mine. May I ask if either of you have dined yet?'

We replied in the negative.

'Then in that case, unless you have something better to do, I shall be glad if you will join me at my own home. I dine at seven, and am already rather late. I feel half-famished and was proceeding to Kensington, where my humble quarters are, when the sight of De Vaux compelled me to discharge the cab. What say you?'

'With all my heart,' replied De Vaux, and since I knew him to be a perfect sybarite at the table, and that his answer was based on a knowledge of Monsignor's resources, I readily followed suit.

To hail a four-wheeler and get to the doors of Father Peter's handsome but somewhat secluded dwelling, which was not very far from the south end of the long walk in Kensington Gardens, did not occupy more than twenty minutes.

Before many minutes he rejoined us, and leading the way, we followed him into one of the most lovely bijou *salons* it had ever been my lot to enter. There were seats for eight at the table, four of which were occupied, and the *chef* not waiting for his lord and master, had already sent up the soup.

I was briefly introduced, and De Vaux, who knew them all, had shaken himself into his seat before I found time to properly note the appearance of my neighbours.

Immediately on my left sat a complete counterpart of Monsignor himself, save that he was a much older man; his name, as casually mentioned to me, was Father Boniface, and although sparer in his proportions than Father Peter, his proclivities as a trencher-man belied his meagreness. He never missed a single course, and when anything particular tickled his gustatory sense, he had two or even more helpings.

Next to him sat a little short apoplectic man, a Doctor of Medicine, who was more of an epicure.

A sylph-like girl of sixteen occupied the next seat. Her fair hair, rather flaxen than golden-hued, hung in profusion down her back, while black lashes gave her violet eyes that shade which Greuze, the finest eye painter the world has ever seen, wept to think he could never exactly reproduce. I was charmed with her ladylike manner, her neatness of dress, virgin white, and above all, with the modest and unpretending way she replied to the questions put to her.

If ever there was a maid at sixteen under the blue vault of heaven, she sits there, was my involuntary thought, to which I nearly gave verbal expression, but was fortunately saved from such a frightful lapse by the page who, placing some appetizing salmon and lobster sauce before me, dispelled for the nonce my half visionary condition.

Monsignor P. sat near this young divinity, and ever and anon between the courses passed his soft white hands through her wavy hair.

I must admit I didn't half like it, and began to feel a jealous pang, but the knowledge that it was only

195

the caressing hand of a Father of the Romish Church quieted me.

I was rapidly getting maudlin, and as I ate my salmon the smell of the lobster sauce suggested other thoughts till I found the tablecloth gradually rising, and I was obliged to drop my napkin on the floor to give myself the opportunity of adjusting my prick so that it would not be observed by the company.

I have omitted to mention the charmer who was placed between De Vaux and Father Peter. She was a lady of far maturer years than the sylph, and might be, as near as one could judge in the pale incandescent light which the pure filtered gas shed round with voluptuous radiance, about twenty-seven. She was a strange contrast to Lucy, for so my sylph was called. Tall, and with a singularly clear complexion for a brunette, her bust was beautifully rounded with that fullness of contour which, just avoiding the gross, charms without disgusting. Madeline, in short was in every inch a woman to chain a lover to her side.

I had patrolled the Continent in search of goods; I had overhauled every shape and make of cunt between Constantinople and Calcutta; but as I caught the liquid expressions of Madeline's large sensuous eyes, I confessed myself a fool.

Here in Kensington, right under a London club-man's nose was the *beau idéal* I had vainly travelled ten thousand miles to find. She was sprightliness itself in conversation, and I could not sufficiently thank De Vaux for having introduced me into such an Eden.

Lamb cutlets and cucumbers once more broke in upon my dream, and I was not at all sorry, for I found the violence of my thought had burst one of the buttons of my fly, a mishap I knew from past experience would be followed by the collapse of the others unless I turned my erratic brain wanderings into another channel, so that I kept my eyes fixed on my plate, absolutely afraid to gaze upon these two constellations again.

'As I observed just now,' said the somewhat fussy little Doctor, 'cucumber or cowcumber, it matters not much which, if philologists differ in the pronunciation surely we may.'

'The pronunciation,' said Father Peter, with a naive look at Madeline, 'is very immaterial, provided one does not eat too much of them. They are a dangerous plant, sir, they heat the blood, and we poor churchmen, who have to chastize the lusts of the flesh, should avoid them *in toto*; yet I would fain have some more.' And suiting the actions to the word, he helped himself to a large quantity.

I should mention that I was sitting nearly opposite Lucy, and seeing her titter at the paradoxical method the worthy Father had of assisting himself to cucumber against his own argument, I thought it a favourable opportunity to show her that I sympathized with her mirth, so, stretching out my foot, I gently pressed her toe, and to my unspeakable joy she did not take her foot away, but rather, indeed, pushed it further in my direction.

I then, on the pretence of adjusting my chair, brought it a little nearer the table, and was in ecstasies when I perceived that Lucy not only guessed what my manoeuvres meant, but actually in a very sly puss-like way brought her chair nearer too.

Then balancing my arse on the edge of my seat as far as I could without being noticed, with my prick only covered with the table napkin, for it had with one wild bound burst all the remaining buttons on my breeches, I reached forward my foot, from which I had slid off my boot with the other toe, and in less than a minute I had worked it up so that I could just feel the heat of her fanny.

I will say this for her, she tried all she could to help me, but her cursed drawers were an insuperable obstacle, and I was foiled. I knew if I proceeded another inch I should inevitably come a cropper, and this knowledge, coupled with the fact that Lucy was turning wild with excitement, now red, now white, warned me to desist for the time being.

I now foresaw a rich conquest—something worth waiting for—and my blood coursed through my veins at the thought of the sweet little bower nestling within those throbbing thighs, for I could tell from the way her whole frame trembled how thoroughly mad she was at the trammels which society imposed. Not only that, the moisture on my stocking told me that it was something more than the dampness of perspiration, and I felt half sorry to think that I had 'jewgaged' her. At the same time, to parody the words of the poet laureate—

Tis better frigging with one's toe,
Than never to have frigged at all.

Some braised ham and roast fowls now came on, and I was astonished to find a poor priest of the Church of Rome launching out in this fashion. The Sauterne with the salmon had been simply excellent, and the Mumms, clear and sparkling, which accompanied the latter courses had fairly electrified me.

By the way, as this little dinner party may serve as

a lesson to some of those whose experience is limited, I will mention one strange circumstance which may account for much of what is to come.

Monsignor, when the champagne had been poured out for the first time, before any one had tasted it, went to a little liqueur stand, and taking from it a bottle of a most peculiar shape, added to each glass a few drops of the cordial.

'That is Pinero Balsam,' he said to me, 'you and one of the ladies have not dined at my table before, and, therefore, you may possibly never have tasted it, as it is but little known in England. It is compounded by one Italian firm only, whose ancestors, the Sagas of Venice, were the holders of the original recipe. Its properties are wondrous and manifold, but amongst others it rejuvenates senility, and those among us who have travelled *up and down* in the world a good deal and found the motion rather tiring as the years go on, have cause to bless its recuperative qualities.'

The cunning cleric by the inflection of his voice had sufficiently indicated his meaning and although the cordial was, so far as interfering with the champagne went, apparently tasteless, its effect upon the company soon began to be noticeable.

A course of ducklings, removed by Nesselrode pudding and Noyeau jelly, ended the repast, and after one of the shortest graces in Latin I had ever heard in my life, the ladies curtsied themselves out of the apartment, and soon the strains of a piano indicted that they had reached the drawing room, while we rose from the table to give the domestics an opportunity for clearing away.

My trousers were my chief thought at this moment, but I skilfully concealed the evidence of my passion with a careless pocket handkerchief, and my boot I accounted for by a casual reference to a corn of long standing.

'Gentlemen,' said Monsignor, lighting an exquisitely aromatized cigarette, for all priests, through the constant use of the senser, like the perfume of spices, 'first of all permit me to hope that you have enjoyed your dinner, and now I presume, De Vaux, your friend will not be shocked if we initiate him into the mysteries with which we solace the few hours of relaxation our priestly employment permits us to enjoy. Eh, Boniface?'

The latter, who was coarser than his superior, laughed boisterously.

'I expect, Monsignor, that Mr Clinton knows just as much about birching as we do ourselves.'

'I know absolutely nothing of it,' I said, 'and must even plead ignorance of the merest rudiments.'

'Well, sir,' said Monsignor, leaning back in his chair, 'the art of birching is one on which I pride myself that I can speak with greater authority than any man in Europe, and you may judge that I do not aver this from any self-conceit when I tell you that I have, during the last ten years, assisted by a handsome subsidy from the Holy Consistory at Rome, ransacked the known world for evidence in support of its history. In that escritoire,' he said, 'there are sixteen octavo volumes, the compilation of laborious research, in which I have been assisted by brethren of all the holy orders affiliated to Mother Church, and I may mention in passing that worthy Dr Prince here, and Father Boniface have both contributed largely from their wide store of experience in correcting and annotating many of the chapters which deal with recent discoveries, for, Mr Clinton, flagellation as an art is not only daily gaining fresh pupils and adherents, but scarcely a month passes without some new feature being added to our already huge stock of information.'

To tell the truth I scarcely appreciated all this, and felt a good deal more inclined to get upstairs to the drawing room, when just at this moment an incident occurred which gave me my opportunity.

The bonny brunette, Madeline, looked in at the door furtively and apologized, but reminded Monsignor that he was already late for vespers.

'My dear girl,' said the cleric, 'run over to the sacristy, and ask Brother Michael to officiate in my absence—the usual headache—and don't stay quite so long as you generally do, and if you should come back with your hair dishevelled and your dress in disorder, make up a better tale than you did last time.'

Or else your own may smart, I thought, for at this moment Father Boniface came in to ask Monsignor for another key to get the rods, as it appeared he had given him the wrong one.

Now is my time, I reflected, so making somewhat ostentatious inquiries as to the exact whereabouts of the lavatory, I quitted the apartment, promising to return in a few minutes.

I should not omit to mention that from the moment I drank the sparkling cordial that Father Peter had mixed with the champagne, my spirits had received an unwonted exhilaration, which I could not ascribe to natural causes.

I will not go so far as to assert that the augmentation of force which I found my prick to possess was entirely due to the Pinero Balsam, but this I will confidently maintain against all comers, that never had I felt so equal to any amorous exploit. It may have been the effect of a generous repast, it might have been the result of the toe-frigging I had indulged in; but as I stepped into the brilliantly lighted hall, and hastily passed upstairs to the luxurious drawing room, I could not help congratulating myself on the stubborn bar of iron which my unfortunately dismantled trousers could scarcely keep from popping out.

Fearing to frighten Lucy if I entered suddenly in a state of *déshabillé*, and feeling certain that a prick exhibition might tend to shock her inexperienced eye, I readjusted my bollocks, and peeped through the crack of the drawing-room door, which had been left temptingly half open.

There was Lucy reclining on the sofa in that *dolce far niente* condition which is a sure sign that a good dinner has agreed with one, and that digestion is waiting upon appetite like an agreeable and good-tempered handmaid should.

She looked so arch, and with such a charming pout upon her lips, that I stood there watching, half disinclined to disturb her dream.

It may be, I thought, that she is given to frigging herself, and being all alone she might possibly—but I speedily banished that thought, for Lucy's clear complexion and vigorous blue eyes forbade the suggestion.

At this instant something occurred which for the moment again led me to think that my frigging conjecture was about to be realized, for she reached her hand deliberately under her skirt, and lifting up her petticoats, dragged down the full length of her chemise, which she closely examined.

I divined it all at a glance: when I toe-frigged her in the dining room she had spent a trifle, and being her first experience of the kind, could not understand.

So she really is a maid after all, I thought, and as I saw a pair of shapely lady-like calves encased in lovely pearl silk stockings of a light blue colour, I could retain myself no longer, and with a couple of bounds was at her side before she could recover herself.

'Oh! Mr Clinton. Oh! Mr Clinton; how could you,' was all she found breath or thought to ejaculate.

I simply threw my arms around her and kissed her flushed face, *on the cheeks*, for I feared to frighten her too much at first.

At last, finding she lay prone and yielding, I imprinted a kiss upon her mouth, and found it returned with ardour.

Allowing my tongue to gently insinuate itself into her half-open mouth and touch hers, I immediately discovered that her excitement, as I fully expected, became doubled, and without saying a word I guided her disengaged hand to my prick, which she clutched with the tenacity of a drowning man catching at a floating spar.

'My own darling,' I said, and waiting for no further encouragement, I pushed my right hand softly up between her thighs, which mechanically opened to give it passage.

To say that I was in the seventh heaven of delight, as my warm fingers found a firm plump cunt with a rosebud hymen as yet unbroken, is but faintly to picture my ecstasy.

To pull her a little way further down on the couch so that her rounded arse would rise in the middle and make the business a more convenient one, was the work of a second; the next I had withdrawn my prick from her grasp and placed it against the lips of her quim, at the same time easing them back with a quick movement of my thumb and forefinger. I gave one desperate lunge, which made Lucy cry out 'Oh God,' and the joyful deed was consummated.

As I have hinted before, my prick was no joke in the matter of size, and upon this occasion, so intense was the excitement that had led up to the fray, it was rather bigger than usual; but thanks to the heat the sweet virgin was in, the sperm particles of her vagina were already resolved into grease, which, mixing with the few drops of blood caused by the violent separation of the hymeneal cord, resulted in making the friction natural and painless. Not only that, once inside I found Lucy's fanny was internally framed on a very free-and-easy scale, and here permit me to digress and point out the ways of Nature.

Some women She frames with an orifice like an exaggerated horse collar, but with a passage more fitted for a tin whistle than a man's prick, while in others the opening itself is like the tiniest wedding ring, though if you once get inside your prick is in the same condition as the poor devil who floundered up the biggest cunt on record and found another bugger looking for his hat. Others again—but why should I go on in this prosy fashion, when Lucy has only received half-a-dozen strokes, and is on the point of coming?

What a delicious process we went through; even to recall it after all these years, now that Lucy is a staid matron, the wife of a church rector, and the mother of two youths verging on manhood, is bliss, and will in my most depressed moments always suffice to give me a certain and prolonged erection.

The beseeching blue eyes that glanced up at Monsignor's drawing-room ceiling, as though in silent adoration and heartfelt praise at the warm stream I seemed to be spurting into her very vitals. The quick nervous shifting of her fleshy buttocks, as she strove to ease herself of her own pent-up store of liquid; and then the heartfelt sigh of joy and relief that escaped her ruby lips as I withdrew my tongue and she discharged the *sang de la vie* at the same moment.

Oh! there is no language copious enough to do justice to the acme of a first fuck, nor is there under God's sun a nation which has yet invented a term sufficiently comprehensive to picture the emotions of a man's mind as he mounts a girl he knows from digital proof to be a maid as pure in person, and as innocent of prick, dildo, or candle as arctic snow.

Scarcely had I dismounted and reassured Lucy with a serious kiss that it was all right, and that she need not alarm herself, when Madeline came running in.

'Oh! Lucy,' she cried, 'such fun—' Then, seeing me, she abruptly broke off with—'I beg your pardon, Mr Clinton, I did not see you were here.'

Lucy, who was now in a sitting posture, joined in the conversation, and I saw by the ease of her manner that she had entirely recovered her self-possession, and that I could rejoin the gentlemen downstairs.

'Do tell those stupid men not to stay there over their cigars all day. It is paying us no compliment,' was Madeline's parting shot.

In another moment I was in my seat again, and prepared for a resumption of Monsignor's lecture on birch rods.

'Where the Devil have you been to, Clinton?' said De Vaux.

'Where it would have been quite impossible for you to have acted as my substitute,' I unhesitatingly replied.

My answer made them all laugh, for they thought I referred to the water closet, whereas I was of course alluding to Lucy, and I knew I was stating a truism in that case as regarded De Vaux, for he was scarcely yet convalescent from a bad attack of Spanish glanders, which was always his happy method of expressing the clap.

'Now my dear Mr Clinton, I wish you particularly to observe the tough fibre of these rods,' said Monsignor Peter, as he handed me a bundle so perfectly and symmetrically arranged that I could not help remarking on it.

'Ah!' exclaimed Monsignor, 'that is a further proof of how popular the flagellating art has become. So large a trade is being done, sir, in specially picked birch of the flagellating kind, that they are hand-sorted by children and put up in bundles by machinery, as they appear here, and my own impresson is that if the Canadian Government were to impose an extra duty on these articles, for they almost come under the heading of manufactures and not produce, a large revenue would accrue; but enough of this,' said the reverend gentleman, seeing his audience was becoming somewhat impatient. 'You saw at the dinner table the young lady I addressed as Lucy.'

I reflected for a moment to throw them off their guard, and then said, suddenly, 'Oh, yes, the sweet thing in white.'

'Well,' continued Monsignor Peter, 'her father is a long time dead, and her mother is in very straitened circumstances; the young girl herself is a virgin, and I have this morning paid to her mother a hundred pounds to allow her to remain in my house for a month or so with the object of initiating her.'

'Initiating her into the Church?' I inquired, laughing to myself, for I knew that her initiation in other respects was fairly well accomplished.

'No,' smiled Monsignor, touching the rods significantly, 'this is the initiation to which I refer.'

'What,' I cried, aghast, 'are you going to birch her?'

'We are,' put in Dr Price. 'Her first flagellation will be tonight, but this is merely an experimental one. A few strokes well administered, and a quick fuck after to determine my work on corpuscular action of the blood particles; tomorrow she will be in better form to receive second class instruction, and we hope by the end of the month—'

'To have a perfect pupil,' put in Father, who did not relish Dr Price taking the lead on a flagellation subject, 'but let us proceed to the drawing room. Boniface, put that bundle in the birch box and bring it upstairs.'

So saying, the chief exponent of flagellation in the known world led the way upstairs to the drawing room, and we followed, though I must confess that in my case it was with no slight trepidation, for I felt somehow as though I were about to assist at a sacrifice.

As we entered the room we found Lucy in tears, and Madeline consoling her, but she no sooner saw us than, breaking from her friend, she threw herself at Monsignor's feet, and clinging to his knees, sobbed out—

'Oh, Father Peter, you have always been a kind friend to my mother and myself, do say that the odious tale of shame that girl has poured into my ears is not true.'

'Good God!' I muttered, 'they have actually chosen Madeline as the instrument to explain what they are about to do.'

'Rise, my child,' said Monsignor, 'do not distress yourself but listen to me.' Half bearing the form of the really terrified young thing to the couch, we gathered round in a circle and listened.

'You doubtless know, my sweet daughter,' began the wily and accomplished priest, 'that the votaries of science spare neither friends nor selves in their efforts to unravel the secrets of nature. Time and pain are no object to them, so that the end be accomplished.'

To this ominous introduction Lucy made no response.

'You have read much, daughter of mine,' said Monsignor, stroking her silken hair, 'and when I tell you that your dead father devoted you to the fold of Mother Church, and that your mother and I both think you will best be serving Her ends and purposes by submitting yourself to those tests which will be skilfully carried out without pain, but on the contrary, with an amount of pleasure such as you cannot even guess at, you will probably acquiesce.'

Lucy's eyes here caught mine, and although I strove to reassure her with a look that plainly intimated no harm should come to her, she was some time before she at last put her hand in the cleric's and said—

'Holy Father, I do not think you would allow

anything very dreadful; I will submit, for my mother, when I left her this morning, told me above all else to be obedient to you in everything and trust you implicitly.'

'That is my own trump of a girl,' said Monsignor, surprised for the first time during the entire evening into a slang expression, but I saw his large round orbs gloating over his victim, and his whole frame trembled with excitement as he led Lucy into the adjoining apartment and left her alone with Madeline.

'Now, gentlemen,' said Monsignor, 'the moment approaches, and you will forgive me, Mr Clinton, if I have to indulge in a slight coarseness of language, but time presses and plain Saxon is the quickest method of expression. Personally, I do not feel inclined to fuck Lucy myself, as a matter of fact I had connection with her mother the night previous to her marriage, and as Lucy was born exactly nine months afterwards, I am rather in doubt as to the paternity.

In other words,' I said, astounded, 'you think it possible that you may be her father.'

'Precisely,' said Monsignor. 'You see that the instant the flagellation is ended, somebody must necessarily fuck her, and personally my objection prevents me. Boniface here, prefers boys to women, and Dr Price will be too busy taking notes, so that it rests between you and De Vaux, who had better toss up.'

De Vaux, who was stark mad to think that his little gonorrheal disturbance was an insuperable obstacle, pleaded an engagement later on, which he was bound to fulfil, and therefore, Monsignor Peter told me to be sure to be ready the instant I was wanted.

Madeline entered at this moment and informed us

that all was ready, but gave us to understand that she had experienced the greatest difficulty in overcoming poor Lucy's natural scruples at being exposed in all her virgin nakedness to the gaze of so many of the male sex.

'She made a very strange observation, too,' continued Madeline, looking at me with a drollery I could not understand, 'she said, "if it had been only Mr Clinton, I don't think I should have minded quite so much." '

'Oh! all the better,' said Father Peter, 'for it is Mr Clinton who will have to relieve her at the finish.'

With these words we proceeded to the birching room, which it appears had been furnished by these professors of flagellation with a nicety of detail, and an eye to everything accessory to the art that was calculated to inspire a neophyte like myself with the utmost astonishment.

On a framework of green velvet was a soft down bed, and reclined on this length was the blushing Lucy.

Large bands of velvet, securely buckled at the sides, held her in position, while her legs, brought well together and fastened in the same way, slightly elevated her soft shapely arse.

The elevation was further aided by an extra cushion, which had been judiciously placed under the lower portion of her belly.

Monsignor bent over her and whispered a few soothing words into her ear, but she only buried her delicate head deeper into the down of the bed, while the reverend Father proceeded to analyse the points of her arse.

Having all of them felt her arse in turn, pinching

it as though to test its condition, much as a connoisseur in horseflesh would walk around an animal he was about to buy, Monsignor at length said—

'What a superb picture.' His eyes were nearly bursting from their sockets. 'You must really excuse me, gentlemen, but my feelings overcome me,' and taking his comely prick out of his breeches, he deliberately walked up to Madeline, and before that fair damsel had guessed his intentions, he had thrown her down on the companion couch to Lucy's and had fucked her heart out in a shorter space of time than it takes me to write it.

To witness this was unutterably maddening. I scarcely knew what to be at, my heart beat wildly, and I should then and there have put it into Lucy myself had I not been restrained by Father Boniface who, arch-vagabond that he was, took the whole business as a matter of course and merely observed to Monsignor that it would be as well to get it over as soon as possible, since Mr Clinton was in a devil of a hurry.

Poor Lucy was deriving some consolation from Dr Price in the shape of a few drops of Pinero Balsam in champagne, while as for De Vaux, he was groaning audibly, and when the worthy Father Peter came to the short strokes De Vaux's chordee became so unbearable that he ran violently out into Monsignor's bedroom, as he afterwards informed me, to bathe his balls in ice water.

To me there was something rather low and shocking in a fuck before witnesses, but that is a squeamishness that I have long since got the better of.

Madeline, having wiped Monsignor's prick with a

piece of *mousseline de laine*, a secret known only to the sybarite in love's perfect secrets, retired, presumably to syringe her fanny, and Monsignor buttoned up and approached his self-imposed task.

Taking off his coat he turned up his short cuffs and, Boniface handing him the birch rods, the bum-warming began.

At the first keen swish poor Lucy shrieked out, but before half a dozen had descended with a quick smacking sound which betokens that there is no lack of elbow grease in the application, her groans subsided, and she spoke in a quick strained voice, begging for mercy.

'For the love of God,' she said, 'do not, pray do not lay it on so strong.'

By this time her lovely arse had assumed a flushed, vermilion tinge, which appeared to darken with every stroke, and at this point Dr Price interposed.

'Enough, Monsignor, now my duty begins.' And quick as thought he placed upon her bottom a piece of linen, which was smeared with an unguent, and struck it at the sides with a small modicum of tar plaster to prevent it from coming off.

'Oh!' cried Lucy, 'I feel so funny. Oh! Mr Clinton, if you are there, pray relieve me, and make haste.'

In an instant my trousers were down, the straps were unbuckled, and Lucy was gently turned over on her back.

I saw a delicate bush of curly hair, a pair of glorious thighs, and the sight impelled me to thrust my prick into that divine Eden I had visited but a short time before with an ardour that for a man who had lived a fairly knockabout life was inexplicable.

I had scarcely got it thoroughly planted, and had

certainly not made a dozen well-sustained though rapid strokes, before the gush of sperm which she emitted drew me at the same instant, and I must own that I actually thought the end of the world had come.

'Now,' said Dr Price, rapidly writing in his pocket-book, 'you see that my theory was correct. Here is a maid who has never known a man and she spends within ten seconds of the entrance being effected. Do you suppose that without the birching she could have performed such a miracle?'

'Yes,' I said, 'I do, and I can prove that all your surmises are but conjecture, and that even your conjecture is based upon a fallacy.'

'Bravo,' said Father Peter, 'I like to see Price fairly collared. Nothing flabbergasts him like facts. Dear me, how damnation slangy I am getting tonight. Lucy, dear, don't stand shivering there, slip on your things and join Madeline in my snuggery; we shall all be there presently. Go on, Clinton.'

'Well,' I said, 'it is easy enough to refute the learned Doctor. In the first place Lucy was not a maid.'

'That be damned for a tale,' said Father Boniface. 'I got her mother to let me examine her myself last night while she was asleep, previous to handing over the hundred pounds.'

'Yes, that I can verify,' said Monsignor, 'though I must admit that you have a prick like a kitchen poker, for you got into her as easy as though she'd been on a Regent Street round for twenty years.'

'I will bet anyone here 50 to 1,' I said, quietly taking out my pocketbook, 'that she was not a maid before I poked her just now.'

'Done,' said the Doctor who, upon receiving a knowing wink from Father Peter, felt sure he was going to bag two ponies, 'and now how are we to prove it?'

'Ah, that will be difficult,' said Monsignor.

'Not at all,' I observed, 'let the young lady be sent for and questioned on the spot where you assume she was first deflowered of her virginity.'

'Yes, that's fair,' said De Vaux, and accordingly he called her in.

'My dear Lucy,' said Monsignor, 'I wish you to tell me the truth in answer to a particular question I am about to put to you.'

'I certainly will,' said Lucy, 'for God knows I have literally nothing now to conceal from you.'

'Well, that's not bad for a *double entente*,' said the Father, laughing, 'but now tell us candidly, before Mr Clinton was intimate with you in our presence just now, had you ever before had a similar experience?'

'Once,' said Lucy, simpering, and examining the pattern of the carpet.

'Good God,' said the astonished Churchman, as with deathlike silence he waited for an answer to his next question.

'When was it and with whom?'

'With Mr Clinton himself, in the drawing room here, about an hour ago.'

I refused the money of course, but had the laugh on all of them, and as we rolled home to De Vaux's chambers in a hansom about an hour later I could not help admitting to him that I considered the evening we had passed through the most agreeable I had ever known.

'You will soon forget it in the midst of other pleasures.'

'Never,' I said. 'If Calais was graven on Mary's

214

heart I am quite sure that this date will be found inscribed on mine if ever they should hold an inquest upon my remains.'

The Loves of Lord Roxboro

Preparing herself for the bath, Caroline heard the murmur of voices from the library next to her bedroom, so stepping to the door, she listened for a moment but could distinguish nothing but a mumble. Searching the door, she discovered a tiny crevice through which she could peep into the adjoining room. Applying her eyes to the opening, she looked into the library and saw her uncle seated in a chair, while standing before him, her hands clasped and a beseeching look in her eyes, stood Marie, the maid.

Caroline stood gazing through the crevice in the door and as she discovered who the occupants of the room were, she found she could faintly hear their conversation, although they were apparently talking in low voices.

'Marie,' said Lord Roxboro, 'you have been with me now for some time. You have served me well and I have no particular fault to find with you.'

'Yes, sir, thank you, sir,' said Marie looking at Roxboro wonderingly.

'I make it a point, Marie,' he continued, drawing a paper from his pocket, which he unfolded and glanced over, 'I make it a point to investigate all of my employees thoroughly. You have been with me now for three months, I believe?' he asked, raising his eyes to the pretty maid.

'Nearly four, sir,' she answered.

'Of small matter,' he remarked. 'You gave references when you came here of people that resided in your hometown, Middleboro, is it not?'

'Yes, sir, that is right,' answered Marie, looking a trifle worried at the trend the conversation was taking, and shifting her feet nervously.

'I find,' he continued, referring to the paper, 'I find that you are well known in Middleboro. In fact, to be quite frank with you, my dear, much too well known in certain quarters! Do you happen to know a certain Mr Montgomery, Marie?'

At the mention of this name, Marie blanched and seemed about to swoon. Her lips paled out, controlling herself with an effort, she stood with downcast eyes before her employer.

'I thought that name would touch home!' cried Lord Roxboro with a satisfied air. 'My suspicions, I see, are well grounded. You know him, do you?'

'Yes, sir,' answered Marie, her answer barely audible to Caroline as she listened at the peephole.

'And this man, this man Montgomery, was he your lawfully wedded husband? Is this right, Marie?'

'Yes, sir,' she answered again, clenching her hands until the knuckles whitened, twitching about as she tried to evade her employer's stern and inquiring glance.

'And you, the lawfully wedded spouse of this man Montgomery, ran away and deserted him? And when decamping, took all of his money and his watch and other valuables?' the lord shot at the shrinking girl.

'Oh, that is untrue, sir!' she replied with flashing eyes. 'He beat me and starved me and made me leave him! I never wanted to be his wife and the act of marriage was against my will. I was forced into a union with the detestable creature!'

219

Lord Roxboro cast a sensual glance mingled with pure admiration at the beautiful creature as she stood radiant in her youthful beauty, denying the aspersions cast upon her honesty.

'Easy now, Marie,' he soothed her. 'You left him, at least, and took with you when you left the money and the jewellery that I have just mentioned. Is that not right?'

'Yes, my lord,' she answered in a low tone.

'And you came into my employ and lied to me about these happenings, knowing very well that this husband of yours, this Mr Montgomery, had already filed charges with the authorities against you for theft and that at this very moment the authorities are in search of you? Have you been honest and fair with me, I ask you?'

'Oh, no, sir,' she sobbed. 'I could never bring myself to tell you of those dreadful happenings. Has he really filed charges against me, as you say, and are the police in search of me?' Here she clasped her tiny hands together and glanced beseechingly at his lordship.

'They are hunting for you at this very moment,' said Lord Roxboro sternly. 'And if I should perform my duty as a landowner, I would call them at once and allow them to convey you back to Middleboro, to jail, where you rightfully belong, you shameless creature!' At this his eyes glowed with righteous indignation.

'Oh, master!' cried Marie, throwing herself on her knees and clasping Lord Roxboro's hand as it lay on the arm of the chair, casting her beautiful eyes, now bedimmed with tears of crystal, upon him. 'Oh, master, I beg of you! Do not turn me off like this, do not give me up! Montgomery was a devil, indeed! I married him at seventeen, knowing nothing of the world or its evil devices! I have suffered for my sins, and I have been so happy during the short time I have worked for you and only want to stay here. Be fair with me, if this doesn't please you, and take into consideration the faithful services that I have rendered to you; and if you will not allow me to remain, at least allow me to depart from here in peace! Anywhere will I flee to escape the machinations of this dreadful nemesis, the man who was my husband! I have been a true servant and have tried to do my best. Forgive me if I lied to you before; what I saw now is the truth!'

'Yes, but you have lied to me once, Marie,' replied the lord. 'Who knows whether you are truthful with me now or not?' Upon her continued protestations that she was indeed telling the truth, he arose and paced the floor nervously.

'Then you don't deny that you stole the things mentioned, Marie?' he said, turning to her as she softly sobbed, her head buried in the chair. 'You stole them?'

'Yes, my lord,' she sobbed, 'I stole just enough to enable me to leave him. He would give me no money and I could not stand his brutal ways any longer. He whipped and beat me!'

'How old are you now, Marie?'

'Eighteen, last month,' she said, turning her tear-dimmed eyes upward to him as he questioned her.

'Go to my desk and procure me ink and paper,' he commanded. She scrambled to her feet, went to the desk and procured the articles, placing them upon the table before which he stood, then took her station a few feet away. The lord wrote rapidly for a moment or two, then, reading over what he had written and making a few changes, extended the pen to the maid.

'Marie, I have written an outline of the charges that have been preferred against you. They are here on this paper and I wish you to sign it. It is what you might term a sort of confession. Come, sign.'

'But, my lord,' she remonstrated, 'you aren't going to turn me over to the police, are you? You wouldn't make me go back to that beast, Montgomery, would you? Why are you asking me to sign that paper?'

'That remains to be seen, Marie,' he replied. 'You have confessed here to me, just a moment ago, that you are guilty of the crime charged against you. I really should have turned you over to the police at once. If you will kindly sign this document, I may give you another chance and allow you to continue here in my employ. Of course, you may use your own judgment. I can summon the police if you wish it,' and he turned to the bell cord as if to pull it.

'No, no, sir,' cried the panic-stricken Marie, seizing the pen and scribbling her name at the lower part of the document. 'I will do as you wish, my lord; you allow me another chance to prove my faithfulness. Oh, thank you so much. There you are, sir, I have signed it as you directed!' and throwing the pen on the table, she burst into a torrent of heartbreaking sobs.

Lord Roxboro made no answer, but picking up the paper, he again read it over carefully, and walking to the side of the room where the safe stood, he twirled the knob and opened the heavy door. Depositing the paper in one of the smaller drawers, he closed the door and twirled the knob. Caroline was a breathless spectator to all of this and stood with her eyes glued to the peephole, wondering what would happen next.

Lord Roxboro again seated himself in the armchair, placing his hand on top of Marie's head as she knelt sobbing upon the floor at his side, patting it for a moment, allowing his fingers to run through the fine tendrils of her dark hair and said in a gentle voice:

'Come, Marie, arise and seat yourself on the arm of this chair. I have several things I want to ask you about.'

The weeping girl arose from her kneeling posture on the floor, and following her employer's directions, seated herself alongside him upon the arm of the chair and with a tiny wisp of linen handkerchief attempted to dry her luminous eyes.

'To think that you, my little maid, Marie, were married!' said Lord Roxboro, grasping one of the girls's tiny hands in his own and softly patting it. 'Why, Marie, I thought that you knew little or nothing about such things. Were you with your husband any great length of time?'

'Nearly a year,' she answered, 'but it seemed a lifetime.'

'Don't think, Marie,' he continued, 'that because I do not turn you over to the police that you are entirely free. You have committed theft and you should be properly punished. You must either work out your salvation here with me, or in the workhouse. I assure you, my girl, that I have no present intention of letting you off scot-free. No, not in the least. You must understand that, don't you, Marie?'

'Yes, my lord,' she answered penitently. 'I am extremely grateful for your generosity in this matter, and assure you that you will have no reason to regret it. I will work for you as I have never worked before. I will do my best to please you. You certainly may depend upon it, my lord.'

'Work!' laughed Lord Roxboro. 'It is not a question of work, my dear girl. I desire you to clearly understand the situation. I have the power, if I wish to exercise it, whenever I desire it, to turn you over to the proper authorities. That little bit of paper that is securely held in that safe, attested with your name, is sufficient to convict you in any court in the land and to bring you a long term in the reformatory. Realize that part of it clearly, Marie! You and I must have no misunderstanding along that line. You are fully and completely in my power. Your punishment for this cold-blooded thievery must be fixed and regulated by myself, your master. Remember that!'

'Yes, my lord,' murmured the girl submissively. 'I understand the situation thoroughly, and whatever you decide will be all right, only please don't send me to jail and don't send me back to that brute, my husband! Anything, anything you say, I will be glad to do.'

'We will see later on,' he said, and throwing his arms about the neck of the lovely girl and drawing her face down to his, he presented an impassioned kiss upon the full red lips. She made no struggle to escape, but seemed to react to his impassioned caress, her soft bare arms stealing about his neck, holding him in a close embrace as he rained kisses upon her cherry lips.

Caroline was by now quite warmed by this tender scene. She saw Roxboro's hand steal to the front of Marie's waist, which he unbuttoned, drawing forth her well-shaped breasts, which he proceeded to fondle

224

and squeeze and finally to kiss and gently bite, then allowing them to hang free in sensual looseness from her waist. Caroline envied the girl these soul-titillating touches, and at the sight of her passionate uncle fondling this beautiful maiden, strange feelings coursed through her body.

'Go lock the door, Marie,' commanded the lord, rising to his feet and gently pushing the now flushed girl toward the entrance to the library.

Marie, her breasts still hanging freely from her opened waist, ran to the door and pushed home the bolt. Returning to his lordship, who had by now seated himself upon a couch, she sat beside him, this move bringing both persons directly opposite to the peeping Caroline's line of vision, and when Lord Roxboro again clasped the palpitating girl to him, she responded to his warm kisses.

Caroline, a close spectator of these toyings of love, saw her uncle's inquiring hand creep up under Marie's skirts. The impassioned girl allowed herself to sink back on the couch, her legs slowly spreading as though to permit her sensual employer to ply his exploring fingers without hindrance.

At this movement, the sensual lord dragged up her skirts to the waistline, and the watching Caroline was rewarded with a full unobstructed view of the beautiful maid's lower person.

Her entire lower body was uncovered, as she wore no drawers, with silken stockings of fine texture, which were held in place by a pair of beautiful pink silk garters, and as the inquiring fingers of the lord pulled apart the girl's willing thighs and one of them inserted itself into the dense hair that covered her lower belly with a soft silken growth, fingering the throbbing cove beneath. Caroline wiggled her buttocks with passion, at the same time her own finger stealing into that centre of femine bliss, which she titillated violently in sympathy with the erotic scene before her enchanted eyes.

Marie lay back, almost prone, her thighs outspread to her employer's busy fingers. Caroline caught a glimpse of the passion-swollen lips as her uncle slowly massaged the dewy interior. Finally, evidently deeming that this provocative handling might cause the beautiful girl a premature orgasm, he slowly withdrew his hand, and Caroline, the entire scene directly before her interested eyes, could hardly repress a cry of astonishment at the gaping cleft that was left exposed to her startled eyes.

What an opening this was! Surely her own was not so dilated as that of this beautiful girl! It beamed with a dewy moisture, and as the enraptured Caroline watched it, it seemed to pulse and leap, probably from the soul-stirring fingerings it had received from her uncle's busy digits.

At this moment Lord Roxboro quickly unfastened the fly of his pantaloons, and the delightful object of Caroline's admiration sprang forth, erect and hard, as though to do battle with the pulsating quim that was so near it. Marie, needing no coaching or instruction in the delectable art, immediately grasped the huge bolus in one of her tendril-like hands and slowly massaged and squeezed its gigantic length, her fingers running quickly from the flaming head to the heavy pendulous balls that depended from this gigantic stabber.

The titillations of the beautiful girl's fingers upon his manly rod seemed to have a thrilling effect upon

Lord Roxboro, and he wiggled and leaped at each compression and relaxation of her dainty fingers. Suddenly pushing the girl backward upon the couch, he sprang astride of her and Caroline saw him bury his flaming prong in Marie's throbbing cunt!

Each and every downward stroke and the accompanying sweet withdrawal was watched with eager eyes by the interested girl, whose eye was glued intently to the peephole; and as she watched the wiggling, twisting, sighing couple, each uttering sweet groans and sighs of pleasure, her busy finger frigged that centre of sensual pleasure on her own person in sympathy with the couple so busy in love's action on the couch before her.

Presently, with a few short, frantic plunges that almost seemed to drive his banger home and that seemed to paralyze the wiggling girl beneath him, Lord Roxboro reached the quintessence of bliss and poured forth into the lascivious maid a full stream of love's elixir; the girl at the same time reached her climax, and with a few short, spasmodic plunges and writhings, the two sank exhausted upon the couch, panting from their exertions.

At the same time, Caroline, seeing that the two were approaching the desired moment, had worked herself into a frenzy with her fingers, and when they reached the apogee of bliss, she accompanied them with a self-induced orgasm that nearly caused her to faint with passion and pleasure.

Lord Roxboro, after lying a moment in that sweet, soothing after-ecstasy, upon the body of the beautiful girl who still sighed softly beneath him, her cleft distended by his throbbing tool, arose staggering to his feet, his noble rod drooping and soft, sticky with their combined dew, and, walking to the bathroom, secured a towel and dried his parts.

Truly, this amorous sport must be extremely exhilarating to some members of the feminine sex. Caroline had never seen the maid look so radiant as now she did.

For a moment Caroline supposed that the episode was finished, in her ignorance little suspecting the calibre of the two persons engaged in this battle of love. She kept watch, however, with the idea of missing nothing that might transpire further, and her vigil was duly rewarded.

After Lord Roxboro had cleansed his parts with the towel, Marie laughingly reached for the cloth. Throwing her dresses high, allowing her parts to become thoroughly visible to the watching Caroline and his sensual lordship, she thrust the towel between her legs and dried herself, vigorously rubbing the towel against her sensitive parts with a grimace of passion as the rough texture of the cloth touched the still tingling centres of sensation. This act finished, she permitted her dress to fall and once more seated herself upon the edge of the couch. Lord Roxboro, buttoning his pantaloons, seated himself beside her, and gathering the charming maid into his arms, smothered her with hot kisses.

'You have been pretty well opened up by your husband.' The girl laughed at this and glued her willing lips to his for a lingering embrace. It seemed that she was in that parched condition so well known to widows, and the recent happenings had only increased her passionate desire.

'You are quite a kisser too, my dear,' said the

recipient of the girl's warm embraces. 'Your devoted husband must have taught you that lingering, soul-searing French kiss that you perform so expertly. What a pretty tongue you have, my dear Marie! Thrust it forth for my inspection and allow me to look at that titillating member that has wrought such sad havoc with my manly feelings.'

The girl thrust out her pink tongue and sensuously wiggled its strawberry tip, darting it to and fro, in and out of her pretty mouth for the lord's inspection. Fired by this lascivious exhibition, he sought to embrace the beautiful girl once more, but she laughingly dodged her head from beneath his encircling arm and bent it forward to the man's lap, holding him tightly about the waist with both arms.

'Aha!' cried the lord. 'I am of the opinion that you are quite accomplished in certain ways and devices of exciting the passions. I feel certain that you are well versed in quite a number of practices that I did not, in my blindness, credit you with, you little teaser!' Patting the back of her head with his hand and running his fingers through her hair and about her shell-like ears, he massaged the back of her neck and head, which she had buried in the front of his lap.

'We will soon see how much you know, my little Venus!' cried her uncle. The breathless Caroline from her vantage point watched interestedly as her uncle leaned back and unbuttoned the front of his shirt, baring his manly breast, covered with hair, the brown nipples of his breast standing forth; then, lifting the fair girl's head, he pressed it against his breast and held her closely to him.

Caroline, profiting by the knowledge imparted to her by her sensual uncle, together with womanly intuition, realized that the beautiful maid was busily engaged in tonguing her uncle's nipples. His hand was busy at the buttons on his trousers, then suddenly the head of his member leaped forth, about half-hard but becoming rampant under the ministrations of the lovely girl.

The man's whole front body was now exposed, and the salacious girl, busy with her adroit tongue, slipped down his bare belly, weaving from side to side in her lascivious downward course, missing not a spot on his entire front, until, slipping to her knees on the floor directly in front of the impassioned lord, she tongued up and down his groin, causing her master to writhe in passion.

In another moment the watching Caroline saw the kneeling maid, apparently flaming with lust, suddenly engulf the man's rod in her rosy lips. Sucking it violently for a moment, she released it and her busy tongue licked its sides and head, thence downward toward the hairy sack which she titillated with her dartlike tongue. Then working back upward again, her tongue slid up and down the now throbbing shaft of the man's resurrected tool; reaching the head, she once more plunged it into her mouth until Caroline wondered how Marie could accommodate the huge member without choking upon it.

The lord's hands slipped down about the fair operator's neck, hugging her head close to his belly, and thrust forth his lower parts to meet the action of the girl's head as it worked up and down upon the shaft of his huge prick.

His hands now worked downward and grasped the girl's beautiful bare bubbies, which he massaged and crushed as the maid sucked and chewed upon his swollen member. This lively encounter raged for a few moments, the girl at times being forced to pause for breath, only to engulf once more that now iron-hard instrument within her distended jaws and move gently yet rapidly up and down upon it with a slight swinging motion.

Under the eager gaze of the interested spectator, the pace livened a bit; Lord Roxboro's grip on the neck of the fair manipulator tightened as though he would crush it between his hands, and he now moved his buttocks with frantic emotion. Caroline saw her uncle's staff leap and plunge as he endeavoured to plunge it to the hilt within the fair one's mouth, she only saving herself from being choked by the massive charger by grasping it firmly at the root with one tightly encircling hand; the lord's face contorted with passion and his eyes closed as the girl now sucked on that fleshy morsel with furious intensity, and as his staff throbbed and panted, Caroline knew that her uncle was now pumping into the eager and willing throat of the pretty maid the very essence of his being!

The lord, trembling as if in an ague, held the fair girl tightly to him as she mouthed and sucked, the convulsions of the muslces of her neck telling of the balsamic cargo that was now oiling her throat; and she choked, grasped, and strangled until the man's sensual grasp finally loosened about her neck and she fell, a sodden, panting heap, upon the carpet, and the lord slumped back upon the couch, thoroughly overcome by his recent passion and exertions!

My Secret Life

In the year 18** I walked up P***l**d P***e at about ten o'clock at night, and saw a tall woman standing at the corner of L**t*e P***l**d Street. Her size attracted me, I spoke, and offering half a sovereign with the understanding that she would take everything off—went with her to a house in L**t*e P*** l**d Street.

She kept her word and stripped whilst I sat looking on.—When in her chemise,—Do you want me quite naked?'—'Yes.' Then she slipped it off and stood stark naked, boots, stockings, and garters, excepted.—I may as well describe her at once, as for quite four years, she satisfied almost every sexual want, and helped me to satisfy every sensual fantasy.

She was with the exception of the second Camille (the French woman) almost the most quiet, regular, complacent woman I had had since that time, and moreoever was most serviceable to me in all my pleasures, ministering to them as I wanted them—but rarely herself suggesting them.—Ready to undertake anything for me, and after some length of intimacy participating in, and well pleased with, our erotic amusements; never attempting to exact money, but always content, and at length getting so accustomed to me that she let me into much knowledge of her private daily life.

She was I should say five feet nine or nearly ten high, which is tall for a woman. Her hips were when viewed from the front, of the proper width for such a

234

height—but her shoulders somewhat narrow. Altho so tall, she was small boned and plump all over, yet she had not an atom of what may be called fatness; had a small foot, a fine shaped calve, and thighs not quite so large proportionately. Her bum with fine firm round cheeks was not heavy at the back, was rather broad across the hips than thick and prominent behind, yet her backside looked handsome.—In fact she was straight and well shaped from top to toe, but if anything might have had broader shoulders with advantage, to make her proportionate to her height; yet only a sharp critic would have noticed that deficiency.

Her cunt, that important part of a woman, was large, but tight, fleshy inside, and muscular. It clipped my prick as deliciously as if it had been a much smaller one, and it was so healthy and deep, that often as I tried, I never could touch the orifice to her womb, either with my prick or my fingers. Nearly black hair, crisp and in full quantity was on her mons, and down the lips, and almost to her arsehole, but not round that brown orifice. The lips were thick and full, yet if she put her legs apart, they widened at once, showing deep crimson facings, and when shut a thin crimson streak.—Her nymphae were small.

She had dark brown, bright eyes, dark hair and good teeth—but her nose had been broken. That spoiled her face which otherwise would have been very handsome. As it was it did not make her ugly, but decidedly spoiled her.

She had the longest tongue I ever saw. She could put it further out of her mouth altogether than any one whom I have seen do that trick.—She was somewhat an unusual woman in every respect, and was I think twenty-four years old when I first saw her.—She had been a ballet dancer at some time, altho I only found that out after I had known her some months.—Her name was Sarah F**z**r.

She laid on the side of the bed, pulled her cunt open, knelt on the bed backside towards me, shewing cunt and arsehole together in quick succession as I asked her, and without uttering a word, but simply smiling as she obeyed. It had the usual effect,—a stiff-stander of the first order. It always is so with me. Objections, and sham modesty, a refusal to let me touch, and feel, or see, instead of whetting my appetite for a gay woman, always angers me and makes me lose desire.—With a woman not gay the case is different. The next minute I was enjoying her with impatience, then I lay on her stiff still, and full up her when I had spent.—'I shall do you again.' 'All right,' she replied. My prick never uncunted, but whilst reviving, my hands roved in all directions. She moved first this leg, then that, lifted her backside up, and seemed by instinct to know where my hands wished to go, and they were restless enough.—She was like Camille.—To something I said, she remarked.—'You're fond of it.'—As I recommenced my thrusts she said.—'Don't hurry, I want it,'—and we both spent together.—I forgot to mention that her flesh was of surprising firmness, and her backside solid and smooth.—I gave her the half sovereign as agreed—she did not ask for more, and we parted—but not for long.

The readiness with which she complied with all my wishes, together with the recollection of her personal charms, and the pleasure of her cunt, dwelt in my mind. I had her next night, and the night after, and then began to see her once or twice a week, and to indulge in voluptuous freaks which I had not done for three years or more, and which my imagination increased in its powers by what I had seen, read, and done, supplied me . . .

I went to the house first. Sarah entered followed by a very tall woman with her veil down, who stood and looked through it at me. Sarah having locked the door said, 'Take off your bonnet, Eliza.'—The woman only looked curiously round the room.—'Take off your bonnet.'—Then she took the bonnet off, and stood looking at me.—'Sit down,' said Sarah—and down she sat.

She was full thirty-five years old, but what a lovely creature.—I think I see her now, altho I never saw her but that once.—She had beautiful blue eyes, the lightest auburn hair crimped over her forehead, a beautiful pink bloom on her cheeks, and flesh quite white.—She was dressed in black silk, which contrasted well with her pink and white face.—She was big all over.—Big breasts jutted out in front—the tight sleeve shewed a big round arm—her ample bum filled the chair.—She was exactly what I wanted.—I never could wait long to talk with a woman whom I liked the look of, without proceeding to see, if not to feel, some of her hidden charms.—A burning desire to see what she had hidden seized me. I don't know if I spoke or not, but filled with desire, dropped on my knees and put my hand up her clothes, one round her thighs towards her bum, one towards her cunt.

As I touched her thighs, she put both hands down to stop me with a suppressed 'oh'—neither action or word, those of a woman who was shamming.—It wasn't the fierceness of a girl who first feels a man's hand about her privates, nor the sham modesty of a half-gay woman. It was the exclamation and manner of a woman not accustomed to strange hands about her privates. The next instant, I had reached both haunch and cunt.—She gave another start, my arms had lifted her petticoats, and I saw a big pair of legs in white stockings, and the slightest flesh above the knee nearly as white.—I placed my lips on it and kissed it—my hand slipped from her cunt round to her bum, and both hands now clasped one of the largest, and smoothest, and whitest backsides I ever felt. Then burrowing with my head under her petticoats, I kissed my way up her thighs till my nose touched her motte, and there I kept on kissing.

The warm close smell of her sweet flesh, mingled just with the faintest odour of cunt, rendered it impossible to keep my lips there long. The desire to enjoy her fully was unbearable—I withdrew my head and hands, and got up saying. 'Oh!—undress dear, I long to fuck you.'—They were the first words I had spoken to her, and she had not spoken at all.—She then rose up, and slowly began unbuttoning looking at Sarah.—'Lord, what a hurry you are in,' said Sarah to me.

Off went the black silk dress, out flashed two great but beautiful breasts over the top of the stays—and a pair of large, beautifully white arms shewed.—Then I saw the size of the big bum plainly under the petticoats. Off went stays and petticoats all but one.—Then she, '*There*, will that do?'

I wanted all off.—'Oh—I cannot take off any more.' I appealed to Sarah, who said. 'Now don't be a fool, Eliza'—Eliza then undressed to her chemise, and positively declared she would keep that on—I had taken off my trowsers and was standing cock in hand.—My impatience to discharge my seed into the splendid creature before me, made me careless whether she stripped or not.—I had drawn near to her—was feeling all round her bum with one hand, and wetting the fingers of the other in her cunt. I placed my prick so that it rubbed against her thigh, and feeling her, was at the same time pushing her towards the bed.

When we touched the bed—'I can't with Sarah there,' said the woman.—'Go out,' said I to Sarah. She looked savagely and replied, 'Nonsense.' Then I had a moment's dalliance and no more, forget what more was said or what took place, but saw Eliza on the bed, threw up her chemise, saw a mass of white flesh and a thicket of light hair between a pair of thighs, the next instant was between them, and my prick was up her cunt.

It was an affair of half a dozen shoves, a wriggle, a gush, and I had enjoyed her. Then I became tranquil enough to think of the woman, in whose vagina I had taken my pleasure. Resting on one arm and feeling her all over with one hand, I looked at her, and she at me. I said a few endearing words, as she lay tranquilly with my cock still stiff and up her.

I could have done it again right off, but had not yet looked at her hidden charms, and desire to inspect her quim made me draw out my cock and rise on my knees between her legs. Few strange women like their cunt looked at, when sperm is running out of it. She pushed down her chemise, I got off her, and then without saying a word she washed. When I had washed my cock it was as stiff as ever. I went to the side of the bed where she had just begun piddling, and held my stiff one in front of her eyes. For the first time she smiled.

She began to dress, but I told her I had only begun my amusement. I had brought bottles of champagne, for I knew how that liquor opens the hearts and the legs of women.—We got glasses and began drinking.—She drank it well and soon began to talk and laugh. When I again brought her to the bed she was an altered woman, but still did not seem to like fucking before Sarah. 'Why I have seen all you have got to show often enough,' said Sarah angrily.—On the bed now for a good look at the cunt.—It was a big one.—An inch of fat at least covered the split, stoutish middle-aged women get I think fat cunt lips, and hers was very large.—She had a very strongly developed clitoris, and such a lot of light hair. Large and fat as the cunt was, I do not recollect if the prick hole was large or little but know that I enjoyed her as much as a man possibly could. I delighted in laying my hand between two, long, fat cunt lips—I rolled over her, played with and kissed her from her thighs to her eyes, frigged her clitoris till she wriggled, and as at length my prick slipped up her cunt again, she whispered, 'What a devil you are.' She pushed her tongue out, mine met it, and then all was over.—She wagged her big arse vigorously when spending.

Ballocks and cunt again cleared of sperm, to the champagne we again went.—Sarah had not yet undressed, I had almost forgotten her. Now I made her strip, and my two big women were nearly naked together.—A little more pfiz and we were all on the spree.—Eliza still had the manner of a woman not accustomed to expose her charms, but insisted on by me and Sarah who seemed to have control over her, off went her chemise at last.—Off went my shirt—and there we all stood naked.

I never before had two such big women together and did with them all that my baudy fancy prompted.—I put them belly to belly, then bum to bum.—Then standing up before the glass. I put my prick between their two bums, making them squeeze it between their buttocks whilst I groped both cunts, and frigged at once both of them. Then putting Eliza at the side of the bed with open thighs, I put Sarah between them as if she were a man—and pushing my prick between her thighs just touched her split.—She laid hold of my prick and slipped it up her own cunt.—But I did not mean that, and pulled it out.—Then I had them both side by side on the bed, and scarcely knew which of the gaping cunts to put into, but the fair haired one again had my attention. Then I put Sarah upside down on the bed so that her arse and cunt were near the pillow, one leg partly doubled up, and one cocked up against the back of the bed, and looking at her thus I fucked Eliza by her side. Sarah said she must frig herself and set to work doing it, whilst with the one hand stretched back she played round my prick stem in Eliza's cunt which was tightening under the pleasure of my shoving and probing. Eliza's amativeness had been awakened, she clasped me tightly with her large white arms, kissed and thrust her tongue into my mouth, in a state of the fullest voluptuous enjoyment.

We finished the champagne and sent out for sandwiches, stout, and brandy.—I had taken the room for the night.—Sarah never was, and her companion was not in a hurry now. We ate, drank, and got more erotic.—Eliza's fat bum was on my naked thighs. She

241

put her hand on my prick, and grasping it for a minute whispered, 'Come and do it again.'—Sarah said, 'What are you whispering about?'—She had been looking at times annoyed at my taking no notice of her.—Again I put Eliza on the bed.—Sarah who had alternately been quiet and then baudy, said, 'It's my turn, why don't you poke me?'—'You will have it another night.'—She then got on to the bed, and on to the top of Eliza, kissed her rapturously, got between her thighs, and my two big beauties were like man and woman in each other's arms.—Eliza threw up her legs until her heels were on Sarah's back. Sarah nestling her belly close up to her, the hair of their two cunts intermingled.—Sarah's arse wriggled in a quiet way. 'Don't now —don't'—said the other—Sarah took no heed, wriggled on, then lay quiet, and after a time rolled gently off Eliza, left the bed, and sat down in the arm chair.—I looked at her very white face. 'You've spent,' I said—she laughed.

I fucked Eliza then, and laying with prick in her asked her in a whisper to meet me again. 'I cannot, I dare not,' said she.—I could not get out of her her name, or where to find her again.

Eliza was now half screwed. No sooner had I fucked her than she began squeezing my prick.—She opened her large thighs, placed my finger on her clitoris, kissed my prick, thrust her tongue in my mouth, and did every thing which a randy-arsed woman does to get more fucking.—I fucked her four or five times, perhaps more, and till neither she nor Sarah could make my cock stand. The house was closed, off I went, but not until Eliza had gone long.—Sarah insisted on that.—Then said Sarah, 'I'm not going without a poke.' With infinite trouble she got a fuck out of me, and both of us groggy, we separated.

Some nights after talking of Eliza, whose legs in boots and silk stockings had charmed me, Sarah laughed.—'Why, they were mine, I lent them to her.' Then I recollected that Sarah had not had her usual boots on.

I wished her to get me Eliza again. She refused. I said I would find her out.—She was sure I should not!—I went to one or two places on the chance of finding her, and Sarah laughed when I told her.—I used to get awfully randy when I thought of the two big women naked together. 'She is not gay, altho you may think so, it was only because she was so dreadfully hard up that she came,' Sarah averred.

'If she wasn't gay, she did all I asked her.' 'As she was getting screwed, and I had told her what you expected her to do.' 'And she spent like fun after the first time.' 'Oh yes I saw, and I told her about it afterwards.' 'Where did she go that night?' 'To my lodgings and slept with me.' 'If you don't bring her, I won't see you any more,'—and for a fortnight I did not—I used to go up to her in the street and ask her. She said she couldn't even if she would.—'You are lucky to have had her at all.' 'I paid handsomely.' 'If you hadn't you would never have had her.'—I expect that now and then married women make a bit of money by their cunts.

Then things went on as before, but as I pulled Sarah's cunt about, I used to compare it with Eliza's.—Sarah seemed to me to know Eliza's cunt as well as if it had been her own.

Just then Sarah met the man with the donkey prick,

whom she told me did then exactly what he had done before with her. This recital made me wild with desire.—I told her I would give her something handsome, if she could find a house, where I could see couples fucking. She had heard there was one, but those who knew would not tell, and some time slipped away.—With a smiling face one night she said, 'If you don't mind a sovereign for the room, and five shillings afterwards for each couple you see, I know now where you can get what you want.'—Off we went the following night to the house, and through a carefully prepared hole beneath a picture frame, I had a complete view of a nice room.—The washing place, bed (no sofa), looking-glass, fire place, were all in sight. In fact only that side of the room in which the eye hole was made in the partition, was not perfectly visible.

I recollect that first night well.—The woman of the house said to me, 'You won't tell people will you?'—Then—'Put out your light when you are looking.'—There was gas in the room.—'Don't make a noise—and don't look till you hear, or think they are on the bed.'—Then she lifted a picture up on to a higher nail in the partition, which disclosed a small hole.—Then she went into the other room, and did the same to a picture there. It was in a huge, old fashioned, projecting gilt frame, which when hung higher up, just cleared the hole but well shadowed it.—There was one good, strong, gas burner in the room, but no candle to enable people to pry about with.

The hole was so high up, that it was necessary to stand on a sofa placed just against the partition. There was no fire in our room when first I went there, and

244

it was dark at about seven o'clock, Sarah had gone in first.—The woman when she had got my sovereign said, 'I don't suppose any one will be there till about eight o'clock.'

I undressed Sarah, and sat in excitement feeling her about, and looking at her legs, and talking.—I heard couples going into lower rooms, and the woman saying, 'This way, sir'—a gruff voice reply,—'I won't go so high.'—At length a couple entered. Sarah turned down the gas in our room, and up I got on the sofa. Oh my delight—how I wish it were to come over again. There was a fine young man and a niceish young woman—I watched them with an intensity of lust quite indescribable.—I saw him first pay her, she take off her things, piss, and then stand naked expectantly. He took off his trowsers, she took hold of his prick, and he felt her cunt.—Then it was kiss, feel, and frig on both sides. I could hear him ask questions, and she reply. Then he put her down on a chair, and pushed his noble prick up against her but not up her. Then he brought her to the side of the bed. I saw her thighs distended, a dark haired cunt opened and looked at. He pushed his prick up it and had a plunge or two. (His back was towards me then.) Apparently not satisfied, he then pushed her straight on the bed—got on himself, laid by the side of her, and then I saw his prick in all its glory.—She wanted to handle it, he would not let her, but fingered her cunt with his hand nearest to her.

At length kneeling between her thighs I saw it again in all its prominence, stiff and nodding—until dropping on to her belly, it was hidden from my sight.—I watched the heavings and thrustings—the saucers which came in his arse cheeks, and disappeared as he

245

thrust up and withdrew his penis, her thighs move up, and then her legs cross over his, as she heaved to meet his strokes.—Then the shoves became mere wriggles, then were loud exclamations of pleasure, then all was still. His limbs stretched out, her legs came tranquilly down to the side of his, a long kiss or two was heard, then absolute silence.—It was a delicious sight.

Almost before he had finished, I had put the cork in the hole in the partition, pulled Sarah to the side of the bed, felt her cunt, and was about to put up it, when alas I spent all over her outside, on thighs and cunt, then with my cock still dripping I got on the sofa again.—Sarah with me, for she seemed to enjoy looking as much as I did.

He had risen on to his knees between her thighs, and held his prick in his right hand, I could just see its red tip.—'Don't move, I'll fuck you again.' 'Well, you must give me some more.' 'I will give you five shillings.' 'Very well, shall I wash?' 'No stay as you are.'—Slowly his bum sunk on to his heels—his head peered forward—his left hand went to her cunt.—'My spunk's running out,' he said. 'Oh you beast.' He flopped down on her without another word—and I saw by the action of his buttocks that he was driving his pego up her.—His hands clasped her again, I saw the saucers in his arse—his short shoves—her wriggles and jerks—and heard her sighs and 'oha's.' Then soon his silence shewed that his pleasure was complete.

During all this I kept telling Sarah in a whisper what I saw—she got as impatient as me and wanted to see as much.—It often was, 'Let me have a look.' 'I shan't.' 'What is she doing?'

'She is doing so and so,'—then I let her peep and

she would tell *me*.—I sat on the sofa whilst she was standing and looking, grasped her arse, put my lips on her cunt, and pulled her towards me, giving utterance to all sorts of baudy extravagances in whispers.—It is odd it occurs to me, that all *she* wanted to see was what the *woman* was doing—what *I* principally wanted to see was what the *man* was doing.—At all times that I was at that peep hole, the same feelings were predominant in both of us.

The man was pleased, gave the extra money, told her he would meet her again, washed his prick and went off—she leisurely washed her cunt, and off she went—then lighting the gas, I ballocked Sarah—not letting my sperm be wasted outside this time.—'It's exciting,' said she, 'I have not seen such a thing since the night you had the fine, tall, fair woman—and it makes me as randy as be damned' (her favourite expression). We finished fucking just in time for another couple. We saw three couples the first night.

I am not going to tell all I saw—much of it was common-place fucking enough—yet some had the charm of novelty, and altho I was there perhaps in the course of a year or two, in all fifty or sixty times, and saw nearly a hundred and fifty couples fucking, never grew tired of seeing.

The most amusing thing to me was that Sarah wanted to see so much.—After a time I put her occasionally with her back against the partition, and my prick up her—and then applying my eye to the hole over her shoulder, fucked her, and looked at the fucking couple in the room, until I lost sight of them, in the excitement of my own physical pleasure.

That was a risky thing to do for they could have heard us, as well as we did them. But usually the couples were so absorbed by lewdness, so preoccupied by fucking or anticipation of it, that they rarely seemed to notice anything.

Two or three weeks after I had used this peep hole, Sarah said she had again met the man with the titanic prick.—We had by that time got so intimate, that she told me any funny adventures she had with men.—He had behaved in just the same manner to her, and was to meet her that day week.—'Oh! I long to see him with you—bring him to the next room,'—and it was so arranged.—The spying room was to be kept for me—the back room I was to pay a pound for, and it was to be kept for Sarah. The old baud knew what we were up to.—I told Sarah to keep the man as long as she could, whether he paid much or little (he gave her treble what I did), and above all to manage so that I could see his prick well.

The evening came, I was there before the time, and thought that they were never coming.—At length I saw them enter—I had been in a fever lest it should not come off.—The whole evening's spectacle is photographed on my brain.—I recollect almost every word that was said.—What I did not hear, Sarah told me afterwards, tho that was but little.

'Take off your things,' said he.—Sarah undressed to her chemise.—His back was towards me, his hand was evidently on his prick.—'Ain't you going to take *your* clothes off, you had better—you can do it nicer.'—He evidently had not intended that, but yielded to her suggestion.—When in his shirt he went up to her, she gradually turned round so that *her* back and *his* face were towards me, and her movement was so natural that no one could have guessed her object,

248

altho I did.—Moving then slightly on one side, she put her hands to his shirt, lifted the tail, and out stood the largest prick I ever saw. 'Oh what a giant you've got,' said she.—He laughed loudly.—'Is it not, did you ever see a bigger?' 'No, but your balls are not so big.' 'No, but they are *big*.' 'No,' she said. 'You can't see them,'—and he put one leg on a chair,—Sarah stooped and looked under them.—Whilst doing so, he tried to give her a whack on her head with his prick—and laughed loudly at his own fun.—'Why,' said Sarah, 'if your balls were equal in size to your prick, you wouldn't be able to get them into your trousers.'—He laughed loudly, saying, 'They're big enough—there is plenty of spunk in them.'

Sarah went on admiring it, smoothing it with her hand, pulling up and down the foreskin and keeping it just so that I had a full view. 'You are hairy,' said she, rubbing his thigh.—Then I noticed he was hairy on his legs, which was very ugly.—'Yes, do you like hairy-skinned men?' 'I hate a man smooth like a woman—take off your shirt and let me see.' 'It's cold.' 'Come close to the fire then.'—She talked quite loudly purposely, tho it was scarcely needed. His voice was a clear and powerful one.—Without seeming anxious about it, but flattering him, she managed to get his shirt off and he stood naked.—He was a tall man, very well-built, and hairy generally. Masses hung from his breasts, it darkened his arms. It peeped out like beards from his armpits, it spread from his balls half way up his belly, he had a dark beard, and thick black hair.—In brief he was a big, powerful, hairy, ugly fellow, but evidently very proud of his prick, and all belonging to him. Her flattering remarks evidently pleased him highly, and he turned round as she wished him, to let her see him well all over.—His prick which had been stiff had fallen down, for instead of thinking of the woman, he was now thinking of himself; but it was when hanging, I should say, six inches long, and thick in proportion. 'Dam it, it's cold, we are not so accustomed to strip like you women.'—Then he put his shirt on and began business.

He made her strip and told her to go to the bedside. She went to the end and leaned over it with backside towards him.—He tucked his shirt well up, came behind her, and with his prick which had now stiffened and seemed nine inches long (I really think longer), hit her over her buttocks as if with a stick. It made a spanking noise as it came against her flesh. Then he shoved it between her thighs, brought it out again, and went on thwacking her buttocks with it.—'Don't it hurt you?' she asked him turning her head round towards the peep hole.—'Look here,' said he. Going to a round small mahogany table and taking the cloth off it—he thwacked, and banged his prick on it, and a sound came as if the table had been hit with a stick.—'It does not hurt me,' he said.—I never was so astonished in my life.

'I mean to fuck you,' said he. 'That you shan't, you will hurt any woman.'—Again he roared with laughter.—'Suck it.' 'I shan't.'—Again he laughed.— Then he made her lean on a chair, and again banged his prick against her arse.—Then he sat down, and pulled her on to him, so that his prick came up between her thighs just in front of her quim.—'I wish there was a big looking-glass,' said he. 'Why did you come here, there was one at the other house.'—Sarah said this was nicer and cleaner, and he had said he wanted a quiet house.—'Ah, but I shan't come here again, I don't like the house.'

'Get on to the chairs—the same as before.' But the chairs in the room were very slight, and Sarah was frightened of them slipping away from under her.—So she placed one chair against the end of the bed, and steadied it; and against another which she put a slight distance off, she pushed the large table. Then mounting on the chairs, she squatted with one foot on each as if pissing. I could not very well see her cunt for her backside was towards me, and shadowed it.

He laid down with his head between the chairs, and just under her cunt. He had taken the bolster and pillows from the bed for his head, and there he laid looking up at her gaping slit, gently frigging his prick all the time. At length he raised himself on one hand, and licked away at her cunt for several minutes, his big prick throbbing, and knocking up against his belly whilst he did it.

Said he again, 'I wish there was a glass,' Sarah got down, and put on the floor the small glass of the dressing table, and arranged it so that he could see a little of himself as he lay.—But he was not satisfied.—He recommended cunt-licking, and self-frigging, and all was quiet for a minute.—Then he actually roared out, —'Oh—my spunk coming, my spunk,—my spunk,—spunk—oho.—Come down—come over me.'—Off got Sarah, pushed away the chairs, stood over him with legs distended, her arse towards me so that I lost sight of his face, but could see his legs, belly, and cock as he lay on the floor.—'Stoop,—lower,—lower-'—She half squatted, he frigged away, her cunt was now within about six

251

inches of his prick, when frigging hard and shouting out quite loudly—'Hou—Hou—Hou,' his sperm shot out right on to her cunt or thereabouts, and he went on frigging till his prick lessening, he let it go, and flop over his balls.

Sarah washed her cunt and thighs, and turning round before doing so, stood facing me and pointed to her cunt. His spunk lay thick on the black hair tho I could barely see it.—She smiled and turned away. He lay still on the floor with eyes closed for full five minutes, as if sleep. Sarah washed, put on her chemise and sat down by the fire, her back towards me partly.

He came to himself, got up and went to the fire—then he washed (his back towards me), then stood by the fire, then fetched the pot and pissed. I saw his great flabby tool in his hand, and the stream sparkling out of it, for it was done just under the gas light.—Again he stood by the fire, his tool hidden by his shirt which he had on, and they talked.—Then he strode round the room and looked at the prints on the wall, looked even at the very picture beneath which I was peeping.—'What a daub,' he remarked and passed on (it was a miserable portrait of a man), then from the pocket of his trousers he gave Sarah several sovereigns.

That lady knew her game, and had thrown up her chemise so as to warm her thighs—and after he had paid her, he put his hand on to them.—She at the same time put her hand on to his tool. 'Oh what a big one.'—nothing evidently pleased him so much as talking about the size.—'Did you ever see so big an one,' said he for the sixth time I think. 'Never—let's look at it well.—Hold up your shirt.'—He did as told.—Sarah pulled his prick up, then let it fall,

252

handled his balls, pulled the foreskin up and down, and shewed him off again for my advantage.—'Why don't you sit down, are you in a hurry?' Down he sat, his tool was becoming thicker and longer under her clever handling, and hung down over the edge of the chair. He was sitting directly under the gas light, and I could see plainly, for Sarah cunningly had even stirred the fire into a blaze. He was curious about other men's cocks—what their length and thickness was.—She shewed him by measuring on his own, and kept pulling it about, her object being to get it stiff again for me to see his performances.—My delight was extreme—I could scarcely believe that I was actually seeing what I did, and began to wish to feel his prick myself. How large it must feel in the hand I thought, how small mine is compared with it, and I felt my own.—As Sarah pulled down his prepuce, I involuntarily did so to mine, and began to wish she were feeling mine instead of the man's.

Then only I noticed how white his prick was. His flesh was brownish—and being so sprinkled with hair it made it look dark generally.—His prick looked quite white by contrast. Sarah must have been inspired that night, for no woman could have better used her opportunity for giving me pleasure and instruction. Repeating her wonder at the size, she said, 'Let's see how it looks when you kneel.'—He actually knelt as she desired. I saw his prick hanging down between his legs. Soon after in another attitude, I noticed that hair crept up between his bum cheeks, and came almost into tufts on to the cheeks themselves.—I saw that his prick was now swelling.—Sarah taking hold of it, 'Why it's stiff again.' He grasped it in the way

I had first seen him, and said eagerly.—'Let's see your cunt again.'

Sarah half slewed her chair round towards him, opened both legs wide, and put up one of her feet against the mantelpiece, as I have often seen her do when with me. He knelt down and I lost sight of his head between her legs—but saw his hand gently frigging himself as before, and heard soon a splashy, sloppy, slobbery sort of suck, as his tongue rubbed on her cunt now wetted by his saliva. Then he got up and pushed his prick against her face.—'Suck, and I will give you another sovereign.' 'It will choke me—I won't,' said Sarah.

Then he began to rub her legs and said he liked silk stockings, that few wore silk excepting French women whom he did not like,—but 'they all suck my prick.'—Again Sarah put up her leg—again he licked her cunt, and then said she must frig him, which she agreed to on his paying another sovereign.

He told her to go to the edge of the bed and he then went to the side nearest the door, which put his back towards me.—He called her there.—'Come here,' said Sarah, laying herself down at the foot. 'No, here.' 'I won't, it's cold close to the door' (she knew that there I could not see his cock). He obeyed, put up her legs (just as I used to do) opened them wide, and I could sideways see her black haired quim gaping. 'Close them,' he cried. She did and lay on her back, her knees and heels together up to her bum, 'I'll spend over your silk stockings,' said he, now frigging violently. Sarah to save her stockings, just as his spunk spurted, opened her legs wide and it went over her cunt and belly.—He never seemed to notice it.

254

I had passed an intensely exciting couple of hours by myself, watching this man with his huge fucking machine. Sarah in her attitudes, altho I had seen them fifty times, looked more inviting than ever. My prick had been standing on and off for an hour.—I would have fucked anything in the shape of cunt if it had been in hand, and nearly groaned for want of one. As I saw her legs open to receive his squirt, heard his shout of pleasure, and saw his violent, frig, frig, frig, I could restrain myself no longer, but giving my cock a few rubs, spent against the partition, keeping my eye at the peephole all the while.

He wiped his cock on her cunt hair, washed, and went away seemingly in a hurry.—Sarah came in to me.—'Don't you want me,' said she.—I pointed to my spunk on the partition. 'You naughty boy, I want it awfully.'—Soon after I was fucking her.—With all her care to save her silk stockings, sperm had hit her calf, and while I fucked her at the bed side, I made her hold up her leg that I might look at it.—It excited me awfully. What a strange thing lust is.

THE
AUTOBIOGRAPHY
OF A FLEA

In the hundred years since it first gripped the imagination of an eager readership, The Autobiography of a Flea *has achieved a degree of notoriety known to only a handful of erotic novels. Though often banned by the authorities – as recently as the early 1980s an innocuous (and inept) video based on the book was regularly seized by the British police – like many other 'dirty' books this one refuses to die, indeed the novel is as difficult to eradicate as the robust vermin of its title. Yet its appeal is not obvious. Based firmly on anticlerical themes made popular in France in the eighteenth century in books such as Gervaise de Latouche's* Dom Bougre *and Mirabeau's* Libertin de Qualité, *it recounts the loss of innocence of a young girl at the hands of those who should be protecting her, namely her priest and her guardian uncle. Inevitably, in a book of this nature, the young lady takes to sexual excess like a drunk to free beer and a wild time is had by all. What distinguishes the story, and doubtless has earned it a permanent place in the affection of generations of readers, is the personality of the narrator. As indicated by the title of the book, the tale is told by a flea.*

Blessed by a 'mental perception and erudition which placed me for ever upon a pinnacle of insect grandeur' our flea lives on the luscious flesh of young Bella – 'a beauty – just sixteen – a perfect figure, and although so young, her soft bosom was already budding into those proportions which delight the other sex.' Poised upon such an adorable meal ticket, the flea is in the perfect spot to recount every nuance of her exhausting adventures. The following excerpt finds Bella reporting for the first time to the formidable Father Ambrose as a consequence of losing her maidenhead to her sweetheart Charlie. The priest has fortuitously witnessed the adolescent tryst and, on pain of disclosure to her guardian, has commanded Bella to meet him in the sacristy the next day . . .

Curiosity to learn the sequel of an adventure in which I already felt so much interest, as well as a tender solicitude for the gentle and amiable Bella, constrained me to keep in her vicinity, and I, therefore, took care not to annoy her with any very decided attentions on my part, or to raise resistance by an illtimed attack at a moment when it was necessary to the success of my design to remain within range of that young lady's operations.

I shall not attempt to tell of the miserable period passed by my young protegée in the interval which elapsed between the shocking discovery made by the holy Father Confessor, and the hour assigned by him for the interview in the sacristy, which was to decide the fate of the unfortunate Bella.

With trembling steps and downcast eyes the frightened girl presented herself at the porch and knocked.

The door was opened and the Father appeared upon the threshold.

At a sign Bella entered and stood before the stately presence of the holy man.

An embarrassing silence of some seconds followed. Father Ambrose was the first to break the spell.

'You have done right, my daughter, to come to me so punctually; the ready obedience of the penitent is the first sign of the spirit within which obtains the Divine forgiveness.'

At these gracious words Bella took courage, and already a load seemed to fall from her heart.

Father Ambrose continued, seating himself at the same time upon the long-cushioned seat which covered a huge oak chest:

'I have thought much, and prayed much on your account, my daughter. For some time there appeared no way in which I could absolve my conscience otherwise than to go to your natural protector and lay before him the dreadful secret of which I have become the unhappy possessor.'

Here he paused, and Bella, who knew well the severe character of her uncle, on whom she was entirely dependent, trembled at his words.

Taking her hand in his, and gently drawing the girl to the same seat, so that she found herself kneeling before him, while his right hand pressed her rounded shoulder, he went on.

'But I am wounded to think of the dreadful results which would follow such a disclosure, and I have asked for assistance from the Blessed Virgin in my trouble. She has pointed out a way which, while it also serves the ends of our holy church, likely prevents the consequences of your offence from being known to your uncle. The first necessity which this course imposes is, however, implicit obedience.'

Bella, only too rejoiced to hear of a way out of her trouble, readily promised the most blind obedience to the command of her spiritual Father.

The young girl was kneeling at his feet. Father

Ambrose bent his large head over her recumbent figure. A warm tint lit his cheeks, a strange fire danced in his fierce eyes: his hands trembled slightly as they rested upon the shoulders of his penitent, but his composure was otherwise unruffled. Doubtless his spirit was troubled at the conflict going on within him between the duty he had to fulfil and the tortuous path by which he hoped to avoid the awful exposure.

The holy Father then began a long lecture upon the virtue of obedience, and the absolute submissions to the guidance of the minister of holy church.

Bella reiterated her assurance of entire patience and obedience in all things.

Meanwhile it was evident to me that the priest was a victim to some confined, but rebellious spirit which rose within him, and at times almost broke out into complete possession in the flashing eyes and hot passionate lips.

Father Ambrose gently drew the beautiful penitent nearer and nearer, until her fair arms rested upon his knees, and her face bent downwards in holy resignation, sunk almost upon her hands.

'And now, my child,' continued the holy man, 'it is time that I should tell you the means vouchsafed to me by the Blessed Virgin by which alone I am absolved from exposing your offence. There are ministering spirits who have confided to them the relief of those passions and those exigencies which the servants of the church are forbidden openly to avow, but which, who can doubt, they have need to satisfy. These chosen few are mainly selected from among those who have already trodden the path of fleshly indulgence; to them is confined the solemn and holy duty of assuaging the earthly desires of our religious community in the strictest secrecy. To you,' whispered the Father, his voice trembling with emotion, and his large hands passing by an easy transition from the shoulders of his penitent to her slender waist.

'To you, who have once already tasted the supreme pleasure of copulation, it is competent to assume this holy office. Not only will your sin be thus effaced and pardoned, but it will be permitted you to taste legitimately those ecstatic delights, those overpowering sensations of rapturous enjoyment, which in the arms of her faithful servants you are at all times sure to find. You will swim in a sea of sensual pleasure, without incurring the penalties of illicit love. Your absolution will follow each occasion of your yielding your sweet body to the gratification on the church, through her ministers, and you will be rewarded and sustained in the pious work by witnessing – nay, Bella, by sharing fully those intense and fervent emotions, the delicious enjoyment of your beautiful person must provoke.'

Bella listened to this insidious proposal with mingled feelings of surprise and pleasure.

The wild and lewd impulses of her warm nature were at once awakened by the picture now presented to her fervid imagination – how could she hesitate?

The pious priest drew her yielding form towards him, and printed a long hot kiss upon her rosy lips.

'Holy Mother,' murmured Bella, whose sexual instincts were each moment becoming more fully roused. 'This is too much for me to bear – I long – I wonder – I know not what!'

'Sweet innocent, it will be for me to instruct you. In my person you will find your best and fittest preceptor in those exercises you will henceforth have to fulfil.'

Father Ambrose slightly shifted his position. It was then that Bella noticed for the first time the heated look of sensuality which now almost frightened her.

It was now also that she became aware of the enormous protuberance of the front of the holy Father's silk cassock.

The excited priest hardly cared any longer to conceal either his condition or his designs.

Catching the beautiful child to his arms he kissed

her long and passionately. He pressed her sweet body to his burly person, and rudely threw himself forward into closer contact with her graceful form.

At length the consuming lust with which he was burning carried him beyond all bounds, and partly releasing Bella from the constraint of his ardent embrace, he opened the front of his cassock, and exposed, without a blush, to the astonished eyes of his young penitent, a member the gigantic proportions of which, no less than its stiffness and rigidity completely confounded her.

It is impossible to describe the sensations produced upon the gentle Bella by the sudden display of this formidable instrument.

Her eyes were instantly riveted upon it, while the Father, noticing her astonishment, but detecting rightly that there was nothing mingled with it of alarm or apprehension, coolly placed it into her hands. It was then that Bella became wildly excited with the muscular contact of this tremendous thing.

Only having seen the very moderate proportions displayed by Charlie, she found her lewdest sensations quickly awakened by so remarkable a phenomenon, and clasping the huge object as well as she could in her soft little hands, she sank down beside it in an ecstasy of sensual delight.

'Holy Mother, this is already heaven!' murmured Bella. 'Oh! Father, who would have believed I could have been selected for such pleasure!'

This was too much for Father Ambrose. He was delighted at the lubricity of his fair penitent, and the success of his infamous trick (for he had planned the whole, and had been instrumental in bringing the two young lovers together and affording them an opportunity of indulging their warm temperaments, unknown to all save himself, as, hidden close by, with flaming eyes, he watched the amatory combat).

Hastily rising, he caught up the light figure of the

young Bella, and placing her upon the cushioned seat on which he had lately been sitting, he threw up her plump legs and separating to the utmost her willing thighs, he beheld for an instant the delicious pinky slit which appeared at the bottom of her white belly. Then, without a word, he plunged his face towards it, and thrusting his lecherous tongue up the moist sheath as far as he could, he sucked it so deliciously that Bella, in a shuddering ecstasy of passion, her young body writhing in spasmodic contortions of pleasure, gave down a plentiful emission, which the holy man swallowed like a custard.

For a few moments there was calm.

Bella lay on her back, her arms extended on either side, and her head thrown back in an attitude of delicious exhaustion, succeeding the wild emotions so lately occasioned by the lewd proceedings of the reverend Father.

Her bosom yet palpitated with the violence of her transports and her beautiful eyes remained half closed in languid repose.

Father Ambrose was one of the few who, under circumstances such as the present, was able to keep the instincts of passion under command. Long habits of patience in the attainment of his object, a general doggedness of manner and the conventional caution of his order, had not been lost upon his fiery nature, and although by nature unfitted for his holy calling, and a prey to desires as violent as they were irregular, he had taught himself to school his passions even to mortification.

It is time to lift the veil from the real character of this man. I do so with respect, but the truth must be told.

Father Ambrose was the living personification of lust. His mind was in reality devoted to its pursuit, and his grossly animal instincts, his ardent and vigorous constitution, no less than his hard unbending nature made him resemble in body, as in mind, the Satyr of old.

But Bella only knew him as the holy Father who had not only pardoned her offence, but who had opened to her the path by which she might, as she supposed, legitimately enjoy those pleasures which had already wrought so strongly on her young imagination.

The bold priest, singularly charmed, not only at the success of his strategem which had given into his hands so luscious a victim, but also at the extraordinary sensuality of her constitution, and the evident delight with which she lent herself to his desires, now set himself leisurely to reap the fruits of his trickery, and revel to the utmost in the enjoyment which the possession of all the delicate charms of Bella could procure to appease his frightful lust.

She was his at last, and as he rose from her quivering body, his lips yet reeking with the plentiful evidence of her participation in his pleasure, his member became yet more fearfully hard and swollen, and the full red head shone with the bursting strain of blood and muscle beneath.

No sooner did the young Bella find herself released from the attack of her confessor upon the sensitive part of her person already described, and raised her head from the recumbent position into which it had fallen, than her eyes fell for the second time upon the big truncheon which the Father kept impudently exposed.

Bella noted the long and thick white shaft, and the curling mass of black hair out of which it rose, stiffly inclined upwards, and protruding from its end was the egg-shaped head, skinned and ruddy, and seeming to invite the contact of her hand.

Bella beheld this thickened muscular mass of stiffened flesh, and unable to resist the inclination, flew once more to seize it in her grasp.

She squeezed it – she pressed it – she drew back the

folding skin, and watched the broad nut, as it inclined towards her. She saw with wonder the small slit-like hole at its extremity and taking both her hands, she held it throbbing close to her face.

'Oh! Father, what a beautiful thing,' exclaimed Bella, 'what an immense one, too. Oh! Please, dear Father Ambrose, do tell me what I must do to relieve you of those feelings which you say give our holy ministers of religion so much pain and uneasiness.'

Father Ambrose was almost too excited to reply, but taking her hand in his, he showed the innocent girl how to move her white fingers up and down upon the shoulders of his huge affair.

His pleasure was intense, and that of Bella was hardly less.

She continued to rub his limb with her soft palms and, looking up innocently to his face asked softly – 'If that gave him pleasure, and was nice, and whether she might go on, as she was doing.'

Meanwhile the reverend Father felt his big penis grow harder and even stiffer under the exciting titillations of the young girl.

'Stay a moment; if you continue to rub it so I shall spend,' softly said he. 'It will be better to defer it a little.'

'Spend, my Father,' asked Bella, eagerly, 'what is that?'

'Oh, sweet girl, charming alike in your beauty and your innocence; how divinely you fulfil your divine mission,' exclaimed Ambrose, delighted to outrage and debase the evident inexperience of his young penitent.

'To spend is to complete the act whereby the full pleasure of venery is enjoyed, and then a rich quantity of thick white fluid escapes from the thing you now hold in your hand, and rushing forth, gives equal pleasure to him who ejects it and to the person who, in some manner or other, receives it.'

Bella remembered Charlie and his ecstasy, and knew immediately what was meant.

'Would this outpouring give you relief, my Father?'

'Undoubtedly, my daughter, it is that fervent relief I have in view, offering you the opportunity of taking from me the blissful sacrifice of one of the humblest servants of the church.'

'How delicious,' murmured Bella; 'by my means this rich stream is to flow, and all for me the holy man proposed this end of his pleasure – how happy I am to be able to give him so much pleasure.

As she half pondered, half uttered these thoughts she bent her head down; a faint, but exquisitely sensual perfume rose from the object of her adoration. She pressed her moist lips upon its top, she covered the little slitlike hole with her lovely mouth, and imprinted upon the glowing member a fervent kiss.

'What is this fluid called?' asked Bella, once more raising her pretty face.

'It has various names,' replied the holy man, 'according to the status of the person employing them; but between you and me, my daughter, we shall call it spunk.'

'Spunk!' repeated Bella, innocently, making the erotic word fall from her sweet lips with an unction which was natural under the circumstances.

'Yes, my daughter, spunk is the word I wish you to understand it by, and you shall presently have a plentiful bedewal of the precious essence.'

'How must I receive it?' enquired Bella, thinking of Charlie and the tremendous difference relatively between his instrument and the gigantic and swollen penis in her presence now.

'There are various ways, all of which you will have to learn, but at present we have only slight accommodation for the principal act of reverential venery, of that permitted copulation of which I have already spoken. We must, therefore, supply another and easier method, and instead of my discharging the essence called spunk into your body, where the extreme tightness of that little slit of yours would doubtless cause it to flow very abundantly, we will commence by the friction of your obedient fingers, until the time when I feel the approach of those spasms which accompany the emission. You shall then, at a signal from me, place as much as you can of the head of this affair between your lips, and there suffer me to disgorge the trickling spunk, until the last drop being expended I shall retire satisfied, at least for the time.'

Bella, whose jealous instincts led her to enjoy the description which her confessor offered, and who was quite as eager as himself for the completion of this outrageous programme, readily expressed her willingness to comply.

Ambrose once more placed his large penis in Bella's fair hands.

Excited alike by the sight and touch of so remarkable an object, which both her hands now grasped with delight, the girl set herself to work to tickle, rub and press the huge and stiff affair in a way which gave the licentious priest the keenest enjoyment.

Not content with the friction of her delicate fingers, Bella, uttering words of devotion and satisfaction, now placed the foaming head upon her rosy lips and allowed it to slip in as far as it could, hoping by her touches, no less than by the gliding movements of her tongue, to provoke the delicious ejaculation of which she was in want.

This was almost beyond the anticipation of the holy priest, who had hardly supposed he should find so ready a disciple in the irregular attack he proposed; and his feelings being roused to the utmost by the delicious titillation he was now experiencing, prepared himself to flood the young girl's mouth and throat with the full stream of his powerful discharge.

Ambrose began to feel he could not last longer without letting fly his roe, and thereby ending his pleasure.

He was one of those extraordinary men, the abundance of whose seminal ejaculation is far beyond that of ordinary beings. Not only had he the singular gift of repeatedly performing the veneral act with but very short respite, but the quantity with which he ended his pleasure was as tremendous as it was unusual. The superfluity seemed to come from him in proportion as his animal passions were aroused, and as his libidinous desires were intense and large, so also were the outpourings which relieved them.

It was under these circumstances that the gentle Bella undertook to release the pent-up torrents of this man's lust. It was her sweet mouth which was to be the recipient of those thick slippery volumes of which she had had as yet no experience, and, all ignorant as she was of the effect of the relief she was so anxious to administer, the beautiful maid desired the consummation of her labour and the overflow of that spunk of which the good Father had told her.

Harder and hotter grew the rampant member as Bella's exciting lips pressed its large head and her tongue played around the little opening. Her two white hands bore back the soft skin from its shoulders and alternately tickled the lower extremity.

Twice Ambrose, unable to bear without spending the delicious contact, drew back the tip from her rosy lips.

At length Bella, impatient of delay, and apparently bent on perfecting her task, pressed forward with more energy than ever upon the stiff shaft.

Instantly there was a stiffening of the limbs of the good priest. His legs spread wide on either side of his penitent. His hands grasped convulsively at the cushions, his body was thrust forward and straightened out.

'Oh, holy Christ! I am going to spend!' he exclaimed, as with parted lips and glazing eyes he looked his last upon his innocent victim. Then he shivered perceptibly, and with low moans and short, hysteric cries, his penis, in obedience to the provocation of the young lady, began to jet forth its volumes of thick and glutinous fluid.

Bella, sensible of the gushes which now came slopping, jet after jet into her mouth, and ran in streams down her throat, hearing the cries of her companion, and perceiving with ready intuition that he was enjoying to the utmost the effect she had brought about, continued her rubbings and compression until gorged with the slimy discharge, and half choked by its abundance, she was compelled to let go of this human syringe, which continued to spout out its gushes in her face.

'Holy Mother!' exclaimed Bella, whose lips and face were reeking with the Father's spunk. 'Holy Mother! What pleasure I have had – and you, my Father, have I not given the precious relief you coveted?'

Father Ambrose, too agitated to reply, raised the gentle girl in his arms, and pressing her streaming mouth to his, sucked humid kisses of gratitude and pleasure.

A quarter of an hour passed in tranquil repose uninterrupted by any signs of disturbance from without.

The door was fast, and the holy Father had well chosen his time.

Meanwhile Bella, whose desires had been fearfully excited by the scene we have attempted to describe, had conceived an extravagant longing to have the same operation performed upon her with the rigid member of Ambrose that she had suffered from the moderately proportioned weapon of Charlie.

Throwing her arms round the burly neck of her confessor, who whispered low words of invitation, watching as she did so, the effect in the already stiffening instrument between his legs.

'You told me that the tightness of this little slit,'

and here Bella placed his large hand upon it with a gentle pressure, 'would make you discharge abundantly of the spunk you possess. What would I not give, my Father, to feel it poured into my body from the top of this red thing?'

It was evident how much the beauty of the young Bella, no less than the innocence and *naiveté* of her character, inflamed the sensual nature of the priest. The knowledge of his triumph – of her utter helplessness in his hands – of her delicacy and refinement, all conspired to work to the extreme of lecherous desires of his fierce and wanton instincts. She was his. His to enjoy as he wished – his to break to every caprice of his horrid lust, and to bend to the indulgence of the most outrageous and unbridled sensuality.

'Ay, by heaven! it is too much,' exclaimed Ambrose, whose lust, already rekindling, now rose violently into activity at this solicitation. 'Sweet girl, you don't know what you ask; the disproportion is terrible, and you would suffer much in the attempt.'

'I would suffer all,' replied Bella, 'so that I could feel that fierce thing in my belly, and taste the gushes of its spunk up in me to the quick.'

'Holy Mother of God! It is too much – you shall have it, Bella, you shall know the full measure of this stiffened machine, and, sweet girl, you shall wallow in an ocean of warm spunk.'

'Oh, my Father, what heavenly bliss!'

'Strip, Bella, remove everything that can interfere with our movements, which I promise you will be violent enough.'

Thus ordered, Bella was soon divested of her clothing, and finding her Confessor appeared charmed at the display of her beauty, and that his member swelled and lengthened in proportion as she exhibited her nudity, she parted with the last vestige of drapery, and stood as naked as she was born.

Father Ambrose was astonished at the charms which

now faced him. The full hips, the budding breasts, the skin as white as snow and soft as satin, the rounded buttocks and swelling thighs, the flat white belly and lovely mount covered only with the thinnest down; and above all the charming pinky slit which now showed itself at the bottom of the mount, now hid timorously away between the plump thighs. With a snort of rampant lust he fell upon his victim.

Ambrose clasped her in his arms. He pressed her soft glowing form of his burly front. He covered her with his salacious kisses, and giving his lewd tongue full licence, promised the young girl all the joys of Paradise by the introduction of his big machine within her slit and belly.

Bella met him with a little cry of ecstasty, and as the excited ravisher bore her backwards to the couch, already felt the broad and glowing head of his gigantic penis pressing against the warm moist lips of her moist virgin orifice.

And now, the holy man finding delight in the contact of his penis with the warm lips of Bella's slit, began pushing it in between with all his energy until the big nut was covered with the moisture which the sensitive little sheath exuded.

Bella's passions were at fever height. The efforts of Father Ambrose to lodge the head of his member within the moist lips of her little slit, so far from deterring her, spurred her to madness until, with another faint cry, she fell prone and gushed down the slippery tribute of her lascivious temperament.

This was exactly what the bold priest wanted, and as the sweet warm emission bedewed his fiercely distended penis, he drove resolutely in, and at one bound sheathed half its ponderous length in the beautiful child.

No sooner did Bella feel the stiff entry of the terrible member within her tender body, than she lost all the little control of herself she had, and setting aside all thought of the pain she was enduring, she wound her legs about his loins, and entreated her huge assailant not to spare her.

'My sweet and delicious child,' whispered the salacious priest, 'my arms are round you, my weapon is already half way up your tight belly. The joys of Paradise will be yours presently.'

'Oh, I know it; I feel it, do not draw back, give me the delicious thing as far as you can.'

'There, then, I push, I press, but I am far too largely made to enter you easily. I shall burst you, possibly; but it is now too late. I must have you – or die.'

Bella's parts relaxed a little, and Ambrose pushed in another inch. His throbbing member lay skinned and soaking, pushed half way into the girl's belly. His pleasure was most intense, and the head of his instrument was compressed deliciously by Bella's slit.

'Go on, dear Father, I am waiting for the spunk you promised me.'

It little needed this stimulant to induce the confessor to an exercise of his tremendous powers of copulation. He pushed frantically forward; he plunged his hot penis still further and further at each effort, and then with one huge stroke buried himself to the balls in Bella's light little person.

It was then that the furious plunge of the brutal priest became more than his sweet victim, sustained as she had been by her own advanced desires, could endure.

With a faint shriek of physical anguish, Bella felt that her ravisher had burst through all the resistance which her youth had opposed to the entry of his member, and the torture of the forcible insertion of such a mass bore down the prurient sensations with which she had commenced to support the attack.

Ambrose cried aloud in rapture, he looked down upon the fair thing his serpent had stung. He gloated over the victim now impaled with the full rigour of his huge rammer. He felt the maddening contact with inexpressible delight. He saw her quivering with the anguish of his forcible entry. His brutal nature was fully aroused. Come what might he would enjoy to his utmost, so he wound his arms about the beautiful girl and treated her to the full measure of his burly member.

'My beauty! you are indeed exciting, you must also enoy. I will give you the spunk I spoke of, but I must first work up my nature by this lascivious titillation. Kiss me, Bella, then you shall have it, and while the hot spunk leaves me and enters your young parts, you shall be sensible of the throbbing joys I also am experiencing. Press, Bella, let me push, so, my child, now it enters again. Oh! oh!'

Ambrose raised himself a moment, and noted the immense shaft round which the pretty slit of Bella was now intensely stretched.

Firmly embedded in his luscious sheath, and keenly relishing the exceeding tightness of the warm folds of youthful flesh which now encased him, he pushed on, unmindful of the pain his tormenting member was producing, and only anxious to secure as much enjoyment to himself as he could. He was not a man to be deterred by any false notions of pity in such a case, and now pressed himself inwards to his utmost, while his hot lips sucked delicious kisses from the open and quivering lips of the poor Bella.

For some minutes nothing now was heard but the jerking blows with which the lascivious priest continued his enjoyment, and the cluck, cluck of his huge penis, as it alternately entered and retreated in the belly of the beautiful penitent.

It was not to be supposed that such a man as Ambrose was ignorant of the tremendous powers of enjoyment his member could rouse within one of the opposite sex, and that with its size and disgorging capabilities of such a nature as to enlist the most powerful emotions in the young girl in whom he was operating.

But Nature was asserting himself in the person of the young Bella. The agony of the stretching was fast being swallowed up in the intense sensations of pleasure produced by the vigorous weapon of the holy man, and it was not long before the low moans and sobs of the pretty child became mingled with expressions, half choked in the depth of her feelings, expressive in delight.

'Oh, my Father! Oh, my dear, generous Father! Now, now push. Oh! push. I can bear – I wish for it. I am in heaven! The blessed instrument is so hot in its head. Oh! my heart. Oh! my – oh! Holy Mother, what is this I feel?'

Ambrose saw the effect he was producing. His own pleasure advanced apace. He drove steadily in and out, treating Bella to the long hard shaft of his member up to the crisp hair which covered his big balls, at each forward thrust.

At length Bella broke down, and treated the electrified and ravished man with a warm emission which ran all over his stiff affairs.

It is impossible to describe the lustful frenzy which now took possession of the young and charming Bella. She clung with desperate tenacity to the burly figure of the priest, who bestowed upon the heaving and voluptuous body the full force and vigour of his manly thrust. She held him in her tight and slippery sheath to his balls.

But in her ecstasy Bella never lost sight of the promised perfection of the enjoyment. The holy man was to spend his spunk in her as Charlie had done, and the thought added fuel to her lustful fire.

When, therefore, Father Ambrose, throwing his arms close round her taper waist, drove up his stallion penis to the very hairs of Bella's slit, and sobbing, whispering that the 'spunk' was coming at last, the excited girl straightway opening her legs to the utmost, with positive shrieks of pleasure let him send his pent-up fluid in showers into her very vitals.

Thus he lay for full two minutes, while at each hot and forcible injection of the slippery semen, Bella gave plentiful evidence by her writhings and cries of the ecstasy the powerful discharge was producing.

CONFESSIONS OF AN ENGLISH MAID

Like Bella, the heroine of The Autobiography of a Flea, *pretty young Jessie takes to the delights of sexual activity at an early age – so much so that her stepmother has her committed to a reformatory for wayward girls. There, needless to say, she learns a great deal more about sex and the way in which her fair face and form can earn her a profitable living on her eventual release. It is her even more experienced friend Hester who turns her on to the pecuniary advantages of not giving it away for nothing – quite apart from the obvious pleasures of going to bed with a lot of handsome fellows. Breathlessly Hester proclaims the pleasures of working in 'a sporting house' and inflames Jessie's overwrought imagination with what she intends to get up to on the first night of her release. 'Guess what I'm going to have,' she says. 'A stiff cock?' suggests Jessie. 'No,' proclaims Hester, 'five of them, all at the same time!'*

With such an influence at work it is no wonder that Jessie is keen to tread the professional path on her release. Eventually Hester's pander, Madame Lafronde, posing as her aunt, collects her from her prison and takes her to her new home – 'a place of quiet elegance, soft plush carpets and tapestried walls. Thus did I cross the threshold of a new life and the doors of the past closed behind me . . .'

A small but furnished alcove with a tiled bath in connection was waiting for me, and after I had examined it Madame Lafronde left Hester and me together, saying that she would have a talk with me later in the afternoon.

A maid appeared with a luncheon tray and as I ate, plying Hester with questions between bites, I learned that Madame Lafronde's 'family' comprised eight other girls in addition to Hester and myself. I would meet them later, they did not get up until after twelve, which accounted for the silence and absence of movement I had already noted.

When Madame Lafronde returned, her first request was that I strip myself entirely so that she could examine my body. I did so with some embarrassment, for though I had often enough exposed myself to boys and men, the impersonal, appraising eyes of this strange old lady filled me with a nervous dread that I might be found wanting in some essential.

I was small of stature and feared that the absence of clothing might accentuate the possible defect. However, to my vast relief, she gave every evidence of satisfaction and nodded her head approvingly as I turned around and around in obedience to her indications. When I had replaced my clothing she shot question after question at me, until every phase of my early and subsequent sexual life had been revealed. To her questions I endeavoured to give frank and truthful answers, regardless of the embarrassment which some of them evoked.

'Now, my dear,' she said, when the interrogating had been concluded, 'I want you to know that we're all one big, happy family here. There must be no jealousy of friction or petty animosities between girls. Our gentlemen are very nice, but men are men, and a pretty, new face always distracts their attention from older ones. I have a plan in mind which fits you as though you were made for it. If you handle it rightly you'll be helping the other girls as well as yourself, and instead of being jealous of you they'll all have reason to be grateful. We're all here to make money and as it must come from the gentlemen our aim is to get them to spend it and then come back and spend some more. Never forget that.'

And Madame Lafronde explained the unique role I was to play, a role which to a more mature mind than mine would have at once revealed the astuteness and subtlety of the guiding genius behind this lucrative business and which accounted for its success, measured in terms of gold. Madame Lafronde was nobody's fool.

In brief, she proposed to dangle my youthful prettiness before the jaded eyes of the clientele as a sort of visual aperitif, much as water was placed before the thirsting Tantalus, in view, but just beyond reach, the psychological effect of which would be to so whet their passions that they would in the end, perforce, satisfy

280

themselves with such feminine fruit as was within their reach.

I was to tantalise masculine passion while leaving to others the duty of satisfying them. This with respect to the regular 'parlour' clientele. Exceptions would be made privately with certain special patrons who were always able and disposed to pay well for favouritism.

Things were not as they had been before the war, explained Madame Lafronde. Even this profitable business had suffered from the falling economic barometer, and too many of the gentlemen who dropped in were inclined to pass the evening sociably in the parlour. Of course, between liquors consumed, tips to the girls, and various other sources of minor revenues, their presence was desirable, but the real profits of the business were garnered in the bedrooms, not in the parlour. It was a case of a bird in a bedroom being worth five in the parlour.

As a sort of stimulant designed to inspire blasé gentlemen with an irresistible urge to make use of the bedroom service, I was to be rigged up in an enticingly juvenile fashion and paraded constantly before their eyes in a semi-nude state. Various pretexts and artifices would ostensibly account for my presence and movements. I would carry a tray of cigars and cigarettes, serve drinks, and be available for general services and accommodations with but one single exception. I would joke and chat with patrons, tell a naughty story now and then, even permit them to fondle me within certain limits, but, because of my youth (I was to pretend to be only fifteen years old!) my services were not to be expected in a professional capacity.

I gasped at hearing that I was to play the part of a fifteen-year-old, but Madame Lafronde insisted that it would not be difficult in view of my small body and the fact that certain artifices in costume, hairdressing and other details would be employed to help out the illusion.

The first step was to call in a barber who trimmed my hair so that it hung just below my ears. It was naturally wavy, and when the work was finished it was quite apparent that Madame Lafronde had not erred in assuming that short curls would lend a peculiarly childish effect to my face. I gazed in the mirror with genuine surprise at the transfiguration.

When the barber had gone Madame Lafronde ordered me to undress again, and after taking certain measurements left the room to return later with several garments and a box which on being opened revealed a safety razor, soap and brush.

'We could have let the barber do this, too,' she commented dryly, indicating the razor, 'but maybe you'd rather do it yourself.'

'Do what?' I asked, looking at the razor in perplexity.

'Shave the pretty little curls off your peek-a-boo,' she answered, with a gesture toward the dark shadow which was visible through the texture of my single garment.

'What!' I expostulated. 'Why ... even girls fifteen years old have ... !'

'Shave it off,' she interrupted. 'If you don't know how, I'll do it for you.'

'I can, I can!' I responded hastily. 'I've shaved the hair under my arms lots of times ... only ...' and I glanced around in confusion for, in addition to Madame Lafronde and Hester, several girls had appeared and were standing in the door watching me curiously.

'Go over by the window with your back to us and stand up, or sit down, whichever you wish, if you're afraid someone will see your love trap. You'll get over that before you've been here long.'

Without further protest I took the shaving equipment, turned my back on the smiling assembly and sitting on the edge of a chair with my legs apart I lathered and soaped the hair and shaved it off the best I could. I had to go over the ground several times before the last prickly stubs were finally removed, and when I stood up, much embarrassed, to let Madame Lafronde view the results she expressed her approval and suggested that I dust the denuded flesh with talcum powder.

The absence of the hair from its accustomed place caused me to feel peculiarly naked, and I turned my gaze downward. The two sides of my cunny stook out prominently like fat little hills, the crease between them tightly closed as I stood with my legs pressed together.

I was now to don black hose of sheerest silk and a pair of tiny slippers with exaggerated high Spanish heels. Around my legs, just above the knees, fitted narrow scarlet garters, each adorned with a little silk rosette. Next came an exquisite brocade coat or jacket of black velvet into which was worked fantastic designs in gold thread.

'What about my bubbies?' I asked, as Madame Lafronde handed me the garment. 'Will I have to cut them off, too?'

A gust of laughter followed and I slipped on the loose-fitting coat. It terminated at a point about halfway down my thighs, leaving a few inches of naked flesh between its lower edge and the tops of my hose. Fastening just below the breasts with three braided loops, it covered my stomach all right, but from there down the folds hung loose and a naked, hairless cunny would be exposed with any careless movement.

The last item of this bizarre costume was a tall, military style cap of astrakhan, fitted with a small brim of shiny black leather and a strap which passed under my chin. Madame Lafronde adjusted the cap on my head at a rakish angle and stook back to view the effect.

I glanced at my reflection in the wardrobe mirror. Without undue conceit I realised that I presented a chic picture, one which undoubtedly fulfilled Madame

Lafronde's expectations, as was attested to by the satisfied gleam in her shrewd old eyes, by Hester's enthusiastic felicitations, and by the half-admiring, half-envious looks of the other girls who were watching silently.

From beneath the edge of the black astrakhan cap my hair hung loose in short, crisp curls. The low bodice of the brocade jacket teasingly revealed the upper halves of my breasts, while its wide and ample sleeves displayed my arms to good advantage with every movement. The jacket itself, fitting snugly around my waist, flared out sufficiently to show my hips to good advantage. Further down, the sheen of glossy silk with the brief variation in colour provided by the scarlet garters gave just the right touch to my legs, and the high-heeled slippers completed the exotic ensemble.

The rest of the afternoon and evening Madame Lafronde devoted to coaching and instructing me. The doors were open to visitors at nine o'clock, but it was never until after eleven or twelve that gentlemen returning from their clubs or other nocturnal entertainment began to drop in in any considerable number, and from then on patrons came and went, singly or in groups, some to linger briefly, others to pass an hour or two, or to remain all night.

I made my debut at eleven o'clock. With inward nervousness at first, but with growing confidence as I observed the electrical effect my entry made upon the half-dozen gentlemen who were lounging about the salon in various attitudes of interest or indifference to the wiles of the feminine sirens about them. As I crossed the room with my tray of cigars and cigarettes and matches supported by a strap over my shoulders the hum of conversation ceased as if by magic and every eye was on me.

I approached a tall, well-dressed gentleman who was sitting on a sofa with a girl on either side of him, and proffered my wares in a timid voice. His startled gaze took in the picture before him and lingered a moment on my legs. Shaking himself free from the arms of his companions, he sat up.

'My dear, I never smoked a cigar in my life, but I'll take all you have, if you go with them!'

This was Madame Lafronde's cue. Entering the room from a side door where she had been waiting. she said:

'Dear gentlemen, I want to present a new member of our family to you. This is Jessie. Jessie is here under peculiar circumstances. She is an orphan and, strictly speaking, not old enough to be here in a professional capacity. Though as you see, she is nicely developed, she is in fact only fifteen years old and I am sheltering her here only because of her orphaned condition. She is to make her living selling you cigars and cigarettes, gentlemen, and serving you in all other possible ways ... except one.'

Madame Lafronde paused.

'In other words,' interrupted a tall, thin young man with a tiny moustache who was indifferently stroking the silk-clad legs of a damsel on his lap, 'she can be only a sister to us. I knew she was too good to be true the moment she came into this room.'

A burst of laughter followed and Madame Lafronde, smiling, answered:

'A sister ... well ... maybe just a bit more than a sister, gentlemen, but not too much more!'

From across the room Hester beckoned to me.

'This is my friend Mr Hayden, Jessie. He wants to know you,' she said, indicating her companion.

I acknowledged the introduction.

'Bring us two Scotch and sodas, will you, honey?' added Hester.

Mr Hayden spoke to me pleasantly and took a packet of cigarettes from my tray, courteously declining the change I tendered him. As I turned to execute Hester's order, the man I had first addressed detained me.

'Wait a moment, Sister. I've decided to take up smoking.'

I might add that the nickname 'Sister' was unanimously adopted and clung to me during the time I was in Madame Lafronde's house.

The gentleman took a handful of cigars and reached toward his pocket. As he did so, his eyes drifted down below the edge of the tray.

'Hold on! I'm making a tactical error!' he exclaimed, replacing all the cigars but one. 'I see right now that cigars should be purchased one by one. You may bring me another when you come back!'

Nothing else was needed to start the ball of my popularity rolling and soon the salon was echoing with hilarity and laughter as all called for cigars and cigarettes at once, each trying to keep me standing in front of him as long as possible.

If this kept up there would be substantial returns on the tobacco concession, for half the profits were to be mine, according to Madame Lafronde's promise, and this in addition to whatever was given to me in the nature of tips or gratuities. Flushed and happy, I ran from one to another, replying to jokes and quips in a half-innocent, half-cynical manner, calculated to fit the role of a fifteen-year-old ingenue.

As the evening wore on new arrivals appeared and I was instantly the first object of their attention. Before long the pockets of my brocade jacket were heavy with silver, I had replenished my tobacco stock several times and received several generous tips for bringing in liquor, and in addition, a gentleman had given me four shillings for being permitted to feel my bubbies, 'just in a brotherly way', as he expressed it.

What the effect of my presence was on the regular revenues of the house I could not judge, for though there was a constant movement of couples in and out of bedrooms I had no way to knowing whether this was a normal or an increased activity.

With the advancing hours the movement gradually diminished and by four o'clock the last guest had departed. The door was locked, the girls ate a light luncheon and prepared to retire. It was then that Madame Lafronde informed me that the bedroom service had showed a decided increase, which increase she was fair enough to attribute to my presence.

She was well satisfied and I surely had reason to be, for when the money was counted up and the tobacco sales checked there remained for me the sum of two pounds and eight shillings, which was duly credited to me and would be at my disposition on request.

I was tired out; I had hardly slept the previous night, yet such was my excitement that I did not feel sleepy and preferred to gossip with Hester for an hour in my room. I had a hundred questions to ask. I wanted to know about the nice-looking, gentlemanly Mr Hayden, and learned that he was one of Hester's regular and most favoured friends.

He had been much interested in me, and Hester had unselfishly confided to him that I might reservedly be at his disposition at some later occasion, to which he had gallantly responded that in such an event he would insist on having the two of us together. How good Hester was, I thought, to be willing to share this nice man with me and maybe risk my supplanting her in his affections. He had appealed to me greatly, and there had been several others whom I would not have been averse to doing something with.

'You made a tremendous sensation, darling,' said Hester. 'You could have a dozen roomcalls. I heard what everybody said. But Lafronde is right. The other girls would have been ready to scratch your eyes out. There's nothing makes them so mad as to have a new girl take their regulars away from them. Did you notice that fellow who went with me? He comes here every three or four nights. I guess every girl here has had him, but now he always takes me. He's got lots of money and he's kind of nice, but, gee, he never has a hard-on and it takes about half an hour of work to give him a stand. Sometimes I even have to put the buzzer on him, but tonight, oh baby, it was as stiff as a poker. I jollied him about it and told him I bet it was thinking about you instead of me. 'My word,' he said, 'you're a deucedly clevah mind reader. That little tart did have a most extraordinary effect on me. Wonder what the chawnces would be to secure her company for an hour or two? I think that's all bally rot about her virginal estate, don't you know!' I told him to talk to Madame Lafronde and maybe it could be arranged. That's two of my regulars that have fallen for you already, but I'm not jealous. You can have Bumpy if you want him. It takes too long to make his cock stand up.'

I laughed.

'What did you mean, putting the buzzer on him?'

'The juice, the electric massage machine. Don't you know what an electric massage machine is?'

'Of course I do. They use them for facials. But how ... what ... ?'

'Facials! Oh baby, you don't know the half. Wait ... you're tired out ... I'll fix your bath water for you and after you're bathed I'll give you a massage that will make you sleep like an infant.'

Hester ran into the bathroom and turned on the water. Then she went to her room and came back with an entrancing little pink silk nightgown, face cream, perfume, and a large leather-covered box.

While I lay splashing lazily in the tub, soaking in the pleasant warmth of the foamy, scented water, she laid out the nightgowns and opened the box to show the apparatus it contained and which was, in effect an electric vibratory massage machine fitted with a long cord for attachment to an electricity outlet. There were several assorted pieces in the box and from these Hester selected one fitted with rubber lips which turned out in the form of a small cup.

When I had got out of the tub and dried myself I lay down naked on the bed. Hester dipped her fingers in

288

the jar of cream and passed them lightly over my face, neck, breasts and limbs.

I thought suddenly of the peculiar aspect the shaving had given me in a certain place and flipped a corner of the sheet over it. Without a word Hester flipped it back and her hands were between my thighs, softly spreading the cold cream over them and down my legs.

'You're awful good to go to so much trouble for me, Hester,' I murmured.

'It's nothing. You can do as much for me sometime,' she replied.

When she had finished anointing my body she connected the massage machine. It began to hum and the next instant the rubber cup was buzzing over my forehead, cheeks and neck. My flesh thrilled to the refreshing stimulation and I lay still, enjoying it to the full. Gradually the rubber moved down over my chest, between my breasts, then up over one of them right on the nipple. I came out of any languid rest with a bound. That bubbling, vibrating cup over the nipple of my breast was awakening sensations quite remote to those of mere physical refreshment.

Both my nipples stiffened up, the sensitive area around them puffed out and radiations of sexual excitation began to flow through my body, Laughing hysterically, I sat up and pushed the tantalising device away.

'Be still, will you? Lie back down!' expostulated Hester, giving me a shove which tumbled me back over the pillows.

'But, Hester! That thing . . . it's positively distracting! Don't put it on my bubbies again . . . I can't stand it!'

Hester smiled.

'You'll think it's distracting before I finish with you. Keep quiet or you'll wake the girls in the next room.'

Down over my stomach, in widening circles, around and around, and then back and forth moved the diabolical apparatus guided by Hester's hand. I had a premonition now of what was coming, and as it slowly but surely crept downward until it reached the upper part of the rounded elevation of my cunny, I clenched my fists and held my breasts.

No sooner was it close enough to impart its infernal vibration to my clitoris than tremors of sexual agitation began to shake my body. It was simply irresistible. I could not have forestalled its action by any conceivable exercise of willpower.

But I did not try. The fulminating intensity of the sensations which now had me in their grip nullified any will or desire to thwart them. I threw my head back, closed my eyes, and surrendered supinely. My legs parted shamelessly beneath the insinuating pressure of Hester's fingers, and the humming, buzzing cup slid between them. Up and down it moved, three, four, maybe half a dozen times, pressing lightly against the flesh.

My orgasm, wrought up to the final pitch of excitation and unable to withstand the infernal provocation longer, yielded, and in a second I was gasping in the throes of sexual ecstasy.

When I recovered my breath, and in part my composure, I exclaimed:

'Hester! You . . . you . . . I could murder you! Fooling me with that thing!'

'Make you sleep good, honey, and keep you from having naughty dreams,' she answered complacently, and she disconnected the device and restored it to its container.

'Does that work on men like that, too?'

'Yes; we use it on them sometimes to give them a stand when they either can't get one or are too slow.'

'Well,' I commented. 'I'll say it gave me a stand I wasn't expecting.'

She giggled, tucked the covers around me, kissed me on the cheek, and turned out the lights.

'Sleep tight, honey. I'll wake you in the afternoon.'

She departed, leaving me alone to drowsily review the stupendous transition which twenty-four hours had wrought in my life. Last night, a hard, narrow cot in the drab and comfortless ward of a reformatory. Tonight, the soft luxury of a beautiful bed with the seductive caress of silk and fine linen about my body and all around me the material evidences of a life of ease, gaiety, and luxury. Gradually my thoughts became hazy and I drifted off into a pleasant, dreamless slumber from which I did not awaken until nine or ten hours later.

A week slipped by quickly, each night a pleasant repetition, without any notable variations, of the one I have described. This was time enough to assure Madame Lafronde that the experiment was a success. The continued approval with which my seminude appearance was received by patrons, together with certain indications, was proof that I really constituted an attraction which was imparting a new popularity to the resort.

But it was not Madame Lafronde's intention to limit my activities to exhibitional purposes. She was already being importuned by gentlemen whose interest in me was not to be resigned to mere optical satisfaction and the subtle old procuress was but biding the time necessary for these gentlemen's inflamed fancies to get the best of their financial perspectives. I was being reserved for the most exacting and best-paying customers. To the rest, including the general run of parlour guests, I was to remain only a visual aphrodisiac.

Into the ample pockets of my brocade jacket these more or less credulous victims of my enticements and beguilings poured their silver, eagerly taking advantage of such opportunities as I permitted them to fondle me tentatively or superficially, bought my cigars and cigarettes, tipped me generously for every trifling service, sighed, and generally visited a bedroom with one of my companions where, doubtless, evoking visions of my naked legs and other presumed charms, they ravished me by proxy.

Of the patrons I subsequently served in a more intimate fashion, five developed into 'steadies,' that is, became exclusively mine, and came with more or less regularity. A sixth, no other than the gentlemanly Mr Hayden, kept his promise to Hester and either by virtue of genuine affection for her or actuated by a kindly sentiment to avoid wounded feelings, insisted upon having both of us with him at the same time and maintained an attitude of strict impartiality.

I think Hester's generous spirit would not have resented a surrender of her priority to me, but though Mr Hayden was one of the nicest men I ever met, I was glad that his instincts of gallantry saved me from being placed in the light of having distracted his attention from one who was beyond doubt my best and sincerest friend. I have never found another such.

Patrons like Mr Hayden, unfortunately always in a minority, were the bright and redeeming features of a life otherwise vicious and degrading. They were the ones who, regardless of a girl's lost social status, always treated her with respectful consideration. Generous in recompensing the efforts which were made to please them, they never exacted arduous or debasing services, nor were they addicted to unnatural vices which went beyond the pale of those sexual practices ordinarily considered acceptable and legitimate.

To my lot fell the patronage of a Mr Heeley, a gentleman of this desirable category though with the minor disadvantage of being much older and less attractive physically than Mr Hayden. There was a Mr Thomas, middle-aged and wealthy, who had garnered his fortune in Ceylon and who always had some interesting story to tell. There was Mr Castle and Mr Wainwright, both of whom were addicted to eccentricities of a peculiar and disagreeable nature. At first I protested to Madame Lafronde that these two gentlemen were personages *non grata* with me and insinuated that I would not be loathe to dispense with their attentions. It was unequivocally impressed upon me that my inclinations were quite secondary to those of wealthy patrons. 'Do whatever they want within the limits of endurance. Satisfy their whims, fancies, even their aberrations if possible as long as they are willing to pay accordingly. Humour them, please them, get the money and keep them coming back as long as you can!' This was the unwritten law in the world of prostitution.

Mr Hayden was, I think, about thirty years old. I could easily have become really infatuated with this pleasant-spoken, educated, and cultured gentleman. We never knew exactly who he was with reference to his place in the outside world, nor even indeed that his name was really Hayden, for it was not unusual that gentlemen frequenting such places of entertainment as that provided by Madame Lafronde prudently concealed their identities under fictitious names. Nevertheless, there was no doubt that he was of the real gentility.

I liked him very much and I think the affection was reciprocated to an even greater extent than was ever manifested, but he was of that conscientious, kind-hearted type, disposed to go out of the way even at personal inconvenience to avoid causing pain to others and he knew that Hester adored him.

To Mr Hayden fell the honour, if such it might be styled, of initiating me into the real service of which I was now a recruit. My absence from the salon was noticed, but Madame Lafronde accounted for the numerous inquiries with the old alibi 'a bad time of the month, don't you know.' Hester and I and Mr Hayden enjoyed a little dinner by ourselves and thereafter repaired to Hester's room where we disported ourselves lightheartedly for an hour, romping and tumbling over the bed in good-natured abandon as the wine we had imbibed warmed our blood and attuned our receptive senses to lecherous ideas.

Mr Hayden was a healthy, vigorous young man, a splendid example of physical perfection. The sight of his clean-cut, well-kept body, and the magnificently rigid and well-formed member which was disclosed when he undressed sent the blood surging through my veins. I did not know by what procedure he intended to make use of two women at the same time, but imagined that he should probably take us in turn, maybe changing from one to the other at intervals.

I waited expectantly for Hester to take the initiative. Inside, I was fairly burning up. Though I had bathed most carefully but a short while before, my cunny was wet with anticipation, my clitoris swollen and pulsing. In excuse of this ardour was the fact that I had not been with a man for three long years and during this sterile period there had been no outlet for my passions except the one provided by my own nimble fingers, an occasional wet dream and, as I have related, the orgasm effected by Hester's so-called massage.

We lay down on the bed on either side of our male companion, Hester and I both naked except for our slips, hose and shoes, which we intended to leave on until done with our play and ready for sleep. Mr Hayden caressed us impartially for a while, passing his hands over our breasts, fingering the nipples until they stood up stiffly, and finally a hand drifted down over each of the two cunnies. The contact of his warm hand as it lay over mine with one of the fingers pressed lightly within the cleft produced in me an effect which was almost sufficient to put my orgastic mechanism into immediate action. I literally had to 'clench' my nerves and strain my willpower to keep from coming. Had he let his finger linger there a bit longer, or had he imparted the slightest friction, my efforts to restrain orgasm would have failed then and there.

But he removed it after a short interval without apparently having observed my delicate condition, and straightening out on his back he drew Hester across his body where, by urging her forward bit by bit, he eventually got her straddled across his chest with her knees doubled beneath her on either side of him. Her dark auburn curls were right at his chin and it required no great imagination to divine that her cunny was going to be licked French fashion.

'If he does that to her before my eyes I'll cream despite anything I can do to hold it back. I know I shall!' I thought to myself.

In the light of experience throughout subsequent years I confess this: that the sight of another woman being Frenched by a man, or a woman Frenching a man, reacts upon me more violently than any other spectacle of a lewd nature. My senses are excited to a frenzy at the sight of this act, and if I let myself go I can have an orgasm without even touching myself, but simply through the impulse conveyed to the genital system through the trajectory of the eye.

Having accommodated Hester comfortably on his strong chest, Mr Hayden reached over and took me by the arm, manifesting by his motions that I was to seat myself across his middle, impaled upon the turgid emblem of masculinity, behind Hester. Obeying his wordless indications I crouched over him, passing my arm around Hester and clasping her plump bubbies in my hand. Then, gently, breathlessly, I sank down until I felt the entire length of that glorious member throbbing within the living sheath I was providing for it.

But, alas, to my consternation, barely had I perceived the contact of his crisp hair on my naked cunny than my emotions, overriding all powers of resistance, as though deriding my futile efforts to hold them in abeyance, rebelling incontinently, loosed themselves and in a second I was gasping, writhing and suspiring in a regular paroxysm of passionate ecstasy.

As the reverberations gradually died away and my thoughts took on a semblance of coherency, I was filled with mortification. What would Mr Hayden think of such amazing lubricity and precipitation? Hester, surprised at first, had twisted around, and now burst into laughter.

'What happened?' she gasped.

'I don't know! I did it . . . I couldn't help it!' I answered, shamefaced.

Mr Hayden was also laughing.

'You're a fast worker, sister,' he said, his sides shaking, and realising that I was momentaruly, at least, exhausted by the orgasm, he added compassionately: 'Better get off and rest a moment while Hester and I catch up with you!'

I discharged myself and threw my still trembling body on the bed beside them. With his hands against Hester's knees Mr Hayden pushed her backward to take the place I had vacated and a moment later his cock slid in between her legs. Crouching over him, supporting herself on her hands, Hester worked gently up and down on the glistening shaft, alternating from time to time, with a twisting, rolling movement of her hips as she sank down upon his member, completely hiding it from view.

As I watched this sensuous play the tide of my own passions began to gather anew. Yielding to sudden impulse I inserted my hand between Hester's thigh and got my fingers around the base of the white column which was transfixing her. With each of her downward lunges my hand was compressed between the two bodies, and each time it was compressed my own clitoris throbbed in sympathy.

Hester began to moan softly. A delicate colour crept into her pretty cheeks, and her movements became more vigorous. As I perceived the more powerful pressure of her moist cunny crushing down upon my fist, and the strong, regular pulsations in the hard flesh about which my fingers were clenched, the fires of reawakened lust again glazed within me. My sexual potency was back in full force.

In this opportune moment Mr Hayden murmured something to Hester. Instantly she ceded the post of honour, slipped forward, and again crouched over his face. A second later I was on the throne she had vacated, and with my arms embracing her from behind, was quivering in response to the throbbing of the rigid shaft which penetrated me and filled me with its soul-stirring warmth.

To the accompaniment of Hester's low moans as a vigorous and active tongue teased her organism into expression I gasped out my own ecstasy and clung to her, half-fainting, while jet after jet of the hot balsam of life flung itself against my womb.

I was no longer a novice. I had graduated from the chippy stage of harlotry and was a full-fledged practitioner of the oldest profession. I was now a professional prostitute.

Mr Hayden came regularly, adhering faithfully to his programme of impartiality, and his visits were interludes in which both Hester and I forgot the sordid, commercialised circumstances under which we were prostituting our bodies and enjoyed ourselves like healthy, robust young animals.

GUS TOLMAN

A short but energetic piece of sexual bravado, Gus
Tolman *is of early twentieth century American origin.
Our hero Gus is a wonder of manhood, 'of commanding
physique' and 'strikingly attractive' who holds every
woman spellbound. More specifically (and like many a
hero of the erotic genre) he is blessed with prodigious
sexual equipment over which he is able to exert such
amazing control that any partner is guaranteed 'transports of the wildest joy and supreme ecstasy'. Added to
which, Gus is a musician – a pianist, naturally – of
such sensitivity and touch that he can play upon the
bodies of his lovers as skilfully as he can upon the
keyboard of a baby grand. In short, despite the anaphro-
disiac effect of his name – often rendered in moments
of supreme emotion as 'Gussie' – he is the kind of super-
lover only to be found in books.*

*His fictional confessions, however, make for some rol-
licking reading. As befits a true sexual opportunist, Gus
is a generous soul and here he is to be found saving
a neighbour from certain solitary vices – in order to
introduce her to more social ones. The boy's all
heart . . .*

Passing in and out of the house where I had a room, I frequently noticed a young lady of attractive face and figure with dark hair, who appealed to me very much.

At the very first I was not so much attracted to her until I noticed how she ogled me and the peculiar expression in her eyes whenever she looked my way. Then I began to get interested.

I began to study her. On closer observation I noticed that she was really quite pretty in a way, and that she possessed a tempting figure. One evening, as we were both returning to our respective rooms, I noticed her attire and discovered that she had the room next to mine, looking out onto a narrow balcony. She was attractively gowned in a light summer dress with short sleeves and the neck was cut low enough to reveal a plumpness of the bust. I tarried in the hall to let her precede me up the stairs.

Her rather short skirts displayed a pair of neat trim ankles and a pretty pair of shapely legs fitted in sheer smooth stockings. A pretty leg always made me long to see more, and I usually got a hunch as to whether or not I could feel of it. I managed to get a long look as she slowly preceded me up the stairs.

When we reached the top I spoke: 'Pardon my intrusion and boldness but I would surely like to know the girl with such a pretty figure. You are most attractive.'

She gasped and turned a frightened look towards me. I then got a good look at her face by means of the light overhead. I noted a peculiar, languorous look in her dark eyes. The face had all the marks of a nature which was more or less sensual.

I detected a look of lecherous longing as her eyes swept over me as if she were sizing me up. I made up my mind right then to get close to this beautiful girl. Her voice trembled and her bosom heaved with apparent emotion as she softly murmured: 'I am Miss Taylor – who are you?' I introduced myself in my usual debonair manner, which seemed to attract her. 'May I have the pleasure of calling on you?'

'Sometime,' she bashfully answered as she passed through her door and closed it.

I noticed that she did not lock her door, having probably forgotten in her confusion. I entered my room and for the first time noticed the very thin partition between it and Miss Taylor's room. I later heard strange sounds like moans from a woman in distress. Then I distinctly heard a one-sided conversation; she was apparently talking to herself and this is what I heard: 'Oh – Oh – if I could only have a lover like that man,' she said trembling. 'He – he – is so big and handsome.'

I could hear her voice shake, as if she was under some great strain or emotion. I remembered the sensual expression on her face as the dreamy, pathetic eyes swept over me. Surely, I thought, the poor girl is in heat and apparently craves relief. While I was

302

preparing for bed, and removing my shoes, my eye caught sight of a register in the partition, evidently used in the winter to allow a circulation of warm air. Upon examining it, I found that it opened very easily and through the grill frame I had a wide view of Miss Taylor's room. In my range of vision I saw the bed and an upholstered chair of generous capacity. Opposite this was a bureau with a large tilting mirror.

Miss Taylor was standing before the mirror, slowly removing the belt from her waist and gazing intently with that same languorous look at some pictures on the wall on either side of the mirror. Peering intently, I discovered that they were pictures of men, three of a stalwart pugilist in different poses stripped, but with a sash to hide his bulging genitals. Other pictures were of actors, presumably matinee idols, but the girl's eyes lingered on the muscular figure of the pugilist.

I saw her full red lips move as if she were talking to the fighter. Lifting up a pair of pretty white bubbies out of her corset, she bounced them up and down, then spoke in a low hysterical voice: 'Oh, Jack, see my titties – come – to – me – and – fondle them.'

I was no longer puzzled. The girl was hot and she was calling to Jack, the pugilist, as an imaginary lover. Her thoughts were lustily centred on the fleshy pleasures such a body would impart if she could but hold it in her arms and feel the strong sexual embrace and enjoyment that might result. In her impulsive emotions the girl tore off her corsets and then slipped out of her dress and drawers. She stood there revealed in nothing but her stockings and under-vest, which she quickly removed. When I saw what a finely built young girl she was, that settled it. She had to be gratified. I lay on my back so I could better contemplate with ease what might transpire in the girl's room.

She was about twenty and I could plainly see her white nude body, rich in lovely contours and graceful curves, together with a very disturbing view of her

303

dark thickly haired pussy and her white cherry tipped bubbies. They made me rampant, and my tool was standing straight up. I doubtless would have made a rush through the door to the girl if my curiosity had not gotten the better of me. I gasped when I saw her press her hand to her pussy and insert a finger and again gaze at the picture of the pugilist as she vigorously rubbed and worked her finger in and out.

Her feelings were getting the better of her and as she worked herself up to a pitch of passionate frenzy, a wave of erotic emotion spread a lovely glow over her shapely charms. As if suddenly thinking of something, she unlocked the bureau drawers and extracted a book and a small packet from which she selected several pictures, evidently an obscene book, as I later discovered.

Reclining on the edge of the bed, with one leg hanging over the side, she switched on a reading lamp over her head, which gave me a brilliantly lighted view of the girl's tempting and sensual body in a voluptuous pose. The line of my vision took in every detail of a plump and well defined cunnie between a pair of lovely white thighs. The contrast of the dark thick curls made her belly and thighs appear like alabaster.

Adjusting her pillow, the girl began reading, holding two of the pictures on the edge of the book, leaving her right hand free. Occasionally she would gloat on her own charms reflected in the tilting mirror. At the same time she would pinch and titillate the stiff red nipples of her firm round bubbies.

The swelling, curly mound and pretty round belly began to rise and fall with convulsions and erotic longings as she gloated over the book and pictures. Inflamed to a frenzy the girl's hand slipped down and covered the restless pussy. Then with her middle finger she sought to appease her passions with a rapid nervous thrust and pressure on the burning clitty. Suddenly, apparently coming to a passage in her book which inflamed the poor girl, she gasped aloud. I heard a smothered cry – 'Oh, how lovely – how I'd – like – to – be – in her place.' Then holding the pictures close she gazed with languorous eyes and clasped the whole of the plump curly cunnie in her hand with two fingers in it, squeezing it hard.

The heavy breathing and groans told me of her approaching crisis. Dropping the pictures, her head went back to the pillows. Her limbs twitched and quivered. The pretty bubbies trembled. Then with a convulsive heave and choking expressions of pleasure, as ' – Oh – Oh – how – good,' spasm after spasm of voluptuous ecstasy swept over her in a thrilling orgasm.

She trembled and shivered terrifically, holding her hand very tightly over her cunnie for a short while, and then seemed to die away in a languorous doze for a few minutes. When she finally picked up her book and continued to read she was so worked up that she was as frantic for relief as before. All the time she had held her hand on her moist cunnie, though without moving it at all. Occasionally she would pick up the pictures again and look at them and then go back to her book. This she kept up for some little time, for the book was apparently very interesting.

Finally, however, she threw down the book and began irritating herself in real earnest. Her magnificent bubbies she could just pull up so as to make her lips grasp the nipples and these she sucked hard, at the same time playing her fingers around her cunnie. Then she used one hand to inflame her clitoris and with the other hand she inserted a finger deep in her cunnie until, judging by her emotions, she was coming, she frantically drove three fingers deep into it and worked them in and out fast until she died away in a glorious spend.

This sight was too much for me. I was lying on my back and was naked. I had become so inflamed and highly sensitised that the scene was like a match to dry powder. My erect and well primed penis went off and shot stretches of pearly juice high into the air. It was all that I could do to withhold a cry of delight, for the spend and the sensations accompanying it were terrific. It fell in little puddles all over my belly as I watched the throes and last tremors of the gratified girl. She got up, put on her nightgown and replacing the book and pictures in the bureau drawer, retired.

I quietly closed the register and crawled into bed. In the morning I awoke with my usual morning hardon and lay awake planning how to have Miss Taylor and to get a glimpse of her book and pictures. I heard her go out at seven-thirty. Getting up and dressing I took the key to my bureau drawer, feeling sure that it would also fit her drawer. Going to her door I found it unlocked. Entering and closing the door I tried the key. It fitted. I found the book that the girl had been reading and the package of pictures. The book was called *The Education of Laura* and was intended to inflame passion and instruct girls in sexual pleasures. The photos were faithful pictures of men and women together in all the known positions of indulgence.

No wonder I thought that she was a masturbator. But why she resorted to it was a mystery to me for she was a girl to attract any man sexually. I made my plans to see her that evening when she would return from work. She returned and dressed for dinner in a most attractive dress, and for some unknown reason left off her corsets and put on a pair of those late fashionable hosettes coming just above the calf, leaving the knees bare.

Apparently she was prone to making herself attractive to men. On this occasion she wore very little under a thin organdy dress, through which could be seen the distinct outlines of a remarkably well-shaped leg and thigh. She also left off her drawers. It might have been that she wanted to make a hit with me, but that I didn't know yet. She was standing in the main hall before the open front door when I came out of the dining room. My alert eye caught the alluring view as the light showed through the girl's skirts, outlining the attractive curves and contours.

Passing out on the large veranda, where there were chairs, all occupied but one, which Miss Taylor took, I seated myself on a step below and facing her. Glancing up I had a tantalising view of the bare knees, which were crossed in careless girlish pose. Several times I caught glimpses of a dark brown tuft between the plump white thighs. I was getting too conspicuously uncomfortable and randy for comfort. Miss Taylor noticed the restless shifting and gloating eyes as I glanced up. She too, got restless. The fact that I was watching her with lustful longing aroused all the sensual fires in her passionate body. Did I really like her, was probably the girl's thought as she watched me out of half-closed eyes. Strategy was one of my strong assets. Suddenly I arose and asked her to take a stroll to get an ice-cream soda. At first she demurred, then bashfully consented. Once out on the street she became a little more sociable.

'If you don't mind, Mister Tolman, I'd like to have a gingerale highball,' she said as we walked along.

'Sure thing, my dear,' I answered, 'sodas are not much good when one is as uncomfortable as we are. By the way what is your first name?'

'Margery – Madge for short,' replied the girl. For an hour she conversed and showed absolutely no signs of the seething desires that were teasing her young pussy. Her nature was not revealed. On the way home I took her arm, delicately passing my hand up and down the soft cool flesh.

'Madge, dear,' I said to her in my tenderest way, 'mayn't I sit with you in your room tonight? I have something most important to tell you.'

The poor girl got so frightened and flushed she

almost collapsed, but answered in a low trembling tone: 'I – I don't know – would – would it be safe?'

'Why, my dear girl, I hope you are not afraid of me, and no one would know anything about it in your room,' I said reassuringly. She said nothing but I could detect a tumultuous storm in the heaving of her firm round bubbies and trembling steps. Reaching the house I begged her to remain on the steps until I got to my room, then when hearing her enter her room, I would call. She followed the instructions to the letter.

I knocked on the door. I then heard a fluttering voice: 'C – Come in.' When I stood before her in a white silk shirt turned down at the neck and short sleeves and wearing blue flannel trousers that displayed my muscular limbs, Margery gasped and almost fainted, but finally said:

'Oh, Mister Tolman, I have never allowed a man in my room before. Tell me what you want with a poor working girl like me? You are so big and handsome that you embarrass me.'

The door was closed and covered with drapery that smothered out all sounds of voices from within. Madge remained standing as I stepped up to her side, and anxious of my opportunity to begin, I said:

'My dear little girl, what I am going to say is for your own good and safety.' She again got frightened, her eyes usually so languorous and wide, her scarlet lips hung apart as she breathlessly waited.

'My dear Madge,' I said tenderly, 'do you know that you are doing yourself an awful injury and injustice every time you indulge your passions as you did last night?'

The frightened and surprised girl gasped, 'My God!' and then fainted. I caught her in my arms and picking her up, I sat down in a large easy chair and held the unconscious girl on my lap. The feeling of her soft corsetless body and pressure of the soft round bottom on my penis inflamed instantly.

My tool stiffened and assumed its splendid throbbing proportions. Reaching a bottle of smelling salts I saw on the bureau, I held it to her nose, then chaffed her hands. Pulling up her skirts I slapped and squeezed the plump dimpled knees. My other hand was moulding a lovely tittie. My lips were grazing a velvety cheek. Presently Madge showed signs of reviving. I fondled her bare knees with affectionate caresses and pressures on the nerves that I knew would excite sensations of passion, moving my hand always further up. Her flesh was like the softest velvet.

My rampant tool was moving and bounding against her little pussy. Of course she could feel it through her clothing. Her eyes opened, she drew a long breath and cuddled closer to me, then in a frightened voice she asked:

'Where am I? What has happened?'

'In your lover's arms, who thinks you are the most beautiful and sweetest little peach in the world. Kiss me, Madge,' I said. She didn't speak, but I could tell that she was gradually warming up from her restless breathing and squirming bottom, but she did not want me to know it. She was shy and somewhat frightened at the suddenness of the situation. Finally when she remembered what I had told her of the night before, she straightened out and putting on an air of injury from the liberty and accusation, she stimulated a resentment, but she knew that she was guilty.

'How do you know – how can you – say – such a thing? How dare you?' I was amused. 'Why my dear,' I replied, 'it was very easy. I was in my room and I overheard your moans and cries. I was alarmed and seeing that register I took a chance of looking through it to ascertain the trouble, and what I saw you doing to yourself made me feel terrible to think that a lovely young girl would injure yourself in that way. Tell me Margery, why do you do it, when you can have a lover?'

'Then with a trembling voice and tears in her dark

eyes, she related how she had been taught to gratify her passions, that all her life she had been a victim of uncontrollable passions – that because a girl friend had once let a man have her and she became pregnant and she was always afraid to let a man have her out of fear.

'Why, Gus, that same girl after that gratified herself with her fingers. She was like me, always hot, and it was she who taught me to do it to myself, giving me naughty books and pictures, she got from a man. Is it any wonder that I do it?'

'Not a bit,' I answered. 'But don't you know that you could have a man without serious results?'

'No! How?' cried the girl. I then explained if a girl indulged her passions with a man in the week before her periods or used a strong solution for a douche before and after each time, she would be perfectly safe.

The effect of my hand on her knees and my throbbing tool had so inflamed Madge she was in a tumultuous flutter. 'OO – oo, Gus,' she gasped. 'I must tell my friend Tessie.' Then winding her arms about me she kissed me with her moist red lips, clinging to me with ardent longing. Suddenly and with impulsive emotion, Madge parted her thighs and whispered:

'Fondle me – Gus – I – I'm – I'm so passionate.' I laid my hand over the curly plump nest. 'Oh, Gus – put your finger into it – and make me – spend.'

'Ah, no, my dear,' I said. 'I'm going to break you of that habit, it's not good nor healthy for you and besides it's not natural. Why can't we have the real pleasures together? It's so much lovelier.'

'Oh, Gus, I'd like to, but I'm afraid. I'd surely get caught and I've never done that in my life. I haven't even seen a real live thing, only the pictures that I have.'

'Well, my dear girl,' I said, 'do you want to see one and even have it in you and make you feel so good –

oh so good, better than you have ever felt when you did it with your finger?'

'Oh, heavens, yes, I'm just insane for it, but I'm too scared of it.'

I had been fondling her smooth round belly and tickling her highly sensitive clitty. I stopped and asked her to let me stand up and show her something that beat a finger or candle all to bits. Curious and eager with passion to see what she had seen in hot lascivious dreams, the girl stood leaning against a long library table as I lowered my trousers and released my prodigious tool. It popped out and stood proudly erect and flaming with fiery vigour.

The girl, with eyes aflame with wonder and interest, just stood and gazed. Her face was a study, first blushing a deep scarlet, then distorted with fear, her face lighting up with a hungry gleam of lustful passion. With a choking gulp Madge managed to speak in a half whisper:

'Heavens, Gus, it doesn't look anything like those in my pictures, but it's glorious – a monster. My God! How can a girl take it? I never saw a real live one before.'

I moved towards the girl and she almost shrank. 'Feel it, girlie,' I said. 'It won't hurt you.' Slyly and with girlish modesty Madge placed her hand on it, her fingers just encircling it. They slipped along until her hand held the turgid purple knob in its palm, she squeezed it, then gasped, her panting bubbies heaving and rising and falling in a tumult of erotic sensations.

Remembering some of the lewd acts shown in the photos and described in her book, Madge became very eager.

'May I kiss it, Gus?' she asked. 'Why, of course, if you'll let me kiss yours,' I replied.

'Oh – where? when? how?'

I quickly cleared the table and placed some cushions upon it.

'Now I'll show you for you are a real scout, Madge, and one of the most lovable and fuckable girls I ever knew,' I said. I picked her up and placed her on the table with her peachy bottom on the edge, and directed her to place her feet on the back of a chair I had drawn up behind me. It was my usual preliminary to this, my favourite position to win a woman over. Throwing her dress back and exposing Madge's delectable charms, I feasted my eyes on one of the prettiest bellies and pussies I had ever seen. Such lovely legs and thighs, such a plump and creamy bottom, spread out under the fluffy bunch of dark brown curls, through which the pulpy lips of her moist cunnie were pouting, opening and closing with hot longing.

A bright red clitty protruded stiff and pert. Altogether, Margery's pussy offered about as tempting a feast as any man would wish to see between a pair of shapely legs. I patted and caressed the round white belly and velvety plump inside of the girl's thighs, all the time gloating on the delicious morsel nestled in a thick tuft of silky curls, till I was hungry for it. 'Oh, Gus,' she said, 'will you do what the book calls – lapping the cunt?'

'Why, of course, Madge, and a lot more,' I replied as I proceeded to lay back the thick soft lips and opened up the red meaty interior, disclosing a small puckering orifice, with palpitant longing. I placed my mouth to the distended gap and the fragrant mellow lips closed about my mouth. At the first thrust of my tongue, Margery almost screamed from the new and novel sensation. The faster my tongue glided in and out, the tighter she clasped my head between her convulsed thighs. All she could utter was a trembling. 'Oh, how good – that – feels – Oh God, don't stop!'

I then began a lively tongue play on the stiff clitoris till the poor girl was almost insane with a desire to spend. 'For heaven's sake, bring it,' she pleaded pathetically.

'Yes, pet, I'll make you go off and spend more than you ever did before. When did you say you were last unwell?'

'Ten days ago,' replied Margery with quickened delight. 'Good,' I said, getting to my feet. I had placed the table in front of the mirror and I tilted it to reflect every detail. Taking a soft shapely leg under each arm, I opened Margery's moist and quivering cunnie and guiding my restless penis, I rubbed the purple knob all about the gap.

'Watch in the glass,' I said, as I titillated the sensitive clitoris. The girl was watching every detail, her eyes limpidly languorous, her crimson lips parted in a sensuous smile. When I began to force the head of the ferocious tool into the tight puckering orifice she gave a smothered groan: 'You'll never get that big thing into me. It'll kill me.'

'Yes, dear, it'll kill you with pleasure.' I got the head well in and then stopped to play with the creamy bubbies and tickle her clitty and wait for her to get accustomed to the stretched feeling. She began to sigh and squirm and then murmured softly: 'Oh, Gus it feels so good – I – I – think that you can go a little farther.'She closed her eyes and then gripped the table when I made a lunge that sent the turgid tool into the juicy depths till it bumped against her womb. She gave a smothered scream, her eyes were swimming and her bubbies heaving with a voluptuous sensation. Slowly and sensuously I moved back and forth now.

'There, Madge,' I said softly, 'isn't that nicer than your finger or a candle?'

'Oh, God, yes,' she exclaimed, 'it's heavenly. Do it faster.' I held her belly and with lively hip action, I twisted and screwed the lustful creature. 'OO – Oh, it's lovely – Oh – I'm dying – hold – me – it's – coming – Oh – how – good – now – now – Oh, darling.' I distinctly felt her throbbing womb as each spasm of her orgasm shook her inflamed body and made her breathe hard and stammer her expressions of voluptuous sensations. The amorous girl was so inflamed that her unappeased passion made her call out in her agony of erotic emotions, 'Don't stop, for God's sake, don't stop – I'm not half gratified – I never imagined – it – was half so – lovely to be properly fucked.'

Suddenly realising my immense tool was still stiff and in full vigour and believing that I had spent, Margery looked at me with amazement and dreamy eyes and said, 'Didn't you come?' 'No, my lovely little Madge, I'll not spend until I've made you go off again, and say – no more finger fucks for me.'

'I'll never do it that way after this,' she replied. 'I shall tell my friend all about it. Will you give her a treat like this some time, too?'

'Sure,' I replied, 'if she'd like me well enough to let me.' And then I continued to feast my fleshy appetite on the girl's lascivious charms. Margery indulged her own sensual nature and revelled in thoughts of lascivious pleasures in company with me and her friend Tessie. 'Oh, she will, Tess will go wild when she meets you and sees your lovely big thing,' she said. 'She is just crazy to have a big strong man. Can't we three make a party some night together?'

'Of course. We'll go to a hotel,' I answered, pleased.

'Oh, Gus, you make me so passionate, I could scream. Do it faster!'

I pressed the turgid bursting head against her womb and made it throb and tickle her, sending thrills of lustful emotions over her trembling body. 'Oh, Gus! Oh!' she moaned, as I worked my tool in and out with a lustful spiral motion.

'How's that, girlie?' I asked.

'Oh, it's great – it's – com – ing – fuck me – fuck me hard – Oh, my God!' And her eyes rolled and sank back into her head, showing only the whites.

I groaned. I had held back as long as I could. 'Oh, baby,' I hollered. 'I'm coming, too – suck it – so – so

– ' I cried, as Margery's nipping cunnie closed with convulsive spasms. 'Ah, – there – there,' as I shot a charge of hot balsamic juice into the girl's belly. She lay still and received the balmy delirious juice in ecstasy.

Before the last sensuous thrill had passed, I picked up the half-conscious girl and carried her to the bed with my reeking stiff still in her. Getting off my shirt, I managed to divest Margery of her clothes and then we lay for some time in a languid sea of blissful content, till I got eager for another orgasm.

Getting on top of her, I placed it in her with frenzied frictional thrusts till we both died away again in a voluptuously complete finish. I got up and returned to my room to let the poor girl sleep off the effects of our dream of pleasures such as she had never experienced before.

Two days later I met Madge and she passed the word to me: 'Tessie will be here to meet you at eight o'clock in my room. Come at that time and knock.'

I made a careful preparation for conquest and a night with my latest finds. First engaging a room at a hotel of unquestioned privacy and then completing a toilet that would prove the way to conquest. I wore a Palm Beach suit over a sheer silk shirt with no underwear. I had, without a doubt, an attractive figure and my close-fitting trousers displayed my muscular limbs and abnormal sexual development to good advantage.

Promptly at eight o'clock I heard Madge in her room, and then a cheery voice: 'Gee, Madge, I'm just wild to meet your friend. How do I look?' asked Tessie as she threw off her cape. 'Say, Tess,' said Madge, 'he will go wild and eat you alive when he sees your bare back, it's lovely.' She had left her entire back exposed to her waistline with but a narrow line over each shoulder, the front being so thin that even the stiff red nipple points of a pair of the prettiest bubbies stuck out alluringly. Tessie was taller than Madge, with remarkably pretty arms and legs – not large but tempting in form and shape. She possessed a bottom that was ravishing in contour and agility. She wore nothing else but a lace petticoat and black silk stockings, gartered well above the knees.

When I answered the call to enter, the vision that met my gaze, startled me. 'Miss Tessie Bangs,' said Margery, introducing us, 'this is Mr. Tolman.' I bowed low as I took Tessie's hand and kissed it. She shivered for she felt a thrill go through her. 'Surely,' I said, 'this is a refreshing pleasure.' Tess was speechless as her eyes swept over my figure and when she could speak, her voice was low and musical, 'I am equally delighted,' she said, 'I do hope your pleasure will be equal to mine.'

'Well,' I said, 'judging from appearance, when I see more of you, I know that my pleasure will know no bounds. You are the peachiest looking and most delectable looking chicken I've met in years.' She resented the term I gave her. Her big blue eyes flashed and with a vivacious but injured dignity she retorted: 'I beg your pardon Mister Tolman, I'm no chicken and you needn't think that because Margery Taylor fell for you and you happen to be a handsome brute, I shall fall, too.'

I saw that she meant every word and that I would be obliged to trim her claws as I had often done with others. I replied, looking steadily and smilingly into her flashing eyes, 'You are a chicken and a deucedly tempting bird to broil, and with proper seasoning you will make fine eating.' Tessie gasped, for she knew well what I meant.

'I never met up with such nerve before,' she said. Her practised eye caught sight of the bulging outlines of my abnormal sexual charm, already showing signs of vigour and life. She jumped back with a twist of her pretty shoulders and shaking her pendulous bubbies. 'My God, man, but you are immense,' she said, still

316

gloating on my tool and balls, which showed plainly through my light trousers.

'Pshaw, Tess,' spoke up Margery, 'you ought to see it out and stiff. Take it out, Gus.' It was my plan to work Tess up until she was at the point of begging for it, but as she seemed curious and willing, I unbuttoned my trousers, but first I stepped up to her and without warning clasped her lithe and willowy form in my arms and pressed her mound to my rapidly stiffening tool by placing a convulsive hand on her plump bottom.

She tried to wriggle loose, but the more she wriggled the stiffer my penis became till it throbbed against her pussy. The sensation was so exciting to her that she just hung limp in my arms and shivered. I kissed her and then when my mouth closed over her ruby lips, I thrust my tongue into her mouth and squeezed her soft bottom with both my eager hands.

She returned my kisses almost unconsciously as she gazed at me with limpid, languorous eyes. Once or twice she half clung to me and when I began to run my tongue between her lips, it was too much for her. She just hung onto me enough to keep from falling.

All of a sudden, tearing her mouth loose, she cried out in a frantic appeal:

'Stop, I don't mean to let you get fresh with me!'

My hands and touchings were doing their work, however. I slipped one hand all over her smooth bare back, tickling her spine at the same time and running my tongue around her neck under her chin and ears. Her eyes flushed, her bottom wriggled – she laughed and then began to scratch. I realised I had an unusually spiteful chicken to deal with. Shaking my trousers loose, my rampant penis came forth in all its passionate splendour.

'Oh, look Tessie,' said Margery, laughing. In her excitement and struggle one of her hands came in contact with it. Like oil on troubled waters, her flush of injured dignity subsided and she melted in my arms like jelly in a mould, and hung limp from surprise and suddenly aroused emotions. At first she couldn't speak, she seemed so dazed. Then with sudden curiosity, her hand went to the prodigious, throbbing weapon, her long tapering fingers closing about it. Gasping she drew back to look: 'Good God,' she exclaimed, 'what is it, a bone or a club?'

'The stick that you are going to be broiled on, my dear,' I said.

'Never, never!' cried the astonished girl, looking at it and squeezing the long hard shaft. 'Why that thing would kill me.'

'Aw, go on,' laughed Margery.

'I'll be,' said Tess to her, 'you never had that brute of a thing in you. You told a fib. I never heard of a man having a tool like that.'

'Ah, Tess, just you wait until it's in you, and you'll see all the stars in creation and go off like you never did before, and I'll bet that you'll never want anything else. Why Tess, it beats a finger or a candle a thousand ways. To be broiled on that darling cock is a treat you'll never forget.'

Then turning to me, Margery kissed me and said: 'Strip, Gus, and let Tessie see.' 'I will if she'll do the same,' I replied. Margery led the way and began to undress. She hadn't much on to be taken off. Tessie was now gay and festive, lively as could be. She and Margery were soon stripped to their stockings and I gazed with lustful enthusiasm on two of the most charming and fuckable damsels I ever laid my eyes on. Tessie was perfect in symmetry and shapeliness. Tall and graceful, she was exquisitely rounded with a pair of luscious, slightly drooping bubbies, not as large as Margery's but just as lovely to play with and mould in the hands. She had a prominent, protruding mound covered with a profusion of thick blonde curly hair like silk, through which the pretty deep slit of a plump pussy could be seen.

I was now more than rampant to get at it. I stripped naked, to my socks. When Tessie's eyes swept over me, she gasped with carnal admiration, her eyes almost popping out of her head as she gloated on my penis, which she expected to be broiled upon.

'My God, Madge,' she exclaimed, 'I don't wonder that you fell for him, he is magnificent, but I'll have to see you take that tool before I'll believe you had it in your little cunnie,' she said, as she again felt of it with trembling hands, trying to pull it away from my belly, where it stood stiff as a bar of iron. It slipped from her hand and sprung back with a thud. Tessie giggled and continued to enjoy the unusual vigorous elasticity of the perky, obstreperous penis.

'Let's get busy,' I said. 'I'm getting too hot for comfort and I'm anxious for a drink. We'll have a round, go out for a highball, and then go to a room I've engaged for the night. You two lovely chickens have to broil on both sides thoroughly, so let's get busy while the bone is in good form.'

'I want to see Madge take it first,' said Tessie with a mischievous and lustful thrust of her naughty handsome bottom. I arranged the table with cushions and directed Margery to lie on it as on the first night when she was initiated.

Margery looked most tempting and desirable as she lay with her legs wide open and her peachy, salacious pussy ready for the stick. Two firm milky bubbies, with their stiff red nipples pointing straight up and out, invited kisses.

'Now, Gus,' laughed Tessie, 'do exactly what you did to her the other night. I want to see how you got that awful thing into her tight little cunnie.'

I seated myself directly in front of the voluptuous little pussy with Margery resting her pretty fat legs on each shoulder. 'My God,' exclaimed Tessie, all curious and getting hotter every minute, 'I've had some fun in my life but I was never kissed there.'

I began my feast with hot kisses on the pretty rounded belly and on the soft white insides of her thighs to arouse keener sensations of desire. I then titillated her with lively tongue play on her perky, red clitoris.

Madge began to moan, but when the ardent sweep of my tongue along the pouting slit penetrated the puckering orifice, she trembled and cried out: 'Oh – Tess – ie – wait – till he does this to you – Oh, it's so good – Oh.' When I thrust my tongue into the salacious meaty depths of her pussy and tickled her womb, Margery suppressed a scream, shook all over and cried: 'Oh, Tessie – suck my titties, quick – I'm – I'm – com – com – ing.' Tessie quickly took a big red nipple in her mouth and tickled the other one with her fingernails. As nothing excites a woman to spend as quickly as that, Margery just moaned and heaved and clutched at her friend and cried out: 'Oh, Tess! There – there – Oh – how good – OO – oo – Oh!'

I received her sweet, creamy spend on my tongue and sucked it up as it flowed freely. She being thoroughly lubricated, I got to my feet, and taking the bursting red tool in my hand I worked the swollen inflamed head all about in the juicy slit, while Tessie stood by holding apart the fat lips and watching the all-absorbing and lascivious act of broiling Madge. Her eyes wide, almost popping out, her snowy bosom heaving with excitement and her pussy itching and twitching, Tessie saw me plunge my frenzied penis into Margery to the hilt. Madge stuffed her fist into her mouth to smother her cries and screams of lustful pleasure. I worked my tool back and forth with sensuous effect and Tessie, watching it as it went in and out, almost screamed herself.

'Hurry, Madge, I'm just dying for a piece,' Tessie again tickled the quivering red nipples. Madge cried out: 'Oh, God! It's coming – what a lovely – fuck.' Her voice died away. I pulled out my inflamed tool reeking with her pearly spend and lifting Madge up I laid her on the bed, telling Tessie to get on the table. I had not spent for I wanted to save it for the excited Tessie.

The table was before the mirror and when Tessie discovered that she could watch herself being fucked, she laughed in glee. I stood for a moment to gloat on the exquisitely lovely charms of this delectable girl, fondling every part of her. Then taking my place again in the chair between the prettily shaped legs out-stretched for the kisses, I gazed lustfully at one of the prettiest and alluring pussies I ever saw. Profusely covered with silky blonde hair, it stood out plump and impudent. Tessie had what might be termed a real hardon, for the outer lips were hard and horny and her clitty stuck out its red nose stiffly. I noted the delectable, sweet scented, savoury condition of her pri-vate parts. Holding the soft cheeks of her fat bottom apart, I gazed fondly at all her beauties when she anxiously wound her fat legs around my neck and exclaimed, 'My God, what a lover you are!'

I now buried my nose in her slit and worked my tongue deep in. She bit her lips and exclaimed with a deep moan: 'Suck me.'

I then gave her the same tonguing I had just given Madge, but I fairly ate the mellow meaty interior with lively tongue thrusts.

I gathered all the ripe parts on her cunnie into my mouth and sucked like mad, with my tongue rubbing her stiffened clitty. Tessie was trembling and quiver-ing all over. 'Wow! Oh! Ouch!' she cried. Her cry aroused Margery from her languor, and she came smil-ing to the side of the table.

'Oh, Madge,' she cried, 'he's sucking the life out of me – oo – oo – Oh, how I'm spending!'

'Isn't it great?' asked Madge, patting Tessie's titties and pinching the little stiff nipples.

'Oh, it's heavenly,' replied Tessie as she died away in another swoon of voluptuous ecstasy. I jumped up then with a terrible hardon that was actually painful. It was forbidding in appearance. Tessie had never seen nor dreamed of a penis like it before. Handsome it was, to say the least, with its splendid appendages like ripe fruit bursting with a wealth of rich juices.

Tessie's eyes, languorous with the sensual after effects of a copious spend, looked with fear as I stood beside her. In a voice trembling with apprehension, she said: 'Let – let me feel it, Gus, it's awful.'

I stepped closer to her, and she felt the awful thing from the balls to the tip of the turgid knob as if testing and measuring its size and power. I took it in my hand and moved the knob around in her neck, under her chin and ears. She murmured:

'Oh, you beauty. Now I'm ready – Oh, Gus, be careful, won't you?'

'Yes,' I answered.

'Then broil me and do it good, I'm hot as a blister,' and to Madge she said, 'don't leave me, Madge,.and give me a handkerchief.'

I took a pretty leg under each arm and Madge stood by to assist. She pulled the inflamed fat lips apart, revealing its red meaty interior and puckering orifice from which oozed traces of her recent spending. I moved my tool up and down and rubbed the quivering inflamed clitty. 'Oh, God! that's exciting,' she cried out suddenly, 'put it in quick,'

I placed the almost bursting knob at the entrance and pushed. She gasped and stuffed the handkerchief into her mouth to smother a cry of pain. With the head just inside, I waited for her to get accustomed to the stretching. The nipping stricture was maddening to me. Tessie relieved her mouth long enough to say, 'All of it, Gus – I – I – want it all!' Replacing the wad of handkerchief in her mouth, she grabbed Margery. I braced myself and clutching the girl's squirming hips, I crammed my penis into the tight hot depths till it was completely sheathed. How she did squirm and writhe. I hollered myself with sensuous delight, exclaiming:

'Oh, Tes – sie – what a perfect cunt you have .'

Her pain had subsided, she removed the cloth from her mouth, her crimson lips parted in a smile of joy. Margery bit and sucked the stiff red nipples whilst I tickled her navel. 'What a pretty belly. What pretty legs. You two girls are the peachiest chickens to fuck that I ever knew,' I whispered as I moved my straining spear out and in, producing a fury of erotic thrills in us both. Tessie could not prolong the delightful indulgence long enough.

'Gee,' she gasped, 'I wish that it could last all night.'

Once her tongue was loosened she became obscene as her erotism increased. I was getting a royal feast of voluptuous sensation. The climax was approaching us both. Tessie's curly blonde head rolled from side to side – she clawed at her stomach and her milky panting bubbies as they rose and fell faster and faster with her quickened breath. I put my most masterful strokes to the frenzied girl with agonising thrills.

She hollered in smothered gusts, 'Oh, God! I'm coming!' Her arms dropped to her side.

'Somebody kiss me! Hold me! I'm dying! Oh – oo – oo.' Margery giggled. I grabbed the exploding girl in my arms, crushed a soft tittie in each hand and smothered her gasping cries with a tonguing kiss. She sucked the tongue almost out of me.

'There, you hot little cunt, take my sap, it's – good for you,' I said as I poured hot streams of delicious juice into the trembling girl, the jets piercing her like needles and bringing a secondary spend in which Tessie's eyes rolled back in erotic delirium. I laid her gently back and completed my own double spend in a blinding orgasm which shook me to my toes.

'Heavens,' cried Margery, 'you've got me so hot I can scarcely wait for another piece.' Tessie wriggled off the table and staggered as if drunk to the bed, where she laid in a half-faint from the effect of the frenzied orgy.

I quickly got a bottle of brandy. We all had a stiff drink and prepared to go out. After Tessie had had two drinks she was as lively as a cricket and ready for a frolic. Like a contortionist she writhed and displayed her enticing charms to excite the lewdest passions. Her sensual nature was thoroughly fired after getting a generous taste of my powers and my skillfully manipulated tool. She was wanton to the core. Before I had completed my toilet, Tessie kissed my penis. Being now soft and normal she drew it into her mouth and cuddled it with her tongue. 'Gee,' she exclaimed, 'I'd like to suck you off.' We were all hotter than blisters and ready for anything. We left the house unseen and were soon in the room I had engaged for the night. I ordered highballs with plenty of ginger. Both girls stripped, and jumping onto the table, they did a most exciting and lewd dance. Tessie was more agile than Madge, but Madge's movements were far more suggestive and voluptuous.

They had often practised together when under the influence of lecherous desire to indulge their wanton passion and to induce a spend would press their pussies together and rub and twist with their titties crushed together till a frenzied orgasm would reward their efforts. I watched the lascivious performance till I was so hot my turgid gun was standing cocky and purple and almost ready to go off. I grabbed both girls and fell with them on the bed. I was about to mount Tessie when she cried out:

'Hold on Gus. I'm hot, too hot for an old-fashioned fuck. I want a hootchie cootchie diddle.'

'How's that?' I asked.

She then directed me to lie across two chairs with my head on the bed and my knees hanging over the edge of the farthest chair while Madge was to straddle my head and press her cunnie to my mouth. This was a new trick but I liked the idea and at once arranged for it. I first drew both girls to the edge of the bed, with their plump bottoms on the edge, with their legs wide apart and knees drawn up.

The quivering swollen cunnies were then gaping open, the orifice of each pouting for something stiff. I took a highball and holding Madge's little hole well open, I poured into it a goodly portion and then held the lips together so it wouldn't spill, to let it soak in and heat up the tight little box. Dropping to my knees, I deftly placed my mouth to the lips and sucked out the warmed up liquor. She screamed and wriggled her fat bottom. She was consumed with longing. I gave Tessie the same treat and when I had sucked out the last drops she writhed and screamed.

'My God, that was brutal. I was hot enough without that. Hurry up and get on the chairs and I'll screw the balls off you while you lap Madge.' I got awful randy as Tessie took her position while I lay as she directed, with my erect penis standing straight and rigid, ready to burst. Tessie cuddled it in her soft bubbies and kissed it again with thrusts of her tongue in the little orifice.

Our passions spent, we fell back on the bed. I was asleep as was Tessie. Madge, in her state of erotic feelings, began working her fingers in her moist slit, but was so passionate and eager for another piece, she knew that she had first to get it stiff. Following descriptions she had read, of a way to get a man's penis to stand, Madge hung over me and lifted my seemingly dead penis into her mouth with her tongue after tickling the wrinkled balls. When she got half of the soft mass into her mouth she slipped her tongue around and around the head as she gently chewed the soft root. I stirred, woke up and not thinking which of my partners was at me, clutched Tessie and kissed her, feeling and moulding her titties, now firm after a rest. She, too, awoke.

'Oh, Gus, do you want me again so soon?' I then perceived that it was Madge who was eating it up.

'Look Tess,' I said. 'Madge wants it. Poor girl, she's hungry.' When Tessie saw Madge frantically chewing the mouthful, she rolled the splendid reservoir of sap in her one hand. 'That's right, Madge,' she said. 'That'll make it come up if you want a piece. I'm ready for one myself.' Tess tickled me, sucked my hard nipples and between the two amorous girls, I began to get stiff. My penis got too big for Madge's mouth. Letting it languidly out, she said:

'I do want a piece. I'm hot from my toes to my hair.'

I handled both quivering cunnies, sticking a finger into each. This would always make me hot. My tool swelled and stiffened to grand proportions till I had one of my characteristic morning hardons.

'Give it to Madge first,' cried Tess. 'She found it first.' I got on top of the plump, passionate girl and gave her the liveliest, hottest fuck I ever put to a girl, till she groaned and screamed in an ecstatic satisfying orgasm. I finished her off and left my rigid tool in her till she swooned off in a sensuous die-away, having restrained my own desire to spend.

I preferred my morning feast between Tessie's soft, shapely legs in her tight excitable little box. I wanted to feel Tessie's long lithe limbs wind about me and once more experience the ecstatic spend by her wriggling bottom and toe curling, sucking cunnie.

'Heavens, you're bigger than ever,' she exclaimed. 'It's just grand. Oh, Gee, how lovely, umm.' She groaned with each straining thrust and throb. Tessie twined her pretty legs around me and thus braced, she not only met my thrusts with effective bucking up motions but could wriggle and twist with a screwing motion that thrilled me with lustful zeal.

Her cries and shuddering frame told of the delightful spends she was having. When I could no longer restrain myself to prolong the voluptuous feast, I gathered the trembling plump form of Tessie in my arms and gazing down in her misty rolling eyes, groaned out:

'Oh, Tessie – there – it – comes – Oh, God! how exquisite!'

Our delicious feeling was ravishing after I shot a long charge of creamy spend into the hungry depths of Tessie's cunnie.

She quickly jumped off the bed and let the stuff escape in a morning pee. Returning to the bed we all had a nap. At six o'clock we all arose and went our way. Tessie remarked: 'Oh, Gus, I never had such a treat in all my life. Madge picked a star performer when she picked you.'

THE WANTONS

It is London in the mid-50s, the era of the Teddy Boy. Sixteen year old Linda is both appalled and fascinated by these flamboyant young tearaways — she'd like to know them better but she doesn't dare. Her home life, however, provides no safe haven. Her mother hates her — or so she feels — and her new step-father ogles her opulent young body in a funny way. On the night her mother stays at her aunt's house the reason for that funny look becomes all too clear as the step-father forces his way into her bedroom and into her bed. This experience, unwanted and repulsive though it is, awakens a rampant sexual curiosity in Linda and when she tells her friend Betty she is no longer a virgin, Betty can't help feeling a little jealous. Thus the two of them are in a receptive mood when they attend a dance and make friends with two swaggering Teds, Des and Jim. The boys whisk them off to a party in Hampstead and introduce them to a whole new world . . .

The atmosphere was pungent and smoky and the softly-tuned jazz from the record player mingled like an aural incense.

Linda and Desmond lay on the floor listening to the music and he stroked her bottom through her dress.

'Let's have another drag,' she breathed, moving her hand slowly towards the thin cigarette between his lips. They had told her not to expect anything from the first one and she had gone on smoking while they smoked, quietly inhaling, taking in a lot of air with the smoke as they suggested. Now she felt tranquilly wonderful. The room around her seemed a world in which she would live forever. She had no idea of the time and didn't care. All around her were friends, all those couples lounging and lying in the big room, hardly speaking, fondling a little, talking quietly. Betty was over there lying on the floor looking up at the ceiling with a smile on her face and Jim was lying with her, looking at the ceiling too.

She felt a great liking for Des and a great intimacy with him. He was stroking her bottom gently, feeling its round bulge lingeringly and he had a kind look on his face. She felt she was safe and at peace with Desmond. She never wanted to go home. Home! She smiled happily. It didn't bear thinking about.

She drew in on the cigarette and the smoke passed in a dry relief down her throat; the sweet, exotic aroma floated to her nostrils and she breathed deeply, with concentration. Then she relaxed and passed the butt end back to Desmond and the music enveloped her softly in an erotic wave of peace the way his arm and his gently stroking hand enveloped her.

Sam was sitting next to the record player. It was he who made possible this peace, this discovery. She felt tender towards him and to his mistress whose money had provided this Hampstead flat.

The record slid to an end and after a while someone put on another. Most of the girls were young – about eighteen and the men a few years older except for Sam who looked about thirty. His mistress was supposed to have a lot of money.

'Linda.' It was Betty's voice. She moved her head and looked over. Jim had undone the top buttons of her dress and had his hand inside. 'I feel good.'

Betty was going to have it tonight. Linda knew that for sure as she smiled back. This marihuana, "pot" they called it, was great stuff.

She listened again to the record. It was very clear. Everything was very clear, even the sound of Desmond's hand stroking her buttocks and Jim rustling Betty's dress.

'How do you feel?'

She looked up at Des.

'I feel wonderful.'

Her heart overflowed with tenderness for him and she knew that she could tell him anything if she wanted to, that he felt the same for her. She leaned up and kissed him suddenly, tenderly, on the cheek and he moved his hand from the full flower of her buttocks down between them over the dress, sharply aware of the sudden cleavage into separate orbs. His fingers between her legs pressed through the dress and briefs to the fleshy line of her labia. The tenderness she felt flushed in a tender, warm desire to give herself. Desmond felt soft warmth under his hand.

'Any room outside?' he asked Sam softly. It seemed to Linda that his voice rang clearly through the room.

Sam jerked his head absently towards the door and resumed his glazed concentration on the music.

'Let's go,' Des whispered to her, pressing his fingers meaningfully against the hot, giving ridge between her legs.

'All right.'

They rose quietly and she was suddenly aware of a floating unsteadiness in her limbs. Nobody took any notice of them. She was vaguely aware that Jim was kissing Betty and that Betty had one breast bare and protruding from her dress. Around the room everyone seemed to be necking or lying still.

With an arm around her, steadying her, they left the room quietly. Outside, the air was cooler, the thickness of the atmosphere cleared and for the first time she felt slightly dizzy and gave a giggle.

'What's the matter?' Desmond grinned at her.

'Nothing – I felt a bit dizzy that's all.'

He caught hold of her then and kissed her, pressing her hard against a wall so that she felt dizzy again as if she were sinking slowly through turns and turns of a spiral staircase.

His hands cupped her buttocks, pushing her hips out from the wall against his hips. She heard the loudness of his breathing. She put up her hands and caught his face and pushed her tongue into his mouth and rubbed her lips against him, murmuring little sounds all the time.

He released her suddenly and drew her along the passage and through a door into a bedroom. Moonlight came in through a window beyond a glass partition which cut the room in two. It all seemed hardly real. She was vividly aware of a number of objects which seemed to come toward her suddenly and unexpectedly and have no relation with one another.

Des pushed the partition back a little without switching on the light and they passed through into the small room beyond. Thankfully she sank down onto the bed, pulling him down with her. The sensation of lying down and the roaming in her head was a delicious combination and she felt tender and generous and her body seemed like an acutely strung instrument ready for ecstatic sensual use.

'Take your clothes off,' Des whispered, in the moonlight.

'Take them off for me,' she whispered back, settling snugly on the bed.

She felt his hands pulling her dress gently up over her hips, her breasts, felt him move her arms and pull it off over her head. The cool air and the cool counterpane refreshed her skin like a shower. She felt him fumbling with her brassiere and he pulled her half up, holding her against him. Her face came up against his loins and she rubbed her cheek against him. But something kept her at a distance from his body, a great, hot bulge in his trousers. She turned her face towards it, looking at it. She felt a tenderness towards it, a desire to caress and fondle. Slowly she moved her hand on his leg as he held her, still-fumbling. The bulge was farther away than she'd anticipated, but her hand reached it and closed over it, creasing the trousers around it. Far above her she heard him gasp and against her hand she felt the flexing of bulge and hips behind it.

Gently she squeezed it through the cloth, trying to

334

fell its length. She kissed the bulge tenderly and on an impulse bit it gently through the clothing.

She saw his hand come whitely down between her face and the bulge and, fascinated, watched it pull at buttons which jerked undone one after the other.

She pushed his hand away and, with her movement, felt her bra slip down off her breasts. There was still a wild floating in her head, but she focused on the opening and pushed her hand through it. Her hand was assailed by the heat of his loins. She searched around with her fingers, pulling aside his shirt, eventually finding the slit in his pants while he strained impatiently against her. She felt the hot, hard length against her hand – hard; but with a soft, delightful surface. She pulled and it shot out through the opening. Des grunted above her.

It felt beautiful in her hand; a long, white, hot, soft-textured length of stiff Plasticine to play with and mould.

She could see it white, almost luminous in the moon-light. He let her feel it, breathing heavily, pressing against her as he held her up on the bed.

The length of white substance was almost the whole range of her vision. Beyond that was only the vague floating and the clear sound of his breathing.

She stroked it and slowly pulled back the skin from the end-knob which glowed redly at her in contrast with the soft folds of the drawn-back whiteness. Gently she moved her fingers on it and held it in her hand, squeezing slightly and then harder to see how hard he could stand it. The object was hot and slightly pliable under her hand – a beautiful thing.

His hand came down over hers at last and he moved her hand up and down with his over his penis. She began the gentle massage and continued when he let go and pushed his hips out at her with a gasp.

He began to squirm and rock on his feet. She could feel the rocking movement against her and it seemed to make her float farther away with her white penis in her hand.

The sound of his passion was like a rushing sea above her and again his hand came down and pulled her hand away. She released him reluctantly and then he had caught hold of her face and was jabbing his penis gently against her soft lips. For a moment she didn't understand what was going on, but the pressure was there, heavily, on her mouth and automatically her lips opened and the white flesh plunged into her mouth. For a moment she fought against it, afraid she would choke, but he held it there and reached down to stroke her breasts. Floating, hardly aware of what she was doing she began to move her mouth against the soft velvet which filled it.

She was aware of a trembling behind her breasts, almost as if it had nothing to do with her directly and she sucked at the heat between her lips, trying to cool it.

Above her was the moaning, rushing from his lips; his hand pressed hard against her hair, forcing her against his loins. She licked the knob with her tongue, enjoying its smoothness. It was like a big, velvety lollipop which she would eventually swallow. She caught it in her hand, holding it against her mouth while she sucked the end; nothing seemed strange in her activity; she sucked as if she did it every day of her life in a normal routine.

In her floating, spiralling mind it seemed that the great thing was expanding, that it would fill her mouth and plunge down her throat, perhaps to emerge through her vagina. She felt a giggle deep inside her and sucked harder.

Above her, his moaning had reached a frenzied pitch and he was no longer rocking, but had locked his thighs together and was rigidly flexing his hips at her while he leaned slightly backwards with the top part of his body.

She heard the moaning break into little barks, coughing barks of sound and he pushed into her mouth, grazing the velvet organ along her teeth, choking her. And she felt her mouth flooded suddenly with a hot, sticky wetness which encircled her tongue and lodged on her palate and oozed down her gullet.

He sank against her and she realized vaguely that it was finished, found the knob, slight and limp now, still in her lips and gave it a few little sucks and licks before letting it flop out against his trousers.

She lay back on the bed, aware of its whiteness, like the whiteness of him. Through the window there was only the silver space of the sky washed in the moonlight. It seemed to envelop her; she felt a great delight in it.

After a little while she felt him against her, naked, warm and soft-skinned and his hands ran fluidly over her bare breasts and pulled her briefs down over her thighs and off her feet. He was sitting up looking at her. He kissed her belly, her breasts, moved his lips moistly over her soft body. He kissed her knees, her thighs and she was tenderly excited.

His lips moved up her thighs. He turned her over and kissed her buttocks, her back, running his lips down her spine. She shivered delightedly and he turned her on her back again and opened her legs. She felt his face there, slightly rough between her thighs. She was floating happily, sensually, and all she had to do was lie there and he would give her joy.

And suddenly his mouth had moved up between her warm thighs to the long lips between her legs, his tongue had darted out and into her vagina. She pulled up her legs, gasping and then reached down to grasp his head as she actively began to move into a rhythm with him, unable just to lie, wanting to float and writhe and twist, unearthly and above the world in a torment of strange passion.

Desmond buried his face in her crotch and sucked

337

her clitoris. He was fairly high, but nowhere near the way she was. What a find! he was thinking. What a hot little bitch! And now he was going to fuck the daylights out of her. God, how she was writhing and wriggling and clutching at him and moaning! It was going to be a real kick hearing her moan all the time as if she were in agony.

Against his lips he felt the soft, ragged moistness of her nether lips, the hard slipperiness of the clitoris and then he withdrew and slithered up onto her, wriggling up between her legs, crawling onto the slim strength of her body.

He lay along her and she lay under him with her eyes closed and her lips moving like prayers in the moonlight. She was pretty, damned pretty. God, what a kick! And her pretty face and excellent body were tormented now in a marihuana maelstrom which was making sex seem like the end of the world.

He was sent by the pot he'd had and the sight of her puckered face and the feel of her body underneath him and he covered her mouth passionately with his, sucking at her moist, lost lips and tongue the way he'd sucked at her clitoris.

Her breasts were like soft, pointed cushions beneath him and her hips like a pillow. He strained against her, crushing his prick against the little lawn of hair down there at the point. She wriggled against him and moaned.

Slipping down on her a little, he guided his prick at her cranny with his hand. It was throbbing with a certain feeling of frustration.

He moved a hand against her thighs and she pulled them higher – and then he had crushed slowly, agonisingly through the labia up into the vagina, high up towards the cervix and was beginning to undulate his behind between her legs. His frustration disappeared on the first entry and all his high excitement zipped down through his body to that one penetrating rod of sensation lost in her fleshy passage.

Up and down, up and down, gently, gently and growing stronger his hips played, while his penis drove in and out, in and out and an explosion of sound escaped his lips on every stroke.

The girl grasped his shoulders and then put her arms tightly around him as if she were hanging onto some whirling machine at a fair; her mouth hung open letting out a stream of low sound. His penis, cleaving into her, had a permanent acute sensation as if he wanted to pee and couldn't. Her tight little passage sucked pains of joy out of his lost flesh with each thrust.

God, oh, what a kick, oh, oh; the words danced in a vague *pas de deux* with a plethora of feeling in his head. Her skin caught and brushed and battled with his as she wriggled against him. Her thighs squeezed and released and as he explored farther and farther, letting the knob lead on into the welcoming tunnel, she swung her legs up and wrapped them around his waist, crushing him in a vise as she gasped out.

She was gone, really gone, with eyes closed, just a body abandoning itself. What a sexy little bitch! And he was half gone and it was wonderful, out of this world, that great sucking pool of joy down there where they met and mingled and he dominated and she gave and begged for more.

He put his hand around her buttocks. What delightful mounds they were – a little too big for his hands, they overflowed and he could lose his fingers in them as they relaxed. When they tautened he pushed his fingers between them and felt the little anus. It was a tiny little slit, like an unopened vagina in a small child. She squirmed, squirming with squirms as he touched it. She contrived to press it against his fingers as with her arms she pulled his hips at her loins. He

339

dug his finger at its resistant surface and felt the little, glossy crack give and his finger worm in a little.

'Oh Des, oh, Des,' she moaned as his finger moved into the soft hole. He moved it around within the tight cavity to bring more passion from her limbs as he shagged her.

As his hips writhed and squirmed, impelling his rigid member up between her hot, flailing thighs he rubbed his chest across her breasts, feeling the hard nipples brush his firm flesh, feeling the full, solid flesh of the breasts resist and give and suck against him.

She brought down her slim thighs from around him and spread them out on either side, horizontally so that tendons showed between thighs and crotch. He rammed into the greater depth that that gave him and she jerked with the sudden excruciating expanse of his filling.

She reached around him with her arms and pulled his head onto hers, biting his lips, thrusting out her tongue, licking him, biting and licking and sucking his neck. When he bit her neck, she cried out and hugged him closer, swinging back her thighs to press him into her.

His rhythm which had grown farther and almost brutal began to slow as he felt the end drawing ecstatically near.

She too began to wriggle all the time, clamping her buttocks together on his hands, pushing her hips flat into his and then relaxing, moaning and gasping and waving her tongue in his mouth.

God, this time he would die! It was too excruciating to bear! He soared slowly, crushingly into her, up and up, never ending, a feast of sensation all the way.

He was vaguely aware that she was almost delirious, rocking and moaning against him and flexing her loins with every stroke. He heard her gasp in a long drone of excitement and pain, felt her wriggle in a sharp, furious movement as he pulled her behind at him and

340

then she was pressing her hips at his off the bed for several seconds as she cried out her fulfillment.

She continued to hold him tightly, with her lips moving in a prolonged ecstasy while he forced his staff up and up in great, grand, final movements, feeling the tissues of her passage clutching at him, drawing the lifeblood from his penis which would surely shatter into total destruction.

'Oh God, God, you lovely bitch, ooh, oh!' His knob seemed to be growing and growing, heavy with its imminent discharge. His whole length of penis seemed to expand, to hurt, to have a needle running sharply down its centre. He dug his nails into her, felt her hands around him, digging, urging, asking for his sperm. His penis had grown to an enormity and she was groaning again. It was going to suddenly turn inside out, it would burst. He gasped, caught his breath and then lost it in a great surging of his lungs as needle after red-hot needle of ecstatic pain shot hotly and wetly from him to her in a culminating blaze.

He wriggled his prick into her even when it was growing limp and empty. He didn't want it to be over, that delight which was better than he'd had before.

At last he lay still on her hot, rounded body, which was still as death, but with a heart he could feel pumping at a declining fury of speed.

She opened her eyes at last and smiled at him, kissing his cheek.

'God, that was wonderful,' she whispered.

'You said it.'

He felt a great contentment and satisfaction; a temporary euphoria in which he wanted to lie for as long as possible.

'You're heavy,' she said after a while, and he rolled off and lay beside her with one arm across the peaks of her breasts.

He felt now the full effects of the pot. He wanted to lie absolutely still and take delight in the fact of being

341

warm and still and able to watch the moonlight and have his arm across her warm, smooth breasts.

They lay for a long time without speaking, perfectly still.

The opening of the outer door and a shaft of light flooding the outer room and cutting across the wall beyond the foot of their bed disturbed them slightly, but not even enough to make them turn their heads. They remained still, looking at the long yellow shaft lighting up the yellow wallpaper and the top of a chest of drawers. They heard the door close.

'Nobody here,' came Jim's voice, hazy and strange, from the other room.

There was the sound of footsteps across the outer room followed by that of someone falling on the bed.

'Oh, I feel as if I'm not really here.' It was Betty's voice, slow and careful as if she was having difficulty in speaking.

Linda stirred, attempting to sit up, but Desmond held her down, putting a finger to his lips.

'Perhaps we'll see something amusing,' he whispered with a wink.

Linda stifled a giggle. What a joke. Betty was about to be fucked for the first time and she and Des would probably be witnesses. How funny!

'Get down on the other side of the bed,' Des whispered. They slid nakedly off the bed and crouched down on the side away from the partition. Des reached up and pulled their clothes down with them.

There was a murmur of voices from the other room. Linda was trying to stifle her growing desire to laugh.

The light flashed on in the other room and filtered dimly through the partition. They heard Jim moving and then his voice saying: 'Looks as if someone was in the other room, but it's empty now. You want to go in there?'

Linda held her breath.

'No, I can't move off this bed. Let's stay here.'

342

There was silence with a few muffled noises for a time and then Betty's voice.

'Why don't you turn the light off?'

'No, I want to see you. God, you're beautiful.'

Gently Des and Linda eased themselves up. The light came through very dimly. They climbed softly onto the bed and lay out flat facing the partition, watching.

Betty was lying on her side, her back towards them, unclothed and Jim, in a similar state of nudity, was leaning over her on the bed.

'Jees, she's almost as good as you,' Des whispered.

She looked pretty good, Linda admitted to herself. Slim shoulders which curved down in a long line to her hip, exaggerated by her reclining position. Her bottom was bigger than Linda's, each separate buttock seeming to belong to the other, cast in an embracing, oval mould. Her thighs were shorter, more muscular – that was what gave her the dumpier, slightly more sexy appearance; her calves were slim and strong.

She saw Jim's body, too, with its hair. It seemed to be almost covered with hair: on his chest, his shoulders, his thighs, his belly and in a great fuzz around his fat, white erection. Linda felt a thrill of excitement to think that a few days ago she'd been a virgin and now she'd seen three pricks and been fucked by two men.

They watched Betty, saw her put out her hand and touch the giant rod. All her nervousness, her inhibitions had disappeared, Linda noticed. That was the pot.

Jim slid down beside her and they saw him kiss her, watched Betty roll back so that she was flat on the bed and her breasts pointed to the ceiling. They were whoppers, Linda thought. She remembered how they had developed before hers and how embarrassed Betty had been about them at first.

Their faces were fused and Linda saw Jim's hand

stray away and flow over first the right breast and then the left. She could hear Betty's breathing quite clearly.

'She's a virgin,' she whispered to Desmond.

'No kidding!'

Desmond looked through the partition into the clearly-lit room with an interest that approached envy. What a feeling of power that was to be initiating someone into the ways of sex. He wondered how long it would take Jim to find out.

They saw Jim's hand stray away over her ribs down over the belly and the film of hair that was just visible. Betty kept her legs together for the moment, but as he fingered her around the sweating vault of her crotch, she opened them for him.

'He's lucky,' Linda whispered. 'If it hadn't been for the pot she'd have been terribly embarrassed – she might not even have wanted it at all.'

'She'll be a damn good fuck once she knows how,' Des murmured. 'D'you see the flesh on those hips.'

'How about me?' Linda pouted.

'Oh, you're tops already.' He risked the rustle to rub his hand over her rump and she hid her face because she wanted to giggle again.

Jim, meanwhile, had pushed his fingers into Betty's vagina. She had cried out at first, but now she was wriggling around with her thighs half open and her head moving from side to side as he kissed her neck.

Jim took her hand at last and placed it around his prick, squeezing it round him. They saw his organ shooting out over Betty's hips as he lay alongside her.

'She's learning,' Des whispered, as Betty began to squeeze and caress the rigid flesh and Jim began to breathe heavily and push his hips and thighs against her side.

Jim moved his mouth down and they saw the outermost angle of her breast with its cherried nipple disappear into his mouth. Betty gave another shriek and clutched his head after having moved as if to push him away.

'I wonder what they'd say if we burst in on them now,' Linda whispered with a grin. 'I don't think I can stand much more of this.'

'Nuts,' Des whispered back. 'Nothing more exciting than being a Peeping Tom. I want to see how she looks when she's having it for the first time.'

By now Jim's penis was flaming red, turning almost purple. He moved as if to climb onto Betty, and they heard the words falter from her lips: 'No, not yet, not for a bit.'

Jim sank down again and they could see his wrist jerking about between her thighs.

'I – I didn't tell you – but I'm a virgin,' Betty said softly.

At first they could see that Jim hardly believed her.

'God almighty,' he said at last. 'Where you been all this time – and with a body like that?'

Linda hid her face in the counterpane again and Des followed suit. Jim had looked comically surprised – almost hurt that she'd never known a man before.

He recovered eventually, while she lay with eyes closed, wriggling quietly against the wrist between her muscular, white thighs, and he began his digital penetration with greater care and relish. He actually looked down towards her slit as if he wanted to see what a virgin's hole looked like. Des, watching, felt a fresh pang of desire.

Kissing her breasts, mauling her, Jim was gradually getting her more and more excited. She'd spread her legs wide, now, and was squeezing his penis so hard that he had to tell her to ease off.

'Do you think we can try it now?' he panted.

There was a moment of hesitation. Linda knew just what fear, excitement and desire for complete abandon were battling in Betty's head.

'Yes, all right.'

Jim knelt up and climbed between Betty's legs. Her knees came up chest high on either side of him. Linda, seeing his fat thing stabbing out like a spar at an angle of 75 degrees with his belly felt a sudden desire to be filled again, but she couldn't take her eyes from the drama of devirgination. Des, too, lay transfixed.

Gently Jim stretched out on Betty, who gave a little whimper of anticipation as she felt his thighs move out under hers, his knees against her upturned buttocks.

They almost lost sight of his prick, as he guided it with his hand, but they heard Betty's sudden shrill gasp and saw her jerk as if she'd been stung.

'Ooooh, oh!' she gasped. 'Oh, please.' Her head was flung back and in spite of her gasps she made no effort to push him off. She was taking it very well after the preliminary fingering.

When Jim's hand came away they could see where his prick had made a bridgehead. Just the knob and a bit more inside her; the rest they could see, white and somehow tense-looking. Betty had a look of strain about her for the moment. They could see the delightfully voluptuous line of her buttocks, tensed, slightly lifted in the strain, waiting for further shock. It hollowed in like a piece of moulded clay.

'What I wouldn't do to have those buttocks in my hands,' Des was thinking. 'I'd give her something she'd remember for her first time.'

'Stop moving, they'll hear you,' Linda squeaked.

He realised he'd been moving his hips on the bed. He grinned and put his hand between her legs. In answer she pushed her hand under him, searching for his prick. He turned over towards her, still watching the others through the partition. She saw his prick had fattened again into its burden of desire. She caught it and began to move the skin softly up and down. Trying to stifle his breathing, Des let her start to toss him off. The pulsation in his penis was the more acute from his watching the spectacle.

Linda, too, turned her eyes back to the partition while continuing to massage the stiff mast of flesh at her side. It gave her a vicarious thrill to be filling Des with sensation, to be able to feel his great, hot doughy thing in her hand, between her deft fingers.

Betty was giving a series of little shrieks back in the other room, while Jim gently edged into her. His face was an open key to his passion. His mouth hung open, panting and his face was screwed up, tense. He won't hold himself back much longer, Des thought, watching and feeling his own passion rise as he followed their movements and felt the relentless hand on his penis.

Jim had placed his hand under Betty's bottom and pulled her hips up towards him a little, ranging his organ. Betty, with her eyes closed, the corners screwed up in a pain which was still half anticipation, was trembling and gasping.

Suddenly, with a firm thrust of his hips, Jim surged into her. They saw his white prick tear right in, disappearing, inch by inch, smoothly and quickly, from their view.

His head went back as he thrust. The tight, resisting passage gave him a sensual joy which was almost unbearable. Betty's head strained back into the pillow and her body arched up in shock as she gave another little scream.

'Oh, oh, oh, you're hurting me!'

But there was no quarter now. Jim had lost his prick in her and there was no going back. He couldn't even if she really wanted him to.

After several slow strokes which brought his penis almost right out into their vision and then plunged it right back again so that they could see where his black bush of hair met the raw flesh of her love lips, Betty's cries of pain calmed and settled into groans which could be a mixture of pain and passion.

Jim lowered his head and they saw her lips move

347

round toward his, as she felt his breath on her cheek. Her face was screwed up with a torture which was exquisite. They were making so much noise now, that they couldn't hear the laboured breathing from the next room.

In, in, in. Betty's virgin body was rifled, her channel scourged by a great, foreign body which marihuana had made her want more than ever. And now she knew the pain and ecstasy of it, the completion of herself, the end of those nights of wondering, fearfully desiring, unknowing.

Linda and Des watched gluttonously, following every movement as the two crushed bodies became one and sank into a single rhythm, sometimes faster, sometimes slower, according to the lead which Jim gave.

They watched the muscles on her thighs contract as they pressed him, saw her buttocks tense and relax, her breasts flattened slightly under his weight. Above all they watched that source and centre of the joy, that strangely naked section where his piece of protrusion fitted into her hollow and their hair mingled and moisture began to run and slide around her crotch and over his prick as it withdrew. Linda watched, fascinated as Jim's balls swung slightly, skinnily with their movement. Her hand moved, still on Desmond's penis, and in her mind it was moving on Jim's.

Desmond was straining. In *his* mind his prick was plunging into Betty, giving her the first experience she'd ever had of sex; his hands held those buttocks, his teats weighed on hers, his mouth on hers, his face hotly against her moist, helpless lips in her hot face.

Jim was gasping for breath as he buried himself in the soft suction of Betty's virginal tautness. He wanted to be brutal now and he pushed her thighs back towards her breasts leaning up from her, pushing with his hips, giving them a last flick into her so that some of his hairs were also sucked in with his flesh and

348

reappeared moistly dripping. Betty writhed slightly, gasping, helpless, lost in herself, hardly aware that it was he, Jim, doing this to her, aware only that her body, that aching channel in her belly, was filled with a strange object which seemed to split it and rub it with an exciting, titillating rhythm which seemed to be growing to a white heat in the wandering haze of her mind.

Desmond, gasping quietly, one hand over his mouth, stared fixedly at the wet, raw area into which Jim's prick was slipping and then fixedly at Betty's tormented face, the face which that raw area was producing, which Jim's raging organ was producing. He watched, stared, fixed his eyes, concentrating until they bulged from his head because he could feel himself coming, and he wanted to be almost feeling that flesh when he came. Beside him Linda was breathing heavily, too, excited by his excitement and by the furious winding up of her friend and his friend in the other room. The air seemed to be filled with gasps and vague, sensual movement.

'I'm coming, I'm coming!' Desmond moaned softly.

Linda wriggled quickly in towards him, surprised that she should think of the counterpane. She turned over onto her back so that she could get her hip under his soaring flesh without changing her grip. He stared and stared through the partition until suddenly he tensed, seized her and bit her neck in a long roar of breath, and she felt a stream of hot liquid make a wet, punctuated path all the way across her belly.

In the other room the locked couple were coming to their climax. That was obvious from the animal noises they were making. Taking advantage of the noise, Linda slipped off the bed for her handkerchief. She wiped the sperm from her belly and wiped Desmond's penis before getting back onto the bed to watch the final throes.

Betty was wriggling like a worm suddenly come into

349

the light. Her face was contorted with a sort of pain. While they watched they saw her lips move very quickly and then her mouth open very wide as she suddenly convulsed against the body above her and inside her.

The pot's pretty good to get a climax for a virgin, Desmond thought.

Now it was only Jim and he was very near the end. He'd moved his hands to her shoulders as if pinning her to the bed against her will and was leaning up, putting the whole of his weight on her drawn-up thighs. His face, too, was wracked with passion, and his teeth seemed to be gritting together. They saw him slow suddenly, thrust, thrust, thrust and then push hard against her as he choked and then again, choking again and so several times until he'd emptied all into her.

When they'd been lying quietly for a while Desmond and Linda went laughing in to them. The pot made it all very funny and Jim and Betty weren't at all offended that they'd been watched.

MORE EVELINE

Eveline is one of the most interesting of Victorian erotic heroines, a lady of quality whose obligatory nymphomania is accompanied by a wicked sense of humour and a thoroughly masculine approach to sexual activity. Her story is told in two volumes, the sequel – More Eveline – being initiated by the crude but effective device of rewriting the ending of volume one (which had consigned her to the virtues of motherhood with her wicked ways behind her). The beginning of the second book sees her spurning the advances of the strapping peasant who impregantes her in the first book and taking off for the delights of London. There she sets about corrupting her rather wet cousin Emma and continuing to assuage her ever-abundant appetite for the flesh.

In pursuit of her amours Eveline is as single-minded and as cunning as any Casanova and she has a particular penchant for tumbling with those lower down the social pecking order than herself. When boredom sets in she is inspired to disguise herself as a working girl and set off on an adventure such as the following . . .

I entered the hotel's dowdy reception hall. The clerk was bemused at the appearance of someone as well-dressed as I. It mattered not. The room I was given was evidently their best. It was small and tasteless, but I intended not to stay too long within it. Scarce had the door closed than I stripped to my boots and stockings and drew out an old dress and bonnet that I had found long before in the attic. How they had got there did not matter. They were sufficiently shabby for my purpose.

The clerk, being engaged, did not see me go out, nor would have recognised me from the back. Down the long street I walked towards Pimlico. I needed the exercise. The late afternoon was warm. Houses alternated with small, poor shops. Women leaning in dark doorways disregarded me. From all appearances I was one of their kind. Several men stared at me. I ignored them just as I did one who drove a cart slowly past and stared into my face.

'What a lovely one! Cor, Miss, want a ride?'

I did indeed, but not of the sort he first intended. I knew not my way in this district and clutched my purse tightly. It was a ragged one. No one would expect to find more than a few pence in it. As I approached the Pimlico district, the houses became a little better. Steps had been cleaned and doorknockers polished. A carriage stood outside one, from which a man of about thirty-five descended. Paying the cabman, he stared at me and then walked quickly across my path.

'Pardon me, but you are exceedingly pretty. Allow me to introduce myself. I am Edwin Pickles, photographer.'

'Indeed? And how would that interest me?'

I placed a nasal Cockney twang in my voice, but my vocabulary evidently puzzled him. He was of neat attire and wore a sporting jacket and modishly tight trousers with black silk bands running down the sides. His shirt was open. Like the corset designer, he wore a cravat.

'I seek models. You would make a perfect one. I would pay you, of course.'

'Oh! ain't you a lark! Naked I suppose?'

'Would you like to talk about it? I pay a guinea for first poses – more later.'

I sniffed. I was remembering the manners and speech of some of the maids we had had. To imitate them amused me.

'As you like.'

We mounted the steps of the house. The hallway was clean within. I was led into a sitting room, as it is called in such dwellings. Scarce had I sat than a woman appeared. She was much of the man's age and had a slightly common but attractive face. He introduced her as his sister, Edwina. Her eyes cast up and down upon me.

'This one will do, yes. A pretty one.'

I affected to look pleased, pretended a bit of sharpness and tried to bargain for thirty shillings, but they would not have it. A glass of cheap sherry apparently assuaged me. I was led up two flights to the studio which had a large roof light. Couches, armchairs, and drapes of various shades lay about. On the floor were cushions. A painted cloth back-drop showed a rural scene. There was even a Penny Farthing, propped in one corner. In the centre of the room stood a large brassbound camera of mahogany on a sturdy tripod. The back of it was covered with a black cloth. A big brass lens gleamed at the front.

'Take your clothes off and I will pose you.'

I had little enough to take off. My dress followed my bonnet. I stood naked in my stockings and boots.

'What a beauty! I swear you are the loveliest girl I have had here!'

'Then you should pay me more, eh? How about it?'

He was close upon me. Poor girls did not struggle very much, I imagined, if there were money in the offing. He made bold to caress my naked bottom. I wriggled it a little and cast my eyes down.

'Will you pay me more if I do?'

His erection was evident already. He pressed it to me, raised my face and kissed me. His hand sought my breasts. It was two days since I had been mounted and I still had visions of Emma in her transports.

'Another guinea, by God, you shall have it!'

'Promise? You got to promise! Oh my gawd, what a whopper, what a big one!'

We were on the cushions. Their purpose was obviously twofold. A shaft of impressive size quivered in my grasp. His mouth smothered mine. I absorbed his tongue. Breeches sliding down, he prepared himself for the assault. I would have preferred some preliminaries, but my lust was as great as his. I panted. I guided the knob to the orifice. It sank within. A gasp of pleasure escaped us both.

'My, you're lovely! What breasts, what a bottom — it's as round as a peach! Put your legs up over mine!'

I obeyed. It would not do to be too forward with my skills. His cock sank in me to the root. I squeezed.

'Oh! you're hurting me with it! Don't go too fast!'

'There, there, you'll like it in a minute. Hold it in. Can you feel it throb? No one ever brought it up so quick, I swear. What a perfect fuck you are!'

'Suck my tits, then — I likes that.'

He began to thresh. His piston moved in my spongy clasp. I closed my eyes and felt a complete delirium. There are occasions when I can be mounted three times in a day and then feel that the fourth is the first I have had for weeks. It was so now. I bucked my bottom to encourage him.

'Do it fast — I like it! Make me come!'

'You beauty! Oh, what heaven!'

His knob seemed to be thrusting up almost into my womb. His balls made a fine smacking sound. Beneath the cushions the floorboards squeaked. I was wet already with my spendings. The perfect, simple glory of the act overcame me. Those who scorn such 'wanton pleasures' know nothing of the richness of experience such as only the truly initiated can enjoy. My pleasure was twice and thrice his own, had he but known it. Lithe in his movements he pumped it back and forth, his cock well oiled by my juices.

'Don't come in me! Suppose I 'as a child?'

Too far gone, he did not care. I pretended of a sudden the same abandon. I heaved to his heavings. Our pubic hairs rubbed together. My nipples were stark against his chest.

'You like it? Have I got a big one? Is it nice?'

'Oh, I loves it! Do it more!'

He shuddered. His words had been meant only as a prelude to his climax. Jets of warm come streamed from his prick and flooded me. The sensation was delicious. I alone, it seemed, could enjoy such pleasures and remain free of complications. I absorbed him like a sponge. He groaned in my velvety depths. Our bellies squirmed. Then he sank down. He panted mightily. We lay soaking until at last he decided to withdraw and rise. I rose and flopped into an armchair, feeling a little pool of sperm issue itself under me where it spilled from my cleft.

His eyes were somewhat rapturous as he covered himself and gazed at me. Indolently I let my thighs fall apart.

'You didn't 'arf fill me up, you did!'

'You'll come again tomorrow? I can photograph you then. The light isn't good now.'

'Tomorrow? I ain't got nowheres to go tonight.'

He looked bewildered. He ruffled his hair. His eyes could not take themselves from my muff.

'Very well. I will speak to my sister.'

He was gone. I looked around, saw a bottle of wine that had been newly opened, sniffed it and drank a little. My throat was parched. I replaced the bottle hastily when he ascended again.

'There is a spare room. You may sleep there.'

'You said as you would pay me two guineas, remember, and I 'as to get my supper.'

'All right. See, I have a half a crown on me. Take that and we will settle in the morning.'

I took it quickly and placed it in my purse where I had otherwise placed only notes so that they would not click together. He would think it otherwise empty. Having put my dress and bonnet back on I went down. His sister waited for me in the hall.

'I suppose he had you? He does that with half the girls. It's disgusting!'

'I don't know what you mean – I'm a decent girl, I am. Don't you go besmirching my name or I'll make ructions about it, that I will!'

I pride myself as an actress. She could not help but be convinced. I take care always with the expressions in my eyes as well as the words that come from my lips.

'Nothing intended. After you've got your supper you can come back. Second door on the left, first landing, is your room. Has he paid you?'

'No. I ain't done no posing yet, 'ave I?'

Perhaps she thought to catch me out. I gave her a stare and departed. I had no need to return. The thought that I had earned two shillings and sixpence by enjoying myself was extremely amusing. I had learned something at least about the economics of copulation among such people. Entering an eating house I had passed on the way I saw a young girl standing there. She had dirty golden hair, a ragged skirt, and worn-down shoes on. I imagined her sixteen or seventeen. Our eyes met.

'Got a penny to spare, Miss?'

'Are you hungry?'

'Yes, Miss. I ain't eaten only but a scrap of bread since morning.'

'Come in with me. I will buy you something.'

I was moved by her prettiness and her poverty. She could scarce believe it when I ordered mutton chops. The grease ran through her fingers. She was in heaven. I gathered she lived in Stepney. Her mother beat her and she had run away from home. There were thousands of such poor homeless on the streets. Her name was Alice.

'Would you like to earn money, Alice?'

Her eyes were as bit as saucers when I explained. No, she didn't mind taking her clothes off. Her brothers had seen her often enough like that, and her father. They all lived in one room. When her mother was asleep she had played with their 'diddles,' she said. They called it tickling. She liked being tickled. It was a rare lark, she said.

I took her back with me, her tummy full. Before leaving I got the man who owned the eating house to wrap some cold meat and pickles for us in a piece of paper. It would serve as our supper or breakfast. Alice danced along beside. I think she was sure I was a lady but would not dare say so.

Edwina received us at first haughtily but changed her mind when she had had a good look at Alice. In the sitting room she lifted the girl's dress and displayed a perfect, chubby bottom, handsome young legs and a fine down of curls.

'She'll do. Edwin can photograph you both together.'

I guessed what that meant. We slept together in a narrow bed, huddling close. I gave her a little 'tickle' before going to sleep. It made her feel nice, she said. My finger worked smoothly in her soft cleft. She hugged and kissed me, then straightened her legs and gave a sigh.

'Did you come?'

'Yes. I like that. Ain't it lovely?'

She would not confess to having had any cocks in her, but I guessed she had. She was a warm little thing, fully amorous when started up. Bread and drippings and a mug of tea sufficed for our breakfast. At nine Edwin began photographing us. We assumed various poses, but it was necessary to remain perfectly still for each one while Edwin counted solemnly. Little by little he encouraged us until Alice lay on her back with her legs in the air and I held my tongue close to her slit.

'I mean to have a young fellow to pose with you girls now. Would you like that?'

I said nothing. Alice stared and giggled. The young man was presented. He was scarce more than a year older than Alice. His eyes would have eaten me up. I wore black stockings and nothing else. Edwin had provided gaudy garters which clipped my thighs tightly. Undressing as if embarrassed, the newcomer, who was named Charlie, presented a slender figure to our view. His penis looked equally thin.

We took our first pose with Charlie between us, he kissing me and Alice holding his cock. In a trice it was up. Though of small girth it was of reasonable length. At Edwin's command I lay on my hip and took it in my mouth. The long seconds passed while Edwin counted. I sucked seductively upon the pear-shaped knob.

'Let him do it? Would you?'

'Half a crown extra for that if I do.'

The photographer frowned. He regarded me obviously as a hard bargainer. By any working girl's standards I would be coming into riches.

'Very well. Kneel up. Have Alice lie under you. Keep your bottom up. I want you and she kissing while he holds it in.'

I presented a bottom as perfect as any that Charlie or Edwin would ever be likely to see. A thought had seized me that I could not resist. Passing my hand under me I took Charlie's stiff little penis and guided it – not in my slit but against my rosehole. Whether he had ever entered it in a girl before I know not, but he made no ado about presenting it there. Edwin, busy with his focussing beneath the black cloth, was at the wrong angle to see what was happening. Charlie groaned. I do not blame him. I was still then a trifle tight there, yet he proved a perfect size to initiate me in this respect.

A sob of pleasure escaped my mouth as it settled upon Alice's. The minx, excited, thrust her tongue. I moved my bottom back carefully on the doughty little rod whose knob was already pressing beyond the puckered rim of my rosette.

'Be still!' Edwin commanded.

Charlie's hands clasped my hips. I dared not move. I wanted it too much. Fortunately at that moment Edwin fussed again beneath the cloth. He was forever rearranging his focussing and twisting the lens about. Quite beside himself meanwhile, Charlie inserted himself a further inch . . . another! Ah! the sensation was beyond description. My tongue twirled about Alice's. If I had measured the corset designer, then I measured Charlie's piston much more sensitively. I had reason too. There was a slight burning and itching, yet the pleasure was immeasurable. A sensation that the breath was being expelled from my body overtook me and then passed. I had absorbed five inches of his tool when Edwin again sternly bid us be still.

We froze our postures – externally at least. Within my bottom Charlie's prick pulsed its pleasure. A gurgling sound escaped him though he managed to keep perfectly still. Within seconds – the very seconds that Edwin was devoutly counting – I experienced the long shoots of Charlie's sperm that for a blissful moment seemed to throb endlessly and appeared to jet right up into my bowels.

The pleasure was rapturous. Too often in my delights I had failed to feel the spurting of the male liquid in my slit. Now in my narrower, tighter passage I could feel it all – ALL.

The photograph was taken. Charlie withdrew as slowly as he could. His sperm trickled armly from my bottomhole. Falling back, he appeared to grow pale, his cock oozing. Edwin – not knowing exactly what had passed – thereupon berated him. The further poses which should have included Charlie's young manhood, were ruined, he said.

'I am tired anyway. You must have taken enough.'

I made my tone clipped and certain. I rose to put on my dress. I wanted to absorb in my mind the experience I had received as much as I had done in my bold bottom.

'Is he going to pay us now, Evie?'

'Yes, he is. Are you not, Edwin?'

I had forgotten my Cockney accent for a moment. All stared at me. A certain furtive look came into his eyes. Overtones of false geniality entered his voice.

'No time to go to the bank today, you see. I tell you

what – come back tomorrow morning and I'll have it ready.'

'You must have some money. Ask your sister. Does she not keep your purse?'

'She is out.' His face was sullen.

'Very well –,we will return as you say.'

Alice looked bewildered. I believe she thought that both the photographer and I had conspired to welsh on her. I gave him no more of my time and let her down.

'He aint' going to pay us, Miss, I knows it.'

'Oh, he will pay us, Alice. You know I am not as you believed?'

'Oh yes, Miss – I guessed you was a lady. I knowed you was doing it for a lark, but now I aint' got a penny and nowheres to sleep or go.'

I hailed a carriage. It was the first one that Alice had ever been in, she said. In a few minutes we were at the hotel. The clerk, perceiving my face and then my clothes, nearly fell off his stool.

'This young lady will stay the night here instead of myself. It is paid for and therefore it does not matter. See to it that she gets what she wants and I will reimburse you.'

He nodded in a surly manner. I threw a note down before him. His expression changed. He stood up.

'Yes, Miss.'

I changed again and settled Alice in, giving her the half crown that I had received from Edwin. She would be able to buy food a-plenty with it.

'You will come back, Evie?'

Her gaze was solemn and anxious. I assured her of my word. She was a charming creature. Papa would appreciate her once she was bathed and cleanly clothed. I felt certain we could find a place in the household for her. She and Mary would get on no end.

I made my way down to the street. Cabs were a-plenty at that hour. One stopped expectantly beside me.

'Anywhere to go, Miss?'
'Yes. Scotland Yard, please.'

'Inspector Barkey is not here, Madam. Would you wish to see someone else? Can you tell me what the matter is about?'

The policeman who received me regarded me so closely that I imagined my dress had become transparent.

'It is a matter of some confidence. Who is the other senior officer?'

'Chief Inspector Ramage. I dunno whether he can see you now or not.'

The matter, however, was swiftly arranged. The Chief Inspector was a man of some physique. He accommodated me in his office. His eyes scanned my figure with more than passing interest. I affected my quietest manner as one who is deeply shocked. I had chanced upon a young girl, I told him, who had fallen into the hands of pornographic photographers. Not only had they made devilish use of her, but had refused to pay her and thrown her out of the house into the bargain.

'The devils! There are a number of these people about now that photographic work has taken on. We shall have them, Madam — I swear on it. Can you explain the nature of the photographs to me?'

His gaze was somewhat expectant. As if summoning himself up for some ordeal he partook of a glass of whisky and offered me one. I sipped my own delicately.

'The photographs were of an extremely intimate nature. I do not know whether or not I dare speak of them to you. In one, for instance, the poor girl – quite naked save for stockings, was bent over a chair. . . . Oh! but I cannot describe it!'

His look was immediately solicitous. He rose and came round his desk.

'Do not fret yourself. I believe I know well what you

363

mean. Allow me to show you. Perhaps if madam could stand a minute?'

I stood. My breasts made somewhat intimate contact with his chest. A slight hoarseness entered into his voice.

'I has to be certain, Madam, that the postures were within the meaning of the Act, if you catch my meaning. She was bent over, you say, right over, and all showing.'

I lowered my gaze. My breasts rubbed across him.

'If I show you, will it clear the matter up for you?'

'Indeed it will. If you turn round now – so. Take no fright now for I am just going to bend you over and draw your skirt up a shade. You say she was naked?'

'Yes. You will have to arrange my skirt higher, I fear, to get the full effect. Oh dear! am I showing all now?'

'All that is perfect. And another scoundrel were right behind her, if my guess is right. Putting it up her?'

'AAAH! OOOOH! Is that your truncheon, Inspector?'

'Not the one I use on the villains, ma'am. This one is to pleasure the ladies. Still now – jut your bottom up a bit. Ah, what lecherous likenesses they must be indeed, yet none would show as pretty an offering as yours. Steady now and we will get the posture perfect. Like so, was it?'

'In . . . In . . . In . . . Inspector, AAAH! Oh my goodness, it is in! You are stretching me! No more, Oh I beg you!'

'We'll never know otherwise, ma'am. Legs apart was it?'

'Yes! A bit more! Be careful of my stockings! Oh, you rogue, you are slipping more of it in. It's too big! Ah, what a thrust! Oh goodness, what a feeling it is!'

'Straddle your legs – keep your ankles firm. Another couple of inches does it. There – steady now – bend a little more. I love a girl who offers it up like this. Younger than you, is she?'

His cock was superb – a genuine ramrod of stiff flesh and muscle. With the last effort of his forcing it all in I felt his balls swing under me. A final squelch and nine inches of his weapon were within. I all but fainted with the delicious sensation.

'Ah, you naughty man, you are making me do it! Do you like my cunt? Is it tight and soft for you? Unbutton my dress – caress my breasts! OH! Yes! AH! Pump me hard!'

Our pretence had ceased. We were in the full throes of it. The buttons of my corsage flew apart. His big palms cradled the gourds of my tits. Bent over well as I was, it is a posture I adore. All propriety left me. I moaned and twisted. My bottom rotated lewdly against his belly. The warm silky orb enraged his lust further. His strokes, powerful and deep, quickened.

'Give it to me! Push it in! Oh, what a monster you have! Do you get many young ladies to do this to?'

'None as you. The working class lassies is easy. Many a one I've had in a dark passageway if she was afeared I were going to arrest her. Little devil! You know how to work your bottom, don't you?'

I was beyond reply. The friction of his big thick cock had already made me spill my libation twice. I was on the brink of another. The room seemed to swim about me. His loins were lusty. I suspected he could run a second bout in as quick a time as any man. And so it proved. Having inundated me, he uncorked and sat me upon his lap.

'Was it true, your story?'

'Of course! I will lead you to the young girl herself – and then to the den of vice. Promise me only one thing. The latest photographs taken must be destroyed. I do not wish them to appear before the courts.'

'I shall find no trouble in doing that. Move your bottom on my cock a little. I never knew a girl to stir me so!'

My nipples attracted his lips. He sucked them greedily. His hair was thick and dark. I stroked it encouragingly while he was about his task. Beneath me the
thick worm stirred and transmuted itself into a small
pole that almost lifted me off his lap. I groped and felt
the girth of it, slimy with love's spendings.

'Do you want to again?'

'Clear your desk. I will lie on it with my legs hanging
over the edge. It will be nice that way. Do not soil my
dress. Oh, you rogue!'

He was upon me again in a minute. A second bout
is often the best. They take longer about it. Their cocks
are less feverish, but even more willing. We panted,
kissed and murmured our delights. After three or four
minutes he inundated me anew. My thighs were wet
with his come. I wiped them as best as I could with
my kerchief while he watched and grinned. I truly
believe he expected me to stay long enough for a third
injection.

'What a lot you do in me!'

I could not help but smile. His pride was obvious.

'And shall do again, ma'am, if the pleasure takes
you. As to the whereabouts of these rogues, now.'

'I would like to accompany you, Inspector. I wish to
assure myself that the photographs of Alice – the girl
I spoke of – are truly destroyed. Unfortunately at the
moment I have another engagement. Can you not
secure the villains tomorrow?'

'As you wish. A few more hours will make no difference. And the young girl concerned? I have to take her
statement down, you understand.'

I hesitated, but it would do no harm for Alice to
have a little company. He would take more than her
statement down, I felt sure. I gave him the name of
the hotel. His eyebrows raised. I hastened to explain
that I had paid for her accommodation as an act of
mercy.

'You are a good 'un, all right, ma'am.'

'I try to be, Inspector.'

He would not leave for an hour or two, I guessed. I hastened back to Alice who sat looking rather forlorn. I apprised her of events. Her first thought was of her money. I opened my purse and gave her a guinea. She clutched it as though it were the last coin in the world.

'The Inspector will call soon to see you, Alice. You will tell him everything and show him what you did. You won't be shy?'

'Oh no – I like a bit of company. When shall you come back?'

'In the morning.'

The next day I repaired immediately to the hotel where I had left Alice. There – not unexpectedly – I found her abed with the Inspector. Or rather he in his shirt-tails was sitting on the bed quaffing coffee while Alice lolled beside him like the princess she undoubtedly felt.

She grinned but showed little dismay at my entrance. The Inspector's doughty tool lolled rather limply. It had done much inspecting evidently. His pleasure at seeing me again at such an early hour was exceeding. With pleasing tact, however, he did not attempt to embrace me.

'What's afoot, Inspector? Do you intend to catch the rogues today?'

'No doubt on it, ma'am. I has six stout officers at the ready to pounce, and a cart to take away the photographic plates. They will be needed in evidence, of course.'

'Of course – save those of this dear girl. It would be a terrible thing if they came to light. May I propose a plan to you?'

'As you wish, so long as it don't impede our entry today.'

'No, it will not do that. In fact it will aid it. I intend to visit there. I shall take care to leave the door unlocked. That way your men may enter quietly and take them by surprise. Meanwhile I will ensure that Mr and Miss Pickles are caught in an unguarded moment.'

He gazed at me with admiration. So much did it show that his penis began to thicken. Its bulbous nose peeped from beneath his shirtfront.

'You've given thought to this matter, I can see that, ma'am'

'I do to all things, Inspector. It is now but nine A.M Allow me until eleven. All shall be ready then. Come, Alice, get dressed and we shall depart.'

'Yes, Miss. Will I gets my money?'

'Of course.'

The little wanton was quite naked. Getting off the bed she drew out the chamber pot from beneath it, squatted, and piddled loudly. She being then out of sight of us, I passed my hand beneath the Inspector's shirttail and held his penis for a moment in my gloved hand.

'You have been most accommodating, Inspector.'

'You, too, ma'am. Perhaps we shall co-operate again.'

His penis stirred. It began to assume alarming proportions. The tousled state of the bed afforded me lewd ideas, but I knew better than to succumb to them then. I gave his weapon a last squeeze.

'It will not be forgotten.'

'Nor yours, ma'am. We fitted 'em together nicely.'

Alice was up and wiping herself with a corner of the sheet. I had stepped away from the Inspector. She had not seen my movements. His risen baton appeared as a tribute to her charms. In a moment her clothes were on. Bustling her to the door I looked back at the policeman who lay extended on the bed, his cock upthrust. It was a farmyard invitation. I smiled and shook my head.

A quick breakfast at the eating house where I had previously taken Alice and we were ready for the fray.

I told her all that I intended. Her eyes were aglow with complicity and excitement.

'We have come to photograph again, if you want us.'

Edwina Pickles, who opened the door, looked more disappointed that pleased at our return. We were ushered in. Edwin appeared, looking rather pale.

'I had not expected you yet.'

'It does not matter. The light is good, is it not? If you promise to give us some likenesses of ourselves we will do this one free. But you must pay us for the others that we done.'

My speech was still an amusing mixture of cultivation and Cockney, but it did not matter. He appeared bemused at the invitation.

'Very well, then, but the young man is not here.'

'We will pose together, Alice and I. You will have plenty of sale for such pictures. I know a few people who would buy them – well-to-do ones.'

Their interest was immediately captured. The mystery of my identity added salt to the offer. Edwina accompanied us up to the studio.

'You are not a common girl, are you? Who are these friends you know?'

'Better to ask no questions, Miss Pickles, I am told they sell for two or three guineas a set – a fortune to some, a small amount to others. There are thirty or more men who would give a lot to see me naked in such pictures. First, though, you must pay us.'

The money came immediately to hand. Edwina could not contain herself for curiosity. The idea of quickly selling thirty sets was obviously uppermost in her mind.

'Who are you really? Are you making a market of us?'

'Shall we have wine first? Let me pour it. I find it quite amusing to serve people instead of constantly being waited on.'

There was no disguising my tone of manner now. I had them entranced. I expounded my themes. I was a high-born young lady of the best Society, I told them. The escapade amused me. I knew other young ladies of rank who would be equally daring, given the chance. Alice remainèd dumb with wonder. I satisfied them entirely as to my credentials without giving away a single name. While talking I refilled our glasses and passed into those of Edwin and his sister a few drops from a small phial that I had in my reticule. Papa had brought it back from India with him. I knew its power.

I continued my lecture, amusing myself no end. I reclined upon the floor cushions, so bringing them to follow suit. I had no doubts about the many poor girls they had cheated as they would have done Alice and I.

In a moment Edwina's features grew somewhat flushed, as did her brother's. Forewarned as she had been, Alice affected not to notice. The eyes of the pair assumed a glazed look. Their glasses lolled in their fingers. In a moment both sank back inert.

'Quickly, Alice!'

Edwina appeared conscious but incapable of resistance. We stripped her to her stockings. Her figure was firm and full. Arranging her neatly on her back, we spread her legs. Edwin was next. He attempted a faint resistance but was beyond strength to affect it. A slight dosage of an aphrodisiac in the drug had made his penis distend to a fine length and girth.

Edwina – unable to move – uttered a strangled moan as we rolled him upon her. Excited herself by the effects of the potion, the lips of her vagina were puffy, and moist. To a hollow groan from Edwin his stiff weapon was neatly inserted. The knob disappeared slowly and was engulfed. Their loins stirred restlessly as if each were in a dream. Fetching some rope which I had spied earlier I bound him tightly upon her beneath their arms, rolling Edwina about until he was couched upon her again. Raising her legs, I brought them to his hips and – with the help of Alice – bound her ankles in such wise that her legs could not slide down.

I rose and gazed upon the spectacle. Had I known how to effect a photograph I might have taken a fine one then.

'Shall we leave them like this, Miss?'

'Look for the plates he took of us, Alice. They will be in those metal slides, I suspect, in the corner.'

A neat pile stood there. Undoubtedly they were the ones. Edwin had not developed them yet. Removing them from the slides we shattered each one into several pieces. The evidence that most concerned us was now destroyed.

I gazed at my watch. There were yet six or seven minutes to go before the Inspector and his men arrived. I hastened down and unlocked the door. A carriage passing outside halted at my wave.

'Wait, cabbie.'

I returned to the studio upstairs. Unable to resist temptation, Edwin had begun to agitate his loins. With her legs bound up about him, Edwina was in no position to say no. Her bottom began to bump merrily on the cushions.

'Quickly, Alice!'

We had just time to effect our escape before the policemen arrived. Inspector Barkey approached with his contingent. I waved and pointed to the front door which hung open. His expression was one of dismay that I was departing . . .

A GALLERY OF
NUDES

Like a previous excerpt in this volume A Gallery of Nudes *takes us back to London in the 1950s – though the protagonists of this particular episode are rather more sophisticated than the gauche teenagers of* The Wantons.

Anthony Grey is a well-known roué, a dyed-in-the-wool bachelor whose reputation as a lady-killer is wearing just a little thin now that he has reached the age of fifty. His interest has been piqued, however, by a woman of half his years whom he meets at a rather grand dinner party. Grey perceives Casilda Vandersluys to be 'a sleek young beast, full of surprise' and naturally his curiosity is further aroused by the knowledge that she is the lover of his hostess, the society heiress Helen. It soon transpires that Casilda's interests are not exclusively homosexual and that she is fascinated by all kinds of behaviour – 'meaning,' as she puts it, 'Sex with a big snaky capital S.' In short, Casilda is keen to indulge in any kind of sexual antics, the more outrageous the better. She arranges for Tony to watch Helen making love to her, she picks up a swarthy young Spaniard in a restaurant and beds him at Tony's flat, she turns the tables on Helen with Tony to that lady's utter horror – the more public the act and the more complex the emotions involved, the happier she is. And so, when Tony renews his acquaintance with an old girlfriend and her husband, Cassie is only too keen to make the most of what turns out to be a very uninhibited occasion . . .

It was at an exhibition of paintings by a young Austrian artist, one wintry February evening, that we ran into Janet, whom Casilda had not met before, though I, needless to say, had related to her many memorable incidents from the annals of our tempestuous, jaunty-blithe, dingdong engagement, which had lasted on and off for nearly seven years and broke up in final disorder, to our immense mutual relief, on the way in her car to the registry. I have a weak ankle still as a result of that thousand-and-first fracas, while Janet wears two wedding rings, a false front tooth, and a big white streak in her dark mane as reminders of what she calls 'the public wars' or 'my grim Grey period.' We were now fond friends, sharing the curious jocular charm that passions spent acquire as a patina with age, but I had not seen her, either, nor her inoffensive Scottish husband, Andrew, since 'the evening you vamoosed halfway through dinner,' as Janet reminded me rather tartly. She shrugged off my apologies. 'I only hope she was worth it,' she said, 'I assume so, as we haven't heard from you since.'

We were standing under the shadows of an elongated Battersea Bridge at sunset, and Casilda drifted in from the next room at that moment, catalogue in hand, looking for me.

'I rather like that,' Janet declared, waving a glove at some bathers on a canal bank and narrowly missing Casilda's nose as she approached.

'Me too,' I said. I introduced them. 'This was the reason why I owe you and Andrew an especially good dinner.' I explained, 'to make up, Janet dear, for my rudeness in leaving you that night a trifle abruptly.'

'Janet, the famous Janet!' Casilda exclaimed. 'Knowing Tony as we do, I needn't tell you how often he drags your name into the conversation. It's a household word with us, if you'll forgive me saying so.'

'Oh, my God, yes, I'm sorry for you,' Janet laughed. 'He's such a tireless reminiscer, isn't he? You must know all – but everything – about me in the most lurid detail, I'm sure. How dismal of you, Tony!'

'Let me give you the lowdown on Casilda in return,' I offered. 'When can you have a quiet, gossipy lunch with me?'

'I insist on getting my word in first,' Casilda stated. 'We girls have a lot in common. What do you say, Janet? Unless we let him come along as well – just to eat, shut up, and listen.'

We took a stroll round the gallery, discussing Klaus Ritter's quite commendable stuff, and gave Janet a few drinks at the pub on the corner before she dived into the Underground for Hampstead, where we were to dine with them the following Thursday. My two darlings, past and present, had taken to each other in a big way, and I was completely ignored in the frowzy saloon bar while they got on like a row of houses on fire, chattering and giggling so gaily that I noticed several staid customers regarding them with greater interest and more frankly amused admiration than any freak or foreigner can normally count on arousing among the British at home. They made a striking pair of beauties, even for the West End, I will admit, in that dowdy setting, though there was nothing bizarre about Janet's lean English looks and Casilda was so un-American an expatriate that she could happily refer to herself as a crossbred mongrel, instead of just taking it for granted.

'I'm nuts about that Janet of yours,' Casilda informed me as the station swallowed my ex-fiancée down its fetid gullet. 'She's loads of fun – and madly attractive, in a famished style of looks. Not much of her, is there?'

'If Janet were ever to shed an ounce of weight off her spare frame, skinny would be the only word for her. But that isn't feasible because there ain't no flesh on her anywhere that she could lose, as I used to tell her, without the light showing through. You'd have to scoop to hollow out even a sliver of Janet. My cronies used to describe her as scrawny, but dressmakers call it 'slenderly built.' She's a sylph – irremediably thin, or, as she says herself, 'thin with knobs on.' That's more accurate. The knobs are all there, and the curves – long and slight and sinewy as a greyhound's, but perfectly in proportion and finely drawn, like a stream-lined, sensitive piece of machinery, a shiny steel instrument of some sort. Janet, stripped, presents a far less gaunt appearance than the fashionable self you saw in her clothes. A bit lanky, of course, but a damned sight more human in shape when she's naked.'

'So I would imagine,' Casilda commented with a smile. 'You and your nudes! You analyse and compare every woman's body you come across. Wouldn't you do better to photograph us all for the record, instead of trying to remember a whole jumbled mass of mental notes?'

Where Janet was concerned, if I wished to be critical,

I would set against her undoubted good points two anatomical flaws that are often found in this tall breed of Englishwomen. Her tits were appealing, firm and excellent, although of course too small – but they also were placed too low and rather too far apart, pointing outwards, which gave her a flat chest at first sight, and yet, almost as a pleasant afterthought, a distinctly feminine bosom. This was charming enough in itself, once discovered; but it seemed to have little, if any, connection with the strongly marked, splendid pectoral muscles that could scarcely be needed to lift those sweet, prancing, miniature breasts. Secondly, under her fork, at the top of her long, lean shanks, though she was not bow-legged, there was an empty space, an unsightly, inverted triangular gap between the thighs, which were devoid of any fat, so that, here, at the vital intersection itself, you got more room for manoeuvre than is usually provided for a man's comfort or the woman's ease in accommodating a visitor's retinue, however bulky. It always struck me that this fault – I would hardly call it a drawback – detracted from the obvious merits of Janet's smooth, pretty concave belly and proud, very prominent mount of Venus, which were among her best features, to my taste.

The Mackenzies lived on the far side of Hampstead. Andrew wore glasses, an incipient paunch, and a canny, good-natured expression, as though all three attributes were as congenial to him as the pink complexion which was a shade darker, if anything, than his now greying carroty hair. Physically he was not prepossessing, but he had the proverbial Scottish traits of dry humour and reserved gravity, though he carried neither to that excess which amounts, in many of his race, to unwarranted conceit and taciturn boorishness. The martinis, after a hard day's work at his printing office, loosened his tongue before we sat down to the delicious, unorthodox sort of meal in which both our hosts, and hostess, as butler and cook, were right to take great pride, for its succession of exotic specialities was typical of the house. Casilda could not conceal her admiring envy and thereby won Andrew's heart, so that no stranger joining us at table would have been able to guess who among the assembled company were intimate friends or had never met before in their lives.

Andrew assured me, when I complimented him on the choice variety of his food and wines, that above all else he had a passion for his trade as a typographer, which took up every moment of his time, he said, apart from weekend gold, because he had allowed it to become his hobby as well. He too was a collector – of books. 'I have a very small library,' he told me, 'but most of the items in it are prize specimens, and some are unique. You'll see – though they may not be much up your street. I only go in for fine bindings and perfect examples of print.'

Andrew kept his cigars also in the cosy little room off the hall, where we retreated with a decanter and plenty of coffee to inspect the shelves that glowed, like a tapestry, with rich tones of leather and gilt. He showed me a wealth of magnificent volumes, among them half a dozen that I had not merely seen before in booksellers' lists or behind glass, and though I did not doubt his word it occurred to me that sometimes perhaps he let the merits of subject matter outweigh the intrinsic value of the production. There was a priceless Aretion, the *Decameron*, Crebillon's *Sofa* and other curious works that may have owed their presence there to outward beauty, but, rubbing shoulders with them, I found a tome or two – a smudgy, tattered copy of Rochester's *Sodom*, for example – whose rarity alone would rate them worthy of inclusion, whereas the few modern editions, maybe a score, in a separate section, belonged to the same single class of illustrated masterpieces intended solely for perusal by adult and discriminating readers.

I was pouring over the pages of Sade's *Justine* when

the telephone pealed out beside me, and the bookworm Andrew answered it. An agitated voice spluttered at length into his ear, eliciting no more than an occasional gruff query or dour affirmative in reply. Finally he snapped: 'Well, all right then – I'll have to go down and cope with it myself, I shan't be long.'

He turned to me. 'I'm sorry,' he said. 'A call from that fool of a head printer. Apologise to the girls on my behalf. I might get back, with luck, before you go.'

He started to ring for a taxi, but I insisted on driving him at least as far as the station. It was a dirty night, and I was glad to let myself into the warmth with his latchkey. *En passant* I picked up another cigar and some brandy from the study before joining the ladies.

There they were, on the sofa together, in front of the drawing-room fire, but I could not say that I caught them in a compromising situation, because they showed no sign of heeding my intrusion in the least. Janet was almost lost to view in Casilda's arms, but both were still fully clothed. Casilda was kissing and fondling my former love, who very evidently relished her attentions, for her head was thrown back, her eyes were shut, and she was sighing and squirming in that abandoned way she had, which I remembered so well. This went on for some time, until Casilda, becoming aware of my diffident presence, looked up and gave me a wink of the most entrancing vulgarity. If she did not wave in recognition, it was because both her hands were deeply engaged, at first on a roving mission and then in a definite pincer movement that appeared to rouse our hostess from uneasy slumbers to a vocal and increasingly active share in the proceedings. Janet's staring peepers opened like a doll's, she suddenly found a great deal to say – all of it highly flattering to her newly acquired friend – and her arms, linked about Casilda's neck, dragged the happy, wide, scarlet mouth down to her own, silencing them both, to some extent, for neither one of the excited pair could speak again for a while in coherent terms, though the language they used was an expressive universal *lingua franca* sound beyond the limits of speech, as they kissed, mumbled, panted, gasped and sighed . . .

I was sitting back in a large armchair, quietly puffing at my mellow Larriñaga, as utterly at ease as a millionaire impresaria watching a deliriously popular stage turn from the wings. The success of the act did not exactly surprise me, though it had never crossed my mind, earlier in the evening, that the girls would fall for each other in such startling earnest, practically on first sight, or that their mutual attraction could produce this happy harvest, before one could say Tallulah Bankhead. Casilda, I realised, might perhaps have been feeling a trifle starved for this special form of love, which no doubt meant more to her than she was prepared to admit. Bless her wicked heart, I couldn't blame her for getting up to her old tricks again so soon, at the drop of an eyelid! But, casting my mind back over Janet's case history, I did not recall that she ever showed much liking or aptitude but rather, on the contrary, a natural distaste for any hint of these naughty digressions, which I would, I confess, have been only too ready to encourage and approve. It was obvious that Casilda had taken the initiative tonight, and was calling the tune, but I was equally fascinated to see that Janet must have welcomed her overtures without the faintest hesitation of demur, judging by their present harmonious pitch of enthusiasm. There had not been time, after all, for any lengthy process of persuasion, and Casilda, with her unfailing sixth sense in sexual matters, had clearly neither delayed nor rushed the pace unduly. They seemed meant for one another – and both were bent on proving it.

I crossed over and sat on the arm of the sofa. Casilda's black jersey dress was off one shoulder. She had undone Janet's shirt and removed her bra. Between them they struggled to get her out of her

381

tight tartan trews. Casilda signalled to me for aid. She
had slithered on to the floor and delved deep into
Janet's lap at once, leaving the upper half of the long,
slim body in my care. Janet's rosy limbs were flung
wide across the cushions, like a starfish stranded helpless on the shore. Hers was the emaciated, abandoned
carcass, we the plundering crows that swooped on her
in unison to gnaw her vitals. Neither of them at last
could bear the strain another moment. Leaping to her
feet, Casilda wrenched off her sombre plumage,
quickly cast the layer of downy silky beneath, and,
launching the full force of all her naked weight into
the saddle, bestrode the eager mount that bucked,
quivered, reared, bounced hard up to meet her with a
wild, savage will of its own. I was thrown off my perch
and was forced to relinquish the tiny, tender, dancing
tits to Casilda's strong grip, as she seized them for
reins and clung to them also for support while she rode
the cleft of Janet's crotch, hitching it fiercely to her
own, twisting and writhing against it, plunging, pressing, thrusting more and more closely, more deeply into
the devil's dripping mouth, the open breach, the
entrance to the loins' dark, leafy-locked, mysterious
cave, to dig within its folds on a hot quest for hidden
treasure . . .

I could have sworn that the violence of this encounter made the roughest moments of the frenzied frolic
I had witnessed between Helen and Casilda seem like
child's play. Among several reasons for this distinct
impression were the fact that here was a new and
unexpected challenge, that it was largely a novel thrill
for Janet, whose physique was particularly well con-
structed to ensure that she should get the utmost
enjoyment out of such an awkward method of fornication, that both girls were conscious of their appreci-
ative audience,so may have been tempted to play up
accordingly, and not only had Casilda lately been
deprived of this pleasurable outlet but probably she

felt that, given the chance to cuckold me a little into the bargain, she must trespass on an ancient light-o'-love of mine with an extra vengeance. She did not stint herself, certainly, nor pull her punches. But Janet was never one to take things lying down – at least not in any metaphorical sense. She gave as good as she got, on principle – and in this case she put up such a gallant show that she succeeded, with all her wiry might and by a swift, wrestling ell-like motion, in turning the tables completely on her more solid opponent. I did not see how it was done, but in a tangled flash, after a brief upheaval of flailing legs and humped muscle, the lightweight came out on top, like a bantam in the cockpit, amid a triumphant flutter of wings, spurs and waving crests. It now seemed better so. She held Casilda in the scissor grasp, and their joint movement, fast and furious, grew, rose, galloped, pounded, swelled to Valkyrian speed... when the door behind me opened, and Andrew walked in.

He must have used the back way. He stopped dead in his tracks and stared at the scene that confronted him, but said nothing. I handed him a drink off the mantlepiece, which one of our women had sipped and left. We stood side by side in front of the fire, watching with all eyes. Still he did not speak. I was glad. Only brute force could have separated them. It would not take long... suddenly there was a single loud, sharp cry from both their throats – followed, seconds later, by a choking, breathless rattle of joy that fell away in the lost, heavy silence. Languidly Janet withdrew, as a man does, quitting the flattened body that has received the gift of his sperm. She staggered slightly and dropped into a chair. I passed her the rest of my cognac. We gazed at Casilda, lying motionless and spent, lax and spread-eagled on the sofa, as uncovered and starkly indecent as a corpse. When she moved at last, and looked at us, it was to clutch at her fork, her throbbing parts, with a quick shiver and a broad, quiet smile; but not to shield the wound or hide her trembling flesh from view. Her playful fingers parted it in fact, lightly toying with the matted curls, stroking the flushed red rim all round, as though applying an oily balm to soothe a gently tickling sore, and skimming down its blatantly bare, gaping length, as in a quick canoe between bushy banks, she sighed, arched her back lazily, with yearning, and rolled her tousled head upon the cushions. We knew what she wanted – a different, immediate and deeper solace. She had made that plain enough.

'Take pity on her,' I said to Andrew, 'since she's asking for it. You have my permission.'

He glanced at Janet, who nodded. 'And mine,' she said.

'No – that won't quite do.' It was Casilda who spoke, to our surprise, as though she could not yet have revived sufficiently to communicate with us directly by word of mouth, but must continue to emply her more expressive sign language.

'Both men – I'll have you both,' she said, sitting up. 'That's it, that's what I want – and always did. Hurry, can't you – get undressed! One in front and one behind. We can manage that if we try . . .'

It took some managing. Andrew had already torn off his clothes, before I could work out what Casilda meant or how she proposed to set about it. She sat huddled demurely on her tail now, a caricature of modesty, waiting. She studied us carefully although of course she didn't need to examine me, it all depended on Andrew. He was enormous. The tool he carried was a long, gnarled, hefty great club – a bludgeon. I was astonished. Casilda's eyes opened wide. She wet her lips. For such a little fellow, upon my soul, you would scarcely believe it possible – the most lavish endowment, and considering that it did not show up to advantage, under that bulging stomach, frankly excessive, an outsized monstrosity. How women can contemplate

384

such repulsive objects without flinching in horror at the sight, they alone know! It had a curve on it like a rhinoceros horn or a hockey stick – and no less vast were the balls, slung in a hideous, wrinkled sack, as big as a cantaloupe. The corona itself was a dark, bursting ripe red plum, stuck on at the end of a thick, knotted bare branch – nothing short of grotesque. There we were, standing to attention, with weapons at the ready, presenting arms for Casilda's inspection. She leaned forward, putting out a hand to each of us, in an unconscious, ribald parody of a royal command soiree, assessing our offers – medium and immoderate – with judicious concentration on the big problem that faced or otherwise intimately concerned her.

In point of fact the choice was obvious; but she anointed us both for her own ends, when Janet's sisterly perception had sent her post-haste from the room, to the medicine chest, on an errand of mercy. The sofa looked a bit cramped, I thought, for the three of us, but Casilda shook her head when I beckoned her to the wide, woolly hearthrug, and, firmly drawing the two members of her party towards the couch, she lay down on her side, without letting go of us, as we loomed above her, wondering what to do next. There was only one solution, which Janet, the idle spectator, promptly advised, though it probably dawned on us all simultaneously. We turned Casilda on to her back. Andrew got up into position with some effort and misguided vigour, yet not so precipitately as the pawing stallion who needs assistance to put him into a proper fix, oddly enough, rather than to pull him out of a hole – and they settled down to it straightaway, going great guns, hard on the job with everything they had.

It was a sight to see, and thrilling to overhear, for they made the deuce of a noise, rootling like stoats, though neither of them said a word. None of us had a stitch on. A lurid light shone in Janet's eyes, as she hovered and circled around the inebriate pair, like a referee. I hopped, in sheer torture, from foot to foot, torn between fiendish impatience and jealousy. My turn would come to repay this lewd, hot-slotted nympho in kind, and I hoped it would hurt the crazy, cock-struck whore – hell take her grinding guts, I'd give it to the bitch till she laughed on the wrong side of her foul, fat fanny, damn it. I'd shoot some decent good sense up her leching, bawdy bum and fill my lovely lady with a jolt from a prick every bit as rich and randy as his ... but when? Would they never stop? She was carried away completely, curse her, she had forgotten all about me. He'd spend, and spoil half our fun in a minute, if she didn't watch out ... ought I to take the risk and cut in? Where was Janet? She'd serve, at a pinch. It was then, praise be, that Casilda rolled over, pushing the chap with her, jabbing him in the ribs, shoving them around, both of them, to lie, still copulating like monkeys, on their sides, with him facing out towards the fireplace, his back against the sofa, and she, in reverse, showing me her buttocks, the white, milky full moon of her bottom turned to me. There it was at last, beaming, big, broad and beautiful, in all its innocence or insolence, bland or crass, according to how one looked on it, delivered into my power as a hostage, meat indeed for the slaughter, rakish and docile, the sinful flesh ...

It was worth a further fleeting delay, a moment's scrutiny. I bent over the two-back beast, ran my hand along the steep ravine between the smooth, cool cheeks, which jounced about distractingly under stern orders from in front, though Casilda thrust her tail outwards as far as she dared while I probed the pursued little brown buttonhole, like the bud of a tiny wild-flower, with my fingertip at first, and then, flinging myself on the sofa behind her, and prising the massive mounds apart, with an inch or so of the old codger himself. Easy does it, in he goes – just as slippery and sweet as you please ... no trouble at all –

for a couple of split seconds, that is, until we got the warhead in place, truly embedded, streaking up her fundament like a dentist's drill through a temporary stopping, an express train roaring full-on into a tunnel, a bull-dozer boring a trench in a stiffly packed squelch of clay. But then, ye gods, what a to-do! What shrill yelps and yells, what wriggling, tugging and dodging, what tearful entreaties, elbowings, fisticuffs, and ghastly oaths! I held on to her grimly by one hip, with the other arm around her neck, and ploughed on, regardless of the cloudburst, which passed and was gone in a few more shakes at the crucial base of the triangle . . .

The last of this trio, however, was the first to quit. It wasn't my fault. I had shot my bolt a little while before the others finished – which apparently they did, bringing it off very adroitly, together. I might have lasted out, too, if Janet had not seen fit to chip in as an auxiliary to our already somewhat overcrowded act by prodding me from the rear and swiping at my backside with her open palm, just when we were all approaching the terrific climax of our intricate three-fold exercise. It's true that I was teetering on the sofa's edge the whole time, and nearly got butted off on to the floor once or twice, because there simply wasn't room for three on it: Casilda had her arms and legs coiled around Andrew in a ferocious hug to keep him in place, the couch was far too short, we stuck out in every direction like a cactus patch. But Janet's well meant intervention hastened my undoing.

I started to dress, and Andrew was about to follow suit, but his wife would not hear of it. She had snuggled up next to Casilda, cooing affectionately, but her hackles rose on the instant when she saw what was afoot.

'Hey, no you don't!' she cried with comic indignation, although quite seriously. 'That's all jolly fine – but what about me? You two stay right where you are,

387

until I'm given just the same treatment as Casilda here. How frightfully ungallant of you, Tony, to try to sneak out on me, again! Really you're both absolute bounders, I do think. But I shan't allow it! I won't have you make such cads of yourselves. Come here!'

'Janet, honey,' I pleaded, 'have a heart! With the best will in the world . . .' I pointed to my cock. It was shrivelled and limp.

Andrew's, as she could see for herself, was in an even more pitiful plight – shrunk to a third of its former size, it hung down only a quarter of the way to his knees, like a discarded old rope end, frayed and soggy. Ugly enough at the peak of its rampant grandeur, now, in this tatty, slack, bedraggled state, it was simply revolting.

'I'd be no lousy use to you, my sweet,' he protested mildly. 'Another day – '

'Come here!' she repeated. 'We'll look into this . . .'

We were leaning against the mantlepiece, side by side, warming our backs at the fire. We did not budge – so Janet dropped on her haunches between us on the hearthrug. She refused to lose faith. She was not going to take no for an answer. We swayed, drooping before her very eyes, our crinkled, deflated organs dangling under her nose. She set to, an ardent revivalist, tackling the desperate, double task with both hands. I got the left, her better one – and she took us to task with both hands at once. She was making a lovely job of it, quite like old times . . . soon it was better still: I got her undivided attention, when Casilda flopped down beside her, and took over half the work. Now Janet could devote herself wholeheartedly to doing one thing at a time – too beautiful for words . . . her undivided attention was nothing if not widespread . . . she flag-wagged signals to Casilda, reporting progress, while simultaneously she massaged my scrotum and slid a hand between by legs, to visit warmer regions, where a venturesome middle finger went on an expedition to

explore the interior ... Janet was never so rash and
clumsy as to frig a fellow at all strenuously until it
was required of her. In my present condition, any but
the most gradual first aid would have proved fatal.
She rubbed and kneaded my testicles, pinching and
playing with them, while merely brushing and stroking my phallus, as though to chafe and polish it, with
a certain curious maternal fondness, for its own sake.
Comparing by results – which are, after all, what coun-
ts- I'd have said she ran rings round Casilda; but I
may have been biased by gratitude in her favour –
especially when she went the whole hog and adopted
heroic measures, with her tongue at first, then her
lips, and finally her mouth, that other vulva, a cavity
as scorching-hot and spongy but twice as clever ...
We were the more advanced; Casilda was finding it
an uphill, gruelling chore to strike a spark into that
dormant, mouldy member, so she consulted me with
an air of punctilious servility. 'May I? she asked. I
gestured dumb assent. She clapped her kisser like a
leech to his gross organ, which had begun to swell and
stretch by infinitely small degrees, like some slow-
waking giant. There, she had something to be going
on with! Personally, my cure was almost complete ...
we looked like queer bookends, the four of us, like
heraldic supporters or carved figures, flanking the
chimney piece, although the caryatids knelt, shoulder
to shoulder, while the quaking male pillars could
barely stand upright, but had to be propped and girded,
fore and aft by sustained, intimate pressures from
below. We were lifted and wired underneath, Andrew
and I, to make a peculiar nude frieze and our two
ministering angels, the fairer and the darker, identical
in their position yet so different in build, the one full-
bodied and shapely, the other spare and lithe. With
heads bent over their labours, noses to the grindstone
their agitated mops of hair were hoisted on our joy-
sticks at half-mast, as though luxuriant, extra fleece

389

had sprouted from his protruding paunch, and my pale belly. Casilda linked the circuit by lending a hand to fiddle with Janet's pussy – a bonus which Janet promptly requited in kind. Andrew's arm lay, lightly touching mine, along the mantleshelf.

Casilda took command as mistress of ceremonies, but Janet jibbed at the sofa, like a horse at a hedge, so our tricky threesome was accomplished this time, in the end and with equal or even greater difficulty, after various vain attempts on the rug, when Andrew was shored up with pillows on the edge of a large armchair, Janet impaled herself upon his prong, to sprawl face down on top of him, crushing him against the springs and hitching herself high up into the air for me eventually to perforate at my leisure, though not with some jabbing and incitements from Casilda, who skipped around the simmering stewpot like a witch doctor. My orgasm was the last – a feather in my cap, I thought – and for a few moments after we were through with the smothered underdog, Janet and I shunted to and fro in ecstasy, a toppling pile of flesh, like a three-decker sandwich, that sagged to rest where it lay, until Casilda called us to get a bit to eat in the kitchen, which Andrew aptly compared to a nudist's canteen.

'Whenever you feel like a return match,' said Casilda brightly as we left, 'just let us know.'

THE ROMANCE OF LUST

The Romance of Lust, or Early Experiences *is one of the world's most notorious erotic texts. Here is a veritable cornucopia of lubricity from the Victorian era featuring possibly the most precocious and prodigious of sexual heroes, young Charlie Roberts. His remorseless pursuit of a thorough sexual education is spread over the course of four volumes, leaving the reader panting with exhaustion and our hero – incredibly – panting for more. It is the youthful Charlie's greatest delight to lure his elders and supposed betters into compromising positions and scarcely a member of his family can resist his phallic charm. However, in this excerpt from the opening of Volume Four, we see the indefatigable Charlie spreads his net beyond his own relations and undertakes the wholesale seduction of his landlady's family . . .*

I had taken lodgings in Norfolk Street, Strand, for the convenience of being near King's College. It was at the house of a Mrs. Nichols, tall, powerfully built, masculine, but a kind and motherly looking widow of fifty-two – an attentive and bustling landlady, looking herself to the better cooking, and having a plain cook, who was also a general servant, to help her downstairs, and two nieces to do the waiting and attendance on her lodgers upstairs. The younger was there alone when I entered the lodgings; her elder sister had had what they called a 'misfortune,' and was then in the country until she could be unburthened of it. She was expected back in about six weeks. Meanwhile, as the winter was not the season, I was the only lodger, and the younger had only me to attend to; her name was Jane; she was but a little thing, but very well made, good bubbies and bottom, which I soon discovered were firm and hard, projecting fully on both sides. She was fairly good looking, but with a singular innocent manner of freedom about her that made me imagine she had as yet had no chance of a 'misfortune.' In a week we became intimate, and after often praising her pretty face and figure, I snatched a kiss now and then, which at first she resented with an attractive yet innocent sort of sauciness. It was in her struggles on these occasions that I became aware of the firm hard bosom and bottom.

Up to this time my flirtations were without ulterior object, but the reality of the attractions of these hidden charms raised my lustful passions. I gradually increased my flatteries and caresses, squeezed her bubbies, when I sometimes drew her on my knee and was kissing her, and as at first she resisted my drawing her to my knee, I took occasion to lay hold of her buttocks, which I found more developed than I could have supposed. Gradually her resistance to these little liberties ceased and she would quietly sit on my knee and return the kiss I gave. Her dress was a little open in front, so from feeling her bubbies outside, I gradually got to feeling their naked beauties inside. I now thought I could attempt greater familiarities, so one day when seated on my knee with one arm round her waist, I pressed her to my lips, and while so engaged, whipped my free arm up her petticoats, and before she had become aware of the movement, had got my hand upon her mount, a very nicely haired one, She started up to a standing position, but as I held her close clasped round the waist she could not get away, and her new position enabled me the easier to get my hand between her thighs and thus to feel her charming pouting little cunt. I began attempting to frig her clitoris, but stooping she drew her cunt away, and looking at me with a droll innocent expression of alarm, and with a perfect unconsciousness of the import of her words, cried, – 'Oh! take care what you are at. You don't know how a lodger this last summer suffered for seizing me in that way and hurting me very much. I

394

screamed out, aunt came up, and, do you know, he had £50 to pay for his impudence.'

I could not but smile at the extraordinary innocence of the girl.

'But I do not hurt you, dear Jane,' said I, 'and don't mean to do so.'

'That was what he said, but he went on in a most horrible way, and not only hurt me very much, but made me bleed.'

'It would not be with his hand, you see I only gently press this soft hairy little thing. I am sure that don't hurt you.'

'Oh no! if that was all I should not mind it, it was when he pushed me on the sofa, and pressed upon me, that he hurt me terribly, and you must take care what you are about, or you too will have to pay £50.'

There was a curious air of innocence in all this; it was evident to me the fellow had got into her, and broken her hymen with violence, and then her screams had prevented his finishing his work. Her manner convinced me that she was really not aware of the consequences, or rather had not as yet really had her sexual passions aroused.

'Well, my dear Jane, I neither intend to hurt you or make myself liable to pay £50, but you will not refuse me the pleasure of feeling this nice little hairy nest, you see how gentle I am.'

'Well, if you will do me no more hurt than that I shan't refuse you, because you are a nice kind young gentleman, and very different from the other rough fellow, who never chattered with me and made me laugh as you do – but you must not push your fingers up there, it was something he pushed up there that hurt me so.'

I withdrew my finger, and as, at my request, she had opened her thighs a little, I felt and caressed her very nice little cunt, and with a finger pressed externally above her clitoris, I could see that she flushed

395

and shivered on feeling me there. However, I did no more than gently press and feel all her hairy mount and fat pouting cunt; she said I must let her go, or her aunt would be coming up.

The first step was now gained. Gradually I progressed further and further; felt her charming bare arse as she stood before me, got her to let me see the beautiful curls she had got on her cunt, then came to kissing it, until at last she opened her thighs and let me tongue it, to her most exquisite delight. I made her spend for the first time in her life, and soon she came to me for it. I had gradually introduced a finger up her cunt while licking her clitoris and exciting her so much that she was unconscious of my doing it; then two fingers, and after she had spent deliciously, I made them perform an imitation of a throb, which made her jump and ask what I was doing. I asked if she did not feel that my fingers were inside of her sweet Fanny.

'You don't say so. It was there I was so hurt.'

'But I do not hurt you, dear Jane?'

'Oh, dear no, it makes me feel queer, but it is very nice.'

'Well, now you know that I have two fingers inside, I will use my tongue again against your charming little clitoris, and work the fingers in and out.'

I did so, and she soon spent in an agony of delight, pressing my head down hard on her cunt, and crying – 'Oh! oh! it is too great a pleasure!' and then died off, half insensible. Another time I repeated this she told me not to forget to use my fingers. Having made her spend twice I took her on my knee, and told her that I possessed an instrument that would give her far more pleasure than tongue or finger.

'Indeed?' said she, 'where is it? I should so like to see it.'

'You won't tell.'

'Oh, no!'

So pulling out my stiff-standing prick, she stared in

amazement. She had really never seen a prick, although it was evidently a prick that had deflowered her, for with my fingers I had explored her cunt, and found no hymen there. I put her hand upon it; she involuntarily grasped it firmly.

'This enormous thing could never get into my body, look, it is thicker than all your fingers put together, and only two fingers feel so tight.'

'Yes, darling, but this dear little thing stretches, and was made to receive this big thing.'

I was exciting her clitoris with my finger, she grew evidently lasciviously inclined, so saying, 'Just let me try, and if it hurts you I will stop; you know I am always gentle with you.'

'So you are, my dear fellow, but take care not to hurt me.'

She lay down on the bed, as I desired, with feet up and knees laid open. I spat on my prick, and wetted the knob and upper shaft well, then bringing it to her cunt, well moistened by my saliva in gamahuching her, I held open the lips with the fingers of my left hand, and half buried its knob before getting to the real entrance.

'Don't flinch, dearest, I shall not hurt,' And I got it well over the knob, and buried it one inch further.

'Stop!' she cried, 'it seems as it would burst me open, it so stretches me.'

'But it does not hurt you, dearest?' I had immediately stopped before asking the question.

'No not exactly, but I feel as if something was in my throat.'

'Rest a little, and that will go off.' I slipped a finger down on her clitoris, and as I frigged it she grew more and more excited, giving delicious cunt pressures on my prick, it gradually made its way by the gently pushing I continued to make without other movements. It was more than half in when she spent, this not only lubricated the interior, but the inner muscles relaxing, a gentle shove forward housed it to the hilt, and then I lay quiet until she recovered from the half fainting state her last discharge had produced; soon the increased pressures of the inner folds showed that her passions were awakening afresh. She opened her eyes and, looking lovingly, said I have given her great pleasure, but she felt as if something enormous was stretching her inside to the utmost. Had I got it all in?

'Yes, dearest, and now it will be able to give you greater pleasure than before.' I began a slow withdrawal and return, frigging her clitoris at the same time, for I was standing between her legs. She soon grew wild with excitement, nature prompting her, her arse rose and fell almost as well as if she was mistress of the art. The novel combination of prick and finger quickly brought on the ecstatic crisis. I, too, was wild with lust, and we spent together, ending in an annihilation of all our senses by the extreme ecstasy of the final overpowering crisis. We lay panting for some time in all the after-joys. Dear Jane begged me to give her some water, as she felt quite faint. I withdrew, still almost in a standing state, got her some water, helped her up, seated her on the sofa and kissed her lovingly as I thanked her for the exquisite joy she had given me. She threw her arms round my neck, and with tears in her eyes told me I had taught her the joys of heaven, and she should always love me, and I must always love her, for now she could not live without me. I kissed and dried her eyes, and told her we should in future enjoy it even more when she got accustomed to it.

'Let me see the dear thing that gave me such pleasure.'

I pulled it out, but it was no longer at the stand; and this surprised her. I explained the necessity of its being so, but said she would quickly see it rise and swell to the former size if she continued to handle it so nicely. It rose almost before I could say as much. She fondled it, and even stooped and kissed its ruby head. We should quickly have got to another bout of fucking if the ringing of the call bell had not brought us to a sense of its imprudence; so after arranging her hair and dress, she hastily descended with some of the breakfast things.

Of course, so good a beginning led to constant renewals and Jane quickly became extremely amorous, and under my instruction a first-rate fucker.

As all my dear friends were not in London, I was fortunate in having such a *bonne bouche* to comfort me. My sisters passed every Sunday with me, and both got some good fucking out of me in every way, without raising any suspicions in the house.

A month after I had taken up my residence at Mrs. Nichols's, Jane's sister arrived. She was a much finer woman than Jane, broad shouldered, wide-spread bosom, which, in after-days, I found had not suffered by her 'misfortune,' but then she had not suckled it. Her hips were widely projected, and she was grand and magnificent in her arse. Naturally of a very hot temperament, when once she had tasted the magnificent weapon I was possessed of, she grew most lasciviously lustful, and was one of the best fuckers I ever met with. Her power of nip almost equalled my beloved aunt's. Jane was fair, Ann was dark, with black locks and black hairy cunt – a very long cunt, with a small tight hole in it, and above it a wide-spread projecting mount, splendidly furnished with hair. Her clitoris was hard and thick, but with little projection. She also became madly fond of arse-fucking, and particularly liked me to spend therein. This was partly to prevent any consequences leading to a second 'misfortune.'

On her first arrival Jane was much afraid she would discover our connection and we took every precaution, although I, in my heart, wished this might occur, for as she occasionally waited on me, I grew lecherous upon one whose charms, even covered, excited me greatly. I always flattered and praised her magnificence of figure whenever she came alone to me, but as Jane generally was running in and out, I did not attempt further action. One morning I overheard Mrs. Nichols tell Jane to put on her bonnet and go to Oxford Street on some errand; I knew thus that Ann would attend on me, and there would be no chance of interruption from Jane, so I determined to come at once to the point. We had become on friendly, chatty terms, and when she had laid breakfast I asked her to help me me on with my coat, which done, I thanked her and with one arm round her waist drew her to me and kissed her. 'Hallo!' said she, 'that is something new,' but did not attempt to withdraw, so giving her another kiss, I told her what a glorious woman she was, and how she excited me – just see. I held one of her hands, and before she was aware, placed it on my huge prick, that bulged out of my trousers as if it would burst its way through.

She could not help squeezing it, while she cried -

'Goodness, gracious! what an enormous thing you have got!'

Her face flushed, her eyes sparkled with the fire of lust that stirred her whole soul. She tried to grasp it.

'Stop,' said I, 'and I will put it in its natural state into your hand.'

So pulling it out, she seized it at once, and most lasciviously gazed upon it, pressing it gently. She evidently was growing lewder and lewder, so I at once proposed to fuck her, and thinking it best to be frank, and put her at her ease, I told her that I knew she had had a 'misfortune,' but if she would let me fuck her I should be on honour to withdraw before spending, and thus avoid all chance of putting her belly up.

She had become so randy that she felt, as she afterwards told me, she could not refuse so splendid a prick of a size she had often dreamt of, and longed for.

'Can I trust you?' said she.

'Safely, my dear.'

'Then you may have me – let me embrace that dear object.'

Stooping, she kissed it most voluptuously, shivering at the same time in the ecstasy of a spend produced by the mere sight and touch. She gave one or two 'ohs,' and drawing me to the bed by my prick, threw herself back, pulling her petticoats up at the same time. Then I beheld her splendid cunt in all its magnificence of size and hairiness. I sank on my knees and glued my lips to the oozing entrance, for she was one who spent most profusely, her cunt had the true delicious odour, and her spunk was thick and glutinous for a woman. I tongued her clitoris, driving her voluptuously wild. So she cried -

'Oh! do put that glorious prick into me, but remember your promise.'

I brought it up to that wide-spread, large-lipped, and immense cunt. I fully expected that big as I was I should slip in over head and shoulders with the greatest ease. So you may imagine my surprise to find the tightest and smallest of entrances to the inner vagina I almost ever met with, it was really with greater difficulty I effected an entrance than I had with her little sister, whose cunt presented no such voluptuous grandeur. It was as tight a fit as Ellen's was to me on our first coition. Tight as it was, it gave her nothing but the most exquisite pleasure, she was thoroughly up to her work, and was really one of the most voluptuous and lascivious fuckers I have ever met with, excellent as my experience has been. I made her, with fucking and frigging, spend six times before I suddenly withdrew my prick, and pressing its shaft against her wet lips, and my own belly, spent deliciously outside. Shortly after it rose again, and this time after making her spend as often as before, for she was most voluptuously lustful, when I withdrew, she suddenly got from under me, and seizing its shaft with one hand, stooped and took its knob between her lips, and quickly made me pour a flood of sperm into her mouth, which she eagerly swallowed and sucked on to my great delight.

We should have had a third bout but for the necessity of her going down to her aunt.

I breakfasted, then rang to take away. Again we had a delicious fuck, and a third when she came to make the bed and empty the slops. This third time I begged her to kneel on the sofa, and let me see her gloriously grand arse, and when I had to retire I would show her a way that would continue both our pleasure. So after fucking her from behind, and making her spend far oftener than me, I withdrew, and pushing it up between the lips over the clitoris, with my hand round her waist. I pressed it tightly against her cunt and clitoris, and continued to wriggle my arse, made her spend again as I poured a flood all over her belly. She declared it was almost as good as if inside.

After this very shortly I proposed to push its nose into her bottom-hole, and just spend within.

With reluctance at first, it ended in her not only liking the point there, but deliciously enjoying my whole prick within, and eventually it was always the receptacle of a first discharge induced by fucking, and a second fuck completely carried on in that more secret altar of lust. She became a first-rate *enculeuse*.

It soon happened that both sisters knew of the other enjoying me, and it ended in their slipping down from their attic, where both slept in the same bed, to my room, and we had most delicious fucking and double gamahuching.

Ann was by far the finest and the most lascivious fuck, but little Jane had a certain charm of youth and also of freshness, which got her a fair share of my favours.

We carried this on for several weeks until use made us careless and noisy.

The aunt, when no lodgers occupied the room, slept

overhead, and, probably being sleepless one morning, when it was early daylight, heard our voices, came down and surprised me in the very act of fucking Ann and gamahuching Jane, who stood above her and presented her cunt to my lecherous tongue. A loud exclamation from their aunt roused us up at once.

'Get to bed, you dreadful hussies.'

They fled without a moment's hesitation.

Mrs. Nichols then began to remonstrate with me on the infamy of my conduct. I approached the door apparently to get my shirt, for I was stark naked, but in fact to shut and lock my door, and then to turn on Mrs. Nichols, who apparently had quite forgotten she had only her short shift on, which not only allowed the full display of very fine, firm and ample bubbies, but not falling below the middle of her thighs, showed remarkably well made legs and small knees, with the swelling of immense thighs just indicated.

My stiff-standing prick in full vigour, and if anything still more stimulated by the unexpected beauties shown by Mrs. Nichols, I turned upon her and seizing her round the waist from behind, pushed her forward, and before she could recover herself I had hauled up her 'cutty sark,' seen a most magnificent arse, and into her cunt — not without somewhat painful violence, before she could recover from the surprise of the attack.

She screamed out murder, but there was no one who could hear but the girls, and they knew better than to interrupt me. I kept fucking away in spite of cries, and passing an arm round her body, with my finger I got to her clitoris, which sprang out into considerable proportions. My big prick and the frigging of her clitoris produced their natural result. In spite of herself she grew full of lust. I felt her cunt pressures, and knew how her passions were rising. Speedily, in place of resisting, she began to cry, 'Oh, oh,' and breathe hard, and then most gloriously wriggled her splendid arse, and as I spent she too was taken in the delicious ecstasy of the final crisis. She lay throbbing on my delighted prick until it stood as stiff as before. I began a slow movement, she made no resistance, except crying out, 'Oh! dear, oh! dear,' as if in spite of regrets, she could not help enjoying it; indeed, at last she said -

'Oh! what a man you are, Mr. Roberts; it is very wrong of you to do this, but I cannot resist enjoying it myself. It is years since I did such a thing, but as you have done it, it makes me wish you should do it again. Let us change position.'

'Very well, but you must throw off this tiresome chemise, or I won't withdraw.'

As her lust was so excited, she made no objection, so withdrawing we stood up; she drew her shift over her head, and displayed a far more splendid form, with an exquisitely fair and dimpled skin, than I could have thought possible.

'My dear Mrs. Nichols, what a fine perfect form you have got, let me embrace you in my arms.'

She was nothing loath, flattered by my praise. She laid hold of my cock with one hand, and closely clasped me with the other arm, while I threw an arm and hand round on her truly magnificent arse, and with my other hand pressed on a wonderful pair of bubbies as hard and firm as any maid of eighteen. Our mouths met in a loving kiss, our tongues exchanged endearments. She said -

'You have made me very wicked, let me have this enormous and dear fellow again.'

I said I must first gaze on all her beauties, especially on her gorgeous and enormous bottom. She turned herself round in every way, delighted to find that I so ardently admired her.

She then lay down on her back, and spread wide her legs, and called to me to mount and put it in.

'First I must kiss this beautiful cunt, and suck this superb clitoris.'

Her mount was covered with closely curled brown silky locks; her cunt was large with grand thick lips and well-haired sides. Her clitoris stood out quite three inches, red and stiff. I took it in my mouth, sucked it, and frigged her cunt with two fingers, which went in with the greatest ease, but were nipped tightly the moment the entrance was gained, and I frigged and sucked until she spent madly with absolute screams of delight. I continued to suck and excite her, which quickly made her cry out -

'Oh, darling boy, come and shove your glorious prick into my longing cunt.'

I sprang up and buried him until our two hairs were crushed between us. She held me tight for a minute without moving, then went off like a wild *Bacchante*, and uttered voluptuous bawdy expressions.

'Shove your delicious prick further and harder. Oh, you are killing me with delight.'

She was a perfect mistress of the art, gave me exquisite pleasure, and, I may add, proved afterwards a woman of infinite variety, and became one of my most devoted admirers. Our intrigue continued for years, while her age, as is the case with good wine, only appeared to improve her. Her husband was not a bad fucker, but having only a small prick, had never stimulated her lust as my big splitter had done.

We had on this first occasion three other good fucks, which she seemed to enjoy more and more.

As I had previously fucked the girls pretty well, my prick at last refused to perform. We had to stop fucking, but I gamahuched her once more after again posing her, and admiring her really wonderfully well made and well-preserved body. She had a good suck at my cock, without bringing him up again.

At last we separated, but not before she made a promise that she would sleep with me that night, and a glorious night we had. I had the more difficult task of reconciling her to my having her nieces. I used to have them one night, and sleep with her the next.

Ann, as I have said, was one of the lewdest and most lascivious women I had ever known. I had told them of the beauty of their aunt's whole person, and of her wonderful clitoris, and how she liked me to gamahuche it. This awakened the tribadic passions of Ann to gamahuche her aunt.

I, at last, persuaded her to let Ann join us, and both were afterwards extremely glad I had done so, for both were thorough tribades, and lasciviously enjoyed each other, while being fucked by me in turns. Mrs. Nichols too, once she got used to arse-fucking, delighted in it, and we had the wildest orgies together.

SPORT AMONG THE SHE-NOODLES

The hearty tone of late-Victorian pornography to be found in The Romance of Lust *rang loud and clear in certain naughty periodicals of the time such as* The Pearl *and* The Boudoir. *This is the origin of the following piece which bears all the hallmarks of this particular style. The narrator, Walter, tells the tale of a visit to his cousins, three sisters and a brother, at his uncle's country residence in Sussex. Walter is a jolly fellow and his cousins sporting types. One thing you can be sure of in a sex romp of this nature – nobody is going to be left out . . .*

Next day being the last representation of a celebrated piece at the theatre of the County Town, by a first-rate London company, papa expressed a wish that we should all go in the evening, but Annie and Sophie, giving me a knowing look on the sly, declared they had already seen it once and did not care to go again. For my part, of course, I had seen it half-a-dozen times in town, so it was finally arranged that Frank, Rosa and Polly only would go with papa and mama; they had a drive of more than an hour before them so started at 6 P.M., and as soon as they were out of sight we three started for the bathing place at the lake. It was such a deliciously warm evening, and it would be just the place for our anticipated pleasures, as I had suggested to Annie and Sophie during the day.

Bolting the summer-house door on the inside as soon as we got in, I suggested first of all to stimulate our mutually ardent desires by a bottle of champagne; this so exhilarated the two lovely girls that we indulged in a second bottle before stripping for a romp. Seven o'clock found us bathed in a flood of golden light from the declining sun, which now shone directly in upon us, this warned us to make haste and improve the opportunity, so each one assisting the others and at the same time indulging in many loving tricks and liberties, we were soon in Adam and Eve costume.

'Now,' I exclaimed, 'Annie dear, you won't be jealous if I make a woman of your sister, as we promised the other day,' taking the youngest one up in my arms with my rampant cock throbbing against her belly, as I carried her to the lounge.

'What a naughty boy you are, Walter, anything or anybody for a change is what fickle men like, but I won't be jealous of Sophie, although I am of Mrs. Leslie. I know you had her yesterday; that sheepish tell-tale look, sir, when you met me on your return, was enough to confirm my suspicions of what would happen when you were *tête-a-tête* with that killing lady,' she replied.

'For shame, Annie darling, you told me yourself the other day love ought to be free everywhere; I don't deny my guilt, but will do my best to earn forgiveness now,' I said, pushing Sophie back upon the soft yielding lounge, 'help me to ease this darling of her troublesome virginity, and I will then repay your own longing cunny for all your love and forebearance; I am sure Mrs. Leslie would like to make you one of our party without any feelings of jealousy; there are so many ways of voluptuous enjoyment that if only one man to three beautiful girls it can be so varied as to give everyone the most intense delight.'

At this both the girls gave me rapturous kisses, with every possible assurance that they would never be selfish, and would be only to happy to extend the circle of those they could be free and loving with, adding with special emphasis, 'We are such noodles, dear Walter, we knew nothing till you introduced us to the arts of love, and as long as you can stay with us shall look up to you to guide us in everything; we know it's wrong, but what heavenly pleasure there is in the loving mixture of the sexes.'

ANNIE, taking my prick in her hand. – 'Now, sir I will show this gentleman the way into Sophie's cabinet of love; be firm, dear, he won't hurt you more than can be helped, and the after joy will soon drown all recollection of the first short suffering.'

SOPHIE, opening her legs as wide as possible. – 'I'm all on fire to taste the real tree of love, don't spare me, Walter, dear, I'd rather die than not have it now!'

The red head of 'Cupid's Battering Ram' was now brought to the charge; Annie opened the rosy lips of her sister's cunt and placed my cock in the exact position, but her touches, together with the thoughts of the delicious titbit I was about to enjoy, caused me to spend in a moment all over her fingers and into the virgin passage in front. 'Push on, push on; now's the time to gain your victory,' she whispered; 'that will make it easier to get him in,' at the same time lifting up Sophie's buttocks with her disengaged hand, so as to make her meet my attack in a more favourable manner. My first lunge lodged the head of Mr. Priapus fairly within the tight folds of the victim's vagina, and I had already won the first outworks of the virgin's defences.

Poor Sophie moaned under the sharp pain of my assault, but biting her lips to repress any cries of pain she courageously placed one hand on the shaft of my prick, as if jealous of her sister's loving help, and anxious to have the honour of herself showing me the way to achieve love's dearest triumph, or perhaps it was for fear of my withdrawing before completely accomplishing my task.

'You love!' I exclaimed, enraptured by this exhibition of pluck, 'I will soon make a real woman of you,' then pushing fiercely on, on, I gradually forced the tight

411

sheath to dilate. Every obstruction gave way to my determined energy, and with a final plunge, I was buried to the roots of my affair, and shooting at the same moment my warm spendings into her inmost vitals. This exhausted me for a few moments, and I lay supine upon the heaving bosom of the lovely Sophie, till I could feel Annie's fingers busy tickling my balls and feeling the shaft of my cock. Just at the same moment Sophie, who had almost fainted under the painful ordeal, opened her eyes, and with a loving smile pouted her lips as an invitation for a kiss, which I instantly responded to, almost sucking her breath away in my ardour. My excitement was now raised to the highest possible pitch by her sister's titillations, and the loving challenge of Sophie herself to renew my motions with her, by heaving up her bottom and nipping my prick in her cunny in the most delightful way imaginable.

This time I prolonged the pleasure as much as possible, beginning slowly, and often stopping to feel the delicious throbbing of cock and cunny in their delightful conjunction. 'Ach! this is indeed love; it repays for all the pain I felt at first. Oh! oh! dear Walter, it feels as if my very soul was flowing from me in ecstasy!' she almost screamed out, kissing, biting, squeezing me with all her might at the moment of emission, which I again responded to with a flow of my own sperm.

I now declared we must refresh ourselves a little before going further, so she reluctantly allowed me to withdraw. A short plunge in the lake had a most invigorating effect. I felt as strong as a giant again, then another bottle of fizz renewed our loving ardour; the girls were handling my prick, which stood again as hard as ivory. So slipping on my shirt, as I intended to be the uppermost of the trio, I laid Sophie on her back, and the telling the obedient Annie to kneel over her sister and gamahuche her in return for Sophie's doing the same to her, I mounted up behind her, saying, 'I've made a woman of your dear sister, and will now treat you, my darling, to a new sensation.' But just at the moment Sophie, who had no idea of my intentions, seized hold of my cock, saying, 'She must kiss the dear sweet thing, which had afforded her such exquisite bliss.' Holding it tight in her hand, she took the head between her pearly teeth and kissed and treated him to such love bites that I soon spent in her mouth, which she greedily swallowed, with all the abandon of voluptuous enjoyment. Meanwhile, I had been frigging Annie's bottom with my two fingers, which I had managed to insert together, and that dear girl was sucking her sister's quim, and wriggling herself in the most excitable way possible.

Sophie was now going to insert my prick in her sister's cunt, but Annie, almost beside herself with excitement, exclaimed, 'No, no, my dear, put him where Walter has got his fingers; I should like to try that, it is so exciting; the very thought of it makes me mad with desire to know what it is like. His fingers have given me such pleasures that I am sure the dear thing in your hand will greatly improve the sensation!'

No sooner said than done; the obedient girl directed my cock to the beautifully wrinkled tight little brown hole of her sister's bottom at the very moment I withdrew my fingers. When I found they so thoroughly appreciated the idea I had resolved to initiate them into, being well lubricated and as stiff as possible, it soon passed the portals of Annie's second virginity. But, Heavens, what a delicious bout we had, she bounded about so with delight, that I had to hold tight round her neck to prevent being thrown out, whilst Sophie, below, gamahuched her delighted sister, and with her right hand continued to press my balls and prick, keeping time to every insertion in her sister's bottom. We spent together, almost screaming with delight, and then lay in a confused heap, enjoying the sensations of our delicious exhaustion.

413

As soon as they could kiss and persuade my rather enervated tool into renewed stiffness, Sophie declared I must oblige her with a taste of the new-found joy, and ravish her bottom as well as her sister's.

This was another delicious love engagement; the sisters gamahuching each other with the utmost erotic ardour, whilst my delighted prick revelled in the tight-fitting fundamental of the sweet girl, who wriggled and plunged about so excitedly that I had to hold fast to keep my place.

After this, we returned to the house, and passed the time very pleasantly till the return of the party from the theatre. I was anxious to hear Frank's account of how he had got on with Rosa during the evening, and especially as they drove home.

'Walter,' he said, as we were once more alone in his room after all had gone to rest, 'I've had a most enjoyable time of it since we started. Of course, as we went, it was daylight, so Rosa and I maintained a proper decorum, but at the theatre, papa and mama were separated from us by Polly, and we all five sat in the front row of the dress circle. How the sight of Rosa's swelling bosom (which her low-necked dress allowed me fully to see) made my prick stand at once; so I took her gloved hand and made her feel how hard and excited I was. As no one could see, she indulged me with quite a gentle frigging outside my trousers, till I spent profusely, to the great delight of the roguish beauty, as I could tell by the smile on her face and the excited looks with which she met my ardent gaze.

'What a shame,' she whispered in my ear. 'I know what you have done, you naughty boy. You should have reserved it for a more favourable opportunity.'

'Look out, darling, as we drive home; see if I don't repay your kind attentions,' I whispered in return.

'Both papa and mama were rather sleepy before the conclusion of the last piece, and to make them go off, as soon as we were seated in the carriage, I offered them my flask of brandy to keep out the effects of the night air. It had a pretty good strong dose of narcotic in it, and they were soon sound asleep in their corners. Polly also pretended to be dozing.

'Rosa was on my lap directly, and my hands were at once groping their way to the seat of pleasure whilst she was equally busy unbuttoning my trousers and handling the staff of life.

'Our lips met in long-drawn rapturous kisses, which fired every drop of blood in our veins, and both were too impatient for the real business to prolong our toyings with each other's privates; besides, I felt she was already spending over my busy fingers. She had my cock in a glorious state of erection; so opening her delicious thighs as she raised her clothes, she was at once impaled on the spike she so burned to have thrust into her. It was quite equal to the first time I fucked her. The long evening passed in expectation of what I might be able to do on our return journey; so it added to the piquancy of my arduous longings that I seemed in Heaven itself, and swimming in a very ocean of love, we spent over and over again; our melting kisses and tongue-sucking continually stimulating us to renewed exertions, till the near approach to home warned us of the necessity of bringing our pleasures to an end for a time. Even now, I tell you, Walter, my cock keeps throbbing and standing at the very thoughts of the delightful pressures she treated me to; her cunt bites so deliciously.'

In the morning, papa and mama had scarcely slept off the effects of the sleeping dose they had imbibed from the brandy flask of their dutiful son, and lay abed very late, in fact, almost to luncheon time; meanwhile, we, the younger members of the family, had privately agreed upon a plan of amusement for the afternoon and evening.

Finding that two pretty girls of sixteen and seventeen were living close by, with an invalid mother, whilst their brother was away, being a Midshipman in the Royal Navy, I proposed that Annie should spend the afternoon with us, en famille, without the least ceremony, and join us in any alfresco tea party at a little hut in the woods, which formed part of my uncle's estate.

At luncheon we informed the governor of what we had done and hoped that both he and mama would join in our outdoor party in the woods.

'No thank you, my dears, we are too afraid of the damp grass and rheumatics. Besides, we have not yet gotten over the fatigue of yesterday. We will stay quietly at home and hope you may enjoy yourselves thoroughly, as we should do if we were younger,' replied the jolly, kind-hearted old gentleman.

This was exactly what we had wished for and expected; so Frank and Annie at once sent off the servants with every requisite for our open-air tea party.

About three o'clock, the two young ladies arrived, and as all were ready, we at once set off for the scene of our anticipated fun, which was a rough bower covered with flowering honeysuckle and clematis, at the end of a long, shady, private walk, more than half-a-mile from the house.

Frank and myself particularly attached ourselves to the two fresh young ladies as being the greatest strangers, and therefore justly expectant of the most attention.

Emily Bruce, the eldest, was a charming dark-eyed brunette, her rather large mouth having a fascinating effect as you regarded her. In fact, such a display of pearly white teeth, I never saw before, and the very thought that they might perhaps be soon employed in love bites on my tender-headed prick filled me with maddening lust to possess myself of their owner.

Nor was her sister, Louisa, a bit less prepossessing, she being almost the counterpart of Emily, except that one could easily see there was a slight difference in age.

Arrived at the bower, the servants were at once sent home, being told that they could clear away the things next morning, as it would be late for them to return in the evening, and at the same time, without asking the consent of her young friends, dear Annie scribbled a pencil note to their mama, to say that if they at all were late, she would insist upon them staying with her all night, and not to make herself at all anxious on their behalf – this was quietly sent off by one of the servants.

As soon as we were alone, Frank and I, uncorking the champagne, lighted our cigars, and saying that the sun was still too warm for outdoor romping, pressed the girls to try some very mild cigarettes of Turkish tobacco.

At last Annie and Rosa set the example by lighting up, and were at once laughingly followed by the others. Our two young friends protested they never took wine. Still, they evidently sipped it with great delight, and we bantered them upon being so tied to their mother's apron strings, etc., till they began to be quite free as my cousins and Rosa.

We had a good stock of fizz, besides sandwiches and cake, so that no one seemed at all anxious to take the trouble of tea-making.

Still we were careful that only enough should be taken to warm our friends up to a slightly excitable state, in fact, just to induce that state of all-overishness, which tingles through a young girl's sensitive frame when she feels the first vibrations of amorous desires, which she can as yet hardly understand.

Their sparking eyes, slightly flushed faces and above all, the dazzling beauties of their teeth, as they indulged in gay laughter at our badinage, set all of us aflame. I could see that Rosa and my cousins were longing to help in enjoying these innocent and ravishing young girls.

Now a game of hunt the slipper was proposed, and we at once joined to the soft, mossy green sward, outside the bower. This was a most delicious and excitable romp.

Whenever it came our turns, Frank and myself indulged in all kinds of quick and startling touches, which made the two little dears blush up to their eyes at first, and when we managed to catch one of them with the slipper we claimed a hearty kiss as penalty, which they submitted to with tolerable grace, yet evidently in a state of great excitement, it was all so new to them. We finished the game, had a little more champagne, then proposed a game of hide and seek in the wood, with the reservation that no one was to go too far off.

We were to be in pairs, I chose Emily, and Frank took Louisa. Polly and Sophie went together, whilst Annie and Rosa had to search for us when we called out.

It so happened that there was an old sand pit close by, in which several years before Master Frank had amused himself by making a Robinson Crusoe's cave, and planted bushes in front of it, so that the entrance was perfectly out of sight, and no one would fancy anyone could be screened by the small amount of cover which seemed to grow on the side of the pit; this was just the place for our purpose, and it had been beforehand arranged that we were not to be found for a long time. Gliding into the cave Frank let fall the old curtain that hung at the entrance, and we were at once in the dark, the place was large enough for us to sit together on a heap of fine soft sand at the further end.

'What a dear girl you are!' I whispered in Emily's ear, as I took a kiss in the dark, and drew her trembling body quite close by an arm around her waist.

'Pray don't,' she whispered in return, 'if you do not keep quiet I won't stop in this dark place.'

'Don't say so, it would be cruel, especially if you knew all I feel towards you, Emily dear. I must call you Emily, yes, and kiss you again and again, I love you so, your breath is so fragrant, what are you afraid of, there's nothing to fear among friends, darling,' I whispered, kissing my partner rapturously.

'Oh, ah, you take my breath away Walter, I'm so unused to such goings on. Oh, fie, sir, for shame, you make me feel all of a tremble, you take such liberties!' as I was working one hand inside the bosom of her dress, and getting possession of two hard round bubbies which throbbed with emotion under my loving caresses.

'It's all love, darling, and no one can see, can't you hear how Frank and Louisa are kissing; is it not delicious to think they are doing the same, and will be sure to keep our secret?'

A deep sigh was my only answer, and again our lips met in a long luscious kiss. My tongue was thrust into her mouth, and tickled the tip of her own velvety organ of speech. I could feel the nipples of her virgin bosom stick out as stiff as little cocks and whispered to her to allow me to kiss them.

'I can refuse you nothing,' she whispered; 'you are such a bold lover. I'm all in flame from head to foot at the numberless liberties you are taking with me. Ah, if mam only knew,' she sighed, as I was now sucking her titties, and running my disengaged hand up her thighs; they were nipped tightly together, but gradually relaxed under the gentle pressure of my hand, till I actually got possession of her cunny, which I could feel was slightly covered with soft downy hair, and soon began to frig her gently with my forefinger. How the dear girl wriggled under the double excitement, and I could feel one of her hands groping outside my trousers over my bursting prick, to return the pleasure

I was giving her. One by one she unfastened the buttons, then her soft delicate hand soon had possession of my stiff affair, naked and palpitating with unsatisfied desire.

'Ah,' she whispered, 'I am satisfied at last! we had a servant at home, a few months ago, who slept in our room, and used to tickle and play with us. She told us that men had a long thing as hard as iron, which they pleased the ladies by shoving up their bellies, and that was how the babies were made. Do you believe it? She was always shoving her fingers into us as you are doing to me now, and – and – and,' here she hesitated and seemed to shudder with delight, just as I spent all over her hand, and I could also feel her spendings come in a warm gush over my fingers. It was delicious. Her hand first held tight the top of my throbbing prick, then gently worked up and down the shaft, lubricated by my spendings. It was indeed a voluptuous treat; I begged her to thrust her tongue into my mouth, and we continued the mutual frigging till she almost fainted away in her ecstasy.

Slightly recovering, I asked her what it was she was going to tell me about the maid servant, when she hesitated.

'Do, dearest, tell me everything,' I implored, in a loving whisper, 'We are now without reserve to each other; you can have no secrets from your loving Walter.'

'It was so funny, I don't know how she could do it, but Mary was so fond of sucking and kissing us where you have your hand, dearest,' she replied, 'but it was so nice you can't imagine how we enjoyed having her do it to us.'

'My love, my Emily, let me kiss you now, and it would be sublime if you would kiss me. I long to feel the love bites of your beautiful teeth in my *Cupid's Dart*. Frank and Louisa are too busy to notice what we do,' I whispered in her ear, as I inclined the willing girl backwards on the soft pillow of sand, and reversing my position, we laid at full length, side by side, both of us eager as possible for the game; my head was buried between her loving thighs, with which she pressed me most amorously, as my tongue was inserted in her loving slit; this was a fine gamahuche, I stirred up all the lasciviousness of her ardent temperament till she screamed with delight, and caused Frank and Louisa to enquire what we were doing, but we made no reply. She sucked my delighted prick, handled and kissed my balls, till I spent in her mouth, as her teeth were lovingly biting the head of my penis. She sucked it all down, whilst I repaid her loving attentions to the best of my ability with my own active tongue.

As soon as it was over, I took Emily by the hand, and we groped towards our companions, who, I found, were equally busy as we had been. Frank thoroughly understood my intention; we all got together, and joined in a grope of cocks and cunnies without the least restrained, till suddenly the curtain was pulled down, and we heard the laughing voices of Rosa and Annie, as they exclaimed, 'See, here they are. What are these rude boys doing to you young ladies?'

Emily and Louisa were covered with confusion, but the girls lovingly assured them they would keep the secret, and introduce them to more fun after they had retired to bed, as it was now getting late, and we must all return to the house.

As I have before observed, the wing of the mansion in which we all slept was quite apart from the other wing in which papa, mama, and the servants were located, so as soon as we had retired, Frank and myself joined the girls in their room, or rather rooms, for they occupied two. The Miss Bruces blushed crimson at seeing us only in our shirts, especially as one was seated on the *pot de chambre*, whilst the other was exhibiting her charms to my inquisitive cousins before a cheval glass.

'All right,' exclaimed Annie, 'my dears, everything is free between us and the boys, but we mean to punish you for allowing the impudent fellows to presume upon such liberties with you in the cave. Your bottoms shall smart, young ladies, I can assure you,' as she produced a couple of light birch rods from a drawer; in fact I had provided them for her, the idea having been suggested to me by reading a book called *The Romance of Lust*.

A fine large bed stood by the wall, facing another at the end of the room, but our programme only required one couch. Annie and Rosa were determined to have their enjoyment now; everyone was ordered to strip off shirt or chemise, then I horsed Emily on my back whilst Frank did the same by her sister.

Sophie and Polly were entrusted with the rods, and gaily switched us and our riders' bottoms as we trotted round the room, the sisters hardly knowing whether to laugh or cry, when a more stinging cut than usual made them cry for mercy; our pricks were as rampant as possible, and we were not in need of any stimulation; still the girls were very hard on our rumps, although not quite so severe with the sisters. The darling Emily had so entwined her legs round me as I held them close under my armpits that her pretty feet in their bewitching slippers were frigging my cock between them most deliciously.

The sight of our red smarting bottoms and bursting pricks was too much for Annie and Rosa, and they were inflamed with lust, so throwing themselves backward on the bed, with their legs wide open and feet resting on the floor, the two dear girls presented their quims to our charge, as with both hands they held open the lips of their delicious cunts, inviting our eager cocks to come on. We charged them at once, under the impulsive urging of the rods, gave a few delightful fucking motions, then withdrew and trotted round the room again, this we constantly repeated to prolong our enjoyment, till at last the dear girls could stand it no longer, their arms clasped us firmly, whilst the rods cut away with extra force to make us complete their pleasure; it was a most luxurious finish, we all spent with screams of delight, and lay for a few moments in a delicious state of lethargic exhaustion till we awoke to find Sophie, Polly, Emily, and Louisa all rolling on the floor in the delights of gamahuching.

After this the two dear girls begged, with tears in their eyes, that Frank and Walter would make women of them, so that they might really taste the wildest delights of love.

'Then, dears,' said Rosa, with a sly laugh, 'you must kiss them, and make their exhausted cocks stiff again, and then we will lend the boys to you.'

We sat on the bed by the side of our late fucking partners, who we kissed, fondled and frigged, whilst Emily and Louisa, kneeling between our knees, sucked our pricks up to standing point, as their hands drew back our foreskins or played with our balls.

Stiff and rampant as we were we entreated them to go on for a little longer, till feeling ourselves almost at spending point, Polly and Sophie arranged two bolsters and some pillows on the floor in the most advantageous manner, the sisters were each placed with two pillows under their bottoms, whilst their heads rested on the bolsters. Annie and Rosa then conducted the victims, who impatiently awaited their immolation to the god of love with open legs and longing cunts. The two mistresses of the ceremonies took our pricks in hand, and directed them to the path of bliss. Emily was my partner again; she threw her legs over my back and heaved up to meet the fatal thrust, which was to be the death of her troublesome virginity. I had no time to see how the others progressed, but heard a smothered shriek of agony from Louisa, as no doubt Frank achieved her fate for her; my partner was more courageous, she glued her lips to mine, sucking in my tongue in the most ardent manner imaginable, even whilst my prick was tearing through her hymen; my spending deluged her wounded quim, and we soon lost all thoughts of pain when we recommenced a lovely fuck, moving slowly at first, till her rapid motions spurred me on to faster plunges, her delicious tight cunt holding me like a hand, in fact so tight that I could feel my foreskin drawn backwards and forwards at every shove.

'Ah! you dear fellow, push on, kill me with delight!' she screamed in ecstasy, as we came again together, and I was equally profuse in my words of endearment.

As we lay still after it was over her tight-fitting cunt seemed to hold and continually squeeze my delighted prick so by its contractions and throbbings I was ready again directly, and we ran another thrilling course before she would let me try to withdraw.

Frank and Louisa had been equally delighted with each other, and thus the two sisters each lost her maidenhead almost at the same moment.

Not a day passed but we had some voluptuous games, whilst as to Rosa and Frank, they were openly engaged to be married, which was an especial gratification to the old people.

Time flew so rapidly that my visit drew to its close, and we were all thinking of devising some signal display of love, to be enacted as a parting scene ere I took my departure from my uncle's hospitable and happy domicile, when one fine morning in June, who should favour us with a call, but my lovely brunette Mrs. Leslie. She had driven over to invite myself and my cousins to spend an early day before the Colonel's return. 'You know,' she said, turning to my uncle, 'how stiff and starch all his ideas are, and I must have one day of real fun before he comes home from Paris. Will you let them come tomorrow and stop till the next day?'

My uncle being too kind to refuse, the arrangement

was made at once, Mrs. Leslie stayed to luncheon, and we took an afternoon stroll in the park afterwards. From time to time her intelligent glances assured me she was anxious for a *tête-a-tête* with me, so asking her to take my arm, we soon managed to give the others the slip, and lost ourselves in a dense copse. Sitting down on the soft mossy turf, under a shady little yew tree, we were quite hidden from observation.

'How I longed to kiss your sweet lips once more,' I exclaimed, clasping her in my eager embrace, and sucking her breath almost away in a luscious osculation.

'If that is all you thought of sir, you have been vastly unfaithful to your protestations of love, and I should really feel awfully jealous of your pretty cousins and Miss Redquim did I not see the unruly state of the jewel in your trousers,' she laughingly replied, as she took speedy steps to release and secure the impatient prisoner in her grasp, continuing, 'I wonder how he has amused himself since that ever memorable day when I first had the pleasure of both seeing and feeling the noble fellow. Now tell me true Sir Walter, have you seduced your cousins and their friend?'

I at once made a full confession of all our amours, and begged she would indulge us in every possible way on the morrow, as it would be the last grand chance I should have before returning to town.

'Most delightful state of things I am sure, but what a shame not to have run over and invited me to join in your amorous festivities. Surely you knew it was just what I should have delighted in. I have a great mind to disappoint you now, only I should also be punishing myself, so come on, you naughty young fellow, and I will consider between this and to-morrow what your penance will be,' she said, reclining herself backwards, her fine dark eyes full of humid languishing fire, which too truly indicated her voluptuous requirements.

Lifting her skirts quickly, I paid my devotions at the shrine of love by a kiss and playful bite of her clitoris, then, unable to dally any longer, placed myself between her readily yielding thighs, and was soon revelling within the soft juicy folds of her divine organ of bliss, delighted beyond expression by the throbbing compressions to which it treated me as I lay quietly enjoying the sense of complete possession, which is so delicious to contemplate, before commencing more vigorous action; our lips met again and our billing and cooing would have lasted some time had we not heard Frank declaring to Rosa and his sisters, 'What a damned shame it was of Walter and Mrs. Leslie to give them the slip, but he would find us and spoil our fun.'

This caused my charming inamorata to heave up her buttocks as a challenge to me, not to waste more time, so I put spurs to my steed, but none too soon, for just as we died away in a mutual spend, Frank, Sisters, and Co. burst upon the scene with a triumphant exclamation of 'here's Walter and his grass widow,' and before we could recover ourselves, the laughing party inflicted an awful slapping on our bottoms, till a truce was made and we all agreed to wait patiently for the morrow's party at Mrs. Leslie's.

Next day, favoured by splendid weather, we were early at the Colonel's residence, and the handsome swarthy Vishnu ushered us into the luxurious boudoir of his voluptuous mistress. 'You have arrived early, it is scarcely one o'clock, my toilette's not yet made, but how very welcome you all are to my house, I need not trouble to say, after the frank understanding we came to yesterday, as to our amusements now you are here. The chocolate is just ready, and I have infused in it an imperceptible something (a secret, my dear, which the Colonel brought from India), which will soon set all your young amorous blood in such a glow of desire that you will not know how to satisfy your intense cravings for the delight of love, and then naughty Walter shall be served out for his unfaithfulness to me.'

This speech made us all smile as we took up the small cups of delicious chocolate which Vishnu handed round, and as he disappeared our hostess, who had nothing on but her dressing-gown, having drawn Frank to her side on the lounge, asked us, as the day was so warm, to throw aside as much as possible of our superfluous clothing, which was speedily done.

'We must have a romp before luncheon, then repose or stroll about during the afternoon, and in the evening we shall, I hope, enjoy some novel ideas I have quite set my mind upon,' she continued during the short time we took to disrobe. 'That's right, only keep on the *chemiserie* now, at night we will discard the last rag; I have no chemise to take off, so will keep this convenient *robe de chambre*, but you may look Frank, if you don't think Rosa will be jealous,' as she opened the front, and displayed to his ardent gaze all the beauties of her person.

'If it makes her jealous, I can't help admiring such charms!' said Frank, 'but Rosa is far too sensible for that, and thoroughly enters into all our fun, in fact I am sure she loves Walter as well as she does me, only she can't marry both of us.'

'Ha! Ha! that accounts for Walter forgetting me, so to be revenged on them both you must have me now,' she replied, lifting up his shirt to see if he was ready, 'why your lovedart is almost exactly the size of his,' and without more ado she was on his lap, and spitted herself on Frank's cock, throwing off entirely the *robe de chambre* that she might enjoy him without impediment.

This instantly excited the girls, who lay down in pairs for a mutual gamahuche and bottom-frig, Rosa playfully telling me to let Mrs. Leslie have the double pleasure by fucking her bottom as she was riding Frank.

'Hold her tight, my boy,' I said, 'and I will let her beautiful little fundamental know what it is to keep a stiff prick waiting for his turn,' as I took a little cold cream from the dressing-table, and putting some on the head of my prick as well as the delightful wrinkled hole exposed to my attack, the head began to slip in at once, despite her struggles and screams, 'that we should injure her between us.' Further and further I gradually worked in, till I could feel my cock rubbing against Frank's with only the thin divisional membrane between them, our joint spendings deluging both cunt and bum, spurting the warm, frothy sperm over our balls at every thrust. This was not enough to satisfy her, but she kept us at our work until we repeated our emissions with screams of delight, and rolled on the floor in a confused heap amongst the dear girls, who were so excited by the sight of our ecstasies that they were revelling in every species of tribadism to allay their lustful yearnings.

After this Mrs. Leslie opened a side door, conducted us into her bathroom, where we refreshed ourselves and indulged in a variety of kissing, frigging, &c., but by her advice the girls refrained from exhausting us too much, and accepted cigarettes of Turkish tobacco to join us in a smoke, as we lighted some of the Colonel's fine cigars. It was a picture worthy of Apelles, as we could see the reflection of all our naked charms on the bathroom walls, which constituted one vast mirror of the very finest silvered glass, two rather good-looking fellows with big pricks, as rampant as could be wished, and five lovely ladies all smoking and puffing pretty curls or rings of vapoury nicotine, alternating that sober enjoyment for more active fun, by trying to burn the tip of their cunts with the fiery ends of cigarette or cigar.

About half-past two, we dressed, and then took luncheon, then strolled in the grounds or on the bank of a small stream, where some of us passed the time

428

trying our piscatorial luck, till the bell rang for dinner, which passed pleasantly enough, and about 9 P.M., we assembled in the drawing-room, for a grand erotic séance.

Mrs. Leslie dismissed all her servants for the night, except Vishnu, who she said would be quite sufficient to attend to our little requirements.

The room was large and lofty, the windows closed and artistically draped with gorgeous black and gold curtains, the spaces between filled up with mirrors and branching candelabra, the opposite side of the apartment being also quite a tableau of flowers, mirrors, and lighted wax candles, which shed a brilliant and yet soft luxurious effulgence over the whole scene; two doors at one end gave access to retiring rooms, where we undressed, and in a very few minutes the whole party, in a state of ravishing nudity, were grouped round Mrs. Leslie as she sat on an ottoman, awaiting her decision as to the programme.

She first persuaded us to sip a little of her chocolate, then went on to say, 'As we are five to two you will find I have a stock of fine, soft, firmly made dildoes to make up the deficiency in males, which alternated with the real article will enable us to thoroughly enjoy ourselves. First, I believe Miss is a virgin, notwithstanding all she knows and has seen; her delicate little pussey must be itching to be emancipated from the thraldom of virginity. Walter must do the service for her at once, on Rosa's lap, so now to business, as I see our gentlemen are in a beautiful state of readiness.'

Polly blushed deeply, but readily seated herself on her friend's lap with her legs wide open, presented to my staff of life, whilst Rosa, passing her hands round the dear girl's waist, held open the lips of her cunny, and guided the head of my affair in the proper direction. Much as she had been frigged and gamahuched, it was a hard task; her cunt was so deliciously small and tight that in spite of her favourable position, I could only just get the head of Mr. Priapus within the nymphae before she started with the intense pain, and gave a supressed scream of anguish, the tears starting to her eyes and trickling over her blushing face.

'Courage, darling, it will soon be over,' I whispered, kissing her excitedly, while Mrs. Leslie encouraged me by saying, 'Sharp and quick, Walter, a good thrust will force better than those gentle pushes; gentleness is not real kindness when taking a maidenhead;' at the same moment I felt she was attacking my virgin bottom-hole behind with a well-lubricated dildoe, its head being well in before I knew exactly what she was doing; this and the desire to possess Polly so stimulated me that I thrust furiously at the opposing obstacle, her heartrending cries adding to my pleasure, and making me mad with desire. At last I was halfway in, then a fierce lunge seemed to break quite through as I, at the same time, deluged the tight passage with a copious emmision.

The poor little victim had swooned, but Mrs. Leslie, working her dildoe behind, ordered me to let my cock throb inside Polly's tight sheath, as it would tend to bring her round, and excite her amorous sensibility to the utmost.

What delightful sensations I experienced, my prick feeling all the spasmodic contractions of her vagina, and having my bottom well dildoe-fucked at the same time, I spent again under the influence of this accumulated excitement just as my partner was coming round under the influence of some cordial which had been poured down her gasping throat, whilst strong smelling salts had been applied to her nostrils. She opened her eyes, giving a violent sneeze at the same time, which vibrated on my delightful prick, who instantly began gently to bestir himself in her tight scabbard; this roused her little by little, till throwing her arms round my neck, and returning my hot kisses with all the ardour of her nature, she cried and laughed by turns, as she begged me to make haste and complete her happiness.

By a side glance I could see Frank was in Mrs. Leslie's bottom, Annie in him with a dildoe, and Sophie doing the same to her sister, a perfect string of pederastic branchings from my own violated bum. It was such a scene as I had never seen before, and added additional fury to my already maddened lust. I came again and again before we finished, each spend more ecstatic than the last. The chocolate had so invigorated us, that we went through an almost interminable series of spendings, till at last the nature could stand it no longer, we rolled on the floor in a confused heap, and wound up in a mutual gamahuche; Mrs. Leslie secured the bloodstained quim of Polly, which she sucked till she had enjoyed the last drop of ensanguined spunk she could extract from the wounded slit of her young friend, who writhed in delight under the soothing touches of such a lascivious tongue.

It was between eleven and twelve o'clock, when just as we were recovering from a state of lethargic oblivion, and thinking of some re-invigorating refreshment, the sound of carriage wheels on the gravel drive up to the house, and then, rat-a-tat-tat on the loud knocker made us all start to our feet and rush for our clothes.

'The Colonel, by all that's unfortunate,' exclaimed Mrs. Leslie, 'make haste or he will catch us; who would have thought of his arriving at this time of night.'

The prudent Vishnu, pretending to be awakening out of his first sleep, so bungled and delayed opening the front door, that we were tolerably presentable by the time the Colonel made his appearance, and whatever his suspicions may have been, he went through the formality of introduction in the most friendly way possible, the presence of so many young ladies evidently quite disconcerting him for the moment.

I afterwards learnt from his wife that under promise

of secrecy she had confessed all to him, and vastly amused her husband by an account of our doings; but, at any rate, it stopped our fun at the time, and next day I was obliged to return to town, and thus brought to conclusion 'My Sport amongst the She-Noodles,' anything but 'Noodles' after I had so enlightened them, in fact quite as knowing as Adam and Eve after they found out they were 'Naked' having tasted the *'Tree of Knowledge'*, which, in my humble opinion, meant found out *'L'Arte de faire l'amour.'*

THERESE

Caught in the pursuit of certain solitary pleasures and in consequence confined to a convent, young Therese embraces religion with a great fervour. Such is her piety that her health begins to suffer – Therese is not a girl to do things by halves – and on medical advice she is sent home to her mother. It is then that she meets the two people who are to become the most important influences in her life – the venerable Father Dirrag and his devoted disciple Eradice. This lady is blessed with the same passionate temperament as Therese and the two become confidants, drawn to one another by their religious devotions. However there is one blemish on their friendship – the jealousy that Therese cannot suppress whenever Eradice speaks of her father confessor. Therese refuses to believe the stories of Dirrag's particular attentions to her friend, the frequent meetings at his home, his promise that under his ministrations Eradice will soon be capable of great miracles. It is only natural therefore that Therese should require some proof of this very special relationship . . .

Eradice must have noticed that I was envious, begrudged her her happiness and, worst of all, did not seem to believe her! I must admit that I was very surprised about her tales of his confidential talks with her at his home, especially since the good father had always carefully avoided talking to me, one of his most ardent penitents, about anything else but mortification of the flesh. And I knew another penitent, also a good friend of mine, who, like Eradice, also carried the stigmata of our Lord. He had never been as confidential to her as he had been to Eradice, and this girl friend, too, had all the requirements of becoming a saint. No doubt, my sad face, my yellowish complexion, my utter lack of any sign of stigmata were enough reasons for the venerable Father Dirrag not to have any confidential talks with me at his home. The possibility existed that he saw no reason to take on the extra burden of spiritual works in my behalf. But to me it was a bone of contention. I became very sad and I pretended not to believe any of Eradice's stories.

This irritated Eradice no end. She offered to let me become an eyewitness to her happiness that next morning. 'You will see for yourself,' she contended heatedly, 'how strong my spiritual exercises are, how the good father guides me from one degree of mortification to the next with the purpose of making a saint out of me. You will be a witness to the delight and ecstasy which are a direct result of these exercises and you will never doubt again how marvelous these exercises are. Oh, how I wish, my dearest Therese, that my example would work its first miracle upon you. That you might be spiritually strengthened to totally deny the flesh and follow the only path which will lead you to God!'

We agreed that I would visit her the next morning at five o'clock. I found her in prayer, a book in her hand. She said to me, 'The holy man will arrive soon, and God shall be with him. Hide yourself in that little alcove, and from there you can see and hear for yourself the miracles of Divine Love wrought upon me by the venerable father confessor. Even to such a lowly creature as I.'

Somebody knocked quietly on the door. I fled into the alcove; Eradice turned the key and put it in her skirt pocket. There was, fortunately, a hole in the alcove door, covered with a piece of tapestry. This made it possible for me to see the entire room, without, however, running the risk of being seen myself.

The good father entered the room and said to Eradice, 'Good morning, my dearest sister in the Lord, may the Holy Spirit of Saint Francis protect you forever.'

She wanted to throw herself at his feet, but he lifted her off the floor and ordered her to sit down next to him upon the sofa. Then the holy man said, 'I cannot repeat too often the principles which are going to become the guidelines for your future way of life, my dear child. But, before I start my instructions, tell me, dear child, are the stigmata, those miraculous signs of God's everlasting favour, still with you? Have they changed any? Show them to me.'

Eradice immediately bared her left breast, under which she bore the stigma.

'Oh, oh, please dear sister! Cover your bosom with this handkerchief! (He handed her one). These things were not created for a member of our society; it is enough for me to view the wound with which the holy Saint Francis has made you, with God's infinite mercy, His favourite. Ah! it is still there. Thank the Lord, I am satisfied. Saint Francis still loves you; the wound is rosy and clean. This time I have with me a part of our dear Saint's sacred rope; we shall need it for our mortification exercises. I have told you already, my dear sister, that I love you above all my other penitents, your girl friends, because God has so clearly marked you as one of the beloved sheep in His flock. You stand out like the sun and the moon among the other planets and stars. Therefore I have not spared any trouble to instruct you in the deepest secrets of our Holy Mother Church. I have repeatedly told you, dearest sister, "Forget yourself, and let it happen." God desires from Mankind only spirit and heart. Only if you can succeed in forgetting the existence of your body will you be able to experience Him and achieve sainthood. And only as a saint will you ever be able to work miracles. I cannot help, my little angel, but to scold you, since I noticed during our last exercises that your spirit is still enslaved by your body. How can that be? Couldn't you at least be a little bit like our saintly martyrs? They were pinched with red-hot irons, their nails were torn off their feet and fingers, they were roasted over slow fires and yet . . . they did not experience pain. And why not? Because their mind was filled with pure thoughts of God's infinite glory! The most minute particle of their spirit and mind was occupied with thoughts of His immense glory. Our senses, my dear daughter, are mere tools. But, they are tools that do not lie. Only through them can we feel, only through them can we understand the evil and the good. They influence our bodies as well as our souls. They enable us to perceive what is morally right and what is morally wrong. As soon as we touch something, or feel, or hear, minute particles of our spirit flow through the tiny holes in our nerves. They report the sensations back to our soul. However, when they are filled completely with the love they owe their God and Creator, when YOU are so full of love and devotion that none of these minute particles can do anything else but concentrate on the Divine Providence, when the entire spirit is given to the contemplation of our Lord, then, and only then is it impossible for any particle to tell our spirit that the body is being punished. You will no longer feel it. Look at the hunter. His entire being is filled with only one thought: his prey! He does not feel the thorns that rip at him when he stalks through the forest, nor does he notice cold or heat. True, these elements are considerably weaker than the mighty hunter, but . . . the object of his thoughts! Ah, that is a thousand times stronger than all his other feelings put together. Would you feel the feeble blows of the whip when your soul is full of the thoughts of happiness that is about to be yours? You must be able to pass this all-important test. We must know for sure, if we want to be able to work miracles, whether we can reach this degree of perfection, whether we can wholly immerse ourselves in God!

'And we shall win, dear daughter. Do your duty, and be assured that thanks to the rope of the holy Saint Francis, and thanks to your pious contemplations, this holy exercise will end for you with a shower of unspeakable delight. Down on your knees child! Reveal that part of your body which raises the fury of our Lord; the pain you will feel shall bring your soul

438

in close contact with God. I must repeat again: "Forget yourself, and let it happen!" '

Eradice obeyed immediately without uttering a single word. Holding a book in her hands, she kneeled down in front of a little prayer stool. Then she lifted her skirts about the waist, showing her snow-white, perfectly rounded bums that tapered into two gorgeous alabaster, firm-fleshed thighs.

'Lift your skirts a little higher, my dear,' he said to her, 'it does not look proper yet. Fine, fine . . . that's a lot better. Put the prayer book down, fold your hands and lift up your soul to God. Fill your mind with thoughts about the eternal happiness which has been promised you!'

The priest pulled up his footstool and kneeled next to her, bending slightly backward. He lifted his cowl and tied it to the rope around his waist. Then he took a large birch rod and held it in front of my penitent friend who kissed it devoutly.

Piously shuddering I followed the whole procedure with full attention. I felt a sort of horror which is very difficult to describe. Eradice did not say a word. The priest gazed upon her thighs with a fixed stare, his eyes sparkling. He did not let his gaze wander for a single moment. And I heard him whisper softly, full of admiration, 'Oh, God, what a marvelous bosom. My Lord, those gorgeous tits!'

Now he bent over and then he straightened up again, murmuring biblical language. Nothing escaped his vile curiosity. After a few minutes he asked the penitent if her soul was prepared.

'Oh yes, venerable Father! I can feel my soul separate itself from my unworthy flesh. I pray you, begin your holy work!'

'It is enough. Your soul will be happy!'

He said a few prayers and the ceremony started with three fairly light blows of the rod, straight across her firm buttocks. This was followed by a recitation from

439

the Bible. Thereupon another three blows, slightly stronger than the first ones.

After he had recited five or six verses, and interrupted each of them the same way as before, I suddenly noticed to my utter surprise that the venerable Father Dirrag opened his fly. A throbbing arrow shot out of his trousers which looked exactly like that fateful snake about which my former father confessor had warned me so vehemently.

The monster was as long and as thick and as heavy as the one about which the Capuchine monk had made all those dire predictions. I shuddered with delightful horror. The red head of this snake seemed to threaten Eradice's behind which had taken on a deep pink colouration because of the blows it had received during the Bible recitation. The face of Father Dirrag perspired and was flushed a deep red.

'And now,' he said, 'you have to transport yourself into total meditation. You must separate your soul from the senses. And if my dear daughter has not disappointed my pious hopes, she shall neither feel, nor hear, nor see anything.'

And at that very moment this horrible man loosened a hail of blows, letting them whistle down upon Eradice's naked buttocks. However, she did not say a word; it seemed as if she were totally insensitive to this horrendous whipping. I noticed only an occasional twitching of her bum, a sort of spasming and relaxing at the rhythm of the priest's blows.

'I am very satisfied with you,' he told her after he had punished for for about five minutes in this manner. 'The time has come when you are going to reap the fruits of your holy labours. Don't question me, my dear daughter, but be guided by God's will which is working through me. Throw yourself, face down, upon the floor; I will now expel the last traces of impurity with a sacred relic. It is a part of the venerable rope which girded the waist of the holy Saint Francis himself.'

The good priest put Eradice in a position which was rather uncomfortable for her, but extremely fitting for what he had in mind. I had never seen my girl friend in such a beautiful position. Her buttocks were half-opened and the double path to satisfaction was wide-open.

After the old lecher had admired her for a while, he moistened his so-called rope of Saint Francis with spittle, murmured some of the priestly mumbo-jumbo which these gentlemen generally use to exorcise the devil, and proceeded to shove the rope into my friend.

I could watch the entire operation from my little hideout. The windows of the room were opposite the door of the alcove in which Eradice had locked me up. She was kneeling on the floor, her arms were crossed over the footstool and her head rested upon her folded arms. Her skirts, which had been carefully folded almost up to her shoulders, revealed her marvellous buttocks and the beautiful curve of her back. This exciting view did not escape the attention of the venerable Father Dirrag. His gaze feasted upon the view for quite some time. He had clamped the legs of his penitent between his own legs, and he dropped his trousers, and his hands held the monstrous rope. Sitting in this position he murmured some words which I could not understand.

He lingered for some time in this devotional position and inspected the altar with glowing eyes. He seemed to be undecided how to effect his sacrifice, since there were two inviting openings, His eyes devoured both and it seemed as if he were unable to make up his mind. The top one was a well-known delight for a priest, but, after all, he had also promised a taste of Heaven to his penitent. What was he to do? Several times he knocked with the tip of his tool at the gate he desired most, but finally he was smart enough to let wisdom triumph over desire. I must do him justice: I clearly saw his monstrous prick disappear the natural

way, after his priestly fingers had carefully parted the
rosy lips of Eradice's lovepit.

The labour started with three forceful shoves which
made him enter about halfway. And suddenly the
seeming calmness of the priest changed into some sort
of fury. My God, what a change! Imagine a satyr.
Mouth half-open, lips foam-flecked, teeth gnashing and
snorting like a bull who is about to attack a cud-
chewing cow. His hands were only half an inch away
from Eradice's full behind. I could see that he did
not dare to lean upon them. His spread fingers were
spasming; they looked like the feet of a fried capon.
His head was bowed and his eyes stared at the so-
called relic. He measured his shoving very carefully,
seeing to it that he never left her lovepit and also that
his belly never touched her arse. He did not want his
penitent to find out to whom the holy relic of Saint
Francis was connected! What an incredible presence of
mind!

I could clearly see that about an inch of the holy tool
constantly remained on the outside and never took
part in the festivities. I could see that with every backward movement of the priest the red lips of Eradice's
love-nest opened and I remember clearly that the vivid
pink colour was a most charming sight. However,
whenever the good priest shoved forward, the lips
closed and I could only see the finely curled hairs which
covered them. They clamped around the priestly tool
so firmly that it seemed as if they had devoured the
holy arrow. It looked for all the world like both of them
were connected to Saint Francis' relic and it was hard
to guess which one of the two persons was the true
possessor of this holy tool.

What a sight, especially for a young girl who knew
nothing about these secrets. The most amazing
thoughts ran through my head, but they all were
rather vague and I could not find proper words for
them. I only remember that I wanted to throw myself

at least twenty times at the feet of this famous father confessor and beg him to exorcise me the same way he was blessing my dear friend. Was this piety? Or carnal desire? Even today I could not tell you for sure.

But, let's go back to our devout couple! The movements of the priest quickened; he was barely able to keep his balance. His body formed an 'S' from head to toe whose frontal bulge moved rapidly back and forth in a horizontal line.

'Is your spirit receiving any satisfaction, my dear little saint?' he asked with a deep sigh. 'I, myself, can see Heaven open up. God's infinite mercy is about to remove me from this vale of tears, I . . .'

'Oh, venerable Father,' exclaimed Eradice, 'I cannot describe the delights that are flowing through me! Oh, yes, yes, I experience Heavenly bliss. I can feel how my spirit is being liberated from all earthly desires. Please, please, dearest Father, exorcise every last impurity remaining upon my tainted soul. I can see . . . the angels of God . . . push stronger . . . ooh . . . shove the holy relic deeper . . . deeper. Please, dearest Father, shove it as hard as you can . . . Ooooh! . . . ooh!!! dearest holy Saint Francis . . . Ooh, good saint . . . please, don't leave me in the hour of my greatest need . . . I feel your relic . . . it is sooo good . . . your . . . holy . . . relic . . . I can't hold it any longer . . . I am . . . dying!'

The priest also felt his climax approach. He shoved, slammed, snorted and groaned. Eradice's last remark was for him the signal to stop and pull out. I saw the proud snake. It had become very meek and small. It crawled out of its hole, foam-covered, with hanging head.

Everything disappeared back into the trousers; the priest dropped his cowl over it all and wavered back to his prayer stool. he kneeled down, pretended to be in deep communication with his Lord, and ordered his penitent to stand up, cover herself and sit down next to him to thank God for His infinite mercy which she had just received from Him.

What else shall I tell you? Dirrag left, Eradice opened the door to the alcove and embraced me, crying out, 'Oh, my dearest Therese. Partake of my joy and delight. Yes, yes, today I have seen paradise. I have shared the delights of the angels. The incredible joy, my dearest friend, the incomparable price for but one moment of pain! Thanks to the holy rope of Saint Francis my soul almost left its earthly vessel. You have seen how my good father confessor introduced the relic into me. I swear that I could feel it touch my heart. Just a little bit deeper and I would have joined the saints in paradise!'

Eradice told me a thousand other things, and her tone of voice, her enthusiasm about the incredible delights she had enjoyed left no doubt in my mind about their reality. I was so excited that I was barely able to answer her. I did not congratulate her, because I was unable to talk. My heart pounded in wild excitement. I embraced her, and left.

So many thought are racing through my mind right now that I hardly know where to begin. It is terrifying to realise how the most honourable convictions of our society are being misused. How positively fiendish was the way in which this cowl-bearer perverted the piety of his penitent to his own lecherous desires. He needled her imagination, artfully using her desire to become a saint; he convinced her that she would be able to succeed, if she separated her mind from her body. This, however, could only be achieved by means of flagellation. Most likely it was the hypocrite himself who needed this stimulation to repair the weakened elasticity of his flagging member. And then he tells her, 'If your devotion is perfect, you shall not be able to feel, hear, or see anything!'

That way he made sure that she would not turn around and see his shameless desire. The blows of the rod upon her buttocks not only increased the feeling in that part which he intended to attack, but they also served to make him more horny than he already was. And the relic of Saint Francis which he shoved into the body of his innocent penitent to chase away impurities which were still clinging to her soul, enabled him to enjoy his desires without any danger to himself. His newly-initiated penitent mistook her most voluptuous outburst of carnal climax for a divinely inspired, purely spiritual ecstasy.

THE LOINS OF
AMON

The Loins of Amon *is an erotic entertainment on an epic scale, a grand costume drama set in a mythical Ancient Egypt where mighty armies clash and priests sacrifice virgins in arcane and bestial rituals. Centre stage in this robust play stands Prince Ineni, an Egyptian noble with a claim to the throne and an outspoken opponent of the cruel and powerful priesthood. Manoeuvred by his enemies into leading a small army on a suicidal mission into Palestine and Syria, Ineni does not expect to return alive. Surprisingly his army is triumphant and he returns a hero, only to be arrested by the priests and sentenced to death. With the help of his favourite harem girl he succeeds in escaping to Nubia and from there he leads a revolt which places him on the throne as Pharaoh. Within a few weeks, however, he orders the virgin sacrifices to be resumed and himself begins plotting against a bold new pretender to the throne . . .*

As can be deduced from this bald account, here is an erotic book whose plot is not primarily sexual – though the narrative flesh that cloaks this skeletal scenario contains incidents that are as brazen and seductive as any other featured in this volume. Here, for example, is the initiation of a Syrian girl into the mysteries of the harem . . .

Riding amongst the last signs of life, touring the city on horse for any sign of trouble, Ineni was suddenly aware of two shadowy figures walking along the foot of the great wall of a noble's house, far from the poor quarter of the city. He galloped his horse towards the faint movement in the shadow and saw two women stepping quickly along towards the entrance of the house.

In the moonlight, he could see that one was well advanced into middle age, the other – taller and slimmer – a mere girl. The older woman appeared not to hear as he approached, but the girl turned while still walking and looked back. Her robe, close around her, tautened into long, suggestive folds, bulging over her breasts, falling away in slim lines to her hips, tightening around her shoulders and buttocks in a twisted clasp.

Ineni drew up his horse alongside them and the old woman drew back in fear. The younger had a sweet, almost child-like face, with a small nose, a pouting lower lip and large soulful eyes, which looked, now, at the Egyptian with nothing but curiosity.

'Where are you going?' Ineni demanded of the elder woman.

She looked pale and frightened as she answered, her voice little more than a whisper.

'We have been watching your glorious troops in action,' she said. 'Now we are retiring in thankfulness that the battle was short and saved us from the northern invader.'

'You have worked your fawning subservience to a nicety,' Ineni said, scornfully. 'Had I been the king of the Hittites you would have been licking my feet here. As it is I suspect you would be glad to thrust a knife between my shoulders.'

'No my lord, that is not true.' The woman was almost in tears in her fear. 'Both I and my daughter here abhor the barbarity of the Hittites.'

It was clear the woman was one of the noble's harem – probably the daughter, too, Ineni decided, as he looked them over. The woman continued to shift uneasily as if she were likely to dart away through the gates at any moment. Her daughter – large undulation of her breasts under the robe, clearer now – continued to gaze at Ineni with a curiosity which amounted almost to boldness. She was a very pretty creature.

'Your lies do not become you, woman,' Ineni said sternly. 'But although I could have you slaughtered, I shall bid you quietly goodnight if you will tell your daughter that she is to come with me.'

The woman clutched the girl's hand, seeming to grow suddenly bolder in protection of her young. The girl's slim fingers twined around her mother's but she didn't take her eyes from the Egyptian prince.

'Oh my lord, she is yet a virgin,' she whispered.

Ineni raised his eyebrows in surprise.

'Indeed the harems must be well filled if a place

450

could not be found for such a dainty morsel,' he said. 'She has, indeed, the face of a child, but her body, I would say, is that of a woman. Tonight she shall behave as befits a woman.'

'My lord, I beg you. I will bring you other more beautiful women if only you will not harm my daughter,' the woman pleaded.

'Why this concern?' Ineni asked with a laugh. 'Your daughter will not be harmed, woman. She will learn what all daughters must learn – how to take a man's weight on her hips, his spear between her legs.'

As he said this, Ineni looked straight at the girl, but her eyes showed no trace of her feelings. The older woman was clutching her arm now. Tears shone in her eyes.

'My lord, I will give you anything within my power if you will not take her. She is my only daughter and she is but sixteen.' A tear flowed gently down the woman's face as Ineni regarded the girl again with surprise.

'A woman, indeed for sixteen years,' he said. 'But how do you feel, my daughter at the thought of making love to the leader of the Pharoah's army?'

The girl spoke, for the first time, quietly, in a voice which made her seem suddenly more mature.

'My fate is in my lord's hands,' she said.

'Words of wisdom, my child. I am sorry for your mother's fears, but they are groundless and I cannot deprive myself of such a pleasant hour or two on their account.'

So saying, Ineni leaned suddenly from his horse, caught the girl around her slender waist, feeling the warm, living flesh against his arm, and whisked her onto the horse in front of him. Her mother, almost pulled off her feet as her daughter was dragged away from her, gazed at them in mute horror, tears coursing down her cheeks, unmoving, as if she knew the futility of movement.

451

Beginning to trot gently away, Ineni called back softly to the woman. 'Don't worry, I will bring her back, safe and happy in a few hours time.'

Jogging back through the city – deserted and quiet now except of the Egyptian guards on the walls – Ineni pulled the girls' dark head back against his lips, feeling its almost liquid texture. He kissed the back of her neck and she moved it against him, completely acquiescent. His free hand, held her against him, moving strongly over the outline of her breasts and ribs, tracing with a fierce tense hand, their firm, springy contours.

Her body, under the robe was wonderful to the touch. It sent a thrill through his fingertips so that his body gave an involuntary shudder of anticipation.

'Such a virgin,' he whispered to her as they rode. 'Your mother must be mad to withhold you from your destiny.'

'It was not my wish, my lord,' the girl said, softly. 'I have longed for the moment although now I am half afraid.'

'Don't be afraid,' Ineni whispered gently. 'You could have no better tutor.'

The girl nestled contentedly against him, breathing slightly, aloud, through parted lips as his lips caressed her hair and his hand her body outside the robe.

Soon they had reached the Egyptian tents and with the bright rays of light splintering the eastern horizon, Ineni pushed the girl gently ahead of him into his nightly shelter.

His heart was thumping fiercely and his hand found an echoing tremble in the girl's quivering flesh. Now that the moment was upon her, she was very frightened.

Ineni turned her and pulled her to him. Her soulful eyes were deep and giving, her body trembling slightly like a felt but unseen ripple on a pool. His hands moved over her, intently feeling her body with its warm

452

vibrations, sensing the roundnesses, the fleshy weight of breasts and buttocks through every pore. He kissed her, thrusting his tongue into her mouth, forcing apart her unwary lips, penetrating her for the first time. In his arms she was like a soft shifting of desert sand, light, slipping and moving in little eddies.

He pressed his hips in against her, clamping them to hers and through hers in a strong, relentless movement. Her loins, for a moment, seemed hesitant and unsure and then his pressure was answered. The soft, hot flesh of thighs and hips pushed against his so that he could feel their tubular imprint, could feel it flattened and spread by his own strong force. And in the centre of this pressure where their central cores seemed soldered together was his pulsing, hot pyramid, which crushed and bent against her triangle of junction; crushed until it was so painful that he had to ease back for a moment to relieve it.

The girl's hands were tentatively pressed on his arms now, moving slowly like searching, timid animals, feeling the long, hard lines of muscles which tensed and relaxed as he moved her against him. Her tongue was answering his, learning readily, flickering softly over his lips and in with a swift determination.

Gently, with hands which she could hardly feel, Ineni eased off her robe. She made no effort to help him, seeming, now, overcome with a stomach-clutching tension which allowed her only to breathe with difficulty. Her body when it rested, nude, in his arms, was shivering.

Again he brushed his hands over her, heat seeming to leap from flesh to flesh at every spot his hand touched. Her buttocks were full – quite fleshy for one so slim – and as his hands explored them, fingers probing gently against the sensitive flesh between them, she tensed them, swaying them involuntarily away from his hand, so that her hips pressed in against his.

He slipped his hands lightly over her back and shoul-

453

ders, drawing it over her flesh to the front of her body where her breasts, large and fragile-feeling, like enormous rain-drops, also trembled at his touch. The nipples were small and hard and as he moved his lips from her neck to kiss them, she gasped, made to push his head away with her hands, but then clasped it closer, wriggling her breast against his mouth as he nipped her gently with his teeth.

Ineni piloted the girl across the room to his bed of hides, leaning her gently backward so that she collapsed on her back on them, soft arms moving automatically around his shoulders as he sank down beside her. Lying on his side against her, he stroked the whole of her body with his hand, running his fingertips down from her shoulders out over the breasts, in again to her waist and then across the slight, smooth bulge of her lower belly.

As his finger explored the outer fringes of the soft hair which dwindled down to a point at the junction of her closed legs she began to wriggle her bottom uneasily. Slight, strangled whimpers choked in her throat.

At her leg junction, Ineni pressed his hand along the flesh of her thighs which felt like the skin of a grape. As he forced his fingers through between her thighs, she involuntarily pressed them closer together so that his hand was caught in a vice of flesh, unable to move up to its goal. But then her legs relaxed and he moved up a little before, involuntarily again, they tightened. Thus his hand continued its interrupted progression until, with the girl straining in thrilled fear, his fingers were brushing the warm, wet flesh of the lips of her vagina. She pushed a hand down at his arm, holding it away, reluctantly, not really wanting to hold it away, but afraid. And then he bent his face down on hers and kissed her passionately, losing his tongue in the depths of her mouth. She gave a little groan, there was a tremor of relaxation – and then his fingers had

454

pushed up and into the hot, moist aperture as the girl gave a gasp of pain.

In the first moments, she jerked his hips away from him, afraid of being hurt, afraid of unknown mysteries. But as, moaning quietly, she became used to the intruding pressure, she allowed her legs to be opened so that his hand no longer brushed against the inside surface of her thighs as he dug into her farther.

For some time, Ineni coaxed her, getting her used to the feeling of a strange flesh inside her passage and then, face and body flaming, he released her for a moment and slipped out of his tunic.

His body compared with hers was huge and rugged and his over-strained penis soared out from his loins like a temple obelisk.

He had risen to climb out of his clothes and he stood above the girl, looking down on her so that she would see the secret body of a man in all its splendour for the first time.

The girl, slim body rising and falling slightly with her disturbed breathing, looked through half-frightened, half-desiring eyes at the rugged nakedness before her. Her gaze swept down his body to the all-important source at his leg junction and there rested in wonder and fear on the great, thick, rigid rod which jutted out at her and over her.

Exploring, timidly, her eyes ranged over the large, dangling testicles, half lost in the shaggy covering of black hair and then her eyes moved up again to meet Ineni's with a look which plainly showed her mixture of willingness and fear.

Quickly he lay down against her once more, running his hand in fluid movements over her body so that she began to tremble. Then her caught her hand and pulled it against his penis, closing her fingers around the stiff, bursting flesh. For a second or two her hand remained limply where he had placed it, making a hot fusion between them and then she began gently to slip her fingers up and down and round the organ, feeling it, squeezing it, wondering at it. Bolder she moved on to his testicles, drawing her finger tips over them in an intuitive recognition.

Ineni, lying taut against her, felt his great projection raging as if it were water boiling and sizzling over a fire. His whole body was alive with thrills and skewers. He could wait for her no longer.

Raising himself, he moved one leg over her, lowering it between hers and then he moved his body onto hers drawing over his other leg in the same movement so that his hips were between the girl's thighs.

Her hands pressed against his chest for a fraction of a second as if she would try to push him away, but then they relaxed again and moved around his neck, pulling his face down to hers so that, she in turn, could dart her moist little tongue into his mouth.

With that indication of her readiness, Ineni raised his hips onto hers, feeling her hot and waiting beneath him. With her smooth, little face pressed against his, cheek to cheek, looking over his shoulder into the gloomy shadows of the tent roof, tensely waiting, he reached down to her leg junction. A soft movement spread her legs a little more so that she was completely exposed and then he had guided his pulsing spear at the moistened cavity. For a moment, in which life seemed to stand still for the girl, he hesitated – and then he thrust into her, holding her tightly in his arms so that she could not wriggle away as he did so.

The girl screamed and squirmed as the mountain of flesh burst into her, but she was firmly caught against his body and he drove into her again.

'Oh, oh, you're hurting me,' she screamed, trying to sway her hips from under the anchoring weight of his. But Ineni's body was now a great yearning, down at his penis the hot, moist relief for the yearning – a hot, jellied feeling – so that he began to grunt and his breath grated in his throat. He held the girl with all

456

his force, crushing her, rendering her body helpless. Her upper body was unable to move, only her legs could writhe and struggle and her central opening slip and jerk against the rigid pain.

Ineni ignored completely her whispered gasps for mercy, her tears. And in a short time the gasps had changed, mellowed into gasps of pure yielding and joining and enjoying as the pain, too, changed and mellowed.

He reached down, grasping a slim, smooth thigh with each hand and drew her legs apart and up around him, plunging deeper into her abdomen. There was to be nothing timid and too-gentle about this union. The girl would remember the first time in a sharp, clear image for the rest of her life.

Her hips wriggled and swayed under him, crinkling the flesh of her belly in little, momentary ridges. Her thighs clasped him as if she would hold him in her for ever. Her moans became the fuller, deeper moans of accepted challenge. Her eyes were closed as her fingers stroked down over his cheeks and drew his face onto hers for his mouth to make an outlet for her searching, giving tongue.

With quick, furious movements of his hips, Ineni thrust into her and into her again, regulating the speed to ensure her satisfaction.

His penis seemed to be burning as if it were on fire and in the tight, tender grasping of her channel he was pushing always against a slight force which agonisingly forced back his skin, contracted around the knob in a painful embrace.

The girl's whimpers became, suddenly, a greater, more prolonged consistent moaning and she caught at his thighs where they pressed against the underside of hers, pulling them at her while her mouth opened as if she were gasping for air. Her whole tender frame began to writhe and twist in an agony and in the rushes of air which burst from her throat, Ineni sensed

457

rather than heard whispered pleadings for speed as she felt the enormity of sweet pain building up, inevitably, in the soft, marshy regions of her genitals.

In turn he felt the pain, as if he were trying, agonisingly, to urinate and couldn't. His breath exploded from his stomach in fierce, coughing gasps and he slowly swept his penis in a great, bulging crush in and in with a painful grinding, forcing it more and more slowly into the depths which felt strangely solid as if he were reaching the flesh of other openings.

And with a sudden, continuous, high-pitched moaning, the girl found words: 'Quick, quick, quick, quick, ooooh!' in a cascade of incoherent emotion. Her hands clutched him with the force of a madman, digging into his shoulders, her knees stretched back, so that her buttocks were wriggling under his thighs, her face contorted and then her whole body was wracked and tormented in a series of convulsions and her mouth opened in a great 'Aaaaaaaaah . . .' and her soft passage reached the extreme of sensation and the liquid juices exploded as the breath was drawn from her body in a furious, aching sigh.

As he had felt the channel grow big around his penis, Ineni forced himself into the girl, holding her, pressing and grinding against her for seconds without jerking his hips, his head swaying in ecstasy on his shoulders and then he withdrew, thrust slowly in again – and again – and with a last deep surge, his entrails seemed to break through his penis and spatter in swift floods high up in the girl's body. He rammed in and into her, gasping, with her pulling his thighs to her, until the very last of his emotion had been dragged from him and then he settled slowly down on her hot, soft body and lay, crushing her breasts and belly with his weight until the immediate exhaustion had dissipated.

He rolled off the girl and stroked her belly gently. There was blood on the hides.

The girl smiled at him through deep, grateful eyes

which knew, now, all of the world that she had not known before.

'You were very cruel to me at first,' she whispered with a smile. 'But I am glad you were. It was a sweet pain.'

Ineni kissed her, stroking her full breasts and she looked down at his penis with a curiosity which contained now, little embarrassment. It was thick and heavy even now and she traced a vein with her finger tip, glancing up at his eyes with a quick, child-like smile.

'Now I am fit for the best harem,' she said with an air of satisfaction.

'There are many things you have yet to learn,' Ineni replied with amusement. 'You must be ready to obey your lord's every whim, his every perversion, to give him the fullest enjoyment no matter what he demands.'

'Is there more he might demand?' the girl asked, raising dark eyebrows, while her hand moved gently, possessively almost, around the thickening penis.

'You sweet innocent. He might demand of you three score positions, or your mouth, perhaps, or your tender behind.'

'What would he want with my behind?' the girl asked in surprise.

'If you like I will teach you,' Ineni said.

The girl looked at him uncertainly, large brown eyes troubled.

'I am a little afraid,' she said. 'But I want to be taught.'

Her slender fingers had continued to caress Ineni's penis, which had swung in gentle stages to a fully rampant position. As he kissed the girl, his organ was crushed, vertically, against the soft flesh of her belly, indenting it with the pressure. He slid his hand down her back, brushing lightly the firm, stretched skin until his hand soared out over the twin smooth mounds

459

of her buttocks. They were full and voluptuously bulbous to the touch and he cupped his hands around them, stroking them, kneading them. He rubbed his hand in little circular motions over the deep inturned join and the girl began to wriggle a little so that her buttocks moved and tautened under his hand, brushing against his palm.

'Turn over onto your belly,' he whispered. And after a moment's hesitation, she rolled gently away from him and over, face flat on the hides, turned to one side watching him, waiting.

Her bottom rounded out below him like a full water bottle and he continued to stroke it, his penis beginning to throb in its heat. His fingers moved gently into the hot ravine and the girl involuntarily tightened her buttocks into taut melons, trapping his fingers between them.

He dug the softer, inside flesh with his finger tips and waited for her to relax. When he felt her muscles loosen again, he brushed his fingers into the depth of the crease, while the girl squirmed with tiny, rippling movements of her hips which creased her buttocks in sinuous hollows and rounded them out again into full moons of flesh.

She began to breathe heavily and Ineni felt with his finger tip for the tight little pucker of flesh. He found it and began to press. The girl seemed to hold her breath for a moment, but then relaxed again and he insinuated his finger carefully and slowly into the loosening bud which was gradually becoming an aperture. His finger moved in and the firm, gristly flesh clasped him like a strong elastic band. As he thrust in, and girl's body flexed rigidly and he eased the pressure for a moment, but continued relentlessly as she slumped again. Soon his finger up to the first joint was warmly enclosed in the tight, rubbery core of her squirming rump, pressing, digging, enlarging in preparation for the greater intrusion.

The girl's face was hot and flushed, pressed tightly into the hides. Her eyes were closed and she breathed heavily and unevenly through open lips.

Ineni's eyes feasted on the creasing flesh of the slim, writhing body as his finger plunged unmercifully into the depths of the girl's bottom. Her breasts were crushed and half flattened against the hides and her hands slowly clutched and unclutched the material as he entered her.

With his penis rigid and pulsing at the very feel of the soft, springy texture of her behind, Ineni felt a surge of power sweep through him. With a sharp movement, he forced another finger into the girl's anus, crushing it in with the first so suddenly that she gave a little squeal and jerked away. But his fierce insistence allowed her no escape and soon she was moaning quietly at the thick ravaging so close to her aching vagina.

Judging the time right and, in fact, unable to restrain himself any longer, Ineni withdrew his fingers and slithered onto the warm skin of the girl's back. His penis rode up vertically between the spheres of her buttocks and he pressed against her for a moment, revelling sensually in the squeezing pressure as she flexed them containing his penis in the deep crease.

'Spread your legs,' he said fiercely.

The girl obeyed after a little hesitation. Her thighs slithered out below his hips until they made an obtuse angle with each other, extended on either side of him in quivering anticipation.

Quietly, Ineni guided his penis down to her anus, raising his hips so that his body pivoted against her on the arm of flesh. He moved her buttocks apart with his hands and prodded gently against the spot.

For some time he lay on her, jerking up and down in little movements while the knob searched, vaguely and without penetration, against a surround of flesh. And then he began to feel a give in the fleshy resistance, a sharp feeling of containment.

The girl gave a gasp, tautened her buttocks and pulled away from him slightly.

He kissed the back of her neck, stroking her hot face with his fingers.

'It will not hurt in a moment,' he whispered.

The girl relaxed again and he resumed the gentle pressure.

This time as he felt the tight containment, the sudden, defined solidity of feeling at the very extreme of his penis, the girl uttered an 'Oooooh!' but did not pull away. Her buttocks went rigid, but relaxed in a moment and he continued prodding gently at the bridgehead. The tiny entrance was clasping at his organ in an agonising grip and he longed to plunge straight into the depths; but he bore the slowness with patience, consolidating gradually for the sake of the girl.

Her anus was broadening, loosening slightly as she became used to the intrusion and although she uttered agonised gasps from time to time, she relaxed almost immediately and Ineni was soon acutely aware of a small section of his penis rubbing in a tight friction well inside the opening.

He pulled her thighs towards a right angle from under his body so that she was stretched away from him in three directions at the latter end of which he was joined to her through the small posterior aperture, leaning more and more heavily onto her bottom with his hips.

The girl began to breathe heavily, lips apart, eyes closed as he explored the outer cavern of her rectum. Her buttocks began to wriggle, apart from her, it seemed, in small intense movements, alive under him, excited by the intimate thickness of him on her and in her.

'Kneel up,' he said in a voice broken with the fierce carnal emotion of the sucking of his organ.

The girl complied, pulling her thighs in a slithering

movement under her, arching her back in a concave and then a convex as she thrust her buttocks up for him.

Now she sloped away before him, from where his great, throbbing rod surged roughly into her back channel, rounding in from her taut, stretched buttocks to her slim, firm waist on which the top part of her body swayed in an agony of half-pain and pleasure, from side to side on the bed of hides.

Her face was crushed in hot helplessness of unseeing, her breasts brushed against the surface below her as she swayed.

Ineni had also moved up between her legs as she knelt and was now firmly pressed against her doubled over buttocks, watching his penis slipping in and out of her anus.

The outer skin slipped like some, thin, sensitive peel on the inner piston as he jerked in and out and the knob, when he occasionally withdrew it completely, or when the girl jerked forward involuntarily at a sudden further pressure, was a furious, outraged red.

Grasping her firmly on either side of her waist, where the flesh creased in thin superfluous folds from her bending, Ineni was overcome with the sheer physical necessity of plunging into her completely, of losing his penis in her so that his whole body, the whole weight of his hips could ram against her, the full length of his rod be clasped to its base in the slim, tight passage.

Squirming her anus on the end of his organ, the girl writhed unaware of the length yet to go. Her breath was issuing in what was almost a continuous thin, low croon at the new experience.

Ineni's grip on her waist tightened. His mouth twisted with the passionate anticipation of his thrust – and then he rammed into her, splitting, like a knife through canvas into the depths of her behind, his penis surging forward like a great, inevitable wave, slower

463

as the thicker base reached the opening, but inexorable and unable to be denied.

The girl screamed at the sharp, painful entry.

Her bottom writhed like an animal trying but unable to reach the spear in its back.

'Oh – oh, it's too much – oh, oh!' The words could hardly form themselves as she tried to escape the pain.

But Ineni held her in a grip against which she flailed in vain. His face, strained back on his neck, was furrowed in passion, his thighs rigidly tensed with his hips as he thrust into her again and again.

The narrowness was agonisingly sensual, seeming to crush his penis, to be tearing the skin from it, leaving it doubly naked and sensitive. His hips pistoned backwards and forwards with increasing rapidity, his penis drawing out and then rushing forward the whole length of her back passage so that she cried out with each hot, furious in-thrust.

Deep in his belly, Ineni was half-conscious of the fierce, unbearable sucking of his entrails. His penis seemed heavy, fully-laden, its very fibre whirling in sharp painful spirals. He rammed his hips against the buttocks of the girl and held them there, crushing against her, wriggling from side to side, while his penis moved in different angles in the depths of her rectum so that she seemed to be almost swooning.

Her anus was larger, easier, now, and between her gasps she was breathing words, indistinct and half-formed.

'Yes, yes . . . hurts . . . wonder . . . oh . . . oh!' They came to him like a far echo in a temple as his head felt tight and crawling.

His hands moved fiercely along the girl's body, grasped her breasts cruelly, clutched them in handfuls, pinched the nipples, returned again to her hips, where they dug deeply into the firm flesh as his hips danced a passionate dance against her behind.

The sucking in his belly had spread like a growing

fire until it seemed that his whole body below his waist was being drawn into the girl, as if the whole of him would disappear into the soft, dark regions of her black passage.

At his penis was the extreme heat of the fire, a painful, burning furnace against which he was helpless, a furnace impossible, now to extinguish, a furnace which he could only go on stoking and stoking in abandoned, willing slavery.

In, in, in he jerked, with his penis expanding and expanding, his mouth opening and closing, eyes fixedly on the face of the girl. Her face, too, was a mask of passion; her buttocks swayed in fury on the end of him; her anus had become a gaping hole into which he had no difficulty of access. He was lost in it to the hilt as his hip movements reached a peak of rapidity, his penis bursting in quick explosions into the waiting sheath, each explosion coming more quickly on the last until they were almost a continuous stream, so that it must have seemed to the girl she was filled with respite with a great thing which was splitting her bottom in two.

His breath was an explosion of gasps. His penis was poised on the brink. The girl was ramming her buttocks back at him. Her mouth was saying 'Go on, go on!' His belly was flooding down to his extreme projection. There was a pause of agony in which the world stood still. And then his organ was undulating in great squeezing jerks which drew sperm in quick jets as when a water-bottle was squeezed.

Ineni went on ramming into her for some time with his penis so concentrated in sensation that it hurt. A gasp accompanied each fresh sucked out release of liquid into her.

As his thrusts dwindled and the dregs of his passion spurted weakly into her bottom, the girl was almost weeping with passion, still thrusting back her hips as if she wanted more.

Ineni withdrew from her at last and rolled over, exhausted, onto his back. His penis slumped, deflated, against his thigh. For some time the girl lay, buttocks crushed together, moving slightly on the hides and then she wriggled towards him, lay her head on his chest and gave a great sigh.

Half an hour later, Ineni, as good as his word, was riding back to the city, with the girl sitting in front of him. She was quiet and thoughtful.

'You have learned well,' Ineni told her with a smile. 'You gave me more pleasure than many an experienced woman of the harem.'

'My lord it was wonderful to me,' the girl whispered. She looked at him sadly. Her hands and lips were trembling.

'What is the matter my sweet little flower?' Ineni asked.

A tear flowed down the girl's cheek and when she answered, the words were a mere, frightened whisper.

'My lord I cannot bear the thought that you are going. I want to stay with you.'

Ineni smiled in surprise, touched by the girl's concern.

'But I promised your mother I would bring you back,' he said gently.

'I don't care. I don't care.' There was a desperation in the girl's voice which troubled him. 'I want to stay with you. Oh, please take me into your harem. Take me with you to Egypt.'

Ineni stroked his chin. This was an unexpected result of his passion. Of course, the girl had been a virgin. She had just endured feelings she had never dreamt of before . . .

ROMAN ORGY

The scene is Imperial Rome and a banquet is taking place at the house of the ambitious senator Lucius Crispus. Crispus is a social climber, a vulgarian who uses his wife's money to buy himself into a the good graces of the aristocracy. His wife, Clodia, is a cool and elegant beauty who watched the antics of Lucius and his slaves with disgust. To please his guests Lucius has squandered a fortune on two erotic dancers from Spain — slim, supple girls with large breasts and no shame. Intoxicated by their sensuous skills, inspired by the plaudits of his guests and egged on by those he wishes to impress, Lucius turns his lascivious attention to his shy new Egyptian slave girl . . .

Like its companion piece The Loins of Amon, Roman Orgy *is a rumbustious sex novel set against the backdrop of history. A creation of the pseudonymous Marcus Van Heller, a stalwart of the Olympia Press stable of erotic writers, it paints a picture of the slaves' revolt in Imperial Rome that is not to be found in any school textbook!*

Among the many pairs of eyes which had witnessed the using of the Egyptian slave girl by Lucius Crispus, was a pair of cool grey. At the moment they were hard eyes, very hard eyes.

They belonged in a face which any Emperor would have been proud of: a broad, strong face with a square jutting chin, a straight fine mouth and a broad forehead from which the eyes looked deeply out, hard and unafraid. A face which could have made a kingdom into an Empire, a face which was going to lead ten thousand men to their doom. The face of a slave.

It was during the lecherous performance of Lucius Crispus that the slave became aware of Clodia's eyes upon him – as they had so often been upon him of late. As Crispus was urged to greater efforts by the licentious crew of Rome's aristocracy, she finally called his name.

'Spartacus!'

He turned his grey eyes toward her and walked over to her side.

As he walked, the muscles in his calves below the tunic bulged; long lengths of muscle stirred in his arms. In spite of his height – he was slightly taller than any other man present – his body radiated a potential dynamism. It seemed unlikely that he could be taken off his guard.

He bent towards his mistress and the cloth of his tunic stretched in wrinkles across his shoulders.

Clodia's eyes held his with a look he could not understand as she said quietly:

'I'm tired of this. I'm going to bathe. I shall need you to stand guard over the door.'

She bade goodnight to her women guests who watched her sympathetically as she left. It was very hard on her, her husband acting like this in public, and Clodia such a beautiful woman and not one man noticing her leave. It was a wonder she didn't divorce him – or get herself a lover.

Spartacus strode silently after her, leaving the noise of the banquet behind, through the portico flanking the huge quadrilateral, which in turn enclosed the gardens with their walks and abours and the baths which Crispus had had specially built to the pattern and proportions of the huge public thermae.

It was not unusual for Spartacus to be asked to accompany his mistress. He was the head of the several hundred slaves which Crispus boasted as his entourage and he occupied a comparatively privileged position. Descended from the Thracian princes, he could boast at least as much culture as his master – which he had to admit was not saying an awful lot – and he knew himself to be more of a man.

But lately, it seemed, Clodia had been singling him out to be with her in nearly everything she did, everywhere she went. He had become virtually her personal bodyguard.

Watching her walk before him through the torchlit porticos, Spartacus wondered why she stayed in Crispus' house. It was well known – even among the slaves – the he treated her badly. There was nothing to stop her leaving.

Spartacus' lips tightened as his mind dwelt on Crispus. His master treated nobody well, in fact, except those he considered of superior rank and birth on whom he fawned his attentions or whom he tried desperately to impress – not without success.

Spartacus was aware that Crispus regarded him with a certain reluctant respect, which he felt sometimes bordered on hatred. For a long time he had been at a loss to understand this, but eventually it had dawned on him that, to his master, he represented the threat of enslaved but superior classes who in different circumstances would have thought him nothing but an ignorant upstart. There were many such slaves; cultured Greeks and Egyptians, many of them.

He wondered why Crispus did not put him in the slave market at times, to be rid of him, but then again it had dawned on him that he represented a challenge. If Crispus got rid of him, he would have admitted his inability to dominate, admitted defeat.

Following Clodia into the bath buildings, Spartacus wondered why she should require him to accompany her. Was she afraid one of her guests might wander away from the banquet and try to take liberties with her? – nobody would dare. Was she afraid of her slaves? They wouldn't dare – besides he was a slave. Spartacus became suddenly aware of the intimacy of leaving the bright, noisy company and disappearing through the grounds with his mistress to guard her while she bathed.

'Wait here.'

Clodia left him with this command and disappeared into one of the dressing rooms just inside the building.

Spartacus stared around him in the flickering torchlight. Beyond was a large vaulted hall, its walls of blue and white stone mosaic. The centre of the roof was taken up by a large space in the vaulting through which the sun poured at noon and the stars glittered at night. In the middle of the floor was the great bronze basin of water, water which steamed now from the heat of the hypocausta beneath.

The slaves were never allowed to use these baths, which had separate hours – like the public baths – for men and women. It was still permissible in the public baths for mixed bathing, but it was never seen. No woman cared to sully her reputation. There had been so many scandals in the past.

In the past . . . How many years had Spartacus been here in Rome, in the great town house of Lucius Crispus? How many years had he listened to the suffering and indignities of the slaves? How many years since he had seen this Thracian hills, those beautiful, free, Thracian hills? How long would it go on? . . .

His thoughts were suddenly stopped dead by the appearance of his mistress. Without a glance at him she ran across the marble floor and disappeared down the stone steps into the warm water of the sunken bronze basin. Spartacus was dumbstruck, a hundred times more so than when he had seen the Spanish maidens dance in the banquet room. Clodia had been quite naked!

He gazed incredulously through the ill-lit gloom of the bathing room. It was so. Through the gloom and the rising vapours he could see her white body floating lazily on the surface of the greenish water. Even now he could make out – how anguishingly vague – the lines of her pale breasts breaking the surface.

Spartacus' mind wouldn't function for some seconds. This had never been known. A Roman patrician woman undressing before a male slave! He turned and peered back through the gloom of the grounds, half afraid that he might be struck down for the sacrilege of having seen what had been paraded before him.

In the fleeting glimpse he had seen the body of one of the most beautiful women of Rome; a body which he knew many noble Romans would have given a fortune to see. Cold virtue in a beautiful woman always increased desire for her.

How could she have been so indiscreet? Why? She could have slipped on her stola and then bathed in one of the smaller baths out of sight. It was as if she had paraded herself intentionally.

Spartacus stood, undecided, at the entrance to the building. He felt he should withdraw to the grounds just outside, but hesitated to disobey his mistress' explicit command. It seemed further sacrilege to remain where he was, particularly as Clodia was making no effort to escape his view, seemed, in fact, to be parading herself quite unconcernedly.

As he watched her misty outline, she turned on her stomach and floated, face down in the water, her long, unloosened hair streaming over her wet shoulders, rounded tips of buttocks showing like some ghostly half-submerged fish.

Spartacus folded his arms. Under his hands he felt the smooth, tight bulging of his biceps and the feeling reassured him. This was Clodia's fault. He would stay where he was.

From time to time, he watched her leisurely lolling in the warm water, he saw her raise her head, or simply turn it, towards where he stood in the shadow of the entrance. Perhaps she was afraid he would go and leave her unprotected. Although why he would was unthinkable. To disobey an order!

Reflecting, with the image of her nudity in his head, Spartacus began to remember little incidents of the past few weeks: the way her eyes were so often upon him, the fact she had asked his advice upon some Thracian vase she had considered buying, that once her hand had rested on his arm, as if absently, when she gave him an order. Spartacus reflected on these things and gazed with his cool, grey eyes through the steam at the bronze basin.

Time passed. To Spartacus it seemed an eternity, at any moment of which he expected some guest to stray away from the noise of the banquet which he could no longer hear, and find him standing his lonely guard over the senator's naked wife.

But when at last the silent worry of his thoughts was interrupted, it was such an interruption as to fill his head with an even darker cloud of anxiety.

From the bronze basin, Clodia's cultured voice reached him. There was a trace of nervousness in the usually firm, imperious tones.

'Spartacus. A cloth and my robe are in the dressing room.'

He hesitated a second or two for her to add something, but she lay back in the water, waiting.

His heart was beating a little faster than normal as he went into the dressing room. There on a wooden seat were strewn her clothes. His face flushed as his eyes passed, in the gloom, from her stola to the under tunic, the brassiere which clasped those proud breasts, the loincloth which contained those virtuous hips.

He picked up the woollen napkin and the blue robe made of the still rare silk from the mysterious Orient.

As he strode toward the pool, muscles flexing and unflexing in his powerful legs, he was filled with the foreboding of strange things. This was no ordinary night. This was no ordinary duty he was performing.

He reached the pool's edge and stood looking down into the opaque green waters where Clodia, still unconcernedly, floated. She seemed to ignore him as he gazed down at the parts of her body which showed through the steam.

Spartacus waited, while Clodia paddled. He could

see the smooth slope of her white shoulders, the deep cleft of the upper part of her breast. Half lying in the water, she turned her eyes towards him.

Her face was radiant with the pale beauty, the clear-cut lines of a Roman aristocrat. Her hazel eyes were bright with a peculiar fire.

'You dislike your master, Spartacus,' she said. Her voice had regained its old, firm tones.

Spartacus said nothing.

Clodia laughed. One of the few times he'd ever heard her laugh.

'Your silence condemns you. He dislikes you too.'

She hesitated and still Spartacus said nothing.

'Today he finally admitted defeat. He decided to get rid of you, sell you in the slave market.'

Spartacus stared at her. So at last it had happened. But her next words astonished him.

'He wanted to sell you, but I put my foot down. Because I want to keep you.'

'My lady is kind,' Spartacus said softly.

'No, not kind,' she said, 'just self-indulgent.'

Giving Spartacus no time to ponder her words, she began to raise herself to the marble floor of the baths.

He stared at her, unable to avert his eyes as she came, like a nymph, out of the water. First her breasts stunned his eyes, large, firm and white with the red smudge of nipples a startling contrast to the colour of the skin. And then her belly, flat, smooth, white; and then her abdomen, with the two pink creases in the soft flesh and the black down of hair reaching to a point between her legs; and the long thighs, themselves like marble, supple, cold and beautiful.

She stood dripping in front if him. Her eyes were those of the sphinx. His lips opened slightly.

'Rub me down,' she said quietly. 'Have you forgotten yourself?'

The whole of Spartacus' skin all over his body seemed to be pulsating as he bent to his task. Clodia stood quietly watching the bunching of his powerful arm muscles as he wiped the moisture from her arms, her breasts, her belly, her back, her buttocks. Spartacus hesitated. Her buttocks were full, contained firmly in long sweeping lines. His hands trembled as he felt their shape and texture through the woollen napkin.

'Go on,' Clodia's voice commanded from above as he knelt. Her voice sounded firm but there was a hollow undertone as if she were steeling herself. He realised suddenly that she was trembling.

His big hands moved down the backs of her thighs, shaping the almost imperceptible down into a slim arrow. His hand contained the rounded calves in the napkin and he swivelled round and rubbed up her legs in the front.

He was more aware of the trembling. Clodia shifted her legs apart, moving on the balls of her small, bare feet. Spartacus looked up at her. Her lips were parted as she looked down on him. Her eyes pierced his with a look which was command and desire and not without a tremulous undercurrent of fear.

'Go on,' she said softly. There was a tremble in her voice as well as her limbs.

Spartacus hollowed his hands around the napkin and moved them up her leg. Astonishment had now given place to a masculine certainty and strength. There was no doubt in his mind, only a deep, luxurious wonder.

His hands moved up over the knee, soaking the moisture from the skin into the napkin. Through it he could feel the solidity of the thigh. He wanted to touch the thigh without the napkin, but he continued pulling the napkin, like a broken glove, up the leg to where it broadened into its fullness and his eyes were on a level with the crease of flesh between her thighs.

Once more he hesitated.

'Go on.' The voice above him was a controlled Vesuvius.

Spartacus held the napkin in the flat of his right hand. With the other he boldly grasped Clodia's thigh, his finger denting the buttery flesh and with a long, slow movement, he wiped the napkin between her legs, dabbing in into the intimate places of her crotch.

As he felt the soft yielding flesh under the napkin flatten out against the inside of the thighs, Clodia's hand moved uncontrollably down to his head and her fingers grasped his long, fair hair and pressed his face to her lower belly.

Spartacus rose slowly up her body, his lips tracing a path up over her navel, the taut flesh of her ribs, resting on the beautiful pearl hills of her breasts, brushing the rich, hard protrusion of nipples, sucking in the hollow of her shoulder, on up the white slender neck, until they found her lips and fastened there, his lips on those of Clodia, famed in Rome for her beauty, Clodia whose slim, smooth tongue now forced its way between his lips, between his teeth and snaked in his mouth, the mouth of her slave.

After a moment she drew away from him, trembling violently.

'Give me my robe,' she said. 'We must not be seen here.'

Spartacus put her robe over her trembling shoulders, she pulled it tightly around her and, bidding him follow her, walked quickly away from the baths.

Walking behind her once again, Spartacus was filled with the joy of incredible discovery, an emotional power which was overwhelming. Here he was following her as he had so often followed her before – but now what a difference! Now he knew those breasts which had vaguely excited him before as they pressed through her stola. Breasts which had excited so many men in Rome; breasts so inaccessible and far away. Now he knew that slender back which shaped into the girdle of the robe as she hurried before him, knew those buttocks which were outlined by the clinging silk, those thighs over which the sulk hung loosely from its swelling over the rump. Now he understood the looks which Clodia had cast toward him. Now he understood the touch on his arm. Soon she would be his, unbelievably his.

Hurrying before Spartacus, Clodia was aware that his eyes were on the tension of her buttocks under the robe. She pulled the robe tightly around her to give him a more exciting spectacle.

Now they were going to her room and she would seduce him. It was no sudden decision Clodia had made. It had been developing in her mind for months.

She was well aware of Lucius' lack of interest in her. She was no longer terribly interested in him. She had in fact made up her mind at one time to divorce him.

But then she had become suddenly aware of the slave, Spartacus. There was some magnetism in him, some superior strength of character which made her, even now, half afraid of her fascination for him.

She had seen Lucius' recognition of the same quality, had watched the battle Lucius, who could not bear to find himself in competition with a stronger man, had fought with himself. She had watched the indifference of the slave to the attempts of an inferior being to degrade him.

It was a fascination, a very physical fascination, which had kept her in Lucius' house. She would sit and watch Spartacus, his big muscles tensing in his big body as he performed his tasks; she would watch the calm, handsome face and if the cool, grey eyes alighted on her she would look quickly away lest he should notice her interest.

The desire had grown in her to touch that athletic muscular body. A desire which had finally found its outlet a few days before when she had allowed her fingers to rest lightly on his arm while directing him in some duty.

And then she had wanted that touch, that physical communion returned. Had wanted to give, to yield under the superior power which she sensed in the man.

Even now it was a desire completely physical which drove her on. The unheard of, forbidden liaison with a slave. That taboo which gave such an emotional desperation and glory to the act.

Although, it was true, a slave could eventually become a freed man – and perhaps rise to office – there was no denying the fact that a slave, as a slave, was the scum of the Empire. Such a liaison would have the whole of Rome howling for the blood of both parties; such a liaison would resound beyond the boundaries of the peninsula to the very outposts of the Empire.

It was partly the knowledge of this that had driven Clodia on in her desire rather than deterred her. She had a will the equal of most in the city and Spartacus, all unwittingly, had driven her towards the inevitable with every movement of his body, every look in his eyes, every one of the few words he ever uttered.

The noise of the banquet, still in progress, reached them as they walked in the shadow of the portico and mounted the steps to the upper story. Without a word, Clodia led the way through Crispus' room to her own. Starlight shone in through the window which looked out onto the quadrilateral. Spartacus moved uncertainly in the poor light and stood silent and still, while Clodia pulled a heavy shutter into place across the window. She lit torches in their brackets on the walls, and while she moved quietly to the door to close it, Spartacus looked with quick curiosity around her room, which he was seeing for the first time.

The room was dominated by Clodia's bed, the bed in which she must have spent so many lonely nights, listening perhaps to the breathing of her husband in the next room. It was a huge bed of oak. The woodwork was inlaid with tortoise-shell, the feet were made of ivory. All three materials shone with a lustre which bespoke much labour from Clodia's female slaves. There were two divans also, strewn with exotically coloured cushions, and in a corner near the window space was a tripod table on which lay Clodia's mirrors of silver and few adornments.

The furniture, as was customary in the grand houses, was sparse but superb.

After Clodia had shut the door she and Spartacus stood looking at each other for a few moments. Her beautiful face was slightly flushed; there was a tint of fear in her eyes which she tried vainly to conceal.

The interval of walking had made Spartacus wary. He was well aware of the penalty for this sort of thing and, although his length of rigidity had itched against his loincloth from the moment he'd seen Clodia run from her dressing room, he now remained where he was, making no move towards her.

Looking at him, Clodia too, felt the slight embarrassment that the interval had built. She had a sudden, fleeting fear that she might be scorned.

She brushed past Spartacus and stretched out on the counterpane and cushions of the bed.

'My bones ache with all that sitting in the banquet room,' she said, holding his eyes again with her own. 'I want to be massaged.'

Spartacus moved towards her, his sandaled feet rustling lightly on the floor. She saw in his eyes the deep unwavering purposefulness that so many were to see and it filled her with a shuddering anticipation.

'Have you seen the women wrestlers being massaged in the palaestrae?' she asked softly. And as he nodded, she added, slipping from her robe: 'Well I am just one of them waiting for the masseur. Clodia does not exist.'

As his fingers began to move over her body and her breath fluttered in her throat, she thought, 'Perhaps this is the *only* time that Clodia exists.'

Once again her full, beautiful body was exposed to her slave. But Spartacus, running his hands over the beautiful tapering arms, the slim shoulders, the glossy swelling of her breasts, knew that he was no longer the slave but the master.

His strong fingers kneaded the firm flesh of her belly, drawing it in little ridges, flattening it with his palms. He stroked the sinuous lengths of her thighs, his chest palpitating, an aching pressure under his loincloth.

His hands rifled her body, knowing the virtuous flesh, all the more sensual for its virtuousness. As his fingers moved between her legs she gave a muffled squeal and jerked over onto her stomach, burying her face in the cushion. Her back heaved as his hands caressed her bare bottom. The white skin of the firm mounds was so smooth it seemed glazed. The hips flowed out from her slim waist, full and receptive; her feet twitched and her thighs rubbed convulsively together has his hands made bold love to her.

Spartacus gazed down, from his ascendant and intimate proximity, on the beautiful rounded lines of her body and choked with a desire to flop his hips down on that filled-out cushion of a bottom and nuzzle his loaded cudgel between the warm, downy pressure of her thighs where they joined her buttocks.

He worked in fingers up between the tight challenge of her thighs, with the flesh giving before his hand, running in ripples up to the arch in which the moist lips nestled.

His hand trembled as he reached his goal, trembled as he was about to touch the intimate secret of Clodia, cold, unfathamable Clodia whose beauty was the talk of Rome. And then his hand, unrestricted now by any napkin, ran along the soft flanges of flesh, savouring their warmth, their heat, their moistness of gentle perspiration.

Clodia gave a sharp intake of breath as his fingers explored, and she slid up the bed overcome with desire.

His hand followed and this time she lay still, breathing wildly as his fingers parted the lips.

As he caressed the little clitoris she gave a squeal into the cushion and the squeal became a gasp as his fingers plunged up through the elastic brim of flesh into the warm depths of her passage.

'Spartacus . . . Spartacus!'

She uttered his name as if in delirium and rolled onto her back. Her hands seized his arms, digging fiercely into their strands of muscle and pulled him down on her. Her lips pressed onto his, working on them as if she was trying to eat them; her tongue jerked into his mouth, gliding like quicksilver.

Spartacus dropped onto her body, her body taking his weight as if she were some complementary part of him, giving in places, resisting in others.

'Spartacus, Spartacus,' her mouth breathed incessantly, as if she had been saying the name to herself for months and it was a relief to say it aloud at last.

He shifted on her, hips grinding on hers, feeling, even through his tunic, the flesh of her belly billowing and swelling under him. The rigidity of his penis hurt him in its confinement.

Her hands moved round his back, arms locking him to her, legs twining with his. Her eyes were closed, mouth open. She seemed more beautiful in her passion than he had ever thought her before.

'Spartacus,' she breathed. 'Don't torment me. You are the master.'

Feverishly, yet with the same sure glint in his eyes, Spartacus raised his hips off her and slithered out of his loincloth. He didn't bother to remove his tunic; it pulled up to his waist. From the foot of the bed his sandals dropped with a thud to the floor.

Her long fingers came down between his thighs and grasped him, making it throb. Then she was stroking his small tight buttocks, urging them at her and her thighs had opened wide.

Spartacus slithered down her. He wrapped his strong arms around her body – and with a swift, full stroke, he shot into her like a Roman legion cutting through the tangled brushwood of a forest in Gaul.

Clodia gave a strangled gasp as she felt the dull pain of his entry. He seemed to split her in all directions. He was bigger by far than Crispus.

He thrust into, splitting her farther and farther as his thickening organ coursed up into the core of her body. She wanted him to fill her; she wanted him to make her ache, make her sore, make her cry with the sweet tears of exquisite pain. At last this man, this silent, magnetic man, was hers, was alone with her in the world, his mind focused only on her and the superb satisfaction of her body.

Spartacus, soaring into her with an unleashed ferocity, felt a tingling in every pore of his body where it touched her. His chest against her sleek, bolstering breasts, his belly against hers, his hairy thighs brushing her columns of marble-smoothness – above all his great, uncovered tool, hot and bursting with sensation, moving tightly, excruciatingly into her lower mouth.

He gasped out his breath, crushing his lips over her face, over all those beautiful features.

Writhing under him, moaning her ecstasy, the cold, virtuous Clodia was in a bitch-heat of passion, pulling her thighs back to her breasts, almost to her shoulders even, wriggling her buttocks so that the counterpane crinkled and dampened under the sweating movement. Spartacus exulted in his raging lust.

His hand roamed over her skin, holding the flesh which belonged to him, doing what he liked with the beautiful body which all Rome would have given its eyes to see.

Gripping her shoulders, squeezing until the white skin turned red, grasping the breasts as they overflowed from under him, holding the waist, cradling the buttocks in his big palms, feeling them overflow from his fingers, so that his fingers dug into them as if they were soft, silken cushions.

Clodia groaned and panted as his hands reached under her buttocks, carressing the soft, sensitive skin, moving down to the source of their liaison.

She spread her thighs to the limit, forcing herself to endure the pain which accompanied the ecstasy, moaning with a masochisitic pleasure under his rough impalement of her. His crushing, aggressive weight seemed to be forcing her through the bed, which creaked under the furious rhythm of their intercourse. She felt inside her belly, as in her throat, a sort of growing restriction of breath, a bubble of sensation which seemed to grow and grow until she knew she could contain it little longer.

The heavy staff which surged in the wetness of Clodia's channel was the only part of himself that Spartacus could now feel. His knees slipped on the silken counterpane as he moved up to try to shove more of its length into the passage.

Her chin was on his shoulder. He could feel the heat of her normally cold cheek on his own hot flesh. Her mouth was fluttering over his face. His own name Spartacus, seemed to mix with the animal noises of her moans. She strained toward him as he felt a heat in his belly move down to his loins. She panted and the gasps became a continuous low-pitched moan which suddenly choked off into a staccato spluttering and screaming as she pushed her belly up at him.

She was still groaning as the tide of life-giving fluid swept through Spartacus making him cry out with the unbelievable ecstasy of it, making him want to destroy this beautiful creature whose body he was wildly ravaging, whose hips still squirmed slightly under his, whose cheek was still against his, whose arms clasped his shoulders tightly, whose buttocks still tensed in his hands.

He wanted to destroy, to make this woman completely his. Passion made his head swim, his eyes glaze. But to his astonishment, Clodia suddenly began to struggle under him, scratching at him with her nails so that thin weals of pain stung his arms.

'Beast, beast!' she cried. Tears were suddenly in her eyes. Spartacus fought down her arms, held them at her sides as her body writhed to escape. Bewildered he recoiled.

It was as he stumbled from the bed, confused and distracted that he heard a gasp from behind him. He whirled around in horror.

In the doorway, a look of shocked disbelief on his face, stood Lucius Crispus.

JACQUELINE

The relationship between teacher and pupil sometimes spills over into life outside the class room and extra-curricular links are forged to the satisfaction of both parties. So it is in the case of the young student Jacqueline, an orphan of noble parentage, now living with her aunt in the family castle. For her niece's teacher, the lady has engaged a young philosopher who is himself an aristocrat, though estranged from his family. It will come as no surprise to the reader to learn that Countess Jacqueline and Baron Francois are soon forsaking the rigours of the intellect for the pleasures of the flesh. A fast learner, Jacqueline is as much a giver as a taker in this interchange of knowledge; and Francois's labours are so appreciated that Jacqueline invents a nickname for his main study aid – she christens his male member 'Francinet'. Thus the two of them (or should it be three?) are happily engaged when Jacqueline's cousin joins the class . . .

As usual, we took our daily afternoon stroll in the park.

After we had said hello to the statue of Leda, who, also as usual, was dying under the caresses of her swan, we wandered into the lane with the nymphs. We always like to look at those marble nymphs who laughingly and playfully surrender themselves to the lustful fauns.

Looking at them gives us a thousand voluptuous ideas, and soon we leave them to their eternal games and go into the bushes to play a few games ourselves, always trying to outdo those marble statues.

This particular day, Francois began his game by putting me down upon the grass without giving me time to take off my panties. His feverish hands groped under my dress and his nimble fingers loosened my garters and began to take off my silken stockings. He loved to hide his head under my petticoat, kissing my thighs impatiently, working his way slowly toward my curly fleece, where his tongue would be lapping the juices and his teeth put tiny marks in the rosy lips. This game usually drives me wild. I put my legs over his shoulders to make it easier for him to get his mouth deeper into my love nest and my feet tap the rhythm upon his back. Francois gets wilder and wilder and finally I reach a climax, giving a loud scream and collapsing into a delicious numbness.

Just as I fainted away I thought I heard something rustle in the bushes. I pushed Francois' head away, and though I thought it might have been a bird or a squirrel, I did not want to take any chances. I pulled up my stockings, smoothed my dress and left the bushes, motioning Francois to follow me.

I was utterly surprised. A charming young girl stood before me. Her blue eyes were wide open and expressed confusion, and the wind had disarranged her hair, which was as golden blond as mine.

When she saw us, she began to blush. But I opened my arms with a wide smile. She embraced me, kissing me upon the forehead. I kissed her ardently, meanwhile looking around if there was someone else present. As soon as I was satisfied that she was alone, I introduced her to Francois.

It was my cousin Amaranthe.

After we had strolled through the park some more we went back to the castle together. Amaranthe told us that she had just arrived, and after she had taken her second breakfast with my aunt, the latter had told her that she would find us somewhere in the park.

My cousin was very vivacious and on occasion her remarks sounded like a pun about what I was afraid she might have witnessed in the bushes. The way she looked at us, I was almost sure that she knew what we had been doing.

Francois did not say a word; he just looked at my lovely cousin who had taken my arm. We must have been a charming couple. Amaranthe was a stunningly beautiful girl, about a year younger than I, vivacious, witty and with a little bit of devil in her.

Despite what had happened, I was very glad to see her again, and I liked the idea that she was going to stay with us for a month. The idea that she would be a stumbling block to our love games did not occur to me. On the contrary! And, since she had not yet indicated what, if anything, she had seen us do in the bushes, I decided to question her about it that evening and make her my confidante.

... Yes! I could even give her a couple of lessons myself! This silly idea flitted across my mind when I felt her warm hand and smooth arm pressed against mine.

This idea made me so happy that I began to laugh, kissing Amaranthe on both cheeks, brushing her lips as if by mistake, but in reality I had planned it that way.

When I turned around to look at Francois, I saw that a curious smile played around his lips.

Amaranthe's room is next to mine. After dinner I decided to pay my cousin a visit. We have a lot to talk about since the last time we saw each other.

Amaranthe told me about her voyage. She vivaciously described the changes of coaches and horses, her staying at the various inns, and all the thousands of little things that happen during a long trip. She told me that she was happy as a child having escaped from her home for a while, and she also mentioned that I had changed so much, that I had become so much of a woman ...

The one question I want to ask her burns upon my lips, but I recognise from Amaranthe's slight innuendos, her behaviour, and especially from the tone of her voice when she tells me that she went out in the park to look for us, that she is fully familiar with our secret and that she has watched us in the bushes from beginning to end.

There is no longer any doubt left in my mind when she begins to ask impish questions about my tutor.

It is no longer necessary to pretend that there is a secret. Smiling, while trying not to blush, I admit the truth to my dear cousin.

Amaranthe laughs, and says, 'Oh, yes, my dear. I have seen the two of you playing around in the bushes. And I must admit that I have seen a lot of things which were very interesting and also ... a little bit shocking.'

'Tell me, my dearest Amaranthe, what did you see?'

'But, darling, why should I tell you! You know much better what you have been doing in those bushes than I. After all, you were a participant, and I was only an onlooker.'

'Please! Tell me ...'

'All right! As you know, I was looking for the two of you somewhere in the park. It seemed to me that those marble nymphs were pointing at the bushes, so I went in to look for you there. When I came closer I heard someone groan and moan; obviously I came even closer so that I could see what was going on. Can you imagine my surprise, darling cousin, when I saw you down on the grass, your legs sticking up in the air, and your dear tutor using his head for a purpose which I had always heard was the task of another part of a man's anatomy. It sure looked funny to see his slobbering face between your thighs ...

'But I also realised that you were enjoying it tremendously because your sighing and groaning became stronger, expressing the greatest joy. Your fists were balled, your feet drummed upon his back, and spasms seemed to jolt your body and jerk your hips.

'I stood there, not moving, frankly shocked, but against my will. My eyes were forced to stare upon the spectacle in the grass. Suddenly you uttered a loud scream.

'I suddenly came to my senses and ran away, very scared. But then, you came out of the bushes, smiling and happy, and I understood immediately . . . I must admit that I am a little bit jealous of you for having such a fabulous teacher . . .'

During those last words my cousin's eyes were filled with lust and desire, betraying far more clearly than words her true thoughts. I knew that she was burning up inside, and could not wait to be initiated into the joys and pleasures of the game of love.

The memory of that afternoon, plus Amaranthe's vivid description of it, had made me very excited, and I embraced my cousin passionately kissing her upon the lips. At first Amaranthe was a little taken aback, but I kissed her so passionately, and held my lips so firmly upon her mouth, that her lips parted and allowed my tongue to explore her mouth. She was soon panting under my feverish kisses and let herself fall back limply upon the couch.

She began to kiss me in return, which gave me another idea! I suddenly wanted to give her the same caresses with which Francois always brought me to a climax. I pulled her legs slowly apart, pulled down her panties and lifted her skirts. For the sake of appearances, Amaranthe put up a very mild struggle which was not too convincing. Her struggle stopped the instant my lips approached her blonde fleece and my tongue went into her little rosy slit.

She shuddered under my caresses and began to moan slightly when I went on to explore her little secret spot which was so much like my own. I did my best to imitate Francois with hands, tongue and lips, and I must admit that I was doing it rather well, because Amaranthe began to groan and buck. I recognised her pleasure, because of the little cries of joy were similar

493

to the ones I had so often uttered when Francois was sucking and licking my love spot.

I was very pleased to be able to give my cousin so much pleasure with my caresses. My tongue was very busy in that little triangle, the warm moist flower which I sprinkled with my spittle, mixing it with the warm juices exuding from her love nest.

Suddenly Amaranthe, who had been trembling like an aspen leaf, cried out loudly. She lifted her buttocks high off the couch, her legs and arms spasmed, her entire body shuddered, and I realised that she had tasted a true climax for the first time in her life. She remained motionless upon the couch, and I pulled my head slowly back, covering her marble-white thighs with ardent kisses.

I was suddenly very tired. It had greatly pleased me to initiate my dear cousin in the pleasures of love. I had passionately made love to her with my tongue and lips. It made me happy, though a curious pain was mixed with my joy; I had not had any real satisfaction. I was about to dampen my glowing desire with my own fingers when I suddenly uttered a sharp cry of surprise which awakened Amaranthe from her slumber.

Francois came from behind the Chinese screen.

I did not even have the chance to ask him how he got into the room, and whether he had seen what Amaranthe and I had been doing. He suddenly jumped towards me and mounted me as if I were a dog.

Looking at the throbbing Francinet, I realised that Francois had seen everything and that it had brought him to an extreme state of excitement. He did not waste time on preliminaries, but shoved Francinet deep inside me and began to push with such vehemence that I could feel his balls slam against my buttocks.

Ooh! It was marvelous. I was roughly taken before

the very eyes of my dear Amaranthe. Soon the passionate glow inside me was extinguished.

I was no longer able to take it, and I pushed Francois away from me. My sweet Francinet left its moist sheath, but it seemed that his excitement was too great because he immediately stretched out and became erect again, as thick and stiff as he had been before entering me.

He went directly toward my cousin; Francois mounted her and Francinet found the way to his satisfaction without any trouble at all. Amaranthe was more than prepared. First, I had whetted her appetite with my moist caresses, and secondly, she was practically under me when I was mounted and taken by Francois. The scene she had watched had more than excited her and her desire was at its peak.

At first I did not enjoy the idea at all. I was aware that my cousin was about to enjoy what I considered the ultimate climax of the game of love, and that she did not have to suffer the long months of preparation which I have had to endure. In short, I felt a tinge of jealousy.

But then I realised that it was, after all, my own fault, and that I had no right to object because of a silly little jealousy. It did not take me long to push those unpleasant ideas out of my mind, because the scene I was about to witness was extremely interesting and I became fully absorbed in it.

I looked at my dear Francois from behind and could see the muscles of his firm buttocks harden, when he pushed Francinet deep into my dear cousin and began to work her over with tremendous jolts. Amaranthe's charming legs were trampling, sticking high up in the air.

And I heard her moan and groan her little screams of joy, her Oohs! and Aahs! and finally, 'Ooh, darling ... I'm dying ... oooh, darling, darling ... it ... is ... too much!'

A scream, louder than all the other ones, announced that the thunderstorm of love was over. I got up from my seat and walked over to the couple, who were now relaxing upon the large couch.

Francinet looked just plain terrible after this double attack. And my dear Amaranthe was in about the same condition I had been in only a month earlier. She silently looked down upon the large spot of blood which announced louder than words what she had just irreparably lost.

For a long time the three of us rested in silence upon the huge couch, and then we began to laugh. Our tiredness had passed. The curious situation which had developed was truly amusing!

My dear teacher complimented me upon the effectiveness with which I had demonstrated that his lessons had not fallen upon deaf ears, and he thought it magnanimous of me that I had wanted my cousin to share my happiness. Then he began a long lecture about love between women, pointing out the things that were missing, though he had to admit grudgingly that their mutual caresses could be infinitely more tender.

To round out his lesson for the day, Francois showed us that three people can act out more love fantasies than two.

The day after this memorable evening Amaranthe insisted upon reciprocating my little service of love and showing her gratitude for having been initiated into those precious caresses which had culminated in her receiving the ultimate delight of making love.

Francois had taken his horse and was riding in the fields to get lots of fresh air and to recuperate from his exhausting labours. He wanted to restore his powers quickly.

Amaranthe and I were alone in my room.

As a matter of fact, I was still in bed when my

charming cousin knocked on my door. She was wearing a charming night gown of lace and silk, and her clear blue eyes still showed the strain from the previous night. But they looked happy and content nevertheless, and a certain glint betrayed that she was already in a certain state of excitement.

She slipped under the covers next to me, cuddled up, and began with the youthful impatience of a beginner to caress me copiously. She imitated as well as she could everything I had done to her that previous night; instinctively she invented the most refined caresses and I quickly reached a point where I felt an intensive lust.

Even though her rather inexperienced caresses and kisses did not have the expertness of my dear Francois, who was a connoisseur in that area, I did reach a very intensified climax.

As soon as I had come to my senses again, I patiently explained to Amaranthe how much her quick approach had spoiled part of the intimacy of my excitement.

And since, by now, we were both naked in the large bed, I could demonstrate my teachings upon her own charming body. I proceeded very carefully and slowly, thereby intensifying her voluptuous yearnings and putting off the climax which she so greatly desired. I carefully went over every part of her exposed body.

I covered every corner with my kisses, the little breasts with the rosy tips, her narrow waist, her flaring hips, the insides of her slender thighs, her flat belly, the blonde curls of her armpits and the delicious fleece which was hiding her moist warm flower.

I stroked with my hands the soft skin of her belly and legs. I turned her over on her stomach and kneaded and squeezed her firm buttocks. Then I let my tongue slowly penetrate her love nest till it had found the little tickler. I rolled it around till it was quite erect, my nimble hands twitching the hardened rosy nipples of her breasts.

Amaranthe was surprised at the effects. She arched her back, her legs trampled in the air, and her fists drummed upon the mattress. I turned her around again, falling upon her and we rubbed our fleeces together. Amaranthe groaned and moaned, went into a jolting spasm and experienced a satisfying climax. When she had rested a while she noticed that the nipples of my breasts were standing proudly erect and that a hot flush covered my body. The dear girl understood immediately. She kissed them and nibbled on them, her hands searched for my fleece, caressing my thighs; in short, she did to me what I had done to her, and I, too, went into a tremendous climax. Our games went on and on till late in the afternoon and finally we fell asleep in each other's arms, completely exhausted, but happy.

The dinner bell woke us up with a start and we were rather late when we appeared for dinner. Francois stared at us with a knowing smirk, and he even used the absence of my aunt for making a few unseemly remarks which were designed to make us feel silly, also indicating that our teacher knew exactly how we had spent our day.

Poor Amaranthe blushed and was red as a peony, but I quickly changed the subject by kidding Francois about his sudden urge to be alone with his horse all day, asking him a thousand questions about his ride into the country.

Fortunately my aunt returned quickly and we sat down to dinner. Needless to say we honoured our sumptuous meal with great appetite, repairing our strength with delicious bits of meat, fowl and fish, not to speak of a reasonable quantity of burgundy wine.

The time during which my dear cousin Amaranthe stayed at the castle was one uninterrupted series of delicious joys. She participated in every respect in my

498

lectures and became an equal partner in our daily strolls through the park.

The botanical excursions in the neighbourhood of the castle were continued and expanded, and Amaranthe was surely not the last who gave herself in full abandon to the wild caresses, kisses and other games of our beloved teacher.

My cousin showed, on the contrary, an ardent desire to learn during those games. But her stay here will soon come to an end, and it seems to me as if she is squirrelling away a great store of experiences before she has to go back to her dull parental home. I cannot blame her that she is trying to cram as much experience as she can into the few remaining days. It is understandable that she desires to know as much as she can about the game of love, because after her departure she will be on her own without the superb guidance of our teacher. She will have to pluck gallant flowers that will bloom upon her life's path without supervision, and taste the joys of lasciviousness guided by her own instincts. It is our holy task to prepare her for the future as well as it is in our power . . .

These are our last outings. The weather is beautiful. The sun's rays are burning the fields golden and bathing Nature in full splendour.

We are searching for the loneliest, most hidden spots to enable us to give ourselves completely and unhindered by curious onlookers to the most voluptuous games our combined fantasies can think of. We wander throughout the entire area; sure of the fact that friendly Nature somewhere has a place for us with a soft bed of grass, with walls and ceiling of thicket and tree leaves. And . . . we find it! The loneliness and the silence of the place are so great that it seems to us as if we are the only three people left on earth. We have no objections to Amaranthe's suggestion to undress completely. In no time Francois, my cousin and I are as naked as the day we were born. It seems as if we were transported back in time to Paradise!

Suddenly the feeling overpowers us and we play the wildest, most delicious games. Amaranthe and I embrace each other passionately, our lips firmly pressed against one another, our fleeces rubbing and our tongues playing a marvellous game.

Francois uses the opportunity to his own advantage. He climbs on top of me and sends Francinet on its natural way. Meanwhile his lips have reached the thighs and his tongue the fleece of Amaranthe; he reaches around till his tongue has discovered her most sensitive spot and Francois begins to buck and slurp at the same time, using both our bodies.

It is marvellous! Excited by the moist caresses, Amaranthe kisses me more devotedly and passionately than ever, and a double joy floods my entire being. I can feel Francinet penetrate me with doubled force. And Francois, too, is enjoying double passion; and glowing passion with which his lips explore the inner secrets of my dear Amaranthe makes itself felt by the double size of the throbbing Francinet who is pushing deep inside me.

We groan and pant, and tumble around and around in the soft grass. Arms, legs and bodies are wildly intertwined. Lips, tongues and hands caress every available part of soft flesh; our fleecy triangles are moist and twitching, Francinet grows harder and stiffer, throbbing wildly with every shove given by Francois. We stay in this passionate embrace, forming a perfect triangle, and each angle is the ultimate passion for the other. Amaranthe and I shudder in this delightful embrace while Francinet keeps pounding unmercifully into me, and Francois' tongue drives deeper and deeper into the fleece of Amaranthe.

Suddenly my cousin and I are in the grip of a long and shaking spasm. Our lips let go of one another to cry out our joy. Our happiness is complete because I realise that the tongue of Francois has given Amaranthe the same climax which I have just been given by Francinet.

The three of us continue our lessons and excursions till the very day that my dearest Amaranthe has to take her leave from us. My cousin's parents have completed their move to Bordeaux, and she must leave now to return into the fold of her own family.

Before she went to the coach she kissed both of us so intimately and passionately that it caused my dear aunt to raise her eyebrows in wonder. Her farewell kisses were obviously far more than convention demanded!

LASHED INTO LUST

Subtitled 'The Caprice of a Flagellator' and introduced by one 'Robert Lovebirch', this frivolous item is set in turn-of-the-century Paris. The great courtesan Diane de Blédor has summoned her female intimates to inaugurate her new home, a 'delicious little mansion', a gift from an English lord. The company comprises a selection of the most exotic (and most exotically named) whores in the city, including Dolores the Andalusian (who comes from Lille), the independently minded Folette Chanteclair, one Gilette Beausourire, and the aggressive Nini Taquin. Before the occasion degenerates into a (topless) duel between Diane and Nini (on discovering that they share the same lover), the ladies draw lots to determine the order in which they will each tell the story of how they lost their virginity. Here follows the story of the unpretentious Gilette . . .

With a shrug of her shoulders, Gilette began her story:

I wasn't bred at Court – I come from Montmartre . . .
I didn't begin with a clergyman, – only what I did
brought me in money! . . . It's not so many years ago
either – only eighteen months . . . I was still able to
call myself a virgin . . . But I didn't make so great a
fuss about it. . . . I was apprenticed to a milliner . . . I
used to be laughed at in the workshop because I had
not yet *jumped over the ditch*. Every morning when I
came to work the other girls used to shove their thumb
between the fore and middle fingers; they pushed it
under my nose, saying: 'Well, has it gone at last this
time? – what? . . . not yet?' And, when I got vexed,
they said to me, shrugging their shoulders out of pity:
'Poor child – You'll never come to anything . . . , what
a lot of time you want to get it cracked . . .' And that
used to make me so wild, to put me into such a rage
as you can't imagine . . . So, one morning, quite beside
myself, I said to them: 'Well now, yes, I've done it this

time – I've *jumped the ditch* at last – But after all, what can it matter to you?'

And the forewoman said to me in a jeering tone: 'Eh! but that's proper! I believe you ... But how was it done? ... tell us all about it, do! ... Show us ... ??' and so on, and so on ... As for me I answered '*Merde!*' 'Eat it darling!' they replied all together ... I had enough of it and, taking up my hand, quitted them and started off for a stroll.

As I was passing through the Passage Jouffroy, I stopped to look in at a jeweller's shop-front, when a gent, pretty well dressed, also stopped at the side of me. 'Mademoiselle' he said to me, 'listen to me, do!' 'Oh! of course, why not?' answered I. He looked at me, I looked at him, and we looked at each other; and then we burst out laughing together. All at once he said to me: 'Will you come and have some lunch with me?' 'What?' said I, 'who do you take me for, you raving idiot? You've forgotten to put your spy-glass up to your bull's-eye? ... Can't you see that I've got none of that, for sale? ... I've still got my ... Godmother ... Look here, old chap, you're out of the run altogether ...' Didn't he just laugh! At any rate, he didn't get vexed and that calmed me down a bit ...

He stood me a good lunch, after which he took me for a drive to the *Bois de Boulogne*. On the way he wanted to make free with his paws, but I stopped him, saying: 'Come now, none of that, hands off! Old buffer! ... I'm going in for a virginity competition, that's what I'm about doing!' He didn't seem exactly to suck that in, the muff. But as after all he'd behaved very nicely to me, standing no end of flowers and sweets, I put on my most serious look and said to him: 'But you don't seem to believe me, that's not nice of you!' He smiled. But I told him all, and as he appeared still to have some doubts, I banged my fist on my knees, crying: 'Damn it all! It's not that I want to go to bed with you, you humbug! ... I want to keep my maidenhead, but as you seem to want to make a fool of me, well, – deuce take it! – I'll go to a doctor's and get myself examined, and then – you may stand dinner!'

Damn me, if the cove didn't then and there order the coachman to turn round . . . He had me driven to a doctor's, a friend of his; there, I was put upon a sort of machine called a spec – , spec . . . let me see – spectrulum –.' 'Speculum!' interposed, rather drily, Nini Taquin.

'Just as you like,' continued Gilette. 'Well, they put me on to the speculum. The other one, the doctor, examines me, messes me about, I think that he even just scratched my button a little, the beast . . . At all events, on leaving, I said triumphantly to my gentleman – I never knew his name, although later on I slept with his friend the doctor – I had his address, – I said: "Was I right, or not? – Am I, or am I not, like *Joan of Arc* . . . ?"'

He began to laugh and said to me: 'My dear, you're as pretty and nice as can be. You've still got it, no doubt, – but you won't keep it for ever. If you like to come to bed with me tonight and stop a few days with me, seven or eight at the outside, I will give you one thousand francs. Will that suit you?'

I turned scarlet. The offer was brutally sudden. But, after all, a thousand francs! That sounded in my ears like the flourish of trumpets of a regiment of cuirassiers. Nevertheless I hesitated. He insisted. At last, I said to him: 'Does it hurt much?' 'Oh! no,' he replied, 'just a little pricking at first, and then afterwards it is so nice, so really nice!' 'I am ready to believe what you tell me,' I said, 'but if I sleep with you and that in the middle of the night you get up and hook it without giving me the money? . . .'

He had a generous idea. He took a thousand francs note out of his pocket-book and handed it to me, saying: 'You see I am not as distrustful as you!'

I thanked him, but, as I was still suspicious, – could he not after all take his note back again when I was asleep? – I asked him to accompany me to the Savings Bank where I lodged 800 francs, for which I got a receipt-book. I kept 200 francs for myself.

My gent took me with him to dinner . . . He made me eat oysters, cray-fish soup, a lot of things that made me feel quite funny. He made me drink champagne only, but only sufficient to make me merry – no more; then he took me with him in a cab to where he resided. It was near the Parc Monceau. On the way he bought me a lot of elegant underclothing; muslin shifts and cambric handkerchiefs . . .

The first thing he did when we got to his home, was to offer me a small glassfull of fine old cognac. He took me on his knees, and kissed me. After which he began conversing with me for at least a quarter of an hour. I had imagined, that once at home, he would have shoved me on to a bed or a sofa and settled my business at once; so that I was somewhat afraid. For, there is no mistake, it *is* rather strange, and makes one feel queer, to go in for it for the first time, when one has no idea what it is. But my fears were soon dissipated . . . he talked to me nicely . . . fetched me some delightful little slippers, of red morocco leather embroidered in gold – he then took out of a wardrobe a lot of linen underclothing, a pretty corset, all perfectly new, which appeared to be quite my fit, besides some lace petticoats and pretty open-work silk stockings.

He gave me all this, saying: 'This was destined for my mistress, but she left for America, where she died. I make you a present of all that, my little dear . . . It is now barely eight o'clock. I will take a turn as far as my club, but by way of precaution, and so that you may not be disturbed, I shall close the door from the outside. Get yourself ready; I shall be back again in an hour. Put on the petticoats, the bodice, one of the new shifts, in one word, deck yourself out; we shall sup together at about eleven o'clock and after that – *Vive l'amour!* ... Should you find the time tedious, here are newspapers and books ...'

I did my best to make myself spruce and afterwards took up a book to read. My unknown friend did not return until ten o'clock. It was now four hours since we had quitted the dinner-table ... He kissed me, told me that I was lovely, and seating me again on his knees, said to me: 'If it is all the same to you, my *bijou*, will you do me a favour?' – 'I will gladly,' answered I 'if it is possible.' Then said he, 'We will take a bath together.' 'Why,?' I asked, 'and where?' 'In my bath-room ... a perfumed bath ... we shall be all the fresher and we shall smell nice!' This explanation convinced me. I consented.

He conducted me, one arm round my waist, into a room feebly lighted, but, pressing upon a knob, he at once lighted three electric lamps fixed to the ceiling and I found myself in the most charming bath-room imaginable. In the centre of the room was a large bath of black marble, and in one of the corners was a white marble toilet-table furnished with all sorts of scent-bottles and silver pots. All around, next to the wall, were arranged low divans and large Venice mirrors, two of which were pier-glasses ...

After closing the door, my lover led me to one of the divans where he lavished caresses on me and fondled me during some minutes ... For the first time he risked a little exploration underneath my petticoats, felt my calves, which he found to his taste, then mounted up to the thighs, stopping finally at my 'pussy-cat', where he played a little with the fur, after which he fairly attacked my 'tickle toby' ... It was thus that he made me *spend* for the first time and, to tell the truth, as he had not gone too far, it set me all on fire, for I found the sensation quite delicious to be thus provoked by the hand of a man ... I began to long for more.

I must tell you at once that he had not yet seen or touched me, for I had not allowed him to be present when the doctor had been examining me ...

'Permit me to undress you,' said he, and without awaiting my answer he begun to undo my bodice. Slowly, and on purpose, he undid button after button. I was always on his knees ... When he had come to the last button-hole, he kissed me several times on the throat, he then took off my bodice. For some minutes he amused himself by showering kisses on my shoulders, arms and hands ... Then he unlaced my stays and taking a full grip of my breasts with his hands he pressed them softly in a rhythmical movement, after which he carried the teats alternately to his mouth, sucking them and fondling them with his tongue ... This made me feel queer all over; my breasts swelled, the teats stood up rigid, and took on a more rosy hue ...

All at once he seized my head between his hands, and after letting my large masses of hair float on my shoulders, he thrust his tongue into my mouth. My tongue encountered his and I felt a sort of electric commotion: I seemed to be seated upon something round and hard, something like a cylindrical tube which almost lifted me up: it could be nothing else than his instrument. I thought as much, and for myself, all alone, I spent a second time, becoming wet all the way down my thighs ...

Little by little, my friend took off all my clothes. It took him nearly two hours to do it. When I had nothing more on me than my shift, he then once more pressed me to his breast and then led me before one of the pier-glasses. There he took off my chemise and began to examine and admire me from every side. To say that I did not blush, that I was not rather ashamed, would be to tell an untruth ... But I was so much excited by his manipulations, by his caresses and kisses; I had been so wound up; my desires had been brought to such a pitch, that I longed with impatience for the moment when I should taste the real thing itself, not the sham...

The bath was ready. He poured some lavender water into it which perfumed it. Then he made me get in: the water was just sufficiently tepid to be pleasant... In a moment he was undressed, and leapt into the bath, as naked as I was myself... His member was fearfully stiff. I have never since seen one better made. Oh, my dears! If you had seen how I looked at it with terror when I thought that he would thrust that big broom-handle into my belly...

He came into the bath and stretched himself alongside of me... For the first time I found myself in contact with the naked body of a man... it made me tremble... he played for some time with me in the water, tickling me, playing with my ahem! – and pawing me all over, then, making me stand up, and standing up himself, he took from a silver shell attached to the wall a cake of very fine scented soap... And, to my great astonishment, began to wash my bush, gentle and delicately, first of all the foliage which played round about it, then the outside, and lastly the inside... the soap frothed... and I felt quite agreeable sensations steal gradually over me.

'It is so that I may love you all the better,' said he, seeing me astonished, 'I want to plant my tenderest kisses upon it. But now, please do the same to me.'

I took the soap, and began with the hairs, then taking hold of his member in my left hand, I lathered it vigorously. It was as hot as fire, and swelled out well-nigh to bursting. During this time he was giving me kisses on the back of my neck, and nibbling the wanton hairs behind my ears, until he fell back exhausted with me into the water, where, in a passionate embrace he bit slightly the lobes of my ears, almost

crushing me in his vigorous arms, and yet I found it
nice ... Oh! it was delicious! ... But the critical
moment was near. My friend soon got over his passionate fit: he left of the bath, wiped himself dry, then,
making me get out in my turn; draped me in a warm
bathing-gown and wiped me dry with care, at the same
time giving me some little furtive caresses ... then
he sprinkled a cloud of violet-scented *poudre-de-riz*
over me, after having first of all, with a vapouriser
transformed my terrified 'puss' into a perfumed
tabernacle ... He now opened a door, which gave into
the bed-room, where, in an instant, I found myself
extended on a low Louis XV bed ... My chemise had
remained in the bath room and the white bathing-
gown he had thrown over my shoulders did not
accompany me to the odorous couch, where his arms
had gently deposited me ...

He had now attained to a state of frenzied excitement. The caresses, which I still remember today, were
as passionate as they were lascivious. He began by
kissing my mouth, then, going gradually down, he
covered my throat, my breasts, my belly with kisses
also, until he reached the sanctuary of Venus. Then
his tongue became astonishingly agile, admirably skilful. It was hard and vigorous ... It seemed to forage
out all the corners and recesses of my cunt, and he,
most beautifully sucking my 'button', whilst I twisted
on the couch writhing with voluptuous spasms ... We
were both of us terribly excited, as can easily be
imagined ...

Without uttering a word he threw himself into position on the top of me, opened out my thighs, which,
docilely enough I let him do, then, putting his member
into my hand, he begged me to show him the way ...
I made no objection, I was mad with irresistible
desire ... He delicately, opened out the way with his
fingers, introduced therein the head of his instrument,
first of all gently, then a little farther, and *then*, with

512

one sharp shove, he sent it in right to the bottom . . .
I gave out a cry of pain, but at the same time, experienced an intense feeling of heavenly enjoyment which shook me to the very marrow of my bones . . . I don't know why, but at that moment I began to cry . . . I was deploring the loss of my virginity . . . Big tears flowed down my cheeks . . . But he drank them up with his eager lips, to shower new kisses and caresses upon me; he came again in the charge two, three, five, as many as seven times . . . and the more he tossed, handled, thrust, battered, rammed, rogered and rummaged me, the more I enjoyed it . . .

In this manner eight days of intoxicating physical bliss rolled rapidly away. On the eve of his departure for America, as he said, he quitted me, after having kept me in bed with him for twenty-four hours and having performed on me the exploits of a Hercules . . . He got the full value of his money, and left me quite smashed up and broken, with a last one hundred francs note as a souvenir . . .

As I could not draw the 800 francs I had deposited at the savings Bank until I was of age, when I had gone through the little money I possessed, I was obliged to walk the streets . . . On the second evening I chanced upon a 'slap up' gent, upon whom I managed to play the *virgin dodge*. He stumped up five hundred francs, which helped me to carry on until I found my present lover. – I have finished . . .

FLOSSIE –
A VENUS AT
SIXTEEN

'Towards the end of a bright sunny afternoon in June, I was walking in one of the quieter streets of Piccadilly, when my eye was caught by two figures coming in my direction.' So begins the story of Captain Jack Archer and his dalliance with the young Flossie Eversley – an example of late Victorian titillation remarkable for the precocious antics of its impossible heroine. The two figures whom Jack encounters in Piccadilly belong to the 'finely-made' Eva Letchford, a lady in her mid-twenties who by happy coincidence is a previous acquaintance of the Captain's, and of course Flossie herself. In Jack's eyes the girl is a beauty with waist-length brown hair, 'deep violet eyes and full red lips'. However, the attribute that makes the most forcible first impression on him is 'the extraordinary size and beauty of the girl's bust'. The Captain, it is evident, is something of a tit-man; he is also a very lucky fellow.

It transpires that La Letchford is only too keen to thrust her young charge in Jack's direction and Flossie herself is only too happy to be thrust. Within a few hours the debauch begins, though sometimes it is hard to decide who is debauching whom. Our Venus, Flossie, is a natural between the sheets and has already acquired some 'French tastes' from her Parisian school-days. She is also eager to share the Captain's favours with her mentor, Eva, and as Jack is not a man to turn down a freebie he takes on the arduous duty of keeping that lady happy as well. The following extract begins on the morning after the night before . . .

'Good morning, Captain Archer, I trust that you have slept well?' said Flossie on my presenting myself at the flat early the next day. 'My friend Miss Letchford,' she went on, in a prim middleaged tone of voice, 'has not yet left her apartment. She complains of having passed a somewhat disturbed night owing to – ahem!'

'Rats in the wainscot?' I suggested.

'No, my friend attributes her sleepless condition to severe irritation in the – forgive the immodesty of my words – lower part of her person, following by a prolonged pricking in the same region. She is still feeling the effects, and I found her violently clasping a pillow between her – ahem – legs, with which she was apparently endeavouring to soothe her feelings.'

'Dear me! Miss Eversley, do you think I could be of any assistance?' (*stepping towards Eva's door.*)

'You are *most* kind, Captain Archer, but I have already done what I could in the way of friction and – other little attentions, which left the poor sufferer somewhat calmer. Now Jack, you wretch! you haven't kissed me yet . . . That's better! You will not be surprised to hear that Eva has given me a full and detailed description of her sleepless night, in her own language, which I have no doubt you have discovered, is just a bit *graphic* at times.'

'Well, my little darling, I did my best, as I knew you would wish me to do. It wasn't difficult with such a bed-fellow as Eva. But charming and amorous as she is, I couldn't help feeling all the time "if it were only my little Flossie lying under me now!" By the way how utterly lovely you are this morning, Floss.'

She was dressed in a short sprigged cotton frock, falling very little below her knees, shot pink and black stockings, and low patent leather shoes with silver buckles. Her long waving brown hair gleamed gold in the morning light, and the deep blue eyes glowed with health and love, and now and again flashed with merriment. I gazed upon her in rapture at her beauty.

'Do you like my frock, Jack? I'm glad. It's the first time I've had it on. It's part of my trousseau.'

'Your *what*, Flossie?' I shouted.

'I said my trousseau,' she repeated quietly, but with sparks of fun dancing in her sweet eyes. 'The fact is, Jack, Eva declared the other day that though I am not married to you, you and I are really on a sort of honeymoon. So, as I have just had a good lot of money from the lawyers, she made me go with her and buy everything new. Look here,' (*unfastening her bodice*) 'new stays, new chemise, new stockings and oh! Jack, *look!* such *lovely* new drawers – none of your horrid vulgar knickerbockers, trimmings and lovely little tucks all the way up, and quite wide open in front for . . . ventilation I suppose! Feel what soft stuff they are made of! Eva was awfully particular about these drawers. She is always so practical, you know.'

'Practical!' I interrupted.

'Yes. What she said was that you would often be

wanting to kiss me between my legs when there wasn't time to undress and be naked together, so that I must have drawers made of the finest and most delicate stuff to please you, and with the opening cut extra wide so as not to get in the way of your tongue! Now don't you call that practical?'

'I do indeed! Blessed Eva, that's another good turn I owe her!'

'Well, for instance, there isn't time to undress *now* Jack, and – '

She threw herself back in her chair and in an instant, I had plunged under the short rose-scented petticoats and had my mouth glued to the beloved cunt once more. In the midst of the delicious operation, I fancied I heard a slight sound from the direction of Eva's door and just then, Flossie locked her hands behind my head and pressed me to her with even more than her usual ardour; a moment later deluging my throat with the perfumed essence of her being.

'You darling old boy, how *did* make me spend that time! I really think your tongue is longer than it was. Perhaps the warmth of Eva's interior has made it grow! Now I must be off to the dressmaker's for an hour or so. By the way, she wants to make my frocks longer. She declares people can see my drawers when I run upstairs.'

'Don't you let her do it, Floss.'

'*Rather not!* What's the use of buying expensive drawers like mine if you can't show them to a pal! *Good* morning, Captain! Sorry I can't stop. While I'm gone you might just step in and see how my lady friend's gettin' on. Fust door on the right. *Good* morning!'

For a minute or two, I lay back in my chair and wondered whether I would not take my hat and go. But a moments' further reflection told me that I must do as Flossie directed me. To this decision, I must own, the memory of last night's pleasure and the present demands of a most surprising erection contributed in no small degree. Accordingly, I tapped at Eva's bedroom door.

She had just come from her bath and wore only a peignoir and her stockings. On seeing me, she at once let fall her garment and stood before me in radiant nakedness.

'Look at this,' she said, holding out a half-sheet of notepaper. 'I found it on my pillow when I woke an hour ago.

' "If Jack comes this morning I shall send him in to see you while I go to Virginie's. Let him – anything beginning with 'f' or 's' that rhymes with luck – you. 'A hair of the dog', etc., will do you both good. My time will come. Ha! Ha!

' "Floss."

'Now I ask you, Jack, was there ever such an adorable little darling?'

My answer need not be recorded.

Eva came close to me and thrust her hand inside my clothes.

'Ah! I see you are of the same way of thinking as myself,' she said taking hold of my fingers and carrying them to her cunt, which pouted hungrily. 'So let us have one good royal fuck and then you can stay here with me while I dress, and I'll tell you anything that Flossie may have left out about her school-life in Paris. Will that meet your views?'

'Exactly,' I replied.

'Very well then. As we are going to limit ourselves to *one*, would you mind fucking me *en levrette?*'

'Any way you like, most puissant and fuck-some of ladies!'

I stripped off my clothes in a twinkling and Eva placed herself in position, standing on the rug and bending forwards with her elbows on the bed. I reverently saluted the charms thus presented to my lips, omitting none, and then rising from my knees, advanced, weapon in hand, to storm the breach. As I approached, Eva opened her legs to their widest extent, and I drove my straining prick into the mellow cunt, fucking it with unprecedented vigour and delight, as the lips alternately parted and contracted, nipping me with an extraordinary force in response to the pressure of my right forefinger upon the clitoris and of my left upon the nipples of the heaving breasts. Keen as was the enjoyment we were both experiencing the fuck – as in invariably the case with a morning performance – was of very protacted duration, and several minutes had elapsed before I dropped my arms to Eva's thighs and, with my belly glued against her bottom and my face nestling between her shoulder blades, felt the rapturous throbbing of my prick as it discharged an avalanche into the innermost recesses of her womb.

'Don't move, Jack, for Heaven's sake,' she cried.

'Don't want to, Eva, I'm quite happy where I am, thank you!'

Moving an inch or two further out from the bed so as to give herself more 'play', she started an incredibly provoking motion of her bottom, so skilfully executed that it produced the impression of being almost *spiral*. The action is difficult to describe, but her bottom rose and fell, moved backward and forward, and from side to side in quick alternation, the result being that my member was constantly in contact with, as it were, some fresh portion of the embracing cunt, the soft folds of which seemed by their varied and tender caresses to be pleading to him to emerge from his present state of apathy and resume the proud condition he had displayed before.

'Will he come up this way, Jack, or shall I take the dear little man in my mouth and suck him into an erection?'

'I think he'll be all right as he is, dear. Just keep on

nipping him with your cunt and push your bottom a little closer to me so that I may feel your naked flesh against mine . . . *that's* it!'

'Ah! the darling prick, he's beginning to swell! he's going to fuck me directly, I know he is! Your finger on my cunt in front, please Jack, and the other hand on my nipples. So! *that's* nice. Oh dear! how I *do* want your tongue in my mouth, but that can't be. Now begin and fuck me slowly at first. Your *second* finger on my clitoris, please, and frig me in time to the motion of your body. Now fuck faster a little, a deeper into me. Push, dear, push like a demon. Pinch my nipple; a little faster on the clitoris. I'm spending! I'm dying of delight! Fuck me, Jack, keep on fucking me. Don't be afraid. Strike against my bottom with all your strength, harder still, harder! Now put your hands down to my thighs and *drag* me on to you. Lovely! grip the flesh of my thighs with your fingers and fuck me to the very womb.'

'Eva, look out! I'm going to spend!'

'So am I, Jack. Ah! how your prick throbs against my cunt! Fuck me, Jack, to the last moment, spend your last drop, as I'm doing. One last push up to the hilt – there, keep him in like that and let me have a deluge from you. How exquisite! how adorable to spend together! *One* moment more before you take him out, and let me kiss him with my cunt before I say goodbye.'

'What a nip that was, Eva, it felt more like a hand on me than a – '

'Yes,' she interrupted me, turning round and facing me with her eyes languorous and velvety with lust, 'that is my only accomplishment, and I must say I think it's a valuable one! In Paris I had a friend – but no matter I'm not going to talk about myself, but about Flossie. Sit down in that chair, and have a cigarette while I talk to you. I'm going to stay naked if you don't mind. It's so hot. Now if you're quite comfy, I'll begin.'

She seated herself opposite to me, her splendid naked body full in the light from the window near her.

'There is a part of Flossie's school story,' began Eva, 'which she has rather shrunk from telling you, and so I propose to relate the incident, in which I am sure you will be sufficiently interested. For most of her school days in Paris, nothing very special occurred to her beyond the cementing of her friendship with Ylette Vespertin. Flossie was a tremendous favourite with the other girls on account of her sweet nature and her extraordinary beauty, and there is no doubt that a great many curly heads were popped under her petticoats at one time and another. All these heads, however, belonged to her own sex, and no great harm was done. But just after her sixteenth birthday there arrived at the convent a certain Camille de Losgrain, who, though by no means averse to the delights of gamahuche, nursed a strong preferences for male, as against female charms. Camille speedily struck up an alliance with a handsome boy of seventeen who lived in the house next door. This youth had often seen Flossie and greatly desired her acquaintance. It seems that his bedroom window was on the same level as that of the room occupied by Flossie, Camille and three other girls, all of whom knew him by sight and had severally expressed a desire to have him between their legs. So it was arranged one night that he was to climb on to a buttress below his room, and the girls would manage to haul him into theirs. All this had to be done in darkness, as of course no light could be shown. The young gentleman duly arrived on the scene in safety – the two eldest girls divested him of his clothes, and then, according to previous agreement, the five damsels sat naked on the edge of the bed in the pitch dark room, and Master Don Juan was to decide by passing his hands over their bodies, which of the five should be favoured with his attentions. No one was to speak, to touch his person or to make any sign of interest.

Twice the youth essayed this novel kind of ordeal by touch, and after a moment's profound silence he said, 'J'ai choisi, c'est la troisieme.' 'La troisieme' was no other than Flossie, the size of whose breasts had at once attracted him as well as given a clue to her identity. And now, Jack, I hope the sequel will not distress you. The other girls accepted the decision most loyally, having no doubt anticipated it. They laid Flossie tenderly on the bed and lavished every kind of caress upon her, gamahuching her with especial tenderness, so as to open the road as far as possible to the invader. It fortunately turned out to be the case that the boy's prick was not by any means of abnormal size, and as the dear little maidenhead had been already subjected to very considerable wear and tear of fingers and tongue the entrance was, as she told me herself, effected with a minimum of pain and discomfort, hardly felt indeed in the midst of the frantic kisses upon mouth, eyes, nipples, breasts and buttocks which the four excited girls rained upon her throughout the operation. As for the boy, his enjoyment knew no bounds, and when his alloted time was up could hardly be persuaded to make the return voyage to his room. This, however, was at last accomplished, and the four virgins hastened to hear from their ravished friend the full true and particular account of her sensations. For several nights after this, the boy made his appearance in the room, where he fucked all the other four in succession, and pined only for Flossie, who, however, regarded him as belonging to Camille and declined anything beyond the occasional service of his tongue which she greatly relished and which he, of course, as gladly put at her disposal.

'All this happened just before my time and was related to me afterwards by Flossie herself. It is only six months ago that I was engaged to teach English at the convent. Like everyone else who is brought in contact with her, I at once fell in love with Flossie and

524

we quickly became the greatest of friends. A month ago, came a change of fortune for me, an old bachelor uncle dying suddenly and leaving me a competence. By this time, the attachment between Flossie and myself had become so deep that she could not bear the thought of parting from me. I too was glad enough of the excuse thus given for writing to Flossie's guardian – who has never taken more than a casual interest in her – to propose her returning to England with me and the establishment of a joint menage. My 'references' being satisfactory, and Flossie having declared herself to be most anxious for the plan, the guardian made no objection and in sort – here we are!'

'Well, that's a very interesting story, Eva. Only – *confound* that French boy and his buttress!'

'Yes, you would naturally feel like that about it, and I don't blame you. Only you must remember that if it hadn't been for the size of Flossie's breasts, and its being done in the dark, and . . .'

'But Eva, you don't mean to tell me the young brute wouldn't have chosen her out of the five if there had been a *light*, do you!'

'No, of course not. What I *do* mean is that it was all a sort of fluke, and that Flossie is really, to all intents and purposes . . .'

'Yes, yes, I know what you would like to say, and I entirely and absolutely agree with you. I *love* Flossie with all my heart and soul and . . . well, that French boy can go to the devil!'

'Miss Eva! Miss Eva!' came a voice outside the door.

'Well, what is it?'

'Oh, if you please, Miss, there's a young man downstairs called for his little account. Says'e's the coals, Miss. I *towld* him you was engaged, Miss?'

'Did you – and what did he say?'

' "Ow!" 'e sez, "engyged, is she", 'e sez – "well, you tell'er from me confidential-like, as it's 'igh time she was *married*", 'e sez!'

525

Our shouts of laughter brought Flossie scampering into the room, evidently in the wildest spirits.

'Horful scandal in 'igh life,' she shouted. 'A genl'man dish-covered in a lydy's aportments! 'arrowin' details. Speshul! Pyper! Speshul! – Now then, you two, what have you been doing while I've been gone? Suppose you tell me exactly what you've done and I'll tell you exactly what *I've* done!' – then in a tone of cheap melodrama – 'Aha! 'ave I surproised yer guilty secret? She winceth! likewise'e winceth! in fact they both winceth! Thus h'am I avenged upon the pair!' And kneeling down between us, she pushed a dainty finger softly between the lips of Eva's cunt, and with her other hand took hold of my yard and tenderly frigged it, looking up into our faces all the time with inexpressible love and sweetness shining from her eyes.

'You *dears!*' she said. 'It *is* nice to have you two naked together like this!'

A single glance passed between Eva and me, and getting up from our seats we flung ourselves upon the darling and smothered her with kisses. Then Eva, with infinite gentleness and many loving touches, preceded to undress her, handing the dainty garments to me one by one to be laid on the bed near me. As the fair white breasts came forth from the corset, Eva gave a little cry of delight, and pushing the lace-edged chemise below the swelling globes, took one erect and rosy nipple into her mouth, and putting her hand behind my neck, motioned me to take the other. Shivers of delight coursed one another up and down the shapely body over which our fingers roamed in all directions Flossie's remaining garments were soon allowed to fall by a deft touch from Eva, and the beautiful girl stood before us in all her radiant nakedness. We paused a moment to gaze upon the spectacle of loveliness. The fair face flushed with love and desire; the violet eyes shone; the full rounded breasts put forth their coral nipples as if craving to be kissed again; below the smooth satin belly appeared the silken tuft that shaded without concealing the red lips of the adorable cunt; the polished thighs gained added whiteness by contrast with the dark stockings which clung amorously to the finely moulded legs.

'Now, Jack, *both together*,' said Eva, suddenly.

I divined what she meant and arranging a couple of large cushions on the wide divan, I took Flossie in my arms and laid her upon them, her feet upon the floor, Her legs opened instinctively and thrusting my head between her thighs, I plunged my tongue into the lower part of the cunt, whilst Eva, kneeling over her, upon the divan, attacked the developed clitoris. Our mouths thus met upon the enchanted spot and our tongues filled every corner and crevice of it. My own, I must admit, occasionally wandered downwards to the adjacent regions, and explored the valley of delight in that direction. But wherever we went and whatever we did, the lithe young body continued to quiver from head to foot with excess of pleasure, shedding its treasures now in Eva's mouth, now in mine and sometimes in both at once! But vivid as were the delights she was experiencing, they were of a passive kind only, and Flossie was already artist enough to know that the keenest enjoyment is only obtained when giving and receiving are equally shared. Accordingly I was not surprised to hear her say:

'Jack, could you come up here to me now, please?'

Signing to me kneel astride of her face, she seized my yard, guided it to her lips and then locking her hands over my loins, she alternately tightened and relaxed her grasp, signifying that I was to use the delicious mouth freely as a substitute for the interdicted opening below. The peculiar sucking action of her lips, of which I have spoken before, bore a pleasant resemblance to the nipping of an accomplished cunt, whilst the never-resting tongue, against whose soft folds M. Jacques frigged himself luxuriously in his passage between the lips and throat, added a provocation to the lascivious sport not to be enjoyed in the ordinary act of coition. Meanwhile Eva had taken my place between Flossie's legs and was gamahuching the beloved cunt with incredible ardour. A sloping mirror on the wall above enabled me to survey the charming scene at my leisure, and to observe the spasms of delight which, from time to time, shook both the lovely naked forms below me. At last my own time arrived, and Flossie, alert as usual for the signs of the approaching crisis, clutched my bottom with convulsive fingers and held me close pressed against her face, whilst I flooded her mouth with the stream of love that she adored. At the same moment the glass told me that Eva's lips were pushing far into the vulva to receive the result of their amorous labours, the passage of which from cunt to mouth was accompanied by every token of intense enjoyment from both the excited girls.

Rest and refreshment were needed by all three after the strain of our morning revels, and so the party broke up for the day after Flossie had mysteriously announced that she was designing something 'extra special', for the morrow.

MY SECRET LIFE

First published privately in eleven volumes between the years 1885 and 1895, My Secret Life *is undoubtedly the most extraordinary sexual autobiography ever to see the light of day. Unlike the other books whose excerpts feature in this volume, this is no work of imagination, it is a chronicle of one man's sexual life as complete in detail as the pseudonymous author, Walter, can make it. This monumental work provides a remarkable picture, not just of one sexually obsessed Victorian, but of a society at work and play fired by the ceaseless dynamo of sexual activity. Inevitably, given that Walter was not a poor man, many of his sexual partners – urchins, maids, street-walkers – were seduced as much by money as by lust, though, as he says, 'Women were the pleasure of my life. I loved cunt, but also who had it; I liked the woman I fucked and not simply the cunt I fucked, and therein is a great difference.'*

The consequence was that Walter forged lasting relationships with many of the prostitutes he favoured. Towards the end of his life Walter became particularly fond of 'Helen M.', a woman he met at the Argyle Rooms in London: 'Of full but not great height, with the loveliest shade of chestnut hair, she had eyes in which grey, green and hazel were indescribably blended with an expression of supreme voluptuousness in them, yet without bawdiness or salacity, and capable of any play of expression . . . I have had many splendid women in my time, but never a more perfect beauty in all respects' . . .

On returning to England I visited Helen and told her of my adventures abroad. She wished she'd been with me, always had longed to see a brothel there, would have gone with me there. She seemed excited about the lubricious cunts, yet calling me a beast all the time. I fucked H within five minutes after I'd entered her house, then laying, telling her these things, she began to frig herself, and almost instantly spent crying out – 'spunk', and grasping my prick. – She'd finished so quickly that I believed her emotion a sham, but on feeling her cunt – washed not long before – it satisfied me she'd spent. She then told me that several times when she'd a great letch come on her, and thought about, that she'd spent involuntarily without touching her cunt. It's not impossible, for in my youth I have spent involuntarily, at the sight of a female whom I wanted – when I was very randy.

One day the following week she'd be alone and would get her 'poor friend to come'. He was usually smuggled in. 'Then you can see him fuck me." – She didn't say what after. 'He'll want me, for Mr Blank has been staying with me, but is going on Thursday, – you mustn't come to the house till you telegraph to *** (a female relative). – If Blank's not left town she'll meet you at the end of the street, and you mustn't come.' – Such arrangements in fact had existed for some time. – I didn't like it, but would have risked anything to have her.

'You want me to fuck you *after* him' – said I. 'I don't, you beast, you shan't do it any more.' – 'You like me to see his prick and to see you fucked.' – She laughed – 'I like to know you're looking at us, and that he don't know.' – 'We men are easily cheated.' – 'It would take a clever woman to cheat *you*,' she replied.

The day came, the coast was clear. In my shirt I stood waiting for my treat, had kissed and gamahuched her, and with difficulty restrained myself from fucking her. Her friend was an hour behind time. H was fidgety and feared her letter hadn't reached him. A ring, followed by a peculiar knock at the street door was heard. – 'It's he,' said she smiling bawdily. Before that, talking about him she said as if she enjoyed the idea, 'Won't he have his cock full, he hasn't fucked for a fortnight.' – 'Perhaps he has.' – 'I'll swear he hasn't, he loves me, he'd wait a month for me and would marry me tomorrow, but what's the good, he can't keep himself, his family only allow him a pound a week – he'd wait to have me any length of time, and he cannot afford a woman.'

She had thrown a gown over her chemise, so as not to seem too ready – and ran down stairs to open the door to him herself. One of her servants had been sent out, and she had let *me* in herself – much maneuvering was now needed in her domicile. Fear of being caught out in intrigues is one of the miseries of ladies who play these pranks. – Leaning over the banisters I overheard much, he explained his delay, they kissed then. 'My friend has just come.' – He was in her secrets and knew some one visited her. – 'He is in my bedroom – don't make a noise.' – 'I'll take my boots off.' – He did. – 'There,' said she, 'wait till I beckon you, I'll go up and see if his door is closed, he is fearful of Blank coming back.'

Upstairs she came, saw me on the landing and nodded. – In I went, closing my door and soon he was in the back bedroom. A few minutes after I was at their door as before. She was exciting him, feeling his prick, both sitting on the bed, his back to the door. Then they nearly stripped. – She said – 'Stand up there, let me see it stiff.' – He complied like a child, obeyed her always I'd found – lifted his shirt, and I saw his powerful machine standing like a prop. – 'You have fucked since you did me last.' – 'I declare to God I haven't.' Then – 'Oh let me do it, dear.' He went towards her, when a powerful gust of wind (it was a very windy day) blew up the staircase, their door slightly moved, and caught his eye, he came and shut it, I retreated in fear seeing him advance, for had he opened the door he must have caught me. – I had I thought lost the spectacle of his fucking her.

But nothing exceeds the cunning of a Paphian. – Soon I heard her loudly calling out, 'Mary, Mary.' – Up came the servant, who was told something and went down stairs. It was a dodge to open the door without his noticing it. Cautiously I'd opened mine and peeped. H was just retiring and winked at me. Her door was now left ajar. – Again and almost directly after, I heard 'Ahem,' as if clearing her throat – her signal; the next instant, I was at the door. He was laying on his back, his big prick stiff as a poker shadowing his navel, his left hand feeling her quim as she stood by the bedside and looking up at her affectionately. He thought not of the door, or of any thing else but her cunt.

She handled his prick, then his balls for a minute.

'Let's fuck naked' and she threw off her chemise, then he his shirt. She laid down beside him for a second, the next he mounted her, and I heard his sigh of pleasure as his prick went up her sex. Then on he went thrusting. — 'Don't hurry,' said she — but he fucked hard. — 'I must,' he sobbed in a gentle voice. — I was mindful of what H had often said in our conversation, and what I now knew from experience, that a man in the full tide of sexual pleasure thinks of nothing else. — I opened the door slightly, then more, and entered the room as his thrusts grew quicker, saw in H's beautiful face that she was spending, heard, — 'Aha — my darling — love — aha' — from him then both were quiet. — I stood there till H opened her eyes. Then closing the door ajar and standing with my prick nearly bursting, listened.

'I must go to him [me], he doesn't like to be left long — I'll tell him some excuse and come back soon — put on your shirt, stay here, don't make a noise.' — Out she came, shutting the door, smiling at me, holding her cunt as French harlots do — and I suppose all do under similar circumstances — and the next instant was lying on the bedside with thighs wide apart. Her quim over-flowing with thick sperm delighted me, the sight made me wild to enter the lubricated sheath, my prick bursting, yet I restrained myself, had sufficient control to do that which whilst waiting I'd resolved. I pulled open the lips, frigged her spermy clitoris, whilst talking bawdily. 'Did you see his prick?' — 'Yes.' — 'Isn't it a fine one?' — 'Yes.' — 'He never fucked for a fortnight, look what he's spent, how thick it is.' — 'Wash it and I'll fuck you,' said I, not wishing anything of the sort.

I'd caught her. She'd before often said she let me fuck her thus solely for *my* pleasure. — 'No — fuck me — put it in.' — 'No. — I'm frightened.' — 'What of? what nonsense — put it up — he's a gentleman.' — (He was) — 'No, wash — you don't like it so.' 'Yes I do, fuck me, I like it so, fuck me,' said she impatiently. 'Get

534

lengthwise on the bed then.' She did, I mounted her, my prick plunged up and revelled in the grateful lubricity of her sheath. 'Ain't we beasts? – Oh – I'm coming – fuck.' – Our tongues joining, stopped further utterance, till my sperm gushed out into cunt. I was as quick as he in spending, certainly his prick hadn't left her cunt seven minutes, before my prick had done its work and quitted her also, tho I lay long up her after my spend.

'Pull it *out* dear, I must go back to him, I told him I would.' – 'He'll fuck you again.' 'That's certain.' – 'Let him fuck in my sperm.' – 'All right, he'll think it's his own, but I must go downstairs first, don't you come out till your hear me cough.' – She went downstairs, and soon returned to his room again. – My door was ajar, again I heard the cough, and looked thro the aperture of the door.

She was just placing herself beside him, he was on his back handling his tool which was half stiff. At once she manipulated it, they kissed and talked. – 'What did he say?' – 'I told him that my dressmaker was downstairs, etc.' – 'He's easily humbugged.' – Both laughed. – 'You must be quick, I mustn't keep him longer. Your prick's quite stiff.' – He felt her cunt. – 'You've not washed.' – She said that she'd not had time 'but must do so before she went to me.' – 'Will he do you?' – asked he in his quiet gentlemanly voice – so they talked for five minutes, kissing and dallying. Then her legs were in the air, thighs clasping his, and the rhythmical oscillation of their buttocks began. He was leisurely enjoying a longer job now. Soon as I heard him sigh and saw his thrusts were quicker, I opened the door, knelt at the bed foot, saw his prick moving and balls as they shook with his thrusts. Had I stood upright he'd not have noticed me in his paroxysm of pleasure – Helen did – I heard soft murmurs, saw his buttocks quiver, her eyes close, knew the

535

spends had come, and went back to my room, closing their door ajar.

This back room was only partially furnished – no water was left there with intent, so that he might go to the bedroom below, next the drawing room. She told me this before. Shortly they both went down there – then to the kitchen where she gave him food – tho well dressed he was glad of a meal. Then up she came to me and stood looking at me with voluptuous eyes. – She hadn't washed, shammed that she didn't want it again, but at the sight of her glistening vulva, my prick stood, and with a deliciously slow fuck we spent together again. Four male libations were in her cunt, and she'd spent at each fucking. – Soon after I left.

The conversations I heard and had with her are nearly word for word. – I wrote them down the same evening.

A few days after, I was there then with pleasure in confessing, for – 'I have no one to tell anything to but you, and him now,' said she. – She told me he had slept with her. 'God knows how often I spent, we were both done up. Come on dear, fuck me – I haven't had it since – he's ill. – I'm making him beef tea.'

At intervals of a week or two this was repeated – I saw him fuck her, and fucked her directly afterwards. Sometimes only once, sometimes twice, and the fun and room were a little varied at times to avoid surprise. She never afterwards denied her liking for the double libation. – 'What beasts we are.' – 'Not beasts at all dear, and if we are, we like it' – this was said regularly whenever the double fucking came off, but I had her at other times when he was not there.

A little before this H's protector was as I'd guessed in money difficulties. She told him that an old kind friend wanted to visit her, that money must be got somehow or they must part, and he consented to me – and only me – visiting her. – She had told him I was too old to poke, and only gamahuched her. Of course I've only her word for that. I never saw him or he me. He was very unhappy about it, but sooner than let her again be gay he would consent to almost anything. – Money and other circumstances, however, prevented my seeing her more frequently, tho I went with greater ease of mind. She also was not under such anxiety, and we had our frolics with increased pleasure – for her lascivious delights with me were greater than ever.

Later on she told me her protector was getting as erotic as I was, tho he was a very much younger man. My impression is that she taught him. – Sometimes it was: – 'What do you think? Phil wanted me to do so and so with him?' – or: 'We poked in this attitude the other day.' – Or: 'He likes hearing how formerly I've been poked,' and so on. – Then she and I had great pleasure in doing the same things together.

One day I wished we had a looking glass to see ourselves in when fucking. I had told her of the glasses at French houses – she excepting in a cheval glass, had never seen herself reflected in copulation, and wished she could. – I offered to buy one, but what would Philip say? 'He'd be delighted, we often wish for one when I tell him I've heard such things, but he's hard up just now – he knows you are the only man who visits me.' – He didn't know of her lovers. – Then I paid for a looking glass which she got. It was nearly as long as her bed, was placed against the wall, the bed nearly close to it, and henceforth we could see our every movement.

I shall never forget the day the glass came. We put it up together at the right level, directly we'd done so we rapidly stripped start naked, mounted the bed, and fucked contemplating ourselves, and that afternoon not a drop of sperm was left in my balls. I gamahuched her, and she frigged herself as well, looking in the glass. At my next visit I heard that Phil had done the same, that night after night they couldn't sleep for the rutting state the glass put them in, so hung a curtain over the glass when they wished to excite themselves no more. To see H frigging herself then was indeed a great treat. Her delight was to make me kneel on the bed naked facing the glass, with my stiff one which she held in one hand, whilst she frigged herself with the other, looking in the glass all the time. It was to me a delight — for her form and face were lovely, — to see her in the venereal spasm — an exquisite sight. — Unfortunately however the bed was so placed in the room then, that I could not see either bed or the reflection from the only door available for peeping, hence the fucking exhibitions were always given in other rooms.

Soon after we had the looking glass, a harlot temporarily out of business was often there. She had been a servant, then seduced, then well kept, then general practitioner in copulation, then lodging-house keeper, and was now impecunious. She had been good looking but was to me plain, yet was plumpish and her breast and leg were not uninviting. She had been a sort of go-between, scape goat and so on to Helen when gay, and of whom she was fond. — H seemed glad of her, for she was the only Paphian who now visited her, and with whom she could discourse of big pricks, etc., etc.

She (I shall call her Miss Def) was a thorough bawdy talker, nothing seemed to please her so much as narrating some meretricious experience, the tricks that she and others had played with men. There was no disguise now before me or between the two women, for that intimacy and confidence which it seems I have the art (unintentionally) of inspiring in gay ladies, had been given me by Helen, as far as a woman who has been gay can. But Paphians whether in or out of the calling never tell *all* to *anyone*, not even to their lovers. — Does a married woman? These narratives were not inventions got up for my edification, there was no object in doing that. — I never gave Def a farthing —

they came out quite naturally in our conversations when sitting together, which naturally turned on fucking.

In that and in amorous reminisceces H was as much pleased as I was. The Priestesses of Venus, I am convinced, all like their occupation, and to talk over past frolics when they have quitted the life, whatever they may aver to the contrary. – When they are sick and plain in face or form, and unsuccessful, they are repentant and virtuous, are 'Magdalenes'. Repentance usually pays better *then* than fucking.

I've seen lots of Magdelenes, but never one in good health or who was good looking. – They were failures in their occupation, they wanted face, form, skill, and go, and I guess had ill-fitting cunts, or certainly something wrong in cuntal quarters. So they repented, turned virtuous, were 'reclaimed', became Magdalenes and got shelter and money – I dare say when better, or at home in the colonies, they didn't forget they'd got cunts, useful for other things besides pissing.

One afternoon after luncheon, we three had champagne which I had taken there, our talk got smutty. Miss Def showed her legs which were good, and then her breasts. 'Show him your cunt,' said H. She did and we talked ourselves into a lewed state, which indeed I always was in directly I set sight on H's charms. What led to it was a tale told by Def, about a man in bed between two women all naked, and there not being room, one woman laid across the foot of the bed the feet of the two touching her, and she frigging herself whilst they were fucking. 'Let's get on to the bed and do the same,' – I suggested.

We all stripped and got on the bed (it was hot weather), Def's cunt was an unusually hair one, a regular well-fucked, and forty-years-old cunt. – She kissed my prick and H's cunt as well, before we laid down. Then our lewedness, and the delicious contact of soft skins, voluptuously suggested all sorts of letches. – Laying on my back feeling Helen's cunt, 'I'll frig you with my foot,' said I to Def. She delighted, let me, and placing my heel against her cunt after she had turned to a convenient position, I pressed and rubbed it there, she clutched my foot round the ankle and guided it, accommodating her cunt so as to get the friction as pleased her. H half sat up still feeling my prick, and watching this foot frigging. – 'Give a poor body a fuck, I haven't had a bit of cock for months,' said Def after awhile. 'Fuck *me*,' said H impetuously and lying down, for she was hot, and desire sometimes seems to seize her impatiently. Taking my heel from Def's cunt, I mounted my beauty's soft belly and began the exercise with my prick, my toes now downwards naturally.

After a few thrusts. – 'Def's frigging herself,' said H – She could see, I laying face downwards could not till I turned my face to the looking glass which I'd bought. – 'Go on fucking, I'm looking at Def frigging.' – Helen's feet and mine were both against the woman's naked body – we could feel the jog of her body as she frigged. 'Put my toe in your cunt and frig with it,' said I, wanting to feel a cunt with my toe, which I'd never well done before. 'Yes, frig with it,' said H with a baudy laugh. – Miss Def caught at my foot quickly without reply, the erotic desire seized her, and I felt my great toe was against the soft slippery surface, could feel distinctly her large clitoris and thick nymphœ, as well as if feeling them with my fingers. H, without letting my prick out of her cunt, managed to twist herself so that she could see that the toe of my right foot was there. 'The hair of her cunt's all round your toes – fuck me, – fuck' – said she with delight and energy, getting straight with a sigh of pleasure, moving her backside voluptuously. – I reciprocated, lunged my prick well into her hot avenue, in which it had got a little displaced in her moving to see where my toe was.

Then we fucked on whilst Def frigged, we thought

of her whilst our pleasure increased. – 'Is your toe on her cunt? – Ahaa' – sighed H – 'Yes, I can feel her frigging her cunt with it.' – 'Ahaa – I'm spending – ahaa – frig *me* – with your toe – some day. – Ahar – won't you? – Ahaa – Aha fuck – bash it up me. – Aharr.' – 'Spend darling, my spunk's coming. – She's frigging – Ahaa' – and in a bawdy delirium our pleasures ended in the ecstacy of the crisis, the woman at the bottom of the bed forgotten. As we ceased fucking Def continued her frig – did what she liked with my foot which she moved on her cunt. – With my other foot I felt her thighs agitated, she sighed, she moaned, my toe and her cunt moved rapidly, and just as we recovered from our pleasures, she gave a sob, a sort of gulp almost as if choking – a most extraordinary noise – and was quiet – my toe still resting on her clitoris, she still holding my foot.

I jumped up as soon as my prick had left H's inundated quim, finding my toe moist with Def's effusion. The devil had spent copiously. My getting up roused her, and she felt H's overflowing quim. 'He's spent a lot, how I'd like a fuck, I haven't had one for an age,' quoth she. All three washed, and after a rest I fucked H again whilst the other handled my balls, delighted with the opportunity of pulling about the testicles, whose juices she so longed to have in her. Then after a glass or two more wine, she asked me to fuck her and H incited me, – begged me – to 'give her a treat' – but I didn't, having no taste for her, and the condition of my toe which I had washed came to my mind and stopped all passion – I have rarely refused a cunt which was new to me; but I did hers.

H's poor lover was still absent. – She and her protector had been in the country and *he* was still. – Donkey Prick then frequently had Helen, then *he* having also been away, she ran short of her delight. I hadn't been in the house five minutes before she said, 'Come upstairs' and began undoing her clothes before she

541

reached the room. Afterwards she named many times for me to be there, when she could have Priapus also, but with difficulty arrangements could be made to suit all. 'I like to know you're looking at us.' – 'Yes and you like me to fuck after him.' – 'Yes I do – ain't we beasts?'

The man was cunning and often shut the door. He was whimsical – wouldn't often undress – and she loving his prick let him have his way. – One day I was there, he as usual in the kitchen – for she cooked for him there and from that place he could more easily escape by the back way. – But the fellow wouldn't come upstairs, and fucked her on the kitchen table – she was so long away that I wondered. – When she came up, she had just got him out of the house, and the sperm was abundant in her quim, tho a quarter of an hour since she'd fucked. She was dressed, and I fucked her from behind against the bed, the only time I think I had then done so on these double fucking occasions – tho I've tailed her in every possible attitude – I delighted usually to see her face as I fucked her whilst we talked. – 'Ah! – isn't his prick a big one?' – 'Yes I should like to feel it.' – 'I should like to feel both pricks at once. – Aha – beast – fuck harder – Ahar.' – 'His sperm's thick today.' – 'Yes isn't it lovely, smooth? – ahaa – don't stop – fuck – I'm coming.' The angelic smile came over her face, her cunt gripping and we spent together. This is typical. We never fucked without talking about pricks and sperm and making all sorts of lewed suggestions to each other, till pleasure stopped utterances.

There was a garret where sometimes the little servant – when she had one – slept. It contained scarcely any furniture but a bed. One day when there was no fear of surprise, she said she'd make him to up there and get him naked. It was in the afternoon of a warm autumn day, he'd had a feast of rumpsteak and had tippled enough whiskey and water, when I heard him going up the stairs, and in time out I stepped and listened. He was jovial and incautious, yet I was fearful of going up until I heard, 'Ahem' – for the carpetless stairs creaked. Then I heard every word as plainly as if I'd been in the room. – He wanted to go to sleep first. – 'Fuck and sleep afterwards. – Piss first.' – 'I don't want' – but I heard the water rattle, and laughter as they got on to the bed, and then, 'Ahem.'

As I peeped thro the door left ajar – the bed had been cunningly placed so as to prevent his looking at the door – he was lying on his back with shirt on only, she frigging his cock, which was thick but pendant. – 'You've fucked before today.' – he denied it – was tired. – She was angry, was sure he'd been fucking hard the night before, and came used up – she'd had enough of him, he'd been like that often lately, she wasn't going to have his lasts – and so on. – 'Suck me.' – She wouldn't – he'd better dress and go off to do it, – get another woman. – 'Show me your cunt.' – Then he frigged himself and got a glorious erection. – 'Lie down.' – She wouldn't now. 'No, stand up naked and let me see it, stand up or you shan't have me.' – He drew of his shirt and stood naked with a donkey sized doodle. It was worth seeing, a noble, well proportioned shaft standing out seven or eight inches from the belly, and perhaps nine from his balls, and looking an inch and a half in diameter. It was white skinned, and had a full plum shaped tip of a bright red, it was circled at his belly with a well defined thicket of lightish brown hair, (he was fairish with blue eyes) which didn't creep towards thighs and navel. His ballocks was ponderous. Altogether, it was the biggest prick but one I've ever seen, and the handsomest. The sight of it made my own stiffen voluptuously, and at the same time desire to handle his – I don't wonder at the ladies who are connoisseurs in Priapean tools, admiring his and wishing to enjoy it once, tho certain it is that a pego of average size gives as much sexual

543

pleasure to a woman as the greatest cunt whacker. – A huge stiff prick when a man is standing naked always looks a little ridiculous, so it's strange that my prick should have stood sympathetically at the sight of his.

H sat looking at it silently. – Once for an instant she turned her eyes to the door where I was peeping. There was admiration, pride, and lust in her eyes. – The expression of, – 'Isn't it a beauty, and it's going up me?' – looking back at it again, her thighs spasmodically closed, then opened, as if a spasm of pleasure was passing through her, and putting her fingers on her cunt she kept them there.

But the prick began to droop. She gave it a violent frig, it then stood stiff, then rapidly fell, and she bullied him – I was pleased to see a man not thirty with his prick not quite ready, as mine has been on one or two occasions, tho I can still fuck her twice in the hour. – After some more angry remarks from her, she threw off her chemise and mounted him, her rump was within six feet of my eyes, and I saw her introduce the prick into her cunt and do the fucking. – His tool kept shrinking – she called him a 'used-up beast' told him to go, but wanted the spend, kept reinserting his machine when needful, and fucking energetically. I had a glorious sight of this grand propagator, which she often brought out to the tip and then plunged up her. Then her bum oscillated quickly, her cunt nestled down till his balls were close up to it – she cried out loudly. – 'Fuck – spend, Arthur. – ahaa' – and was quiet.

In a minute. – 'You've not spent.' – 'I was just coming.' – 'You haven't any spunk in you,' and moving her buttocks, out came his prick shining with her spending and stiff enough. – I saw H's face, which was lewed. Without a word turning on to him again, up went the long thick gristle into her, and she oscillated her splendid buttocks till she'd spent twice more without his spending once; she after each crisis ballyragging him, he making all sorts of excuses. More than half an hour had she been at the work, and yet went on till at length she got a spend out of him – I never saw her so hot before, her face was moist and scarlet, her eyes humid, with her spending, yet fierce, and as she rolled off she gave his prick a slap. 'You've been fucking before today, you liar, get off as fast as you can, you don't bring your fucked out balls into my house again – you won't fuck me again, you mean beast.' – All his sins came out, she'd already told me of his meanness.

He made all sorts of excuses but she wasn't pacified. She put on her chemise, came down to my bedroom landing and called out, 'Arthur's going, let him out – don't let him go into the kitchen.' – He heard this, came down dressed and still excusing himself – she replying to all, – 'It's a lie. – It's a lie' – till he was out of the house. Then she came to me and smiled. – 'Isn't it a splendid prick?' Then she told me she'd heard the stairs creak, but he'd not noticed it. – 'I'm quite wet, I spent three times, he spent at last, the black-guard is fucked out, yet he knew three days ago he was coming – my cunt's wet – won't you have me?' I said no, but was wrought up to the highest pitch of lust, and in half an hour had fucked her twice. She declared donkey prick should never have her again, but I was sure he would. – 'He has a noble prick hasn't he?' said she admiringly. – 'Yes, but he's a coarse brute, not even handsome, not a gentleman.' – 'Certainly not a gentleman, but he's a noble prick, all the women want him, he pays none, I'm told.' – I fancy Miss Def – now with a house of her own again – was the informant.

I never yet saw a woman fucking a man so plainly, as on that bright afternoon. The beams of the sun at last struck right across her backside, her arsehole, cunt, his prick and balls I saw as plainly as if I had been within a foot of them, and had held a candle to look. – How I longed to feel his tool as she fucked him, and how delighted she would have been. But she was annoyed when afterwards I said, 'Your bum furrow is getting brown, H.' – 'You beast – what if it is, so is yours.' – 'I know it.' – She never could bear to be told about her furrow browning, or later on that hairs were beginning to show round her bum hole, as they do in most women after five and twenty and in southern nations earlier. It detracts from the beauty of the region.

On both occasions, *she* had covered *him*, to prevent him going quickly to the door and his chance of catching me. The next time for some rason of her own – who fathoms a woman's dodges? – she had him in her own bedroom which had now been changed. I waited in the backroom. He was still enough and full, laid on her, half fucked her, and then she made him finish with her rump towards him. H laughed as he got off his bed with his great tool sticking out. Then it disappeared up her, and I thought must have hurt her. The fucking was soon over. How beautiful it was, how exciting it looked! They remained coupled for a minute, then she uncunted him saying, 'You lie down, I must go to my sister and will be back in a minute.' He threw himself on the bed, giving her rump a slap as they parted and the next second she was with me on my bed. 'Don't talk loud, he thinks my sister's here, he's never seen her.'

Her eyes shone with voluptuous light and softness. 'Hasn't he spent? my cunt's full, hasn't he a lovely prick?' said she sighing and laying down. I looked at it, pulled open the lips, pushed one finger up, then my balls could wait no longer, I had been stiff since I saw his prick, and plunged my pego up her. Ah! my delight – to feel my prick up her and his sperm all round it. – H put her hand to feel, then clasping my bum, and heaving her arse. – 'Ohoo – fuck' she cried and glued her mouth to mine. Furiously our backsides oscillated, far too soon my sperm rose. 'Hurt me – shove hard,' she whispered, heaving her cunt up, and the next minute both were spending, her ecstacy as great as mine. then quickly back she went to him, her cunt full as before, her motte and thighs wet with our essence. – 'Make him fuck you in it.' – 'If I can, but he likes it washed before he does me again' were the last words.

She closed their door with a bang, cunningly giving the handle a turn so that it was left ajar, but so close that I could see nothing. To facilitate that a fortnight before she'd cut away, at eye height, a slip off of one edge, and painted it afterwards. We had arranged this together after the manner at the French lapunar. She laid down on the bed for *me* to see *her*, then I for her to see *me*, and we moved her bed a little to give the best view of those upon it, both delighted at the dodge. I couldn't see their heads when they were fucking, but saw all from their breasts downwards. – Now she took the side furthest off, and nearer the fireplace, and he turning to her had his back to me. – 'Ahem' – I pushed the door slightly open and saw them both well.

She began frigging *him*, then he felt *her*. 'You've not washed.' – 'No, how could I? – I will.' – 'My spunk's on your thighs.' – 'Yes, did you spend?' – 'My ballocks were damned full,' – said he with a coarse laugh. – Both laughed, and went on talking about some woman who had one of the smallst cunts he'd ever fucked, and about some swell Paphians she had known formerly, whilst she went on frigging him till, 'It's stiff, let's do it.' – 'Wash it.' – She got up, and holding the ewer, – 'There's no water.' – 'Ring for Sally and I'll show her my prick' – said he laughing and handling it. – 'I shan't – you'd better not – never mind washing' – getting on the bed again and frigging his tool. – In another minute after lewed chat he mounted her, she'd pulled her chemise off and tried to pull off his shirt. Saying it was cold, he refused but tucked it up to his waist.

They were fucking in an instant. Is the spectacle of even a handsome couple fucking beautiful or not? – Is the sight of a beautiful creature, all modesty and grace – whom one has walked, talked, and danced with, to be admired when on her back, heaving her buttocks up, her thighs high and round the man's while under is a thick gristly stem protruding from his belly, and going like a steam piston in and out of a bush of hair round her cunt – is it beautiful? – Both rumps jog, and heave, and thrust and meet, till with sighs and murmurs both are quiet. Is it a spectacle beautiful or not? – No. – Yet an entrancing one. – One that no man or woman would hesitate to look at, enjoy, and envy, none whose cunt wouldn't yearn – whose prick wouldn't stiffen at the sight. – Yet it's not beautiful, tho exciting, stimulating, entrancing to all the sense.

This was really a fine couple I must say, much as I disliked his vulgarity, but to know that that big tube, with its inner tube of discharge, was thrusting up *her* tube, with the intensest pleasure to both, made my prick, without frigging, stand till I heard their murmurs, knew that their pleasure was over.

He rolled off of her, she didn't hurry him. 'Get me a glass of whiskey and water.' – 'I shan't, you've had enough, get it yourself in the kitchen if you want it, don't make a noise, I don't want my sister to know a man's here.' The scout – Mrs **** – took care the man shouldn't know I was there. Hastily he put on his clothes and went off. 'Hush' said she as he went downstairs and she waited till he got to the kitchen.

In she came and I looked at her sexual treasure. Sperm is now to me clean, wholesome. It's the outcome of life – the issue and cause of the greatest human pleasure to giver and receiver. – I no longer mind my fingers being in it, but like to feel a cunt which is lubricated with it. – I opened hers, felt up it, wiped my fingers on my balls, and on her motte – the salacity of the act delighted me. 'You beast, you,' said she but looking pleased with the lascivious act. Then up into her my prick went, and prick and cunt then revelled in the unction and the thrusts, and the lubricated friction of our movements, till both sobbed out our joy in the delicious crisis – her cunt discharged, my balls shot forth their sperm, and we mixed this essence of male and female life in her sweet channel – oh happy woman!

Pressing her sweet form to mine, her hand clasping my buttocks – in the lubricious conjunction we lay. – Slowly I still kissed her, our wet lips mingling moistures there as we lay conjoined – eyes closed – baudily thinking – vague visions of lust dreamily passing thro our brains. 'Aren't we beasts?' – the first words spoken. – 'Damn it, Helen – don't say that again – it's nonsense – nothing beastly about it – what beast could do or care about dong what you and I have done? – it's heavenly, divine – don't – I've often told you you annoy me by saying it.' She laughed, her belly jogged, her cunt moved, and out came my prick, and at once as many and as much as I could get of my fingers up her cunt I put there – lewed still.

This again was on a warm autumn afternoon, for it suited us both to meet at that time – the master of the house was then away. Soon Donkey Prick was got out of the house. I dressed, we had tea and toast, then I licked her cunt till she was exhausted with pleasure, then left.

I had now told Helen all the erotic incidents of my life. She, with her fertile brain, voluptuous temperament, and experience in amorosities, both approved, desired to emulate them, and herself to invent. She wasn't – as already said, – at first frank about her letches and lusts, hiding them somewhat and throwing the suggestion of the gratification upon *me* making *herself* but the complaisant partner; but the mask was now pretty well removed – tho probably women in all classes never quite tell their letches or the truth about their bawdy wishes – who knows? When guessing *her* desire, after talking about some luxurious fancies, I passed them over then finding I did not initiate anything, she referred to them again on other visits, and I met them by some such questions as 'Would *you* like so and so to gamahuche you' – or 'Like another man or woman with us?' – or 'Like me to see you fucked by another?' – 'Yes I should' came frankly at last. Then it was, 'Let's have a woman to gamahuche me, but *you* ask me to let her, I don't want *her* to think I wish her.' Singular modesty, it seemed to me.

Then we got our lascivious tastes gratified and to the full. That kept me from other amours, and to her almost alone, for she had youth, supreme beauty of face and form, was clever, conversable, voluptuous, and enjoyed every lewed device in body and mind – aye to the extreme. She agreed with me that every amorous trick might be tried, and we gratified our desires to the limits of possibility. I wanted no other woman, excepting when away from town, or on a sudden letch, or out of mere curiosity. These I nearly always told her of. Some of our amorous play I preserve in this narrative, some will never be even whispered about – the knowledge of it will die with us.

Helen soon had great pleasure in talking of her former tricks – would tell what she'd done or had heard of – reserve was utterly gone between us. She pronounced mine to be the most wonderful amatory career, when she had read a large part of the manuscript, or I had read it her while in bed and she laid quietly feeling my prick. Sometimes she'd read and I listen, kissing and smelling her lovely alabaster breasts, feeling her cunt, till the spirit moved us both to incorporate our bodies. Her sexual passion was strong, her strength great. I have fucked her thrice, and gamahuched thrice, yet seen her frig herself after that, and all in four hours, without showing a sign of fatigue.

Having now no harlot acquaintances, it was a real pleasure to her to have some one to talk with on these subjects. – Telling her of Camille one evening and talking of gamahuching, she said, tho the little servant whom I fucked had done it, it was a long time since a *woman* had gamahuched *her*. She liked a fine, fattish woman to do it to her and took a letch for Camille from my description of her. Camille was long past forty yet wonderfully well preserved, and one evening solely to gratify H I got Camille to visit her.

We had a lovely little dinner at Helen's, then adjourned to her bedroom, both women stripped and looked at each other's cunts – they were so quiet about that – and then Camille gamahuched. 'Fuck her, fuck her whilst she's licking me, let me see it,' H cried – But I wouldn't – I couldn't bear my sperm to go into any cunt but her own, and after she'd spent thrice under Camille's active tongue, I fucked her. Then after half an hour's rest Camille again licked H's quim till she screamed with the exhaustion of pleasure, and Camille could lick no longer. After repose and wine I wanted Camille to suck *me*, but she refused, telling H she'd never done it. – A lie, for she has many times minetted me tho she never liked it, and always wanting me to fuck her. – Poor Camille liked me to the last.

Again I then stroked H who excited by wine and lewd to her marrow made Camille feel my balls whilst fucking, she grasping Camille's motte, or feeling her buttocks whilst she was handling my stones. 'Why a lovely skin,' cried H as she felt Camille's buttocks. Indeed she had still that exquisite skin and her pretty, tight, deep cunt. Never were two more lovely skinned women together. I then fucked Camille at the request of both of them, which finished the night. Taking Camille home in my cab I paid her handsomely. She could do nothing but talk of the unparalleled charms of H I never brought them together again. H's letch was satisfied, and she did not want gay women.

I told her one evening how I had turned Nelly L's cunt into a purse, and she wondered if her own would hold as much. I had doubts, for it did not feel to me as large inside as the other woman's did, but I had H naked one day and tried. The silver brought was carefully washed, and the argental cunt stuffing began. I was so delighted and she also with the experiment, that I prolonged the work, not putting in five and ten shillings at a time as I did with the other, when my lustful curiosity was to ascertain a fact, but a shilling or two at a time only, feeling them of her cunt, then glorying in seeing her exquisite form promenading with the silver in her. When about forty shillings had disappeared up the belly rift, I put my prick up her, and felt with its sensitive tip the difference between a shilling which it struck against and the soft round compressive end of her cuntal avenue. She was as pleased with me at that trick as I was. I nearly spent, excited by my operations, and now with the idea of spending against a shilling up a cunt, but I didn't — wouldn't.

I resumed the silver stuffing, she her ambulations, and it is extraordinary that within a shilling or two, she held in her cunt the same number that Nelly had. She several times walked up and down the room with her cunt so full, that I could see the silver when I gently opened one lip. – The grip and tenacity of her Paphian temple seemed truly wonderful. – What muscular force, what a nut cracker! – But that indeed I knew, for her cunt was perfect in every way, a pudenda of all the virtues, powers and beauties for fucking, or doing anything voluptuous with – a supreme pleasure giver.

Then over the basin she squatted to void the argentiferous stream. It was beautiful to see her squat, her thighs then rounded into the fullest, loveliest form, it

always delighted me to see her in that attitude washing her cunt or micturating. The silver tumbling out
of her gaping hirsute cleft, with a clatter against the
basin, made us laugh, some refused to quit the
lubricious nook in which it found itself, I felt up for it,
and she at last by muscular contraction of her cunt
aided by her finger, got it all out. Then with a syringe
she purified the receptacle, we went to the bed, and
after a little mutual fingering, fucked, – the bawdy
trick just finished enhancing our sexual delight.

The silver was washed and stored away. 'When you
pay any one, tell them that the silver's been up your
cunt.' – 'You beast, I will.' The servants and a female
friend – for she had now a female friend – were told
of this. We talked about it all evening, and she put
one shilling well up for me to touch with my prick
which I did, but did not spend whilst the shilling was
in its lubricious receptable. [I wish now I had, it would
have been something to remember.] Eighty-six or -
seven shillings did her cunt hold.

Available now

The Captive
by Anonymous

When a wealthy Enlish man-about-town attempts to make advances to the beautiful twenty-year-old debutante Caroline Martin, she haughtily repels him. As revenge, he pays a white-slavery ring 30,000 to have Caroline abducted and spirited away to the remote Atlas Mountains of Morocco. There the mistress of the ring and her sinister assistant Jason begin Caroline's education—an abduction designed to break her will and prepare her for her mentor.

———

Available now

Captive II
by Richard Manton

Following the best-selling novel, *The Captive*, this sequel is set among the subtropical provinces of Cheluna, where white slavery remains an institution to this day. Brigid, with her dancing girl figure and sweeping tresses of red hair, has caused the prosecution of a rich admirer. As retribution, he employs the underground organization Rio 9 to abduct and transport her to Cambina Alta Plantation. Naked and bound before the sadism of Col. Manrique and the perversities of the Comte de Zantra, Brigid endures an education in submission. Her training continues until she is ready to be the slave of the man who has chosen her.

———

Available now

Captive III: The Perfumed Trap
by Anonymous

The story of slavery and passionate training described first-hand in the spirited correspondence of two wealthy cousins, Alec and Miriam. The power wielded by them over the girls who cross their paths leads them beyond Cheluna to the remote settlement of Cambina Alta and a life of plantation discipline. On the way, Alec's passion for Julie, a golden-haired nymph, is rivaled by Miriam's disciplinary zeal for Jenny, a rebellious young woman under correction at a police barracks.

Available February 2001:

Sadistic Impulse
by Jack Spender

Professor Jack Spender is hired to teach a group of amoral sorority honeys in the French Riviera, but must also regiment their heedless sexual frolics under the brooding, lustful shadow of the Marquis de Sade. More devastating yet, Spender knows that beneath the surface glitz and fleshly opulence of the Azure Coast lies older traditions of Greek orgiastic rites. Continuing his passion for the beautiful Mlle. Kore, he finds a "yearning libidinal welcome rooted in the very earth itself."

Eveline II
by Anonymous

Eveline II continues the delightfully erotic tale of a defiant aristocratic young English woman who throws off the mantle of respectability in order to revel in life's sexual pleasures. After returning to her paternal home in London in order to escape the boredom of marriage, she plunges with total abandon into self-indulgence and begins to "convert" other young ladies to her wanton ways.

Elaine Cox
by Richard Manton

Elaine Cox is an adolescent tomboy of short skirts, bare thighs and snub-nosed insolence. Her misconduct puts her under the command of her middle-aged admirer, and as punishment and seduction alternate, a dark romance begins in the soundless vaults and tiled discipline rooms. Soon Elaine is a tomboy well-chastised, the recipient of passionate punishments.

Slaves of the Hypnotist
by Anonymous

Harry, son of a well-to-do English country family, has set out to "conquer" all the females within his immediate reach. But no sooner does he begin his exploits than he encounters the imperious beauty, Davina, who enslaves him through her remarkable power of hypnotism. Thus entranced, Harry indulges in every aspect of eroticism known to man or woman.

Available March 2001:

The Sensualists
by Frank Mace

Who are these young, beautiful women who willingly display themselves in the most degrading and defenseless position for their sex? And who is this man who provides them with prolonged spasms of ecstasy, leaving them whimpering, limp and grateful things? They are otherwise ordinary people, but share the same relentless need to reach the heights of sensual pleasure by submitting to the lowest of degradations. Marc Merlin can unleash their erupting sexuality—but by appointment only.

Yakuza Perfume
by Akahige Namban

While still recovering from their ordeal in the Kiso Mountains of Central Japan, Japanese American brothers Jim and Andy are surprised by a female agent of the Clouds and Rain Company who seeks refuge with them. After she leaves they are accused of having stolen the secret of the sexually intoxicating pheromone perfume that is the basis for the company's power. They set out to find the real thieves and prove their innocence, while embarking on lustful adventures along the way.

Rough Caress
by James Holmes

This erotic collection tells of the strange seduction of Isabel Seaton, who keeps her passion corked like fine champagne, under the mistaken notion that it, too, will improve with time. But writhing in the caresses of her abductors, her illusion is shattered as she succumbs to quivering bliss. There are also Miss Clarke and Miss Franks, two young maids who inventively satisfy each other's rampant lust—as well as the pubescent passions of squealing schoolgirls, to whom they apply the birch.

Mistress of the East
by Dean Barrett

Captured by Taiping women warriors in China, a young lieutenant, Thomas Rowley, is flagellated into a docile and obedient slave. As he becomes immersed in the exotic world of the Taiping warriors, he witnesses the carnal needs of these fiercely powerful women. He becomes enraptured with the beautiful and indomitable Sweet Little Sister, and is introduced to new realms of erotic pleasure.

Order These Selected Blue Moon Titles

Souvenirs From a Boarding School $7.95	Shades of Singapore $7.95
The Captive $7.95	Images of Ironwood $7.95
Ironwood Revisited $7.95	What Love $7.95
Sundancer $7.95	Sabine $7.95
Julia $7.95	An English Education $7.95
The Captive II $7.95	The Encounter $7.95
Shadow Lane $7.95	Tutor's Bride $7.95
Belle Sauvage $7.95	A Brief Education $7.95
Shadow Lane III $7.95	Love Lessons $7.95
My Secret Life $9.95	Shogun's Agent $7.95
Our Scene $7.95	The Sign of the Scorpion $7.95
Chrysanthemum, Rose & the Samurai $7.95	Women of Gion $7.95
Captive V $7.95	Mariska I $7.95
Bombay Bound $7.95	Secret Talents $7.95
Sadopaideia $7.95	Beatrice $7.95
The New Story of O $7.95	S&M: The Last Taboo $8.95
Shadow Lane IV $7.95	"Frank" & I $7.95
Beauty in the Birch $7.95	Lament $7.95
Laura $7.95	The Boudoir $7.95
The Reckoning $7.95	The Bitch Witch $7.95
Ironwood Continued $7.95	Story of O $5.95
In a Mist $7.95	Romance of Lust $9.95
The Prussian Girls $7.95	Ironwood $7.95
Blue Velvet $7.95	Virtue's Rewards $5.95
Shadow Lane V $7.95	The Correct Sadist $7.95
Deep South $7.95	The New Olympia Reader $15.95

ORDER FORM
Attach a separate sheet for additional titles.

Title	Quantity	Price
_____	____	_____
_____	____	_____
_____	____	_____
_____	____	_____

Shipping and Handling (see charges below) _____

Sales tax (in CA and NY) _____

Total _____

Name _____

Address _____

City _____ State _____ Zip _____

Daytime telephone number _____

❏ Check   ❏ Money Order   (US dollars only. No COD orders accepted.)

Credit Card # _____ Exp. Date _____

❏ MC   ❏ VISA   ❏ AMEX

Signature _____

(if paying with a credit card you must sign this form.)

Shipping and Handling charges:*

Domestic: $4 for 1st book, $.75 each additional book. International: $5 for 1st book, $1 each additional book
*rates in effect at time of publication. Subject to Change.

Mail order to Publishers Group West, Attention: Order Dept., 1700 Fourth St., Berkeley, CA 94710, or fax to (510) 528-3444.

PLEASE ALLOW 4-6 WEEKS FOR DELIVERY. ALL ORDERS SHIP VIA 4TH CLASS MAIL.

Look for Blue Moon Books at your favorite local bookseller or from your favorite online bookseller.